DEAD WOMAN
SCORNED

1/10/20

Sarah—

Thanks for your
precious time !

—Michael Clark

DEAD WOMAN SCORNED

The Patience of a Dead Man—Book Two

MICHAEL CLARK

Don't fall asleep! Stay in touch:
https://www.michaelclarkbooks.com/
https://www.facebook.com/michaelclarkbooks
michael@michaelclarkbooks.com

PROLOGUE

October 1971—One year before the Open House

Tim Russell banged his palm against the steering wheel in frustration—he'd forgotten his wallet. He wondered for a second if he really needed it before tomorrow, then looked at the gas gauge—near empty. Not even enough gas to make it to Holly's house in Laconia. He stepped on the brake and pulled over to the side of the dirt road to make a U-turn, then hesitated.

It shouldn't be a problem—to simply turn around, drive the quarter-mile back, walk into the house and retrieve the wallet—but it was undeniably *harrowing*, even though their struggles with the murderous Mildred Wells were over. They'd beaten her, and she'd been taken away weeks ago, but even so, Tim's stress level was off the charts as he worked alone each day, watching over his shoulder, restoring the old house as fast as he possibly could.

He looked back before making the turn, his heart picking back up to the level it had maintained the entire day. *Here I go—I'm going back in,* he thought, as he postponed thoughts of the cold beer waiting for him at the convenience store a mile down the road. *Best to hit and run.* He stepped on the gas and made the turn, never taking his eyes off of the house and, more specifically, the turret, his designated office space during the reconstruction—the room where he'd left his wallet.

Rip that band-aid he thought, as the truck climbed the small hill up the driveway. Quickly and carefully, he pulled around to the side of the house, then backed up and parked in front of the porch, facing the road. Now he had the shortest path inside the house to the turret and the shortest path to the road once he was back in the truck. Annoyingly, he had to kill the engine because the house keys were on the same damned ring—something he would remedy tomorrow with a quick stop at the hardware store.

He jogged up to the door and inserted the key as quickly and quietly as possible. His actions were nothing like the words he used to soothe Holly. She worried about him each and every day as he worked alone, and he did his best to persuade her that it was a "totally different place now"—Mildred was gone, and it "seemed as if she'd never been there." Holly didn't believe a word. She hated the house now—it would never be the same for her, no matter what work he did to disguise it.

In seconds he was inside the front porch, opening the front door, faking as though there was nothing to be afraid of. Once inside, he noticed that it seemed very dark in the kitchen. It was late May, and the longest day of the year would be here in less than a month. Sunset should be at around 8 pm today, with the twilight keeping things well lit for another half-hour at least. *Strange.* He turned to look out the kitchen window.

It was pitch black outside, and his truck was already gone.

In a panic, he spun for the porch, deep down, becoming aware that forgetting his wallet was the greatest mistake of his life. The smell hit him right then, and he wondered why he hadn't noticed it sooner. The front door was closed and locked, even though he'd left it open on purpose. He grabbed the knob and began to work it when three flies landed on his hand and wrist. *No. She must be close.* Tim turned to the dark dining room to protect his back. She stood in the far corner, motionless.

She knew he'd forgotten the wallet. She knew he'd be back, and then she set the trap.

Tim gave up on the front door and bolted through the kitchen. As he rounded the breakfast bar and headed for the side door, he stopped dead. What was once a sliding glass door to the carriage house was now literally—a brick wall. *No, how could this—?* He had one last option, *to somehow get past her and—*

Mildred Wells had moved to the center of the kitchen, blocking passage, cornering him. She approached slowly, driving him into the bricked-off dead end. Flies followed, filling the room, interfering with his vision and his thinking. Her smell intensified, and Tim watched as the old hatchet appeared in her right hand.

She raised it high, coiled to strike. Her face was bone-white, and Tim thought she might be smiling under all the dead skin. There was nowhere to go, and nothing left to do but fight. He charged her, screaming with fear as he lunged.

"*Tim, Tim! TIM!*" Mildred screamed back, but it was not at all the voice he'd imagined her to have.

On second thought

…it wasn't Mildred's voice at all—it was Holly's. Was this some sort of cruel taunt on Mildred's part?

"Wake up, you're dreaming again!" Tim opened his eyes, realizing that his dreams were steadily running contradictory to what he told her each day about Mildred being "gone for good." She very well *might be* gone for good—and there was no evidence to believe she wasn't—but now Holly knew that his "beliefs" were only empty words to make her feel better.

CHAPTER 1

November 1ˢᵗ, 1863

As strange as it sounds, Mildred Wells committed suicide in an attempt to reconcile with her son.

Her thinking was that if they were kindred spirits, the healing could begin…or at least that was the idea.

The horrible truth that she wanted to ignore, however, was that any sort of reconciliation with Elmer would not be easy. He did not want her. Every time he saw her, he ran away. He was rightfully afraid of Mildred, but even so, she hoped deep down he could someday forgive her.

Elmer was dead and had made it a point to haunt her ever since she drowned him in the pond in front of the house. The drowning was an ugly exclamation point on a series of events that she felt she had no control over. Thomas had left them— *abandoned* them really, to selfishly satisfy his ego and fight in the Civil War. To make matters worse, it wasn't a month before the news came that he died—*in training*—and would not be coming home. Mildred struggled with the consequences, and with life as a single mother. Anger roiled beneath the surface.

Deeply disturbed, and missing the touch of a man, she had committed the most unforgivable sin. Now the boy taunted her, sabotaged courtships, and made life a living hell. Why hadn't

Thomas come and taken him away? Even in death, he was a terrible father. Finally, when she could no longer tolerate the situation, she made the necessary arrangements to end her own life.

After the suicide, she and Elmer were now equivalents, and she figured she should be able to catch him. Alternatively, maybe her suicide would end his reason to haunt, and she would be free of him—either way would work—as long as he gave in. Perhaps they could begin a conversation and one day reach an understanding, Thomas Pike, be damned.

It didn't work out the way she planned, however. Even in death, the boy eluded her, like a frustrating nightmare. He was there one moment and gone the next, and the same rules didn't seem to apply to her. *Where did he go? Was he that fast?* He would pass between two bushes at full speed and then seemingly disappear, leaving her searching.

Mildred spent a great deal of her time wandering and looking for Elmer. Her anger kept her focused on her second life, and by force of will, she avoided letting her mind drift to her previous life—the one before Elmer and Thomas. Before Sanborn. One thing at a time. Fix the current situation.

With nothing better to do, she began to track patterns in Elmer's movement. Every fifth day he would repeat himself. Every fifth day she would know exactly where to expect him, so she tried ambushing, but he would somehow adjust and successfully elude. Perhaps this was a punishment. Maybe there was a higher power after all, and she had gotten it all so wrong.

Elmer's schedule became disappointing, so she developed some patterns of her own. In an attempt to relive the only happy years of her life, she developed a mental calendar for things of which she had fond memories. It angered her to think of Thomas, so she filtered him out whenever possible.

One of those happy times was the barn raising. Back then, they were about to build the first house she could call her own. In her re-creation of the scene, she swore she could hear the hammering as if it was 1860 again. She wondered if it was real or a product of her imagination.

Little did she know the sounds *were* real, a byproduct of her tragic past. Many things were lost on her because she refused to reflect in any way. Years of brainwashing blocked out most of her ability to remember, bolstered by her determination to forget.

She could see his shape in the back of her mind on occasion, but she didn't want to. Every time the ethereal figure began to solidify, she went searching for Elmer. Her past, the childhood part, could not be fixed. She had no control over it, but she might be able to fix Elmer—and that was what she chose to believe.

Mildred knew that her house would not remain vacant forever, and surprisingly, she found it amusing. It gave her something to do and someone to watch. She decided in general not to make their lives hell as long as they stayed away from their graves, well hidden in the last row of the old grove.

The first family (The Millers) bought the house only one month after her suicide. She had no way of knowing if they knew about the deaths, nor did she care. As soon as they moved in, she broke into the town hall and scrubbed any records with the Pike family name on them. She wanted to erase the memory of the Pike family and the reminder that she had been a part of it. Everyone else could do the same.

The Millers were typical farmers and provided little entertainment. They had two boys, which reminded her of Elmer somewhat—A largely unpleasant turn-off. She spent very little time eavesdropping as the Miller family had shockingly little to offer intellectually.

Mildred spent the early nights of their ownership listening in on their lives as they talked in the kitchen or the bedroom. She couldn't seem to avoid spooking the horses, however, and because of that sadly didn't get to spend any time in the barn.

As time passed, rest eluded her. Elmer eluded her. Thomas was gone. Mildred wandered the woods aimlessly, disheartened and defeated wondering, *what next?* Suicide was impossible. With no imminent chance of Elmer's forgiveness, she dropped to her knees, curled into the fetal position face down, and listened to the forest around her.

She was cursed, and it must be Gideon Walker's fault. Yes, perhaps it was time to revisit that can of worms. The thought of him angered her. His dabbling in dark *magick* surely must have given him afterlife powers—at least similar to hers and perhaps more. Would he crave eternal life? The tyrant that he was, the answer was *most likely*. He would be roughly sixty to sixty-five years old now. It would be very satisfying to pay him a visit and watch him suffer first and then die.

But still, there was Elmer, the son she had murdered. He would never forget the drowning, but might forgiveness someday be in the cards? The fact that he was still on-property must mean *something*. The pain of not having a true direction was debilitating for her. As she knelt, face planted in the leaves, blocking out the light with her arms, she meditated. Passion and hope had left her, and she wished her body would simply dissolve to ash. Mental fatigue battered her soul. Oddly, she felt the need for sleep, which made no sense. *Why on Earth would a dead woman need sleep?*

No longer able to think clearly, she rose wearily in an attempt to find a proper spot to lie down. It didn't have to be fancy. A bear cave. A coyote den. *The grove.* Yes, the grove was idyllic. Beautiful and mysterious, she had always enjoyed the dark mystery of the grove. Letting the Christmas trees go wild was one of the best decisions she had ever made. The grove matched her mood—most of the time. It was a hiding spot, a private *symmetry*—all to herself. It would forever be a part of her.

At that moment, she imagined the spade hanging on the wall in the back of the barn and wished she had brought it with her. Suddenly and surprisingly, it appeared in her hand. Unsure if she was hallucinating or not, and too tired to question, she found a spot between four densely packed spruces and began to dig. As soon as she reached a comfortable depth that somehow seemed just right, she gathered piles of fallen wood and branches, creating a thick mound over the shallow hole. Over the deadwood, she threw bushel after bushel of natural mulch: Leaves, sticks, briars, and stones. When finished, the heap resembled an ordinary forest knoll.

Her task complete, she tunneled back under the porous pile and lay down in the shallow pit, pulling the earth over her, not perfectly but sufficiently, burying herself for the second time in her existence. Safe in the cocoon, she closed her eyes, and before she slipped into the deep sleep, she let her mind drift. It had been hard. All of it, her entire life, and her entire death. So much evil in her life, and so much anger.

CHAPTER 2

1843

On a breezy day in October of 1836, a quiet, dark-eyed little girl named Mary was born somewhere along the Pennsylvania countryside. She was the second healthy daughter for the happy couple, and despite their meager lifestyle, they felt blessed. Unfortunately, they only got to enjoy their lives together for another six and a half years before things took a tragic turn. The father (Elmer) suffered a fatal heart attack behind the family barn just before the sunset on a cold January evening.

It was an out-of-the-way location to fall; he had been examining the remnants of a large hornet's nest that he'd avoided during the summer months. The hive was up high on the building and was hard to get at, not a great place to go to war with an army that outnumbered him two thousand to one on any given summer day. He would have taken the hive down in November, but had forgotten.

Because he lay dying in an out-of-the-way spot, he was hard to find. Help was miles away, and the mother (Alice) suffered a long lonely night searching for her husband while simultaneously keeping her two young girls away from the hot woodstove.

Help didn't arrive until the following day, and when they finally did, they found the husband and father dead and half-frozen within an hour. Elmer's death spelled the end of the happy homestead. Alice missed his love and guidance. He could make any situation work. Sarah, who was nine years old at the time, was just old enough to carry the loving memories of their happy family with her for the rest of her short life.

Mary, who was seven years old, was just under that age line—a little too young to remember the caring he provided, so important to a healthy child's development. For Mary, the hardship years would take a much firmer foothold in her upbringing. Alice, suddenly underprivileged and financially crippled, was forced to sell the farm.

The consequences of Elmer's death were long-lasting. Like a pebble in a pond, the after-shock of his passing would set them on a dark, difficult path. Years later, both Alice and Sarah would die prematurely. Mary would survive, although it could hardly be called a coming-of-age tale. As a teenager, she would be forced to flee and change her name to hide from those that might decide to hunt her.

CHAPTER 3

1844

Elmer's death made life difficult for the mother, Alice. The burden of her two children, along with her plain looks, rendered her nearly invisible to other men. Money was tight, and the resources dwindled. Desperation haunted her dreams, and sleep eluded her. She began to look for work, a job that would provide room and board above all. She could no longer afford or maintain a house of any size.

Two years later and merely days away from bankruptcy, came a knock at the door. It was a man...a very large man with a dark, bushy beard. He towered over her as he filled the doorframe. He introduced himself as Gideon Walker. He told her he had heard of her plight from the clerk at the general store and was willing to help if she didn't mind moving further into the country.

The new job included room and board, and Gideon Walker, although very persuasive, didn't have to twist her arm to say yes. Not only did the job sound like it would solve many of her problems, but...might there be an even deeper connection happening? Alice felt for the first time in a long time that a man might be looking at her...as a woman, and it felt good.

He cooked for them, which was non-traditional, to say the least; men didn't usually cook, but were more often seen in the field, or tending to the animals, or maintaining the structures on the property. This farm, a full day out in the middle of nowhere, was different than any she had seen. Gideon didn't seem to care much about the condition of the buildings, and there were very few animals…in fact, there were no cows to be seen. What meat and milk they had came from roughly eight to twelve goats on any given day. *Was it because he was just starting out?*

His food was…thin and unsatisfying, but it was enough to nourish their bodies. *Barely enough.* Beggars can't be choosers; she reminded herself. Gideon confessed that he had only purchased the farm two months before her arrival, and money was tight, but things would get better as long as they worked hard and as a team, consistently. He was a bit of a controlling man and liked things a specific way, meaning he liked *everything* a specific way.

As time passed and Alice got to know him better, she felt pressured (*persuaded*) more and more to do things his way. She did her best daily to keep the girls occupied. He could be single-minded at times. Sarah, the daughter, sensed this too, and Alice, on more than one occasion, witnessed her eldest daughter physically avoiding him. Mary, however, was as headstrong as her father and seemed on some level to rub Gideon the wrong way. Overall, Alice felt as if she needed him more than he needed her, and feared that if she didn't comply, they might be asked to leave, and that was something she couldn't risk.

The workdays were long—longer than at any time in her life. He would wake her at 3 am every morning, and they would go to bed very late. It was an inordinate amount of work for a tiny garden and a dozen goats. The days and nights began to blur.

At the end of her thirty-seventh evening on the farm, Gideon Walker appeared in her doorway as she prepared herself for bed. The girls were already asleep, nearly an hour before. They, too, were kept up longer than they rightly should be and had a daily list of chores that kept them exhaustingly busy. Gideon approached her and began to play with her hair; she was too tired and too intimidated to think things through or attempt to decline.

Her mind buzzed as she saw stars in her peripheral vision. Before she knew it, Gideon was on top of her. He made no effort to undress or get into bed. Oddly, she felt numb and indifferent to the entire episode. The last thing she remembered was the sight of him leaving the bedroom still completely dressed, buckling his belt. He and the candle he carried disappeared down the hallway, leaving her in the darkness.

He shook her, not three hours later, to get up for work. She would be alone today; he was headed into town and would be back by evening. He told her to work fast to get everything done in his absence and that there would be guests with him when he returned. Exhausted and in a daze, she dutifully rose to do as she was told. After he left, she woke the girls at the customary time she had been trained to and didn't think twice about it.

The only food in the house was what he had left from the previous evening; a gruel-like bowl of goat and—herbs and such. She didn't know what it was and hadn't thought to ask, even though they had all been eating variations of the same thing since they had arrived. There was never any fruit or vegetables in the house, at most a squash or a potato every so often. There were also no fruit-bearing trees in the yard; there had been an apple tree once, but it seemed to have perished. She wondered for a quick second about the history of this farm, but then her mind drifted off again. She couldn't seem to concentrate these days.

CHAPTER 4

1845

Gideon returned that evening with two guests, a mother and son pair. Alice didn't have the strength to be social or even care about the two new people on the farm. He carried a slaughtered goat over one shoulder and a small bag of provisions, a very meager haul for the only trip to the store in over a month.

Alice took the bag and looked inside; more of his herbs, the bitter ones he used to season his bland food. Just a bag of herbs, and a goat, despite the fact there were already a dozen of the creatures on property. She decided not to care. Food had lost most of its attraction anyway. She didn't feel sharp, always in a daze, and nearly accustomed to hunger. She turned her back on the new people and brought the herbs into the kitchen. Gideon dropped the goat on the ground and herded the new people off to the guest house.

He returned a few moments later and instructed her on how to prepare dinner; this was a new and different chore, but the change of pace didn't excite her in any way. He opened the bag of herbs and instructed her on how much of each she should add to the dish before leaving again.

Two hours later, when the food was near ready, she went and found him. He was behind the guest house, standing very close to the new woman and her son, talking directly into her face with a calm, smooth tone. He stood oddly close, filling her field of vision. It was similar to the way he had spoken to Alice when she arrived three, four...*how long ago was that now?*

The new arrival mother was humorless and had dark circles under her eyes. The boy was slightly more animated but was too thin for his age. He looked to be about eight years old. Alice, who used to be cordial to strangers, was indifferent. Gideon occasionally took his gaze off the woman and gave the boy his face to rein him in and perhaps intimidate him. Alice announced dinner in monotone fashion then turned back for the kitchen.

Dusk was falling, and one candle (Gideon's rules) lit the dinner table. He didn't eat very much but instead controlled the conversation from start to finish, keeping the candle near his face so that it would be the only thing on which anyone could properly focus. Alice's girls, used to the routine, said nothing the entire meal. The new boy seemed upset that every one of his attempts at conversation was snuffed by Gideon. The big man had stolen his mother's attention. The boy's self-esteem plummeted, and he sulked in silence. Martha (the mother) appeared desperate, trusting, and hopeful all at the same time, much the way Alice used to feel before the ingredients in Gideon's cooking and lack of sleep neutralized her ambitions. Gideon produced a large cup of tea that he passed around and required everyone to drink.

When dinner was over, Gideon instructed Alice to clean up while he helped the new guests settle. He escorted them out of the main building and back to the guest house while Alice tended to the extra chores that he used to handle exclusively. Her promotion was apparent, but still, he monitored her. She was allowed to go to bed at midnight but not before. He warned that he would be checking, and he did. Alice made a conscious decision not to fight him; she knew not to test his patience. He had not been violent with her except for the encounter in the bedroom (*it might have been rape*), but underneath his surface was something seething she didn't want to see.

Months passed, and Alice was given more and more responsibility—stretching her workday even further. Mary, who was always moody even on her best day, seemed mostly unchanged, but Sarah was markedly different from her first day on the farm. The laughter and joy that used to come spilling out were all held in check, replaced by nerves. Her eyes were dull and disinterested, but she got all of her chores done, so Alice brushed it off. She was worried, but not worried enough to leave the farm for the cold outside world.

In addition to the cooking, Alice was taught how to properly set up the altar in the living room where everyone gathered every evening near midnight. The altar was a new addition to the house. One day the living room was empty, and the next, there it was. There had been no hammering, no construction, and no recent trip into town. Alice guessed it must have been somewhere in storage.

Every night was something different, and she began to look forward to the gatherings. Anything different was stimulating. Sometimes there were rituals; some days there were ceremonies and sermons, and on occasion, a baptism. The goblet of odd-tasting tea made the rounds. Alice didn't recognize the denomination of service or even the name "God" or "Jesus" at any time. Sometimes one of the children would nod off mid-ceremony, and either Alice or Martha would be required to rouse them.

Weeks later, Gideon went back into town, this time for three full days, leaving the two women in charge. They weren't aware, but he doubled back immediately and set up camp in the woods where he was able to watch them make sure they followed his every instruction. Their numbed minds dutifully completed their ingrained to-do lists. The women passed the test. They kept everyone awake as long as he had instructed, and no changes were made to the diet. The children were not seen out in the sun, and he could hear the chanting coming from the living room every evening. His following was growing.

One year and eight new members later, Gideon left the farm once again for a personal pilgrimage to Salem, Massachusetts. It was his dream to congregate with other minds similar to his own. He had heard rumors that some of the *best in the field* were in Salem. Of course, none of this was advertised to the general public or even printed on paper.

The small city in Massachusetts was a magnet to those interested in studying the occult. It wasn't all about witches, but the witch reputation that Salem had earned in 1693 captured the attention of...*enthusiasts*...worldwide. It became a gathering place for dark thinkers. An unknowing visitor would never realize what Salem had become. The downtown area was as normal in appearance as any of the surrounding towns, and its port was a boon to business, but in the woods, and the suburbs and in odd houses, dark minds communed, swapping stories and making plans.

During his trip, Gideon, discreetly poking around, came to meet an old drunk in one of the local pubs. According to the man, there was a book that existed that could enhance the power of the mind. Gideon's ears perked up as he felt a tingle; this was the reason for his trip; he had heard the legends. The *Book of Shadows,* as the old man called it, was said to be a virtual how-to guide that offered (to those that followed it religiously) physical enhancement and even immortality. Gideon, in his soul, was skeptical but wanted it to be true. Perhaps this was the next step in his journey.

The drunken fool he was talking to soon made it known to Gideon that to "purchase" his copy, he would have to endure several tests run by the powers that be, a group of living-dead men who made their home in the woods. These tests were no joke, and according to the drunk, "many people" had backed away from them—and then disappeared—when they heard how dire the consequences could be. Disfigurement, torture, abduction, murder, and often the death of the initiated were the rumors. Furthermore, the tests were always different, making the roadmap to success nearly impossible to navigate.

Not used to being denied or limited in any way, Gideon was intrigued and wanted to know more. He could pass this series of tests or any series he set his mind to for that matter. The "Book of Shadows" called to him. It was real. He could feel it in his bones.

Suddenly the drunk gasped and winced at the same time. Behind him, the crowd in the busy bar backed away as he slid off his chair and collapsed to the floor. A maroon stain began to spread on the back of his coat.

Gideon registered his surprise as he scanned the mob for a man with a knife and prepared to fight. At that moment, the crowd parted, and the bartender passed through, grabbing the dying man by the feet and dragging him through the building to parts unknown. Gideon stood up and backed slowly toward the exit.

"You're a stranger, ain't you?" the man asked.

"I am," he answered. "What happened here?" He put his hand on the butt of his knife under his coat.

"None of your business. What you just saw was a fool that doesn't know when to shut his mouth. Forget what he told you and head back to Pennsylvania, or wherever you're from."

"How did you know I'm from Pennsylvania?" he looked wild-eyed at them…not from fear, but excitement. *They knew*, he thought. The powers *existed*. The man who had spoken realized his tactic had failed.

"It's time for you to leave, Mr. Walker. And we don't want to see you back." Nearly a dozen knives glinted in the dim light of the bar. And they all knew his name. The entire bar knew who he was and from where he had come. Gideon thought it best to leave and regroup. Live to fight another day—and there would most definitely *be* another day.

15

"Thank you; I'll be leaving now." With that, he bowed out. No one followed. *They probably don't intimidate easily*, he thought. *I'm not the first person to come looking and then turn tail*. He smiled, knowing full well that they had underestimated him.

Intrigue turned to obsession as he took the road out of Salem. As he rode, he began to dream of plans for his next visit. He was a big man, a determined man, a smart man, and a ruthless man. Once he got his hands on that book, he would be an unstoppable man. They had no idea with whom they were dealing.

After arriving home, checking his flock, getting in the faces of disobedient children, and making sure provisions were sufficient, he turned himself around and headed back, hell-bent on avoiding the mobs in the bars this time. This time he would seek one-on-one encounters, where he could defend himself properly and get the answers he needed. He would demand to meet the people who held *The Book of Shadows*.

A bald man with a mouth full of broken teeth surprised him on his third afternoon in town. The man was thin, and his mouth was so ugly from neglect that it was off-putting; he resembled a rat in many ways. As Gideon passed two houses in a residential neighborhood, the man popped out of the alleyway between them and followed him for three blocks. They were the only two men on the street, and Gideon sensed his presence. Again, he was surprised when the man used his name.

"Gideon Walker," the man bleated.

Gideon turned slowly and with confidence, preparing for the customary reaction anytime someone faced him for the first time. Because of his size, and perhaps the look in his eye, they always drew back...but...this little ugly man did not—despite being outweighed by nearly a hundred pounds.

"Yes, that's me. Who gave you my name, and what do you want?"

The rat-man looked at Gideon unblinking. He appeared disheveled, and despite the dozen feet between them, there was a strong odor. He wondered for a second if it was from the rat-man, or something else dead in the bushes.

"We know your name, and we know you've been asking around. We also know about your farm in Pennsylvania, and what you're doing with it. We know about New Orleans too. And we told you to stay away."

Gideon's stood still, aghast. Nobody knew about New Orleans. Anybody who knew anything about New Orleans was dead and buried. His control of the conversation was gone, and the rat-man had the floor. He was usually the intimidating one. The last time he'd been intimidated was during his childhood. Now before him, this ugly man's confidence was indeed greater than his own. He stared back at Gideon, seemingly uncaring, all business. Gideon paused. For the first time in his life, *he listened.*

"How..." he stumbled, "Alright. I want to learn. I want to learn everything. I want to read the *Book of Shadows.*"

"We don't need you to read the book. There is no *Book.* We don't need you at all. Turn around, or you'll end up like your friend at the bar."

"Wait...I have a following. If you need *resources,* I can help with that. I..."

"Resources? We don't need your *resources,* Mr. Walker. Keep your hags and their pups. Go back to them while you still can. As I said, we don't want you."

Gideon noted that the man had not blinked since the conversation had started. The wind had changed directions, however, and he realized full-well why the man was not afraid of him.

He was *dead*—

—one of the people to which the old drunk was referring—a *living-dead man.*

Gideon trembled, reflexively. The rumors were not nearly as shocking as the reality. The Book of Shadows must go much deeper than he'd imagined. He stopped thinking about the Book

17

for a moment and began to wonder how this conversation would end. He hesitated speechless.

"Last warning Mr. Walker. Turn and go." The man pulled out a long knife. Gideon began to wonder if he would be slain right there in the street, in broad daylight. This was no idle threat. But it couldn't end this way. He was destined to be more than this, and he believed it to his core. He had seen and done many things, many bad, bad things, both in Pennsylvania and in New Orleans. He had devoted his life to darkness, and this was the next logical step. Why should he fear these people or anything related to them, including the man standing before him?

Their element of surprise was over. Who cared if the Dead Men knew his name, or about his farm in Pennsylvania, or the basement in New Orleans? They were parlor tricks if you had the tools. And they had more tools. And he wanted their tools. He decided then and there that he would rather die than live without the *Book of Shadows*.

Decision made, he told the rat-man to put his knife away—and as the words left his lips, his brief moment of fear disappeared. With his mind's eye, he pictured a symbolic fork-in-the-road; he had just chosen the newer and more exciting path. The rat-man sprung.

He came at Gideon like an animal. The strength in his body was inhuman, but Gideon half-expected as much. A memory popped into his head, something he had read in New Orleans long ago. A creature like this would not die easily. He sidestepped the lunging revenant, adeptly avoiding the dead man's powerful limbs and dangerous blade. While the rat-man whirled, Gideon sank his blade directly into the man's chest, precisely where his heart would be. He followed with a powerful kick, and the beast hit the ground, losing his knife.

Moving quickly, he kicked the blade away and worked fast, cutting the heart out of the body while the dying revenant pounded and gouged at him with ungodly strength. If he hadn't known to remove the heart, he would have been dead. If things had not gone perfectly, down to the quarter-second, it would all be over. Perhaps he *was* here for a reason, as he had always believed. All this in broad daylight. Where were the townspeople? It was a side street, but this was too good to be true. Perhaps another trick from *the Book*. He had to have it.

Gideon sat down, hands covered in rancid blood, arms slashed from fingernails, nose broken. He decided not to remind himself how foolish the ordeal had been and how lucky he was—"*big man*" or not. Realizing he was holding what was once a human heart, he tossed it into the bushes.

Just then, another man appeared from between the same two houses. Gideon froze. Perhaps this *was indeed* his last day on Earth. Lightning could not possibly strike twice for him; if this were the end, then he would have to relax and allow it to happen. He would even ask them to make it quick. The second revenant walked up and stopped ten feet in front of him.

"It's time to move your cult to Massachusetts," he said, holding out his hand, making Gideon get up and approach him for a piece of paper. Gideon approached slowly, flexing his smashed nostrils, trying not to catch too much of the man's air. The eyes had life, but there was a glaze, akin to the beginning of cataracts. His skin was mottled. Spider veins showed on his neck, and a large purple bruise covered the left side of his head. His hands were worn and damaged as if he had been in a fight with an animal and never healed properly. Either that or he had been digging. Yes, that was it, and it made sense—*he most likely had to dig himself out of his own grave.*

On the piece of paper was the address of a farm with directions on how to get there.

"What happens after that?" said Gideon.

"You wait," said the second revenant. He turned and walked back to the alleyway between the two houses, stopping only to retrieve the rat-man's heart, and Gideon Walker knew better than to follow.

CHAPTER 5

1847

The first thing Gideon did after cleaning up was head to the address written on the paper. Trips back and forth from Pennsylvania were neither short nor leisurely, and he intended on economizing as much as possible. He had confidence that the women had his cult under control—if they didn't—they would pay dearly. The farm on the paper was not located in Salem but the next settlement north—an area called Beverly Farms.

Beverly Farms (a rural community inside the town of Beverly), was not as developed as Salem and was still nearly ninety-five percent forest. The farm on the paper handed to Gideon was located somewhere smack in the middle of the map, and it reminded him of his place in Pennsylvania—chosen for its seclusion.

A man sat waiting in the window as he rode in as if he already owned the place. This man was still alive, as best as he could tell.

"Welcome home, Mr. Walker," he said. Gideon laughed briefly at the man's presumption.

"I haven't even seen the place yet. Can I ask your name, since you know mine? Then we can take a look around."

"I'm not here to show you around, Mr. Walker. I'm here to hand you the keys. I'm also here to help you move your things up from Pennsylvania. And in case you haven't figured it out yet, this is the deal. Non-negotiable. It's not my farm to give you; I work for *them*—and apparently, *so do you*. Now from what I also hear, you've got some people to move, and move quietly. I'm here to help you with that, no questions asked. I suggest you unpack your horse and get some sleep. We head south tomorrow early. You can call me Fenerty." With that, the man disappeared deep into the house and closed a door.

Again, Gideon didn't enjoy taking orders. He would succumb for now, but as soon as he got his hands on the Book of Shadows, learned its secrets and figured out the whole situation, things would change. He took a look around before bunking. It was a small farm with a guest house and a medium-sized barn. There were no fields for crops per se, but there was a small patch of land that might have at one time been a family-sized garden. The guest house was close to the main farmhouse, and there was also a shed across the property near the edge of the woods.

The buildings were in disrepair, and Gideon suspected that the farm had never been anyone's pride and joy. It was more like a camp, intended for dark things like his Pennsylvania farm was, namely meetings, retreats, training, learning, and following orders. The revenants, or whatever they called themselves, had most likely taken over this property generations ago and had used it as a way to traffic, hide, and erase people ever since. It would do just fine.

CHAPTER 6

1847

Gideon heard Fenerty moving around outside the bedroom before the sun came up and dressed to join him; it would be a long day—never mind that—a long *week*. To his surprise, a large covered wagon sat in the driveway, a pair of horses ready to pull it. Fenerty sat in the driver's seat prepared; Gideon wondered for a moment how long he had been waiting but then discarded the thought. It didn't matter. He saddled up, and the wagon followed dutifully.

It took eight days to get to Pennsylvania. Fenerty would not yet allow him to put his property up for sale; he even threatened to cancel the deal and return to Massachusetts without him if Gideon did so. This trip's purpose was to get Gideon's cult moved up to Beverly Farms safe and unseen. Once again, Gideon didn't like being the "helper," but kept it to himself, as he could sense that Fenerty was answering to a more intimidating employer.

The women (all six of them) greeted the wagon like slaves as they pulled up. There was no joy in their eyes, nor was there any hesitation tending to whatever needed doing. Fenerty looked around, took a headcount then borrowed Gideon's horse. He then left immediately and was gone overnight; Gideon began to wonder if this was a test. *Move thirteen people to Massachusetts all by yourself, and you can read the Book of Shadows.* But he was wrong.

At two o'clock the next morning, he heard Fenerty return, this time riding a different covered wagon, leading Gideon's horse behind it.

"Let's go, Walker. Load it all up. Get everybody moving. Nobody should see this wagon in broad daylight." Gideon realized that Fenerty had stolen the wagon. He got up and woke the women. They all loaded one wagon with goods and, when finished, woke the children and piled them into the second. Gideon didn't know it, but he would never see Pennsylvania again.

CHAPTER 7

1847

They arrived in Beverly Farms ten days later, well after dark. As soon as the horses stopped walking, Fenerty got down off the wagon and mentioned something about paperwork to tend to on the women, then walked into the dark forest without so much as a goodbye. Gideon watched him go, assuring himself that he was here for a reason. All of his questions, including the reason there were living people working with revenants, would be answered eventually. The women set to work unloading the wagons, feeding the horses, and directing the children. They hadn't heard one of Gideon's sermons in weeks, so he began writing one after mixing a strong tea.

He found a quiet room on the second floor of their new farm and sat down at a desk to write by candlelight. When he was halfway down the page and fully lost in thought, there was a sound outside the window; he stood up to take a look.

A white face outside the upstairs window caught him off guard, startling him badly; he nearly dropped his candle. Staring in through the glass was another revenant, clinging to the side of the house, nearly twenty feet over the lawn below. His eyes met Gideon's, and his head nodded, gesturing for him to open the window. Gideon, surprised, was intimidated once again. How he had defeated the rat-man, he didn't know…the whole event now seemed surreal, as if it were a dream. He had bested a supernatural creature in a ten-second fight, but if it had gone eleven—it would have been his own heart in the bushes, and he knew it. Surely they would not underestimate him twice.

Knowing full-well that the fragile window was no protection, he reached down with both hands and lifted. A stench filled the room instantly, and he gagged before blocking his nose. Gideon backed away, heart racing as the creature crawled in. He attempted to start the conversation, albeit nervously.

"I want to read the Book of Shadows."

"I know that," said the being.

"Who are you?"

"Names aren't as important as they once were, but my name used to be Lyman Helms. That information doesn't help you much, does it? What else do you think you need to know?"

"Are you the boss? I want to speak to someone in charge."

Lyman Helms shook his head, and a half-dozen flies took wing.

"I suppose."

"How many of you are there?" asked Gideon.

"Enough to haunt your dreams. No more and no less. We'll tell you exactly how many if and when we decide the time is right. What other questions do you have before I tell you how things will proceed?"

Gideon had once again lost control of the conversation. He thought for a second about what to ask next but was too distracted by Helms' misdirections. Finally, he repeated his original question:

"How can I see the Book?" But the dead man changed the subject.

"Gideon—this sort of situation doesn't happen often. Maybe every once a millennium for a wild guess. You caught our collective eye early on. When someone begins studying the occult—we know it. Whether it's here or Louisiana—we know.

And when someone starts a cult, we watch even closer…but until now and to the best of my knowledge; no human has ever beaten a revenant one-on-one. Mobs of townspeople have done it, but never one-on-one. You're a special man, but don't count your chickens; you'll be dead in less than a minute if we don't come to terms right here and right now." Gideon swallowed hard.

"I'm listening."

"Two dozen, over ten years. Any more is too fast and would be risking unwanted attention."

"Two dozen what?"

"Two dozen people, of course. Five upfront. Nineteen more over the next ten years. To use as we like—which means we kill them, and use the parts."

As disgusting as that was, Gideon didn't blink, and began to do the math; he would have to recruit roughly two downtrodden souls per year, but he was surpassing that pace already. If recruiting in Massachusetts was anything like Pennsylvania, he should have no problem.

"So you *do* need bodies. I knew it. The rat-man said you didn't need my services when I offered them. What will you do with them?"

"Almost the same thing you were going to, except we don't keep them alive. We can put the parts to good use immediately, and over time we'll show you how. Recipes, if you will, from the Book of Shadows."

"Why wouldn't you just take what I have now and kill me?"

"We could. We certainly could. The fact that nobody even knows you are here would make it very easy. We try to be discrete because of our appearance. We don't need the townspeople burning down the forest, hunting us with pitchforks."

"What are you? I thought you were revenants, but you seem to be more. You're not just hell-bent on revenge and revenge alone."

"We are no strangers to revenge, and we *are* revenants…but

better put, revenants *evolved*. Four hundred years ago, a wise man named Claude Allemand arrived from Europe with his *Book of Shadows*. He had devoted his entire life to collecting all things occult: Spells, talismans, runes, symbols, and that sort of thing. He traveled the world for decades, putting it all together, translating it, and when he had gathered all the information he needed, he decided to make the transition himself—from living to immortal so that he could continue his studies virtually forever.

Instead of a simple bloodthirsty beast driven by vengeance, which is the original definition of a *revenant*...he had applied spells and procedures necessary to enhance not only himself but for others like him. He is dead now, but what he left was a race of ever-evolving revenants adept in *magick*. Not parlor tricks mind you. The fake type of magic I refer to ends with the letter "c." I'm talking about real *magick*, and that ends with the letter "k." Real spells—real results. We are now revenants, enhanced by the powers of witchcraft." Gideon was more than intrigued.

"What happened to Allemand?"

"Something along the lines of what I've already told you. We, as a group, got greedy, dipping our pen once too often. The townspeople were waiting for us one night, and Allemand was ripped apart by a mob. He killed nine before he fell, but they'll never forget it—or us. That's the reason we moved out of Salem. It's a magnet for the insane. Anyone who has used a Ouija Board considers it a pilgrimage. Allemand's death was only fifty years ago—just the blink of an eye for us, and things haven't been the same since."

"What do you mean by that?"

"Turnover...and recruitment. Without his leadership, we became weaker as a group. We made a rule after his death to be stealthier and avoid detection whenever possible. We began to lean more toward the *missing persons* business rather than *smash and grab*. We put a cap on our population to help avoid detection. Allemand would have never recruited Sandberg—the revenant you killed. He had an eye for talent, and he was an even better teacher."

"So, the only reason you won't kill me now and take my followers is that…you want me to join?"

"That remains to be seen, but we see the potential. I may still kill you and take your following, but yes—because Sandberg is dead, we have a vacancy. Your commitment is imperative. If you waver, then we will go in another direction. Also, if you become primitive and bloodthirsty like the revenants of old, we will kill you. You look like the sort of man who likes giving the orders, am I right about that?"

Gideon nodded but did not comment.

"Put it out of your mind, Mr. Walker. There is an order here… one that puts the entire race over the individual. Our evolution is ongoing. We learn and grow together. Am I clear on this very important point?"

Again Gideon nodded, but deep down, he would have liked to hear more about Claude Allemand, a man after his own heart. Gideon was a leader; Helms had him pegged correctly. His entire life had been spent taking things over; it would be a hard habit to break.

"You remind us of Allemand, and your victory over Sandberg could perhaps be considered an omen. Because of your dark background, you have potential. But I won't let any of that sway my decision. What's important is what happens from now on."

"Will I live forever?" Gideon asked, somewhat excitedly.

"Most likely not. The odds are against it, especially considering your inherent nature to harm others. Sooner or later, these things usually catch up with you—if you are foolish. Perhaps you can *change yourself*. For the most part, that is up to you, but immortality is deceptive. Many falsely come to believe they are indestructible."

"Where will I live?"

"You will live here for at least the next ten years as a mortal.

After that, if things go well, we will finish the process for you. I have given you enough information. Now I want your answer."

Gideon didn't have to think about his response. There was only one answer.

"My answer...is, yes, of course. Has anyone ever said *no*?"

CHAPTER 8

1847

Gideon delivered a distracted sermon that evening. He had accepted his wait-list position but couldn't tell his current employees that there would be ten more years of passion-free sermons because his heart was no longer in it. Helms had waved *magick* under his nose, and his old gig of brainwashing lost souls now seemed unfulfilling at best. He knew, however, that if he didn't live up to his end of the bargain, all would be lost.

The meeting had ended with Gideon's acceptance of the deal. As soon as the word "yes" had left his lips, Lyman Helms turned and climbed down the side of the building. Several dozen flies buzzed Gideon's head searching for their lost host. No other words had been spoken. What came next? He went to bed, perplexed and somewhat agitated.

Three hours later, he woke to the sound of screaming. He rose angrily, tired, burdened by problems that now seemed nagging and unimportant, even though his life depended on fixing these same problems—for at least ten more years. The person making the racket was Martha, who lived in the next room over. He entered the room, and she stood there—alone, looking out the window, shrieking into the night.

Her son Marcus was missing. He was gone, and Gideon fully understood why, although he was somewhat surprised by the speed and manner of the exchange. He did his best to comfort her, pretending not to know why. As he false-comforted her, he realized that the screaming was also coming from several other rooms in the house.

Shrill, desperate voices filled the air; Martha's was not the only one, and he fully understood that Helms had come early—very early—striking while the iron was hot. He took the first five souls before the townspeople of Beverly Farms even knew they existed; smart and safe. The entire upstairs was howling with people who had lost family members, taken in the dark of night.

What surprised Gideon—but shouldn't have—was that all five taken were children. *Of course, it made sense*, and he should have seen it coming. While he didn't have the Book of Shadows, he had read a few other books and knew a thing or two about the occult. He knew the blood of an innocent was worth more than the blood of a sinner. He also knew that nothing would go to waste. They would use every bit for something. Blood, marrow, organs, brain, skin, fat, eyes, tendons; every bit, put to use somehow—some way. Even ashes had value in some rites. Helms himself had mentioned virgins and children. *Of course, of course, of course.*

There was no sleep to be had in the house that night. Gideon was handed a fine mess to deal with, a fine first test for an eager new hopeful. He grabbed his rifle and headed into the woods—alone—under the guise of "getting the children back." As soon as he was deep enough into the trees, he pulled the blanket he had stashed under his coat and made camp. There *were* no more children. It was time for sleep, and this would be his only break from the chaos. Tomorrow would be a long day getting the women back in line, and it would take more than a few herbs, teas, and sleep deprivation to make them forget the abductions.

As he pulled the blanket up, he criticized himself for not nailing down more of the specifics of the deal. A warning would have been nice, as well as his input on how to stagger the abductions and make them look like accidents. The women were in a frenzy now. He would most likely have to get physical with several of them to calm their emotions. He did a headcount in his mind; five children missing meant that there were only two left on the farm. He hadn't had time to figure which two.

CHAPTER 9

1847

The next morning, Alice hugged Mary tight; her eldest daughter Sarah had been one of the five children taken, and Mary was all she had left in the world. Gideon Walker had bravely marched into the forest to find the missing kids, and the six women all waited impatiently for his return. He was gone so long some of the women began to wonder if he ever would.

The wailing continued. Four of the six women were now completely childless. Only Mary and Cora's son (Edward) remained. Cora and Alice did the only thing they *could* do; hug their children, but the other four women were manic. Their minds and bodies, accustomed to the routines and muscle memory of tending to a child, were left unemployed, forced to fumble for love lost. They burned their excess energy by pacing and grieving uncontrollably. This and the added fatigue of a lost night of sleep made the overall atmosphere toxic.

Quiet Mary, who was now eleven years old, cried for her missing sister. Sarah had always been the one who did the talking for her; the sister who was perhaps the only person in the world that understood her shyness—her introversion. Millie, Mary's ragdoll, was badly damaged, and she hugged her tight, the same way her mother hugged her. The now twice-broken family was beyond repair—shattered, and down to just two. Mary had not accepted Gideon Walker as any sort of father figure and had never trusted him. She knew for sure that he would return from the woods empty-handed.

CHAPTER 10

1847

Near mid-morning, Gideon emerged from the woods with his rifle. Alice looked at him, crestfallen, as did the other five. The children were still missing, and the odds of finding them alive had fallen exponentially. Oddly, He threw a blanket by the door and approached the despondent, diminished clan.

"I'm sorry. I couldn't find the children. Neither hide nor hair. I'm afraid—they're gone."

Margaret, one of the mothers who had lost her daughter (Anna), ran at him and began beating his chest violently.

"Why, why!? They were terrible! They smelled of death! Go and get a dog! Surely they can be tracked! I will go! I will go right now! I can still smell them. I will never forget that scent!"

Gideon wrapped his large hands around her tiny arms and pushed her back. When he let her go, she came at him again, and he sent her to the grass with a powerful slap.

"Tell me about them," he said. "Tell me exactly what happened." He did this not only to stall but to learn more about how they worked.

"I didn't see a thing!" said Clara, who had lost her son Robert. "I was having a dream about a dead deer's body we found in the forest. When I woke up, the window was open, and Robert was gone!"

"I felt George pulled from me in a dream. I smelled them too. I thought it was a nightmare—I WISH it were only a nightmare… and now…" Rose burst into tears and could not finish her story.

"I was awake when they opened the window," said Martha. I only *thought* I was dreaming. I thought it was a hallucination from something that you were putting in our food, things I didn't care about because we had a roof over our heads and were safe—but now Marcus is gone, and—*you didn't protect him!* Why did I… why did I let you take over our lives! Marcus is gone. I don't want to be here anymore! You're evil! You're terrible! You couldn't even *find them!* A big, strong man like you!"

"Enough!" he bellowed. Despite the herbal measures taken to numb their minds, Martha had known all along and was apparently only here for the roof over her head. *Some people get by easily on little sleep and very little sustenance*, he noted. Martha appeared to be one of these people—only there for the room, board, and protection. She would have to be filtered out sooner than later. Her independent thinking was more than dangerous, especially considering the latest developments.

Gideon turned next to Cora, mother of Edward. The revenants had spared Edward, and Cora hugged him tightly but remained silent. She was the only mother not to lose a child at all—the others would surely show their envy later if she were to demonstrate thanks.

Alice was the last mother to which he turned. She was the very first sheep in the flock, and Alice had lost Sarah, leaving her with only Mary, the quiet one. Gideon frowned; he would have preferred Mary to have been taken. She was hard to read— unpredictable at best. He often wondered what she was thinking. Was she *slow*, or just quiet?

He would have to address this with Helms at his next opportunity. Check with me first, let me pick the names. Alice sat sullen crying, while Mary stood clutching her doll, her sunken eyes hidden by her stringy hair.

"I didn't see anything,"—said Alice—"I was on the floor across the room, and Mary and Sarah were in bed. The first thing I remember was Martha screaming from the other room. I smelled them—It was horrible, like a dead animal, or like a dog that rolls on one."

"Mary, what did you see? What did you hear?" said Gideon. The gaunt-faced girl moved a quarter turn to face him, but did not look up. She said nothing, as he had frustratingly anticipated.

"Mary...*Mary!* What did you see? You were lying right next to your sister." Alice unconsciously pulled Mary's arm and wrapped her in a hug.

"Did you see anything, sweetheart?" she whispered.

Mary's trance ended, and she locked eyes on her mother's, shaking her head "no." Gideon didn't care for the fact that little Mary had never acknowledged him in any fashion—since day one. Quiet people were hard to read. Were his herbs having any effect on her? If not, surely, the Book of Shadows would have stronger remedies. He made a mental note.

CHAPTER 11

1847

Time passed, and Gideon Walker managed the nightmare of damage control. Jarred by the abductions, his cult temporarily lost focus. The proverbial sheep were wandering, and it was impossible to dismiss outright, the common-sense reactions people had when faced with such a catastrophe.

"Where is Martha? He asked.

Martha was missing—Martha the *volunteer*, the one who was fast becoming a problem. Nobody knew where she was. He checked the horses. One was missing. A moment of rage filled his neck with hot blood, and his temples pulsed. No one had ever escaped him. He prepared the cult for visitors.

When law enforcement from Salem finally arrived as he knew they would, the women—previously oblivious—flocked. Here, after all, was hope for their lost children. Martha rode into camp just behind them, looking somewhat triumphant. Gideon glared but let the women do their talking. He filled in the gaps of their stories as the helpful and caring custodian.

As soon as the marshal heard the term "dead men," he nodded as if he had heard something like this before, and wrote faster. Gideon couldn't tell whether it was because the man knew of Helms and his group, or because he had heard similar stories and hadn't believed them. The authorities were at the farm for over three hours. Helms had thankfully not left any evidence that he or his dead men were ever there, and the marshal and his crew had nothing to find.

They interviewed everyone and performed a perfunctory search of the nearby woods. Gideon silently sweated Martha's performance. If anyone might say too much or mention the word "cult," it would be her, yet she depended upon him heavily for her general well-being. She also believed, however, that she was entitled to have a say. Luckily she kept her mouth shut, perhaps choosing to give Gideon another chance at taking better care of her before selling him out and living life in the gutter. Later in the day, like a battered wife, he heard her even complimenting him, describing him as "father-like" to the marshal.

After the individual interviews and the failed search, enthusiasm amongst the women waned, and they retired to their rooms disappointed. When the last of them had left the living room, Gideon spoke:

"Marshal, I'm so sorry you had to be called out there today. I can explain everything. When you arrived, the women surrounded you, and I couldn't say anything, but now I can speak freely." Gideon described the farm as a religious retreat. He also made up a story that he was caring for women who had already lost their children years back and ever since would recreate or "relive" the episode.

"Have you heard of the Hoernerstown Tragedy? Four years ago?" Gideon looked at him intensely. The marshal had not, and it was not because Pennsylvania was so far away—but because it was made up and no such thing had ever happened. Gideon acted as if it pained him to retell the story.

"Ah, well. Bad news does not always travel fast, and sometimes that's a good thing. Four years back, a pair of brothers got it into their sick minds to take over a schoolhouse in Hoernerstown, Pennsylvania. They carried knives and guns, barricaded doors, and took the children hostage. They held the authorities off for more than a week, and the children never made it out alive.

Soon after, the church hired me as a sort of caretaker because my wife had recently passed away. In desperate need of a social life, I offered my assistance. I made a promise to God to see these ladies live into their golden years and keep them at peace. Lord knows they've already seen enough pain and suffering. Marshal, what I'm telling you is, there were never any children here. The clothing, the shoes, the toys…all just props to appease the women.

I wouldn't have had Martha call you out here to waste your time, but…she is not well, understandably. They are all this way—and as for this latest horrific tragedy—I'm telling you it happened *years ago,* to each of them—*individually.* They relive their nightmares. They can even have them communally, as they did this time. Panic spreads, and the only thing I can do is help them ride it out. If it is any consolation, they will only have trouble sleeping for a *few* days now. If you had not come, it would have been much longer."

The marshal looked at Gideon cynically for several seconds. Gideon kept a straight face and met the man's gaze evenly.

"Mr. Walker, I do not have the time or the resources to come out here for any more false alarms. What happened to these ladies is indeed tragic, but if you need us for anything similar in the future, please make sure your horses are locked up, and they have to go through you first!"

"Indeed I will, marshal. Once again, my apologies to you and your crew, and thank you for coming out."

The marshal and his men saddled up and left. As soon as they were out of sight, Gideon turned back to the house. It was almost time to correct Martha.

CHAPTER 12

1847

Mary lay next to her mother, who had only recently cried herself to sleep. It wouldn't be long before she woke again, so for a few moments, Mary had the sounds of the house to herself. She missed Sarah badly, and the bed—while still cramped, seemed empty without her. Mary felt anger more than sadness, which was an unusually perceptive intuition for an eleven-year-old. Her anger meant that she knew Sarah was gone for all the wrong reasons. It was wrongful, and someone was at fault.

Mary blamed Gideon, but she didn't know exactly why—it was nothing she could prove, in other words. She had never liked him, and he was such a poor substitute for her beloved father, Elmer. Gideon was shady. He moved them all here, and bad things happened. Agitated, but not daring to move lest wake her tired mother, she stared at the ceiling with a busy head full of thoughts.

Suddenly, in the bedroom next door, she heard several rapid, muffled thumps followed by silence. As she lay there quietly listening, a moment later, she heard several long strides across the farmhouse floorboards. It was Gideon's gait, she would recognize it anywhere. The women didn't move the same way he did. They used smaller steps—lighter ones. He was up—and in Martha's room. Minutes later, the house was quiet again, and Mary fell asleep.

CHAPTER 13

1847

The next morning Gideon made an announcement. Martha had left camp again, having enjoyed her "sojourn to Salem" the previous day—as he sarcastically put it. One of the horses was missing. Gideon spent the next five minutes uncharacteristically throwing things and punching walls. He gathered everyone and prayed for her safe return. Margaret and Clara began crying again. There had been so much turmoil and so much stress these last two days—all this on top of the fatigue and malnutrition was too much for their emotions.

Mary (quietly) wasn't having it. The things he was throwing were not breakable, or of any value. None of the walls he punched were damaged. The missing horse was the one with the gimp. It was all too staged. Mary decided it was time for her to think outside the box, both for herself and her mother.

She already knew the food was weak. She knew her mother was more tired and helpless than she was, very perceptive for such a young girl. Deep down, she knew this farm situation was wrong. Then and there, in the wake of Gideon's spectacle, she made her mind up to do some investigating.

During the daylight hours, it was easiest in between chores to check out the different buildings on the property. The main building was where they all slept. There was a small two-story barn next to the main house, a small separate guest house, and way out in the corner of the property was a shed. She would see Gideon poking around out there from time to time, and to her knowledge, he was always alone when he did. She could ask her mother about it, or one of the others, but they all seemed so…indifferent.

One afternoon, Mary decided to check and see what might be out in the shed. When no one was looking, she bolted through the shin-high grass. When she arrived at the door, she turned to look back. *Had she been seen?*—No. She looked up: a padlock secured the door. Mary shook it with her little hand, but it was locked tight. With no recourse, she walked the perimeter of the small building, and for a moment, with the shed between herself and the farm, she started into the deep woods.

The forest seemed to call for her. There was no fear, only a sense of—freedom. The urge to run through the trees into the cover of foliage was strong, and a spark of inspiration struck her; if not now, then one day—and this would be the way to go. She could not, however, *ever* leave her mother behind. A mother should never lose one child, never mind two. After one last look into the depths of the trees, she turned back to the dark side of the windowless shed.

She pressed her ear to the clapboards and listened, expecting nothing, and nothing was all she heard. Everything was quiet, both inside the mysterious shed and behind her in the vast woods. Not a bird nor a squirrel disturbed the silence. She began to search the clapboards and spaces between them for any opening, or perhaps a lazily hidden key. The search proved fruitless. *It would have been too good to be true anyway*, she thought. Out of time for today, she ran back to her chores before being missed.

CHAPTER 14

1847

Mary spent the next three days inconspicuously combing the farm for the key to the padlock. It had to be here unless he kept it on his person, and there must be something important in there worth locking up. Near the end of the third day, after she had meticulously checked everything else, Mary very coolly and calmly walked directly into Gideon's bedroom while he was out in the yard and searched it.

The room was almost bare, so there weren't many things she had to move or look beneath. The desk held only a single fountain pen and two sheets of blank paper. There were only two (identical) sets of clothes; one on Gideon's body and the other in the closet. Just as she was about to leave the room and abandon the search, she closed the bedroom door. There on the wall behind the door hung a nail. Off of the nail hung a key.

CHAPTER 15

1847

Very patiently, Mary waited. She did not take the key from its hiding place and sprint to the shed, but rather left it on its nail and ran to the barn. She knew there was a key stuck in an old rusted padlock on a shelf out there from her previous adventures. She pried the key from the old lock and examined it. Compared to the lock, it looked relatively new…but to the key she *wanted* it to resemble; it looked worn and rusty.

For the next six days, she buffed and shined the key with a horse blanket and some oil from one of the lamps. After she had finished, it was still not an exact match, but close enough for her purposes, which would be short term jaunts of an hour or so, or in the dead of night.

At around four o'clock, she waited for Gideon to speak with Cora's son Edward, who had a habit of acting like a normal five-year-old boy. Gideon didn't like the way he acted around his mother, who allowed him a much longer leash than he preferred. As a result, both received a double-dose of Gideon's programming.

As they conversed, Mary rushed out to the shed and tried the key. Thankfully, the lock popped open effortlessly. The door swung open, and her eyes adjusted to the darkness. She stepped in and closed the door so that no one from the house would see it left open. Slowly the room revealed itself to her.

There were shelves of food; things not found in the main kitchen of the house: dried cod and dried beef…proteins she hadn't seen in years. There was a small wood stove for cooking. It was cool now, but atop was some beef, rehydrating for Gideon's private dinner that evening after they had all gone to bed. There were fresh pumpkins and dried corn, and nothing resembling the mush they had all eaten like zombies for most of the life she could remember.

She left the soaking beef alone because he would easily notice the shorted portion, but went through the rest of supplies, skimming small quantities that he would never miss, filling her pockets. Across the room from the stored food was a bench. On it were many of the herbs that went into her food that she had grown to abhor. There were also pretty rocks, sticks, feathers, candles, several liquids, some which appeared to be oil and some not, and an assortment of beads.

Next to the bench, in the darkest part of the room, was an altar, similar to the one in the living room of the main farmhouse. In the center of the altar was a thin book. Mary opened it and turned to the first page, being careful not to tear it. There were no words on the cover, no author's name, and no table of contents. The first page was also the *only* page. On it was handwritten what looked to be a poem, or a recipe, or hybrid of the two, to the best of her knowledge. In the margins were handwritten symbols, and the text seemed to be in a different language. She could make out some words, but only perhaps one in five. The single-page was not a simple leaflet tossed into a folder but was a dedicated page, sewn into the binding in a clean, professional manner. *Odd to make an entire book for just a single page*, she thought.

She sensed she was running out of time and should call this session short and closed the book. She wouldn't squander this gold mine by getting greedy on the first day. Besides, it gave her something to look forward to tomorrow. Very carefully, she placed the book exactly where she had found it. Then she quickly scanned the floor for any kernels of corn that might have fallen. She slipped out and locked up, then jogged along the tree line back to the house, emptying her pockets into a burlap sack and hiding it under the bed after a few more bites later on. This food would help her recover from his brainwashing all the faster.

CHAPTER 16

1847

Mary skipped visiting the shed the second and third days as she worked on eating what she had taken, bite by secret bite. As she did so, she wasted no opportunities continuing to observe Gideon and all of his patterns and habits. She had known many of them before, but now that they shared a common interest, she wanted to be sure they didn't share that common interest at the same time. He barely ever slept. Maybe he caught up on his sleep on his monthly trips into the city? She couldn't be sure.

Alice had been sleeping slightly better of recent (perhaps her mind had given up), so Mary was able to sneak out of bed and into the den where she would sit in the window and watch Gideon from the time he left the farmhouse until just after dawn when the oil lamp in the shed went out. At that time, she knew to begin very quietly sneaking back to the bedroom before he got back to the house to wake everyone. He never left the shed once he entered it until dawn. She made a mental note.

On the fourth day, once her supplies had run out, she snuck back in. Everything was the same inside as it had been on the first day, so she unfolded her burlap bag and once again skimmed an imperceptible amount of food from each item's bin. As she finished, she took another look across the room at the altar, wondering what he had been up to all by himself out here.

She picked up the thin book again and opened to its only page, but to her surprise, this time, there were *two*. Once again, the second page, like the first, was not a leaflet tossed into the book but was a dedicated page, as if sewn in the day the book was created. She wondered for a moment if the pages had been stuck together the last time—(?) Before putting the book down, she double counted and made sure she had checked the number of pages correctly. Suddenly, a noise coming from just outside the shed pierced the nervous silence.

"Baaaaaaaaaaaaaaa!"

"Baaaaaaaaaaaaaaa!"

Mary nearly dropped her burlap bag but recovered quickly. *This noise must stop immediately. The kid goat that had unknowingly followed her to the shed must not give her away.* Her plan, the plan she had for her mother—to one day walk into the woods and never look back, was in jeopardy because of this noise. Freedom, health, and normal life were at stake.

Without hesitation, she grabbed a long knife off of Gideon's bench and stepped outside into the daylight. With two quick jabs, the kid dropped noiselessly to the grass, where she scooped him up before he could begin to bleed and leave a large red clue for Gideon. She took him around to the back of the shed and continued walking, deeper and deeper into the forest, making sure to keep the shed between her and the house.

The kid goat, while very tiny, got heavy before one hundred yards had passed. Realizing her limitations and also concerned the dead goat would bleed on her work dress, Mary made another very practical decision. Taking the knife, she slit him up the belly and let the gut fall out of the body cavity. Now the blood was everywhere, and it wouldn't take long after dark for the coyotes to find him and—remove the evidence.

Examining herself and her clothing, she realized that she

had worked clean. The knife, however, needed to be washed and returned. She unemotionally wiped the blade on the animal's coat and wasted no time returning it to Gideon's bench, locking the door and smuggling the burlap bag up to her bedroom. Once there, she replaced the fake key with the real key, and the episode was over. She felt no remorse.

CHAPTER 17

1847

Gideon noticed the missing goat but did not suspect anything of his cult members. It was not uncommon to suffer the loss of an animal to a predator on any farm; it was simply the cost of doing business. He made a comment under his breath about getting another goat the next time he went into the city two weeks from now. Mary was nearby and heard the whole thing. She began to make plans.

CHAPTER 18

1847

It seemed like forever for the two weeks to be over and for Gideon to leave for Salem. Mary counted the days, and diligently budgeted the contents of her burlap sack until then. She wanted to share the food with her mother, but Alice was not strong enough mentally to be trusted. Mary feared that Alice was so far gone she might even turn her in. If they were going to escape, it would be Mary's job to get it done; this, she felt in her bones. In this miserable situation, the child had to be the adult—the stronger of the two. Mother was not well.

Gideon left for Salem that morning. Mary, who planned on raiding the shed at some point during the day for a snack, was unable to shake her mother's gaze, which surprisingly seemed to have intensified in Gideon's absence. Mother confided in Gideon too much. He had her trust, and Mary did not. She was still just a child in her mother's eyes. Mary would have to be patient for the right moment to break them both free, and it would not be easy.

She waited until after her mother fell asleep, which was slightly after 1 am. This would be the most time she had ever spent in the shed. A thorough inspection was tops on her list, then a light snack, followed by a decent night's sleep back in the farmhouse... the first one in quite some time.

It was a quiet night. She enjoyed her walk across the overgrown lawn with a slight breeze blowing in from the forest. The cabin was, of course, dark as she approached…the first time the interior had been unlit at this time of night in at least a month. Mary, cautious as ever, considered for a second that this was all a setup and that Gideon knew of her plan—knew everything—all along—and lay in wait for her to disable the lock. He knew everything—about the key(s)—the food skimming—the dead goat in the woods—and the book that somehow grew new pages every time she looked at it. At least that was her paranoia—but with almost nothing to lose, she marched on.

The lock popped as always, and she was inside in an instant. Over the window, she hung her mother's black dress so that if one of the brainwashed souls in the farmhouse happened to wake up and look to the shed, they would see nothing but darkness. With the matches she had stolen from the kitchen, she struck one and lit the lamp. It was time for her thorough inspection.

She started with the book itself, which now—contained *four* pages.

What *was* this book—that seemed to grow its pages?

She opened it to examine the new material. To her, the pages were the same as the others, illegible, yet different. She chose a page randomly and began to read aloud.

"Vinculum coniuro te nomine nel margine superiore nomen Iaya et nomine quod nominavit et agnovit. Admirate in domine in nomine et in nomine quod nominavit et sacrificium eius erat acceptu et per quod nominavit et obtinuit oleum misericordiae; et per nomen quod nominavit et mbulavit."

She paused when she was done and looked around, expecting something—anything—but nothing happened.

Disappointed, she put the book down and continued. On the

bench were three tiny wooden cubes—or beads—with strange writing on them. All the "dice" for lack of a better word had different symbols written on each side. She picked them up and rolled them around in her tiny palm—and they were comfortably warm. She didn't want to have to leave them, but she did. There was an odd feeling in the air tonight, something she hadn't felt during her previous visits.

Hungry, she couldn't wait any longer to dig into the food; but she had become so accustomed to the extra rations that she felt she might be in danger of looking a little *too* healthy. However, she could never give it up. Her mind had become incredibly sharp, and clear thinking gave her a feeling of power. Mary opened Gideon's dried beef container, disappointed to see that there were only three strips left. He must have taken the rest when he packed for travel.

She put the lid back on and tried the salted fish instead. Usually, this protein was soaked in water for a few hours, greatly reducing the salinity, but Mary couldn't wait, nor spend time fetching water. Only three bites in, she quit. As hungry as she was, the salt was overbearing. Two carrots later, most of it had been neutralized.

All but finished, she wondered what to do next. The other visits had been rushed and incomplete due to the danger of being caught. Now, the grand inspection was over much sooner than she had expected, and she feared the result of the evening might be anticlimactic.

With her nerves calming, she yawned, prematurely fatigued. If Gideon were in here right now, and she was trapped in the house, she would be dying to trade places with him. It would be a pity to go to bed earlier than expected after a disappointing snack. Torn, she decided to take a break and think a moment outside.

Mary looked up at the stars and took a few steps through the grass toward the forest, letting her eyes adjust to the dark. It was, of course, dark and ominous, but peaceful, and because Gideon was gone, she had no fear. She looked at the house, which was also completely dark. It would be several hours before the weak-minded prisoners rose to do their tedious chores. This midnight walk was a good example of the freedom that Gideon had stolen from them. *They had been wronged.* She vowed on the spot to change that not only for herself but for her mother.

She peered into the woods, attempting to see what could not be seen in this light. Her ears were the sharpest sense right now. She heard leaves flapping in the gentle breeze, and maybe an owl, with bats overhead picking off insects. Her eyelids grew heavy. The cool night and the two weeks of anticipation had taken their toll. The farm was far more relaxed without Gideon, despite the lasting effects of his malnutrition and programming on the others. It was time for sleep.

She stepped back into the shed prepared to snuff the flame in the oil lamp, but something caught her eye. She jumped back because it was so close to her…a dark flash down near her feet.

It was her nightgown. The white, frayed rag she had been wearing was gone, and in its place was a fresh black farm dress. She grabbed it as if it were climbing her, but of course, it wasn't, it was just a dress. *Where did this come from?*

Her eyes went to the only other magical thing she knew of— the *book*.

She picked it up and leafed through it. There were still four pages; it hadn't grown any new ones in the past hour. She turned back to the page she had read from tonight—the third one. She still had no idea what it all meant, and now she had a problem. Her new dress would be noticed immediately. It would stick out like a sore thumb, and they would tell Gideon, and he would know she'd been snooping.

She spent the next twenty minutes digging through the dirty clothes basket in the main farmhouse looking for her only other nightgown, the one that had been rendered unwearable by her mother when she spilled some of Gideon's gruel on it. She hid the black dress in the barn, and using a pail of well water, did her five-minute best and hung the gown quietly behind the bedroom door. Hopefully, there would not be a puddle on the floor for her mother to see in the morning. She then crawled into bed naked, planning to wake before her mother did so she could get dressed.

CHAPTER 19

1847

Gideon Walker tied his horse in the woods just off of Broad Street in Salem. Staying hidden, he waited patiently for the young boy to come running by. The schoolhouse was letting out, and he had spent the last two days observing from afar. One particular boy was a slow-moving loner, which was exactly what he was looking for. Most of the children had already left the schoolyard, excited to head home, but this boy always left later than the others and took his sweet time walking.

It was still year one of his contract with Helms, who had already taken his first five victims and would be looking for number six soon. Gideon didn't enjoy this part of the deal, but it wasn't because it bothered him morally, he just didn't want to get caught before he got his shot at immortality. The new pages in the Book of Shadows piqued his curiosity, and he wondered what would happen if he fulfilled the deal early. Would the book fill itself up? Would all of the spells be made available to him?

The Book of Shadows had originally appeared in his bedroom with just one page, and he read the spell over and over, wondering what the words meant. He read it five times out loud, waiting for something to happen, believing nothing had. And then he looked at his writing desk. A small wooden die sat in the center. He read the spell again, and twenty minutes later, when he wasn't looking, a second die—or bead—appeared. He was elated. If everything was going to be this straightforward, he was hooked. He read the spell again, and as soon as he turned his back, a third cube appeared. *Confirmation.*

The very next night, a second page appeared in the book. How or why he didn't question, but it was if both pages were sewn in when the book was assembled. Again, Gideon read the words, this time out loud in the privacy of the shed, and then closed his eyes. He held them closed for nearly two minutes, praying (to no god in particular) that he would not be disappointed when they reopened.

There on the bench next to the three beads was a medicine bottle with a cork in it. An amber liquid filled the bottle up to the neck. Gideon wondered if this was a potion of some sort. *Do I drink it?* He wondered. Still excited by the wonderfully interactive *Book of Shadows*, he crossed the room and removed the cork. Cautiously he sniffed the contents and dropped to the floor immediately, spilling the entire contents of the bottle. He even cut his hand when it landed on the broken glass.

Four hours later, when most of the potent liquid had evaporated, he came to with a splitting headache and a bloody palm. Whatever this bottle was, he had never dreamed of such a thing. Even doctors did not possess such a drug—if that was indeed what it was. Perhaps it was simply a bottle of pure magick—but doctors could never possess such a thing—only him and his kind. In any event, the bottle lay broken on the floor, so he read the spell out loud again just before sunrise. This time he didn't remove the cork.

The slow boy approached, and Gideon took one last look around; nobody was watching. He assumed Helms wanted the boy alive, or he would have killed him in an instant. He would have killed him, drained the blood, wrapped him neatly in a horse blanket, and returned across the Essex Bridge, but Gideon knew that Helms had taken the first five people alive. He didn't want to "waste" an abduction, so he pulled the boy into the bushes while placing a liquid soaked rag over his mouth and nose. The boy collapsed as if his bones were gelatin.

Gideon rolled the boy into his horse blanket and threw him over the back of the horse. On top, he placed his purchases and a second horse blanket for camouflage. If the boy woke during the long journey, he would drug him again. He didn't dare take the boy back over the Essex Bridge though—it was too busy, with no escape routes. Instead, he would take the long way through Danvers, which offered multiple paths and the cover of trees—far less revealing than the scrutiny he would receive on the bridge.

CHAPTER 20

1847

It wouldn't be long before the city missed the boy, so Gideon got out of Salem quickly. Once he had crossed the town line and gotten through the busy part of Danvers, things spread out again, and he felt safer. He skirted Danvers Plains, and from there on out, he practically had the road to himself until he got to Beverly Farms.

Two hours from home and nearing dusk, he began to wonder where to—deposit—the boy. He had not been given instructions for the transfer and had no way of contacting Helms. He couldn't very well ride into the farm and ask the women for help; certainly, they were under his influence, but this would cause a ruckus.

He could say that the boy was sick, that he found him by the side of the road and that he was only helping. But the boy would not be unconscious forever, and when he woke, he would scream, and then he would talk. Alternatively, he could—

Ahead in the road, stood a man. Most travelers had reached their destinations by this hour, as night was falling and the temperature cooled. He was in the middle of the woods on a road barely wider than a trail. Gideon squinted, attempting to see clearer, but he already knew who the man might be.

Just then, he heard a stirring in the blanket behind him. The boy was waking up, and with his arms pinned to his sides, suffered claustrophobia. The air could not be plentiful in there either, Gideon thought. Not to mention riding in the same position on the back of a horse for half a day. Come to think of it, the memory of the abduction itself would also be horrifying.

Gideon looked ahead at the waiting man in the middle of the road. As he did, he passed through a perimeter of odor—the smell of dead things. He wrinkled his nose. Things were about to turn even worse for the boy in the horse blanket.

CHAPTER 21

1847

Gideon returned that evening, and Mary took note. There would be no trip to the shed tonight, and she felt robbed as if something that belonged to her had been taken away. She did know, however, that the shed didn't belong to her, and there was nothing to do but simmer in frustration. She didn't know it, but she felt the same pull, the same addiction to the shed (or the Book) that he did. Gideon, of course, spent his night in the shed. Mary, wise beyond her years, picked her battles, and went straight to bed, waiting her turn.

Gideon hung close to the barn and the surrounding area the entire next day. Lots of lessons, sermons, one-on-one instructional, and catching up to do. His presence in the area meant Mary couldn't even entertain the thought. She went to bed, hungry and angry.

CHAPTER 22

1847

The following day, Gideon announced he would be going on a turkey hunt. Mary couldn't recall even one time in either Beverly Farms or Pennsylvania when they had dined on turkey. It was out of character, and so, she became suspicious. Was this a ploy to catch her visiting the shed and catch her red-handed?

He left for the "hunt," and despite her fears, she went and achieved her goals before the goats had even finished their breakfast. Her first stop was the dried beef, and she polished off two slabs immediately, pocketing a third for the afternoon. Then, *The Book*. She was surprised to note that there were now a total of six pages. With her budgeted time running out, she began reading the last page aloud:

> *In hoc carmine non poterit legere librum. Tantum phrase iterare: ego dominus, et non sunt locuti estis ad me sollicitat.*

Nothing seemed to happen, at least, not that she was aware. With that, she shut the book and locked up, leaving undetected with the nutritious protein digesting in her stomach, bolstering her body, mind, and spirit.

CHAPTER 23

1847

Gideon—*of course*—returned empty-handed. Mary skeptically wondered where he had gone. She went to bed with her mother once more with one more question on her mind: *What was it she had read in the Book this morning, and what was it supposed to do?* What did any of the spells mean? One spell had inadvertently changed her clothes. *What did the others do?* There were no apparent answers that evening, so in the name of mental health and self-preservation, she let the thought go and closed her eyes. Better sleep now meant clearer thinking tomorrow.

CHAPTER 24

1847

Morning came, and the women rose for work. Mary, always watching for Gideon's whereabouts, couldn't find him immediately. Still, she tended to her chores. Twenty minutes later, someone screamed from inside the house. Mary emerged from the barn to see what the commotion was and saw Rose (the mother of missing George), crying hysterically.

"She's gone! She's gone! Clara is gone! I thought she had gone to look for fox grapes, but her shoes are still in her bedroom!" Rose and Clara had become close since their shared miseries. Now Rose had lost not only her son but her friend. Panic ensued.

Gideon burst from the shed, appearing as if he had been napping and was upset to be disturbed. It was damage control time, a job he now loathed now that the carrot of bigger and better things had been dangled. If it were up to him, he would give the entire cult to Mr. Helms immediately for an early ticket to the revenant afterlife.

Gideon (this time) already knew about Clara. He had walked into the forest the previous day in search of a meeting. Helms appeared behind him out of nowhere, apparently accepting of the idea.

"Helms, how can I speed up this process? Ten years is too long.

I can give you the entire group today if you like." he had forgotten the incredible odor. It was powerful, even in the outdoors, and the flies buzzed actively. Helms frowned.

"You aren't ready. The process will kill you if you are not properly *seasoned*. Why do you think we've only given you a few pages? Have you practiced? I know the answer, and the answer is *no*. We know you are not putting in the time. You're doing what you always do. You do it your way. I told you I would not have the patience for this attitude."

Gideon dropped his chin and looked at the ground, frustrated. He had always been impatient, and the answer he was looking for had not come to pass, leaving him with a ten-year chore in his lap and no way around it. On top of that, dead men were *watching* him, and they knew he hadn't been doing his homework.

"I understand. But if I practice more, spend extra time with the Book, can I accelerate the process? Can it be less than ten years, or is that set in stone?"

"It's not the number of years; it's the progress. It is remotely possible to shorten the time, but it has never been shortened. Ten years is just a heartbeat to us, and it's what you should expect. It might even take longer. One more point I want to make about the souls you bring us; we can do more with innocent blood. It is richer, stronger, and more powerful than the blood of a copulator. We make better magick with the harvested parts. We expect better quality than your offer of your adult followers." Gideon, desperate to find a way out of his old job sooner than later, grasped at straws.

"Yes, yes, we've been over that again and again. What about Edward and Mary? We have two children left. They could count towards my tally. What about them?"

"Again...even if you had nineteen children right here and right now, you are not ready. On top of that, this doesn't include the vow we made to ourselves when Allemand, our forefather, died. The conversation was becoming tiresome for Helms, and he began to regret his deal with Gideon Walker. The saying about the leopard changing its spots came to mind.

"Helms, the last boy from Salem, was very risky and a lot of work. Eighteen more over ten years is a daunting number. Take Mary and Edward."

"You are in danger of losing control of your followers as it is. You have talents—that you retained the mothers after they lost their children on your watch was no small feat; however, you have short-timer syndrome, and we both know it. You think this is almost over, and you don't want to fulfill your duties. You could be losing your grip. More chaos now might break up your little farmstead, and if they talk, well, you might find yourself in jail. If you're in jail, the deal is off."

"I'll kill them before they talk. No one leaves me."

"And what if the marshal decides to pay you an unannounced check-back? How will you hide so much evidence? Where will you say they all went—alone, without the company of a man? You don't see women traveling unaccompanied on these wooded roads. It's too dangerous."

"I'll bury them deep in the woods…or perhaps you could help me hi…"

"We will not help you. This is your job. Consider it the *price of admission*. And a word to the wise; the marshal is not a stupid man. If he even gets a *whiff*, you can bet it won't be easy to get rid of him. If he gets involved, then we terminate our contract. One random leg bone dropped by a coyote in someone's cornfield, and you're *done*. That doesn't mean we go away either, Gideon. No more farms, no more cults, no more freedom. If the marshal gets involved, we will kill you."

Gideon found himself getting angry at the dead man, and then wisely stifled his displeasure. He brooded for a few moments before speaking again.

"I have given you six. You need eighteen more. The marshal may very well have me before this is over despite your threats with a number like that. Make Mary and Edward numbers twenty-three and twenty-four. That leaves sixteen I have to find. Do we have a deal?"

The dead man hesitated. He knew Mary had been to the shed even though Gideon did not.

"No deal, we don't want them. Mary and Edward need each other. The women also need them, and you need the women. Leave them be. You're pushing things. Be patient. Pretend you're dead already, and time means nothing."

"I'm not dead like you. And I'm not used to taking orders," said Gideon. Helms stiffened and walked closer, bringing the flies. The aura filled Gideon's sinuses, and he gagged. He had forgotten to whom he was talking.

Helms stopped six inches from Gideon's face, and he got a good look at every detail of the rotting flesh and peeling skin. The teeth, the breath—He forgot about everything for a moment.

"Would you like to be dead?" It was official; Helms did not like Gideon Walker. But he only counted as one vote.

Gideon backed away slowly, a stunned look on his face. When there were seven feet between them, he stopped.

"I'll do it." Halfway through his sentence, he turned and started walking back to the farm. Helms called after him.

"Walker."

Gideon turned.

"There is someone you didn't mention that we could make use of—*Clara*. She was *not* the mother of the boy we took. That was her brother. She's a virgin."

"How do you know?" asked Gideon. Helms' eyes narrowed.

"You mean you haven't read the book?"

Gideon, embarrassed, mumbled under his breath.

"Take her."

CHAPTER 25

1847

"**S**he's gone! She's gone! Clara is gone! I thought she had gone to look for fox grapes, but her shoes are still in her bedroom!"

Gideon would have rather taken out his eyes than deal with the aftermath of Clara's abduction, but he was one eighteenth closer to his goal, and there were consequences for that, like a hangover after a bottle of wine. Rose continued her rant.

"Where were you?! Why are you always in that shed? Clara is gone. She's gone! Another one of us...taken! We aren't safe here. We aren't s..." Gideon grabbed Rose and clamped his huge palm over her mouth. A hush fell over the barnyard. *That was easy, now comes the hard part*, he thought.

"Clara is not gone! We cannot panic! Get to work, Rose! You attack me, and I haven't had a chance even to wake up and piss! Don't you ever...*ever*...question me! Do you understand? Does everyone understand? I can't hear you, speak up. Does everyone understand?"

A low murmur of shocked understandings broke their silence and then went quiet again quickly, as they awaited Gideon's next move.

"I'm going out to find her. Alice, there is a shotgun in the closet of my bedroom. Get it and guard yourselves. All of you wait in the house until I return."

He left the yard and disappeared into the forest. The women and children moved as one body like a herd of sheep and filed into the house. As soon as Gideon had entered the forest and walked a half-mile or so, he took a seat at the base of an oak tree and put his face in his hands, trying to imagine how to make it all work when he returned. Suddenly he remembered something; *the Book*.

Surely there would be an answer in its pages. Using the sun as a guide, he made his way through the forest to the far side of the shed and approached stealthily. He did not want the women to know he had returned so soon, empty-handed, and he needed time to read.

When he had successfully entered the shed undetected, he walked across the room and picked up the book. Counting, there were now seven pages. What should have been a feeling of relief was only dread; he would be in here much longer now, reading gibberish, trying to guess which spell did what. It had taken him nearly twenty minutes per page up until this point, not counting the time spent unconscious on the floor after sniffing the predecessor to *ether*.

With no better ideas, he grabbed the book and sat down. It was a tedious mess, and he hated it. It would be a long ten years if he had to read things he didn't understand and then have to search for the results and piece them together. Page one, he knew, was all about the wooden beads. Page two was about the medicine bottle (he turned the page quickly). Page three, well, he hadn't read page three yet.

Gideon took a look, read it, and searched his surroundings. It seemed nothing had happened. He felt his blood pressure building, the way it used to when he was a child in school, and he didn't understand the lesson. *Damn it*, on to the next page. Again, it was all gibberish from top to bottom, but as he finished the last word, something happened. The text turned to plain English.

"*This spell, when read, will enable the believer to see the ancient writings as though written in their native tongue.*" The text continued, but the first sentence was the answer he was looking for. *Eureka,* Gideon thought. *As long as I know what I'm doing, and what the intent is, I can read all day long.*

He flipped back to page three; the spell that hadn't seemed to do anything, and read again:

> "*One who reads this spell aloud will have the power to change their attire. This basic skill has proven most valuable in such instances as shaking followers and deceiving victims. It is also used by the dead on the occasion they outlast their clothing. User taste in clothing comes with time.*"

The moment he finished the page, his clothes *popped* in front of his eyes, startling him. His usual dark shirt, pants, and coat had become something a typical Salem businessperson would wear. Gideon hated the frilly jabot worn around the neck and tore it off, frustrated by surprise.

Now he knew the first four pages of the Book. *Why the hell do they put the instructions on the fourth page?* He wondered briefly but knew the answer. It was a test. Everything was a test. With that, he turned to page five.

"Whichever believer reads and chants this text shall come to the knowledge of whether or not those around him are clean or unclean in spirit and blood." The text again was followed by more Latin, or Olde English, or Wiccan, or whatever it was. Helms had been talking about this the day before they took Clara. Gideon felt like a fool. But wait…was he even in possession of page five on that day? He couldn't be sure. He turned to the sixth page and read intently.

"It may become necessary to sap the motivations of human workers or slaves from time to time. For this purpose, I devised this temporary spell. Speak the names of those you wish to compel. Recast as needed."

Gideon read the following spell excitedly, albeit effectively. He sat back in his chair and breathed a sigh of relief. The effects of this one would be an absolute delight, and he couldn't wait to see. He had confidence now that he would return to the main house to be greeted by a crew of docile zombies. He put the book aside to go and check.

CHAPTER 26

1847

Mary felt Gideon's spell wash over the household and knew something was amiss. Her mother stood guard in the window with Gideon's rifle, waiting dutifully for his return. Mary, who was used to her freedom, was agitated by the droney buzz it caused, but she knew it was artificial—part of a sham. Gideon wasn't looking for Clara. There *was* no Clara anymore. He had most likely sold her off—or even worse.

She had trouble fighting the unknown spell, and its effects on the others were immediately noticeable. Rose stopped crying. Alice let the rifle rest on the floor. They looked like tired dogs waiting for dinner. Gideon walked through the front door tentatively. As soon as he saw Rose's eyes, he smirked. Mary witnessed his reaction and promised herself to get to the shed as soon as possible.

"Rose. Come here." Rose got up dutifully and approached Gideon as if nothing had happened.

"Yes, sir. What can I do for you? And, if I may ask, was there any sign of Clara in the forest?"

"Rose, the first thing I want to say is how sorry I am for having to discipline you this morning. It was the stress of the situation, it's very tense for all of us, of course, and, well, I'm certain it will never happen again. But, to answer your question, no. I could not find our beloved Clara. I'm sorry, but it was as if the forest swallowed her up."

"Well, thank you for trying. I know you did your best."

"Things will be back to normal in no time, I'll make sure to it," he added, and no one thought to question him...including Mary, who had finally succumbed. The next morning she didn't recall the details—she only knew that Gideon had cast a new spell, Clara was still missing, and he didn't seem to be doing anything about it.

CHAPTER 27

1847

Mary woke before dawn, finally clear-headed. She knew Gideon would most likely be in the shed, probably close to the end of his time there. She strongly considered leaving the bed, sneaking into the forest and entering the shed the moment he left it, but she realized that he would still have the only real key. She stifled her impatience.

Just after mid-day, she saw Gideon speaking with Rose one-on-one in her bedroom. Fearless, she snuck in and swapped the keys and headed straight for the shed. To her amazement, there were now seven pages in the book, but she was most surprised that she could read and *understand* each one. *The spell that hadn't seem to do anything was coming in handy now,* she recognized.

Thumbing through the pages, she found what she thought she would: The spell that turned the women to subservient zombies the previous afternoon. She flipped backward past the chapters on blood and fainting drugs because of her lack of time, but would surely revisit them later. Her curiosity as to where the book came from was still the largest question in her mind, and that would have to wait too. There were so many things to do. *Was there ever time?*

With a few minutes to spare, she started at the beginning

of the book to skim the contents and catch up; perhaps she had missed something basic that would put it all together for her, like—*making cryptic wooden beads. They must come in handy later on, but no purpose was listed. Knock-out medicine sounds dangerous. The changing of clothes (she remembered that one vividly)—the ability to read the spells in English—Finding the pure blood of…virgins? Whatever that meant. Making people obedient (she'd return to that in a minute). And immunity. A-ha.*

She read the seventh spell aloud and added her name to it. Before she left, she read number six again and added Gideon's name, hoping he had not yet seen the seventh spell. She closed the book and put it back, then locked up and walked straight into the woods, running through the trees and bushes like a deer until she emerged near the back of the house, right next to where Helms had climbed the building the very first night.

Gideon was in the kitchen. He looked tired. Mary asked him if he needed anything and stared directly into his eyes. He slowly shook his head no.

"The goat's pen hasn't been raked yet." She made it a statement just in case.

"Alright. I'll be back." He went straight to the barn and fetched the rake, then went straight to work. She'd never seen him lift a finger outside the kitchen. Mary smiled for the first time in years, wondering what the women would do when and if they saw him. The humor died quickly, however when she considered all the damage he had done to them. This man had stolen their lives. This small victory wasn't even close to satisfying.

Mary returned the key to the nail behind his bedroom door, took out the last strip of stolen dried beef, and enjoyed the chore-free afternoon.

CHAPTER 28
1847

Weeks passed, and the next time she tried the obedience spell, it didn't work. He'd caught up on his reading. Mary spent more and more time caring for her mother as Alice and the other women endured Gideon's periodic zombie-spell castings. Adding their names to the end of the spell hadn't worked. Mary played along to make it look right. She became concerned—Alice appeared to be aging prematurely. Whenever possible, she stole away to spend time educating herself in the shed.

Once more, she started over at the first page with the wooden beads and made a bunch of her own. With no idea of where to put them or what to do with them, she found a spot under the corner of the house and stashed them—she could figure the rest out later. She rechecked the book often for the answer, but only one new page appeared of late, and it had nothing to do with the beads.

Spell number eight was the ability to kill something and make it decompose immediately. It didn't seem like a very useful spell. She couldn't understand what it might be for or why it was as high as number eight on the list. Then she remembered the noisy kid goat she had to silence. It might have been useful at that time to skip the messy, heavy lifting into the woods. She tried it on some chickens. There were only sixteen of them on the property, so she didn't get much practice.

The first, she scooped up by its feet and sprinted to the far side of the shed as the bird flapped and squawked. Feathers flew everywhere, creating a virtual trail of breadcrumbs to her exact location. Angry at herself and the chicken, she pointed at the bird and applied the spell, but it didn't go well. On top of the excess noise, the decomposition didn't go as planned.

At best, it looked like the bird had been dead a day or two—just past the rigor mortis stage. Maggots somehow appeared, filling the eye sockets, and the carcass began to stink, right outside Gideon's shed. This was not an easy spell, and she learned that it was not enough to read a page and check it off as mastered. Quality mattered, and practice made perfect. Hurriedly she scooped up the mess and ran a hundred yards into the woods with it. When she returned, she made sure the coast was clear and then picked up each and every feather.

Two days later, nobody seemed to miss the chicken, so with ice in her veins, she selected another. This time she did not bother to run past the shed but separated the chicken from the others with her body and forced her will right there in front of the barn.

She focused hard, and the second bird dropped silently. The head slumped as if pushed down with an invisible hand, and the decaying process began. It seemed to deflate, which showed progress, but it stopped halfway. Suddenly Little Edward, Cora's son, appeared.

"What's wrong with her?" he asked.

"It's a disease," she replied. "You'd better run." Edward was afraid of Mary, so he did.

Angrily, she grabbed the mess and made her way once more into the woods to dispose of it. A chattering squirrel scaled a tree nearby and paused to watch. Still angry, she directed her full focus, and he fell to the ground dead. Once there, she intensified her will, reducing the squirrel to a length of tail and a tiny skull. *Success.*

She felt somewhat better because of the surprise squirrel, but as a result, was now exhausted. If she had tried this on the kid goat, it would have taken all of her energy and wouldn't have gone well. This skill would be difficult to hone, so she decided to shelve it for the time being. The uses were few and far between, it was risky, and there was a lack of test subjects.

CHAPTER 29

1848

Time passed, and fall turned to winter. Trips to the shed were tricky after a snowfall because of the footprints. Luckily it was not a harsh winter, and the ground cleared completely a few times. The turf remained frozen, meaning Mary would not leave impressions, which was even better. Springtime would be a different story. She would have to make the most of her opportunities now.

Six more pages appeared in the Book before she got caught.

The ninth spell was fun. Mary learned how to create sounds and distractions. The first time she tried, it was on her mother, a simple crash in the kitchen, as she was told to get ready for bed. The best one was scaring little Edward from behind with horse whinnies when no one else was around. She pretended not to hear the horse and convinced him he was crazy. Mary was careful never to try this spell anywhere near Gideon.

The tenth spell was useful, or, could become useful in certain circumstances. It was the ability to detect a weapon on a person.

The eleventh spell was something she enjoyed practicing. It was the ability to call something to your hand, as long as you knew its location. She tried it out the first time in the privacy of her bedroom with a button while her mother was outside working.

First, she set the button on the bureau. Standing five feet away, she called to it silently, and it miraculously rolled itself out from between her fingers. It did not fly visibly through the air but rather resembled a sleight of hand trick. She tried it several times in a row successfully. Either it was a very easy spell to master, or she was very good at it—there was never a drop or a fumble.

She watched closely for twenty minutes, trying to recognize the exact moment the button entered her hand, but it was impossible. For sure, it did not fly, nor did it materialize as if particles in the air were coming together. She had to be moving, at least somewhat—a flick of the wrist perhaps—and the button would appear as her hand changed positions. *Fascinating.*

From there, she experimented with distance. She placed the button on the ground about a hundred yards into the forest. Before leaving the spot, she took a good mental picture and walked back to her bedroom. *It worked.* For the next several days, she tormented poor Edward by leaving his teddy bear on the ground in front of the barn where it could easily be trampled. Cora, Edward's mother, scolded him the first two days it happened, and Edward protested, swearing up and down he had never taken the bear from the bedroom. On the third day, however, Mary was questioned by Alice as to whether she was the one stealing the bear and thus ended the pranking.

This was not the end of the spell, however. It worked with anything: A stick, a comb, a nail—even a small pumpkin. It took extra concentration, but Mary learned to call them all individually in succession. As she practiced, her speed increased. She liked it so much she stole a long kitchen knife from the kitchen and brought it into the woods. At the base of a large oak, she stuck the knife into the ground and with her shoe, pushed the weapon below the forest floor, blade, handle, and all.

There were two more spells that she read but never got a chance to experiment because she ran out of time. The twelfth spell was the ability to disguise a dead body, or more specifically, make it look like it had died from natural causes. Mary took this to mean the body would have to begin the process in bad shape. This spell might have come in handy when she killed the goat, or the chickens or the squirrel, but she didn't care to start that up again.

The thirteenth spell was the ability to shut the body down for long periods, or in effect, hibernate. It wasn't exactly clear how long it could last, or be programmed to work, but Mary got the sense that it could be much longer than just a season, and it didn't appear to be related to the winter months.

One cold February night in 1848, Mary left her bedroom again, carefully and quietly to not awaken her sleeping mother. Gideon had left for Salem the previous afternoon, and Mary was hungry. All-day long, she looked forward to the strips of beef and whatever new information that might be waiting for her in Gideon's Book. Hopefully, there would be at least a fourteenth chapter.

Mary was twelve now and beginning to formulate a plan to break her and her mother out of Gideon's cult. Her mind and body were strong, as was her magick. She knew that he, too, had the benefits of the Book on his side, but she would have the element of surprise on hers. Her goal was to practice until perfection, and when the moment arrived to hit him between his ribs with the blade from the forest, he would not see it coming.

Mary inserted the key into the lock on the shed and popped it open. She let herself in and covered the window with the black farm dress. Then she helped herself to two strips of beef. It was so good compared to the food her mother had been surviving on for so long; it was a pity Mary couldn't trust her brainwashed mother enough to share with her. Slightly upset by the thought, she put the last bit of beef down on the bench and picked up the book. Excitedly, there were four new pages.

She began to read the fourteenth spell and realized only a third of the way down the page that it would be a huge problem. It was so huge in fact that she would have to accelerate her plans and escape the farm immediately, right now, in the dead of winter. Her heart sank. The spell granted the reader the ability to sense a mortal involved in the study of magick.

This bit of bad news meant that Gideon could walk by Mary in the barnyard and at once know that she had been practicing. She froze: *Had he already read this? If he had, he wouldn't be in Salem*, she rationalized, calming herself. To be safe, she decided that she would carefully rip the page out before she left tonight— but whether or not that was possible, she didn't know. Greatly upset, she finished reading the rest of the page.

Upon completion of the last word, she heard a small tone in her ear...a gentle, steady pinging. She picked her head up and began to look around. It seemed to come from within her, and therefore would not be audible to others. As she turned to search for the source, the faster the pinging became.

Mary had carried the shed's only oil lamp to the bench to read by. The back half of the shed was dark, and at the edge of the darkness, she saw the tips of two riding boots.

He sat in a chair in the back corner, and he'd been there the entire time. He saw it all. She'd been discovered—he knew everything now—maybe even more than she did.

"That's a useful one, isn't it Mary? Don't you wish you'd read it before me? I, for one, wish they had given it to us *much sooner*. I didn't realize you had been undermining the good faith of our family. The betrayal hurts, but I can't say I'm surprised. We never really liked each other...*am I right?* If I'd known all this would happen, you would not have made it to Massachusetts."

Mary, still shocked, listened intently but said nothing.

"There are some new pages in there that you're not going to get a chance to read. Good, powerful stuff. No, you won't read it, but you'll feel it. Some of it looks painful—and I have to be sure I know what I'm doing before using it out in the field."

Mary realized her mistake was fatal, and things would never be the same. How it would all end, she didn't know, but in her last moments of freedom, she tried to force herself to remember the possible scenarios.

How will he hurt me without mother knowing? Will he hurt her as well? Will we become prisoners under lock and key? Is the entire cult in jeopardy?

In her last free moment, she decided she would not surrender. Gideon stepped forward to grab her, and in an instant, the knife from the woods found her right hand. She stabbed downward, connecting with his left bicep. Gideon howled as his massive body lunged, and his right hand swatted the knife away—he crashed heavily on top of her.

With her arms pinned by his legs, Gideon shifted to a half-kneel as he fumbled blindly on the bench above. As he did, the stick, the hammer, and a pair of scissors all found her hand in succession but fell harmlessly to the floor as he stepped down hard, causing her to cry out.

"You've been practicing. How long have you known?" Mary relaxed underneath him as he sat on her abdomen, his arms completely free. Rather than answer, she stared into his eyes, attempting the decomposition spell. He knitted his brow then slapped her hard when he realized.

"This makes it easier for me. I don't like people who I can't read. A lot is going on in that head of yours, but you never share. You're a cold fish, little Mary."

With that, he scooped the beads he had gathered at the edge of the bench and cupped them in his hands, then pressed them into her eyes and forehead. One dropped to the floor, but Mary felt the process immediately. There was a buzzing in her skull, a vibration, and some pain as the little cubes indented her forehead and eyelids. She did her best to turn, but Gideon's powerful arms—even the one wounded by the knife—overpowered Mary's frail neck all too easily. She passed out after an intense two minutes.

When it was over, Gideon picked up the beads and put them back on the bench. Mary lay on the floor as if sleeping. There were no burns or welts on her skin as he had suspected there might be. It was fortuitous to have a test subject, or so he thought. She was alive but unconscious. This would be the first of many such nights for her—at least until the first sign of scarring or disfigurement.

Gideon opened the dried beef and took a bite. He hated to waste even a scrap of it on the girl, but to make things look right, he placed the uneaten half-strip in her hand and grabbed the Book of Shadows. First, he read the seventeenth spell and healed his arm. Then he flipped back one page and made Mary forget everything that happened. Finally, he hid the Book under a floorboard and left.

CHAPTER 30

1848

Mary woke up cold on the floor of the shed, wondering how she had gotten there. Was there something in the dried beef? She pocketed the remainder of the strip in her hand for later disposal. Perhaps Gideon was using the food in conjunction with the knockout drug for some horrible purpose. Her head was dizzy, and she checked her other dress pocket and felt the key; Gideon's key from behind his bedroom door that she mistakenly believed she had very recently discovered.

Mary believed this was her first trip inside the shed. *What was he up to?* The only thing out here was a delicious personal stash of food that he wasn't sharing with the rest of the farm. She couldn't even remember the trip out here, which was very dangerous. He had to have laced the food. She would never touch it again.

CHAPTER 31

1848

Gideon was curious to see Mary's reaction the next morning. He'd watched her leave the shed and sneak back into the house, so he knew where she was, but he wondered what she was thinking. Would she remember anything? Would she look at him differently? Or would she remember the entire incident, forcing him to do something drastic in front of the whole clan?

He chose a chair in the den with a clear view of the staircase and waited. At a few minutes past four in the morning, Alice descended the stairs followed thirty seconds later by Mary. As soon as Mary's foot hit the second stair, Gideon heard and felt a low, dull tone in his head. He had forgotten.

"Mother, what's that noise?"

"What noise, Mary?"

Gideon got up quickly and went outside. Such an odd "skill" to have. Why the hell had the revenants invented it? Right now, it was a nuisance and did not suit his needs. He would have to avoid Mary as much as possible during the day. And what about at night? How could the experiments continue if she was to be warned of his presence every single time? He would have to enter the shed after she did, restrain her before she figured out that the tones were warnings, and then recast the memory spell after each episode—a monumental inconvenience.

CHAPTER 32

1850

Two years passed while Gideon experimented on Mary nearly every night. It was all too easy to abduct her as she heard the warning tone and wondered anew what was happening to her ears. *The perfect diversion*, he thought—a *silver lining*.

He began to want her—sexually. Gideon, not happy with seven-plus more years of waiting, took his frustrations out on Mary, who was now fourteen. She wasn't pretty, but she would do. Now there would be something extra to look forward to at the end of each day. The best part was he didn't even have to fetch her… she came to him like clockwork without even a whisper of déjà vu.

Mary's body shrank back to its malnourished state. Her ribs began to show, her eyes sank deeper into their sockets, and her hair became stringy. Alice, still deep under Gideon's influences and aging rapidly, called out to Mary one day—thinking she was *Margaret*—as she crossed the yard headed for the barn. Margaret had been ill for months and had even been bedridden for several long stretches. When Alice saw "Margaret" up and about, she was pleasantly surprised.

"Margaret, you're up! It's so good to see you out of bed!" But when Mary turned to face her mother, Alice's jaw dropped. Gideon had even mentioned that he thought Margaret might have to be taken to see Dr. Helms soon—but this was not Margaret; it was *her daughter*. Mary stared back blankly at her mother like a dull-eyed scarecrow, and for the first time since she'd met Gideon Walker, Alice began to truly *see*.

CHAPTER 33

1851

That night, Mary set out for the shed, seemingly for the first time. Gideon's memory-wipes worked flawlessly, and although she had been to the shed almost five-hundred times, she believed this was the very first.

As always, she stayed close to the tree line and amongst the shadows, practically tip-toeing. Her eyes were glued to the shed door, ready to duck into the trees at a moment's notice. This familiar approach made her an easy target for the revenant that grabbed her. He clamped a rotten hand over her mouth and pulled her deep into the woods.

A half-mile in, Helms waited in a small clearing with two more revenants. The two helpers each grabbed one of Mary's arms while the kidnapping revenant kept his hand over Mary's mouth. Helms held his copy of the Book of Shadows. Mary couldn't see a thing and was naturally terrified.

"Hello, Mary. We'll be quick, I promise." Helms opened the book and began to read aloud. The words made no sense to her. She guessed it might be Latin or some foreign language. Whatever it was, it was too much horror for a young girl, and she kicked one more time but gave up quickly when the grip on her wrists tightened to the point of pain.

Later, she awoke in the barnyard, wondering where she was and how dangerous it was that she had passed out on her way to the shed. If Gideon had found her first, well, she didn't want to imagine what might have happened. Nervous, she stood and ran back to the house. She wasn't even sure what time it was. Had she missed her window of opportunity? A half-hour, either way, could mean disaster. Badly shaken and confused, she snuck back to bed.

CHAPTER 34

1851

Gideon waited, but Mary didn't show. He confronted her the next morning when he found her alone peeling a potato in the kitchen.

"What are you doing?" he asked.

"Peeling a potato," she answered.

He stared, formulating his next question. It didn't matter what he asked Mary—she was alone, and he could easily erase her memory again.

"Where were you last night?"

"In bed with my mother. Where was I supposed to be?"

Gideon frowned and left the house, wondering if he had misread the spell the previous night, but that didn't make any sense. He would not be able to tell if their little routine was truly broken until tomorrow.

CHAPTER 35

1851

Alice slipped back under Gideon's influence and did absolutely nothing about Mary's health for two more years until one day on a crisp autumn afternoon; she saw her exit the shed at the far end of the property. Once again, Mary had a blank look on her face and walked with her head hung low. It was a moment very similar to the time she had mistaken her for sickly Margaret, except this time, Alice believed she might have seen her usually coldhearted daughter brushing away tears.

"Mary...are all you all right? What are you doing in the shed? You know that we aren't allowed to go in there."

Mary looked up at her mother, and for the second time in—*how long now?*—Alice feared for her daughter's life. Mary's eyes stared straight through her. The daily haze that clouded Alice's mind burned away again, and once and for all, Gideon's trance was broken. She could finally see her surroundings for what they truly were. Gideon's compound was unhealthy, to say the least— not fit for Mary or anyone else. Her brain struggled to come to terms with the weight of her decision. How could she have been so blind? She rushed to Mary and wrapped her arms around her.

"Mary...are you alright? You look pale. Are you sick?" Mary shook her head, no.

Just then, the shed door opened, and Gideon emerged, still adjusting his belt. His eyes met Alice's as Mary pushed through her mother's arms and headed for the farmhouse. Alice dropped her eyes but realized in that very moment that she and Mary were leaving—and leaving soon.

CHAPTER 36

1851

Mary continued to walk the grounds lethargically, and Alice, even weaker than her daughter, couldn't bear to watch. For Alice, the past forty-eight hours had been about finalizing the plan, and the pressure was overwhelming.

Before bed that evening, Alice confronted Mary.

"You're not leaving for the shed tonight, darling. I've made plans for us."

Mary stared at Alice blankly, like a convalescent. She was distant—gone emotionally—and Alice saw it. It broke her heart.

"At midnight, we're going to head for the road, and we're going to walk until someone picks us up. The man who picks us up is the man who delivers the hay. He's going to pick us up, and he's going to take us to Lowell. He knows people there who can help us—and that's all I know."

Mary did not react. Not used to being the strong one in *any* situation, Alice put her daughter to bed and shut the bedroom door. She felt ill and started a coughing fit. More than anything, she was worried about falling asleep and missing the pickup. She would have to stay awake the entire night—a near impossibility in her state. Six years of malnutrition, the death of her eldest daughter and Mary's ongoing trauma had taken their toll on Alice's heart. All this, with the pressure of the upcoming escape was far too much.

CHAPTER 37

1851

Mary heard her mother's directions and stayed awake, if for no one else but Alice. Minutes crept buy as she stared at the wall six inches from her face; just a half-hour more until the hay man arrived. Just then, Alice coughed three times. Mary sat up, itching to move, becoming nervous and agitated. *Would Gideon hear them? Would he hear the hay man's horse?* If they were both awake, now was as good a time as any—they could meet their ride further down the road. She turned to Alice and poked her. Alice didn't move. Mary poked her again, but Alice would not stir. Quietly she put her ear close to her mother's mouth. Ten seconds… twenty. Thirty.

Mary's original plan had been to unlock Gideon's shed and explore it while he slept, but her mother had surprised her with a much better plan that stirred her to her core. Now Alice was dead, and Mary would have to leave her body behind, with *the enemy.*

The goodbye tears poured down her face in the dim candlelight. She gathered her things, and in one final intimate moment, kissed her mother on the forehead and tucked her in properly. She mouthed a *thank-you*, then slipped out quietly.

CHAPTER 38

1851

Helms waited alone, hiding by the end of the driveway. Desjardins, the second revenant on assignment, signaled to him that the mother was dead, and the girl was coming out alone. They had been monitoring Alice's health for the past several weeks and knew that the older woman was not well. The escape would have to happen soon if she was to survive, but in the end, they were a day late. Tonight marked their eighth consecutive watch.

If Gideon caught the women escaping, Helms and Desjardins would have to allow it and pretend they knew nothing. The revenant vote was 6-5 in Gideon's favor, but Helms felt better with Mary as a potential insurance policy. Now that Mary would be leaving the house alone, Helms didn't have to worry about the frail mother's reaction to his sudden appearance.

As soon as Mary passed his hiding place in the bushes, he leaped out and grabbed her gently around the neck and began whispering rapidly in her ear. Mary winced at the odor and tried to cry out but couldn't.

"Be quiet, or Walker will hear you, and you'll be right back upstairs. Listen carefully:

Et ultimum carmen brevis est, sed est maxime momenti.
Ut pars fiet ex mortuis vivos, unum oportet esse current
sponsored per socius. Et plangent membrum est: We
welcome tibi. Nos receperint vos. Nos receperint vos.

When Helms finished, he loosened his grip on her neck but secured both shoulders. As he held her facing away from him, he chanted the memory-wipe and released her.

Mary ran down the road as if Helms hadn't even been there, and he watched her go. His plan was a longshot—a *stash and hope.* If things with Gideon got out of control, he would have to hope that her hatred for him would be enough to tip the scales.

CHAPTER 39

1851

Mary cried silently until the hay wagon left Danvers and entered Middleton. The farmer that picked her up heard her sobs throughout the night, and his heart went out to her. As soon as they hit the border of Middleton, she suddenly fell silent, as if flipping a switch. There were several long stretches of road when he wondered about her in the wagon behind him. He looked around several times but could not catch a glimpse. It was an odd feeling. He finally guessed that she must be sleeping.

Mary shut her emotions down all at once. This was not a time to be weak; it was time to reclaim a life stolen, and even make up for lost time. She would find a new life to erase her past. *The best revenge was living well*, after all. She realized now that people were inherently evil—and selfish—and could take control of others' lives. There were givers, and there were takers, and if you let them take—there was only yourself to blame.

Then and there, she vowed to take back her life and never give that power to another human being. She had already lost enough and watched her family lose even more—but never again. Never—*ever*.

She stopped for a moment, realizing she was only applying these thoughts to her future—then she amended the thought.

She would also never forget Gideon Walker, the man who had taken more from her than any human should ever take—Gideon Walker; the vulture who had preyed upon her weak and wounded family. Perhaps one day they would meet again.

The hay farmer left Mary off at a street market with two well-worn Liberty quarters, donated in sympathy, even though her silence during the last half of the journey had spooked him more than anything. Looking to erase any possible trail, the next thing Mary did was find another farmer. This one was from New Hampshire, selling wool he had sheared to the local textile mill. With only the two quarters to offer, she persuaded him to take her with him—anything to put more distance between her and Beverly Farms.

Because the farmer didn't want his wife or anyone who knew her to see him with a young woman as he rode into town, he left her off a town early—a tiny town named Sanborn. Mary had to walk the final half-mile, but it made no difference—it was the first time she had walked freely in as long as she could remember.

The first thing she did was search the skyline for steeples. She spent the entire first day visiting the only two churches in town. She looked for shelter and for families that might be interested in fostering. When they asked for her surname, she used Clara's, so that Gideon could not track her down. For her Christian name, she pondered using Sarah or Alice for a quick moment but decided against diluting the memories of her dead family.

After nearly two seconds of deliberation and an awkward, waiting audience, she found the perfect name, going back to the last time they were all happy together. Despite Gideon Walker's best efforts to erase her memory through malnutrition and dark magick, she still remembered quite a bit. She vaguely remembered her father Elmer, and their happy farm in Pennsylvania, but there had been many things that were part of that happy time: Her father, her mother, her sister, her cat, and her doll, Millie.

CHAPTER 40
1851

Mary had escaped, and Gideon Walker was beside himself. If she ended up going to the marshal, the farm would be in jeopardy, and he would have to tactfully work his way out of a jam or risk the wrath of Helms. It would be tricky, no doubt, but when he thought about it, there were no crimes to cover up that could be proven. Most of the crimes had even been erased, but he would treat the flock once more to be sure.

As far as the authorities were concerned, the remaining followers were all just that—devoted—here on their own accord. The recently deceased Alice was long gone, taken by Helms, and disposed. If Mary came back, he could deny her claims and perhaps even apply another memory wipe to everyone on-scene, including the marshal.

The rapes, well, they hadn't occurred, at least as long as the memory spell had no shelf-life—he would check with Helms about that. The six souls abducted by Helms as part of their deal never existed, at least not in Massachusetts. Maybe Pennsylvania perhaps, but the police, in general, were not set up for interstate investigation. Yes, he would pass inspection, but it would be much better to avoid it.

He considered looking for Mary and consulted Helms. Helms

told him he would go looking himself and keep him abreast of the situation. Perhaps there was no reason to worry. What could the girl remember that would prompt her to call the authorities anyway?

Poor living conditions? Maybe. Suspect food? Fanatical sermons having nothing to do with Jesus? It would be uncomfortable, but he could wriggle out of the interrogation. Still, the loose end bothered him. No one had ever left him.

Helms calmed his nerves two months later when he reported that the girl was back in Pennsylvania and had been taken in by a church and was on her way to a quiet and peaceful life where she would mind her own business. This bit of news made him feel somewhat better, yet he wanted to know in what town she had settled. Helms reminded Gideon that he was monitoring the situation and that a murder investigation—should he kill her—would be potentially detrimental to their arrangement. Was risking his immortality worth it? The laws of the living would be practically meaningless on that fine day. With that, Gideon let Mary go.

CHAPTER 41

1852

Mildred Wells began her new life helping her foster parents run their farm. In the evenings, she homeschooled. William and Claudia Downing were concerned that Mildred was abnormally gaunt and had gone through *something*—but the girl wouldn't open up about it. For the longest time, she would barely leave her bedroom. The night terrors were horrific. It took several months of love and care before they even announced that they'd fostered her and would pursue adoption.

Mildred blocked out her past to the point that she had forgotten her old name. Mary was gone, and in her place was Mildred—a sort of alter-ego. She shut the door on everything, including the remaining cult members and the idea of bringing Gideon Walker to justice. It was all too painful for her, and everyone she cared about was already dead. Letting him see her again seemed unnecessarily dangerous not only to her mental health but also to her sleep, so she let it all go.

In February, when she had gained some weight back, they began to take her into town and socialize her—slowly introducing her to the townspeople. Like a rescued dog, nobody knew or dared to ask what Mildred had suffered. Claudia spent some odd hours inquiring in Salem (where Mildred told them she was from) but never got anywhere trying to trace her roots.

By April of 1852, Mildred had opened up considerably. Winter was over, and the change of seasons did wonders for her spirits. The nightmares had abated somewhat. The confidence that she was under the care of a loving family began to pay dividends. Finally, on one of her trips into town with William, her eyes fell upon a tall young gentleman in the baking aisle of Philbrick & Mull. Five minutes later, they not-so-coincidentally bumped into each other and struck up a conversation. His name was Thomas Pike.

Thomas was the son of Herman Pike, who owned the local sawmill. He attended the Sanborn School, a well-to-do boarding school for the privileged children of the area, and was sure to inherit his father's fortune when the time came. Mildred transformed. For the first time in her life, she knew what she wanted—a family— with Thomas.

He swept her off of her feet, and vice versa. Mildred, now healthy and sporting girl-next-door looks, turned on the charm like never before. Her adoptive parents were overjoyed—their lowly depressed girl surprised them by showing a completely different side.

The Pikes were charmed, and Thomas didn't stand a chance. The one or two girls in competition with Mildred for Thomas's affections quickly fell by the wayside. By September, he asked for her hand in marriage. Sixteen was a bit on the young side, but the girl had an answer for everything and a very mature answer at that. It was to be a June wedding, and the wealthy Downings even offered to foot the bill. Her power of persuasion was almost supernatural.

She had not only put her horrible past behind her but believed her bad luck was over. She looked forward to getting on with her life—her own house and her own land. Children too! Hopefully, a little girl.

CHAPTER 42

1854

Mildred gave birth to a son who they named Elmer—after her father, in January of 1854. Much to her surprise, she was disappointed—her first disappointment of any kind in nearly three years. But it was not the end of the world. The young family lived with Thomas's parents while he finished school. Mildred spent the majority of her time attempting to bond with little Elmer.

The plan was this: After Thomas graduated, he would work in the sawmill for a few years and learn the trade properly. While he worked, they would save for a place of their own. Things slowed down quite a bit after the whirlwind courtship and wedding. Motherhood proved to be hard work, and the mother-son duo struggled. Mildred figured that a little girl in the mix might be just the trick.

They tried, but nothing happened. Mildred's spirits took a nosedive, and she skipped meals—beginning to resemble the girl who had gotten off the hay cart in Lowell. The dark circles reappeared, as did the dark cloud over her head. Claudia Downing became concerned about her daughter-in-law; this was a completely different Mildred. The mood swings were hard on her son, her grandson, and the entire household.

Three years passed with no new pregnancy. Claudia spent her

days actively avoiding Mildred but took Elmer every chance she got, for fear he wasn't receiving enough love and attention. The fact that Thomas had graduated and had begun work was a small blessing, however.

The Downings as a team collectively saw to it that Mildred was given as many mental health breaks as they could manage, even enrolling her in some classes—abnormal in those days for a woman—to take her mind off whatever was bothering her. Privately, and much to her concern, Claudia suspected that it was Elmer.

CHAPTER 43

1856

Ten hard years crawled by for Gideon Walker. Ten years—and eighteen risky abductions. He planned them out on a map to make them appear unrelated, at the pace of two per year. Salem was crossed off the list for good because he had already taken from that community. The next place was Somerville, and then Woburn, before taking from Lynn, and then Gloucester. Boston was too busy. Too many eyes.

The Georgetown job got messy, and he had to kill the child's parents when they saw him hiding in their barn. That wasn't good; it was big news, and it was close to home. He had to take a roundabout way out of town to minimize the odds of getting caught. As he rode, he cursed Lyman Helms. He hated the entire nerve-wracking process. One misstep and his life would be over; *both* of his lives—this one and the next.

The Book of Shadows had stopped growing, and he wondered if it was because they were making him wait. He asked about it twice and was given the same vague answer both times:

"Much of the book has to do with your afterlife."

Still, he practiced on, mastering the existing pages. It became boring. Even a child could do them, as he had witnessed. After the fifth year, he asked again about accelerating the process.

"I have delivered sixteen children—only eight more to go over five years. I have mastered the Book or at least the portion of it that I have been given. It's easy. Too easy! Why should I wait five more years, risking getting caught when you could have me now? I'm ready to work."

"Because *im*patience is not a virtue. Impatience got our founder, Allemand, killed. Impatience attracts attention. We're not concerned with your agenda. Many of the later skills focus on removing the bloodlust ingrained in us, and when you get to that point, you will understand. You won't want the next newcomer to ruin it all for you—make you run from the mobs, or get you killed, just because he can't wait a fraction of a century. Before you can join, you have to master patience."

CHAPTER 44

1859

At Christmastime of 1859, Thomas's parents presented the young couple with an extra special gift. They had purchased a nice piece of land on Lancaster Hill Road, only four miles away. In the springtime, Herman would send help from the sawmill to not only build a house but a big barn next to it. They would plant a spruce grove to serve as a Christmas tree farm for fun and extra money while their kids were young, and a money crop for the sawmill when the kids grew up and moved on.

Mildred seemed to cheer up with the news, and everyone was silently excited by her change of mood. She hadn't lived in her own house since childhood. The last was the one her father fell off the ladder—when she was only four years old. The darkness of the thought began to wrap itself around her, and she pushed it away. Tired of being depressed, she made up her mind to change her attitude, promising everyone—including herself—that she was *back*. She would work to make this an exciting new beginning for everyone.

CHAPTER 45

1860

Winter came and went faster than usual because of all the positive anticipation and the plans and arrangements that had to be made to prepare for construction the following April. They ordered the supplies and scheduled the vacation time amongst the sawmill employees. Little Elmer was six years old now, not as needy as when he was a toddler. Mildred largely ignored him, and he kept out of his mother's way as she planned out her bedrooms, the kitchen, and a turret.

They broke ground during the last week of March while the ground was still slightly frozen. Construction went swiftly with the help of the mill employees, and they raised the barn in late April. Mildred smiled ear to ear as things began to take shape. While the men worked on the framing, she helped plant the seeds for the grove. She took Elmer down to the pond and watched him try to catch bullfrogs. Thomas saw how much fun they were having and came back from town one afternoon with an old rowboat for them to drift the afternoon away.

Secretly, Mildred was bored in the boat and couldn't wait for the men to finish so she could get back to work, turning the house into a full-fledged home. By mid-June of 1860, she got her wish, and they moved in, with the interior far from being finished. It was close enough, however, for the happy-but-fragile family. Now at least they could pick on rooms one by one to refurbish during the winter months.

CHAPTER 46

1860–1861

June was a great month. And so were July, August, and September, but in October 1860 there were rumors of war, should Abraham Lincoln be elected president. Thomas began to pay way too much attention to the news in Mildred's opinion. He began to speak of things like patriotism and the abolishment of slavery as if people from Sanborn had to deal with this sort of thing every day.

Having been somewhat of a slave herself for a time, she could empathize, but at the same time couldn't help but think selfishly. Thomas's commentary was a little too passionate and political, and she began to get testy. He was a husband and a father with a new house, with hopefully more children down the road. She implored him to stay focused on her and the family.

In November, much to Mildred's chagrin, Lincoln was elected, and some of the southern states began to secede. Thomas was beside himself. Some of the men who had helped them build their home were of color—lifelong employees of his father's mill. They were good friends—*practically, family! They celebrated the holidays together! Played together as kids!*

By February, word spread that the Union Army was organizing. Two of the men who helped build the house on Lancaster Hill

Road were talking about signing up. Mildred continued to try and get pregnant again, but it wasn't happening. Thomas had mysteriously stopped talking about the tension between the North and South, and Mildred wondered if it was only to hide it from her. On April 23, 1861, Thomas came home late from the sawmill, extra quiet and looking guilty. Mildred knew.

"Did you do it?" she scowled. Thomas furrowed his brow searching for calming words that did not exist. "You did. *You damn well did—didn't you!* You volunteered! Look at me, Thomas Pike. *Look at me!*" Thomas looked up and met her eyes.

"It's not right, Mildred…they…"

"It's not…*RIGHT?* What's not right, Thomas? Tell me! Is it right to abandon your wife and son and *future* children so that you can go and feel good about yourself? I can't do this alone, and you know that. You're going to regret this, I promise you."

Thomas started to address the threat, but she tuned him out immediately. He saw her face and knew there were no more words. Suddenly she had his hatchet in her hand. *Where did that come from?* For a moment, he thought someone was going to get hurt, most likely him—while he subdued her…that way he couldn't join.

Instead, she turned and walked out of the kitchen. Thomas heard the front door slam. He stood in the window to follow her. Elmer was upstairs playing, and that was a good thing; his mother looked as if she had lost her mind…again. Mildred crossed the driveway and down the front lawn headed for the pond. In moments she managed to snag two Canada geese with her bare hands, then suddenly slaughtered them on the stone wall.

A new low. When they had lived with his parents, Mildred's tirades were child's play in comparison. Thomas had no idea what would happen next, and Mildred still carried the hatchet. Elmer came bounding down the stairs—bad timing.

Thomas Pike continued to watch, preparing to shield his son's eyes. Mildred stopped just in front of the kitchen window, the headless geese still flapping nervous wings as the blood drained. She dropped the hatchet in the grass and raised the geese high, spraying herself and her surroundings crimson. Thomas was so shocked that he had forgotten about Elmer, who also watched, just under his right arm—seeing everything.

"What's mommy doing? Why is she doing that? She's all bloody—she looks scary!" Thomas grabbed Elmer's head and shielded his eyes while stepping back from the window. Her behavior was indeed frightening—and he began to reconsider his decision.

When the bodies of the geese finally shut down, Mildred slowly lowered her arms and transferred both to her left hand, and picked up the hatchet. Their blood dripped off of her face and dress. As soon as she made her move to the front door, Thomas and Elmer headed out the side door to the front of the barn. They stayed there wondering what to do—Thomas proposed a game of catch, preoccupied with the talk to come.

"Elmer, come with me. We'll go in the front door and get you upstairs to clean up for dinner. While you're doing that, I want to talk to mommy alone for a few minutes, okay?" Elmer did as he was told and followed his father inside. Thomas made sure to block the kitchen doorway from view as Elmer headed up. Then he turned to face Mildred.

CHAPTER 47

1861

"Mildred, what are you doing?" The walls were splattered with blood, as the death spasms persisted. Mildred did not respond, and Thomas pressed. A pot boiled on the stove. Mildred stood, her back to him, cutting something.

"Mildred. Talk to me. What is this? Are you ill? You're scaring Elmer. Whatever you're feeling, hold it together for his sake—please!" He searched the kitchen—the hatchet was missing. "Are you not *well*? Do you need *help*?" Mildred slowed her chopping and then stopped altogether. She turned slowly and spoke evenly—an entirely different mood as if she were an entirely different person.

"What are you going to do, Thomas? Tell them all I cooked you dinner? We aren't the only farm around here that eats their animals, you know."

"It's not that, Mildred; it's the way..."

"Don't worry about us, Thomas. We'll be fine without you. Go die in the war."

"It's only for three months. Then I'll be back. It's for Wesley and Abel. I've known them my entire life."

"You won't be back," she replied. "You'll die on the battlefield." Thomas felt a knot in his stomach. Things were not right—for Elmer. She turned her back to him again and began plucking feathers. It was nearly eight o'clock. These geese were never intended for dinner. She never cooked ahead. Thomas quit the fight and backed out of the room.

CHAPTER 48

1861

Mildred didn't speak with Thomas for two straight days. He realized that she had truly shut him out of her life. On the third day, he was scheduled to report for training in Concord. His parents showed up early to say goodbye and wish him luck. Mildred showed up too—and put on a show—an over-the-top sarcastic display that embarrassed them all.

She was overly vocal and dominated conversation, shades of her courtship years, except this time off-balance. Crocodile tears flowed, and only Thomas knew the whole story, he hadn't yet had the opportunity to confide in his parents.

Mildred capped the farewell off by bursting out the front door one more time, dramatically attempting to block his horse, then running beside him, tugging at his sleeve for more than twenty yards. As he rode, the most he got out to his parents was a quick, "Please help Mildred with Elmer." Otherwise, she dominated the occasion. Mildred finished the episode by collapsing at the end of the driveway as he rode away.

When he was gone, she picked herself up and acted as though it was just another day. The Downings were worried.

CHAPTER 49

1861

Gideon Walker delivered the twenty-fourth innocent to Helms four months shy of the ten-year-mark, but *still*, they made him wait. Nervous, he found things to occupy his time while he tried to forget that his glorious day was fast approaching. Every once in a while, paranoia whispered in his ear: *What if they stiff me?* If he didn't curb his thinking, he would begin to get angry, and the day would be ruined.

If he asked Helms again, they would surely delay, so he kept his mouth shut and quite literally practiced patience—although it wasn't easy. On the very day, Gideon woke up before dawn and strolled the edge of the forest, peering in. All was quiet, and he did his best to control his excitement. *It's going to be a long day. Find something to do.*

Noon came and went, and Gideon began the bad habit of checking the time. Pressure built at his temples, but again, he pushed the thinking away. At one point, he envisioned Helms laughing at his expense and wondered briefly if it was his doing, *or theirs.* Was it a torturous spell they had hidden from his copy of the Book, saving it for this very day? If so, it was clever and effective, but perhaps not the best idea. Gideon Walker did not like being the butt of jokes. In anguish, he went to the shed until dinner.

When mealtime came, he couldn't eat, so he got up from the table, surprising the rest of the cult. After telling them to finish eating and clean up, he put on his coat and took another lonesome walk along the tree line, looking for some sign that they would honor their agreement. A twig snapped behind him as he neared the shed. He whirled, and a revenant he had never seen before stepped out of the woods and began to follow him. Gideon stopped.

"Where's Helms?"

The unnamed revenant pointed into the woods. Gideon followed his direction and began to walk through the brush. His heart beat excitedly; *it was happening*. Visibility in the forest was good this time of year because most of the leaves had fallen, but the sun was setting, and it would soon be dark. If this were *not* his long-awaited ceremony, it would be one hell of a trap. *Either way, I die*, he nervously joked to himself.

All at once, they appeared around him, as if parts of the forest. There were ten in all, with the follower right behind him. *I make them an even dozen*, he thought. *This is it*. He kept quiet so as not to ruin anything. *Helms should talk first.*

"Good evening, Walker. What brings you here?" Some of the surrounding revenants chuckled.

"Hello, Helms...hello, everyone. I've been waiting a long time for this. Not just today, I mean, but..." he stumbled on his words, shaking. He was, after all, supposed to die here, if all went well. Helms spoke:

"Ten years is a long time for the living. We've all been there. Tonight is indeed the end of your wait, but unfortunately, I have a bit of bad news, and it wouldn't be right if we weren't here to tell you face to face."

Gideon's stomach sank, and the blood drained from his face. Despite the cool fall evening, he felt hot. *Don't do this, Helms.*

"The vote is in, and you did not make the grade." Helms stared at him grimly, his dead eyes meeting Gideon's. Gideon didn't even have time for anger; he was too afraid. The surrounding revenants shifted ever so slightly, and the woods went still as they waited for his reaction. Gideon's attention was divided. Any of them could be a potential attacker. He stepped back just an inch or two, instinctually. It wasn't completely clear that Helms was done talking. *Was that it?* Finally, Gideon found the words.

"What are you saying? I *delivered!* I gave you the twenty-four! I waited for *ten years.*" No one moved, and Gideon saw the first blade shimmer in the dying light. One of them had his knife out—now two.

They sprang simultaneously. Powerful leaps that covered the distance between them in an instant. Helms got to him first, and for a second, they were nose to nose. Gideon felt the blade enter under his sternum and travel up. He gasped, eyes bulging. The air left his lungs as the rest arrived, knocking him to the ground. Knives flashed, and everyone took their turn. He was dead in seconds.

CHAPTER 50

1861

Gideon's eyes opened, and the dirt fell into them but did not sting. He was immobile, pressed from all sides, and he attempted to take a breath, but suddenly realized he didn't need to. Frozen in place, he recalled his most recent memory, *the betrayal*. Like a person waking from a nightmare, he suddenly realized, it was not betrayal at all. The induction ceremony he'd imagined was simply a far cry from the real thing.

If he were not a revenant now, he would not have awakened. Their knives had perforated him, stabbing nearly every vital organ, except his heart. He felt no pain, and thankfully, no claustrophobia. They had murdered him, then buried him—as part of their hazing ritual.

Now his climb to power could begin. The first step was to dig himself out.

CHAPTER 51

1861

First, he wiggled his thumb, then his hand. His arms were noticeably more powerful. The left-arm poked through the surface of the shallow grave first, while the right arm worked to catch up. The legs kicked, and finally, he stood, clods of dirt falling off of him, landing down around his thighs. The whole process took two days. When he was completely out, he assessed the damage to his body—there was little to none. Finally, a voice from his left:

"Welcome back." It was Helms, standing behind a tree. Gideon turned his head slowly, managing a smile.

"Any more surprises?"

"Did you enjoy it? We don't usually have *arranged* transitions. We thought we'd bring you over in style."

"I'm sure you enjoyed it more than I did—fun at my expense. I haven't been the butt of very many jokes. I can't say I liked it."

"Relax. This is a sort of brotherhood, and it was an initiation. Webb stuck you through the temple before you could feel much of anything." Gideon subconsciously rubbed his temples; they were smooth and unbroken.

Gideon knew they were on equal ground now, and that it was only a matter of time before he flexed his muscles. In the meantime, he would wait, watch, and listen. He would get to know the whole tribe, one-by-one—their ages, their experiences, and their alliances. He would also learn the rest of The Book of Shadows, and how they—*processed*—their victims.

"How long was I dead?" he asked.

"Only a few hours," said Helms.

CHAPTER 52

1861

Now that he was one of them, Gideon was taken to a simple cave amongst an outcropping of rocks in the middle of the forest. The entrance was small and discreet, but the inside opened up. There was nothing to light the space, yet he could see perfectly.

"This is—*headquarters?* How long have you been in this location? Undetected?" he asked.

"Forty-nine years here. When Allemand died, we moved. They came after us. We used to be in a house on the outskirts of Salem." *Downgraded*, thought Gideon. Poor leadership. The cave was impressive—for a cave, but far below Gideon's expectations. They lived like coyotes and bears.

"How many chambers are in this cave? Do all eleven of you live here?"

"Of course not. We don't sleep, so no one needs a room at all unless you're shutting down for an extended period. You *will* require downtime now and again. It is not always necessary, but your body will deteriorate if you do not. Coordinated breaks are recommended, but sleep is no longer daily."

This explained how they got by with so little space. Helms ducked under a low threshold and led him into a larger back room. There were jars, baskets, and canisters everywhere, filled with bones mostly, sorted by type. Femurs, ulnas, and skulls, most of which were leftovers from missing people.

"This is the parts room. We waste nothing. The blood and the organs decompose first, so we use that first. Bones last forever. Some spells call for bones, and when we need them, we come here."

"Where is the original Book of Shadows?" asked Gideon. Helms looked at him with disgust for his ongoing lack of patience. *He wants it all, right away,* Helms thought. *All the secrets and all of the power with the least amount of effort.*

"I was about to show you," he hissed, then led Gideon out of the parts room and into another much smaller room. There were only two items in the room; the Book and the table it sat on. Gideon picked it up and inspected it.

"It looks almost exactly like my copy; is this all there is?" He opened it and skipped the first fifteen or so pages. "There can't be more than thirty…forty pages in here. Is there more?"

"That is four centuries of work, Mr. Walker. If you think you can add something of value, then be my guest. It's not easy to do. Allemand himself put together all but three pages. Crafting a useful spell is a lengthy process."

Gideon was frustrated at the scant amount of magick. He expected much more, much sooner. *They're still primitive,* he thought—*still cave dwellers.*

"I thought there would be more. I waited ten years and—" Helms grabbed his arm.

"We all know you waited ten damned years. We waited ten years too—some of us even longer. Two hours, and you're already complaining." Gideon didn't appreciate the scolding and grabbed Helms' hand off of his arm, pushing back steadily.

"Don't touch me, Helms." Gideon towered over him, but Helms held his ground.

"Occlusis oculis," he replied, and Gideon fell to his knees, blind. "As you can see, Gideon, you still have a lot to learn. This is a

pretty useful spell, isn't it? I've been practicing for one hundred and thirty-four years, and I have read the entire book, which you seem to have judged by its cover. *Conversus in oculis vestris.*" Gideon's sight returned, and he knew Helms could have killed him while he was blind. Embarrassed, he remained quiet. His plan would take longer than he realized.

CHAPTER 53

1863

Two years later, Helms walked alone through the forest on his way for a seasonal check on Bardelli, his hibernating friend. The leaves had fallen, and visibility through the trees was good. Snow would fall again soon, and it was time to make sure Bardelli's digging hand had not come uncovered. It would be a quick trip for Helms, most likely with no maintenance necessary, as Bardelli always did a good job of building his bed.

Depth of pit and ability to cover one's self were of the utmost importance, but Bardelli had mastered those skills ages ago and on top of that, had chosen an excellent spot between two maple trees and a stone wall. Years back, he chose the spot for its impassibility, then chopped through the obstructing roots and dug himself a very nice pit. Near the head and foot of the pit, he planted a series of pine seedlings to make his plot nearly impossible to walk over in the coming years, never mind sabotage.

With about ten minutes' walk to go, Helms heard something from behind. He stopped and listened. The only beings that made it out this far were animals, revenants, and hunters. Bardelli would have to wait, as the man himself had given strict instructions that Helms tell no one where he slept. The footsteps were abnormally careless for these woods.

Helms chose an appropriate hiding spot and waited. One minute later, he saw a ragged figure rushing between the trees, coming his way. It was Desjardins. After making sure Desjardins was not fleeing something, he stood.

"What are you doing? Why the hurry?" Desjardins turned, saw him, and stopped dead, twenty yards away.

"I was looking for you. Have you checked your runes?" Dejardins referred to the beads they all carried, sometimes on a string, sometimes in a pocket—a witchcraft-based tool of divination, powered by the Book of Shadows. Helms hadn't checked, and he reached into his pocket and pulled them out. He counted; two revenants were hibernating and—*eleven*—were up and around. His first thought was suspicion; Gideon Walker had gone unnaturally quiet in the two years since their confrontation, and Helms thought he might be working on something.

But then he remembered.

"I remember now. She had a hard life. Only twelve years have gone by, and she's already dead."

Desjardins nodded his head.

"What would that make her—thirty years old? Or less? Never met the right people. A tortured life. Well, those problems are over. She's probably very confused right about now." Both revenants pondered Mary's situation.

"How long until she figures things out?" asked Desjardins.

"I have no idea, but don't say a word. If you see Pratt or Sterritt, remind them too. Bardelli's asleep and probably will be for a while. If the others ever find out, they'll be angry that we tampered. Remember to feign surprise. They'll be shocked that there's an extra one of us roaming around."

"Do you know where?" asked Desjardins.

Helms shook his head.

CHAPTER 54

1863

Word of the thirteenth revenant spread quickly. Nearly every one of the conscious revenants reported except for McKenna, who was rumored to be in Maine. Gideon Walker even made his way back for the first time in two years, wondering what it all meant. There was an awkward moment between him and Helms before Gideon asked his questions.

"What does this mean?" he asked.

"I've seen this happen before. It could be one of two things; either somebody took advantage of the Book's instructions and converted a human without our authorization, or it's someone from overseas."

"Overseas? What makes you say that?"

"Allemand came from Europe, and he was there for a long time. He left quite a few bastards over there, and they show up once a century or so. The runes can't read the other side of the world. The magick is not without limits."

"Who would convert someone unauthorized? Would they be punished?"

"It's...*our* rule to keep the group to twelve until we refine the magick, but we do not govern all revenants. We don't know who this is. I'm hoping it's a European, and if it is, I'd like to meet them and find out why they're here. Perhaps it's just another Salem enthusiast. Keep a lookout."

CHAPTER 55

1865

For two years, Mildred tried to catch up to Elmer. Frustration gave way to depression and debilitating fatigue. She found a random spot in the forest and instinctively began to dig.

CHAPTER 56

1865–1875

Gideon stayed close to camp for a while and was often seen studying. Helms noticed that Gideon seemed to listen better now. Perhaps he had matured. Two years later, after everyone became used to the idea of a mysterious thirteenth walker, he began to slip away again, which in itself was no cause for alarm.

Helms hoped that Gideon had fallen in line. There was no need for a so-called *"leader"* anymore in his opinion, and Gideon may have finally come to realize it. The community was fluid and continuously evolving; they were freelancers who at times, joined forces.

Helms, however, still suspected that Gideon was the type driven to lead. Freelancing would not be enough for a taskmaster like him. Helms hoped that as the years passed, they could find a way to coexist, as slim as those chances may be.

He had voted against Gideon's inclusion, and Gideon would most likely come to know that if he didn't already. Helms—and four others—were outvoted. The raw potential, drive, and physical presence of the intimidating Gideon Walker had swayed the other six to voting him in. It was water under the bridge now, and Helms knew that it was only a matter of time before their chemistry as a group would change. He feared Gideon's lust for power would set them back fifty years. His ambitions, whatever they were, would change everything.

Helms shook his rune beads in his palm to take a reading. It was October of 1875, and he figured through the process of elimination that Gideon had been sleeping for two full years. Two others, Bardelli and Thayer, were also sleeping. The remaining ten (including the extra revenant believed to be Mary) were awake, spread across the continent—precise individual locations unknown.

Bardelli had been sleeping for nearly eleven years, the victim of an experiment gone wrong. He was the most scientific of the group, often sacrificing personal health for the advancement of the race. He argued that time meant nothing, and there was no other way to test new ideas. Allemand himself had been known to take long absences for the same reason.

Helms and Bardelli were close friends and had even given each other a sort of *power-of-attorney*. Bardelli had been working on a method to reverse decay, potentially paving the way to mixing with the human population. With less smell and no flies, they would be nearly undetectable. Bardelli's spell-in-progress had, in the end, done the opposite of its intention, thus requiring the long rest. By shutting down, he would suspend the decay, and in time, the healing would overcome the mistake.

Thayer had been asleep since just after the vote to include Gideon. His was a case of routine maintenance, more or less. Thayer was a reluctant revenant, still emotionally attached to the life he led nearly two hundred years before. He took more breaks than any of the others, preferring the escape that hibernation offered. Helms did not know Thayer's location.

Gideon Walker had taken five extended rests in his first fourteen years, which struck Helms as odd. The first rest was just after his first year, perhaps simply trying the spell on. The last four rests had all taken place over the last six years, and in total, Gideon Walker had been asleep for fully five of the six. When the third sleeper in the rune beads finally showed as awake again, Helms sent word that he was looking for him, and when Gideon caught wind, returned to meet.

"Have you been busy, Walker? Working on your magick?"

"Yes, Helms, thank you. I'm working on something you'll all like. I'm doing wonderful things with *blood*. I've tried many things with the other organs, but for me, it's about the blood, and once in a while, the heart. I think I'm onto something."

"Tell me what you're working on, and I can help you. We're a community after all."

"Would it be improper to save it as a surprise? I want to be remembered for this. The only one, if you don't mind. I want to create spells that rival Allemand's work. He's the only one I ever hear getting credit for anything. That is going to change, I promise you."

"We don't look at it that way, Gideon. There is nothing to gain by claiming 'credit.' Allemand gets more credit than anyone, but he's dead now, and we move forward…as a *group*. It's impossible not to give him so much credit because he was at it for so many years, but now we collaborate. There's nothing to be gained—no money and no rights—there's only *ego*, and ego is not our way."

Gideon frowned subtly and did his best to stifle disappointment, then rather abruptly continued.

"I suppose you know I've been hibernating. The reason for it is I believe I am on my way to refining Bardelli's work. If we can heal our flesh, we'll lose the damned flies. If we lose the flies, we can buy properties and live in houses again. I've been working hard on this, and—I'm close. Within ten years. Maybe fewer."

Helms grinned.

"Did you hear what you just said? You said you were 'close.' *Ten years 'close'*. Remember Gideon, not so long ago when ten years seemed like a lifetime?" Gideon false-grinned and pretended to enjoy Helms' joke at his expense.

"You were so right, Helms. You were so right."

"How can I help you finish your work? I think you've got me dreaming of living in a house again."

"Uh, well...I haven't split it up into segments yet. You've caught me unprepared. Until now, it's been a solo project, but we could use more blood if you want to collect some. The pure kind, of course. While you do that, I'll go over my notes, and we can divide the work properly."

"How much blood do you need?"

"Well—it's an ongoing process, and we'll *always* need more. Just get *one* to start us off. Oh, and I've been scouting this—I was about to go out and get it myself. My last one was from Rockport about a year back so don't go near there. There's a small schoolhouse in Boxford in a wooded area with lots of hiding spots. They take off in all directions when school lets out. You might want to try that first." Helms considered the request.

"Alright. I'll meet you back here in four days. Be ready. Sometimes they die of shock, as you know." With that, Helms made off for Boxford.

CHAPTER 57

1875

Helms found the schoolhouse Gideon told him about. He scouted it himself for a day and memorized the student's paths. He checked for police and adult presence in the area and then finalized plans.

Just before school let out the second day, Helms took his position just in the woods a quarter-mile down the least traveled road. A single child came down this way, and her home was only an additional hundred yards further. He peered from the bushes—no sign of her yet.

Another five minutes passed, and he checked again, but still nothing. To his left, from the direction of the girl's house, a commotion...the whinny of a horse. He peered left, but there was nobody on the road at all. Suddenly, not one but three horses burst between the trees at the end of the driveway in full gallop—headed his way.

Helms ducked back, still of the belief the horses had other places to go. Very soon, he realized his error. They reared up directly in front of his hiding place, and the men began to dismount with rifles and swords. He knew immediately he had been betrayed—confirmation that the bad feelings between him and Gideon were mutual.

He ran powerfully through the woods as two shots rang out, followed by a third a few seconds later. One bullet struck him in the back dead center, turning two vertebrae to bone chips. The second shattered his left shoulder blade just over the heart. The third bullet missed altogether, whistling past his left ear, embedding itself in an oak tree as he passed it. A human being would have died on the spot, but Helms kept running.

Going for the heart, he realized. He wondered how Gideon had coordinated all this—*working with humans.* How does a rotting dead man team up with parents—and police? Perhaps an anonymous note explaining years of abductions—blaming him. *Be ready. He's after your children.*

It didn't matter how he did it—only that it was done.

Helms ran on and continued to process what had just happened. How could Gideon have known which child he would select? It could have been any one of three strong candidates. Perhaps Gideon had bet on the most likely, based on his own scouting trip. Or might he have been *watching* as Helms scouted? If he had managed to spy on Helms, while Helms chose his candidate—the whole process—*the entire day—*

It was nearly unthinkable.

And nearly impossible. Gideon had been uncharacteristically solo of late, no followers of any kind. Not even a sidekick. Tyrants like Gideon need people to boss around, Helms thought. He'd been out of character for a long time, or so it appeared.

Helms ran four miles non-stop, finally stopping in a clearing. The broken bones in his back did not hurt, but he could sense the disfunction and lack of support. Now only muscles and sinew held the upper portion of his torso in place. There was too much movement and shifting in his upper body, and it would only get worse. When he lifted his left arm, he heard a bone-on-bone grinding sound. He would survive but would need a long sleep to repair. If he were to fight Gideon in this condition, he would not last.

CHAPTER 58

1875

Helms' instincts told him he was in trouble. Something wasn't right; Gideon had betrayed him and would be looking to finish him off. On top of that, Gideon had some *new magick*, the limits of which he had no idea. Sensing danger, he began to run again, this time north, away from Beverly Farms. If Gideon's new magick were some sort of tracking spell, it would be the end of him. Hibernation would mean death. He ran for nearly a day, further damaging his shattered spine, extending the required recovery time.

The further he got from Beverly Farms, the safer he felt. He trusted his instincts. He decided to walk on and on and on—which he continued for nearly two months. When he began to smell the Pacific ocean, he knew he'd reached the end of the continent. On the side of a mountain in the middle of a dense forest, he dug his bed under some overhanging rock. Even if Gideon did somehow know exactly where he was, it would take him an inordinate amount of time to come and get him. But hopefully—he didn't know.

It was still possible that Gideon *would* come to get him, but there was nothing he could do to help it. The possibility chilled his blood. He hoped briefly that his escape would make it look as if he had left for good, but realized quickly it was wishful thinking. He had one final thought before he closed his eyes. *What in the world had become of Mary?*

CHAPTER 59

1875

Gideon stood over the body of Fenerty, one of the four living human candidates hopeful of one day becoming a revenant. He watched the pool of blood expand on the kitchen floor as his rage died and left him with a mess to explain. His temper had gotten the best of him. Now Fenerty would never join them, and the others would wonder what happened. He would have to cover it up.

It had been Fenerty's job to inform the Boxford authorities of Helms' presence and to let them know that Helms was responsible for all of the abductions over the past ten years. Everything went according to plan until the ambush, when Fenerty caught a foot in his stirrup during his dismount and fired too late. To make matters worse, he had been the first horse to arrive and had blocked the two Boxford officers from potentially better shots.

Now Helms was—missing, and he would be aware of Gideon's betrayal. Gideon read the beads. Ten revenants were walking, which meant Helms was alive and awake, although where he could not tell. Most likely, he was running somewhere to heal. Fenerty's mistake was a potentially fatal flaw. Helms would be back sometime for sure—but didn't know when, and the idea of watching his back for a century was harrowing.

He didn't have the political support of the other revenants to hunt Helms down; in fact, they would never go for it. Gideon was still the new guy with no pull other than his looming physical presence. Helms had been until now their unofficial leader and was well-liked. Revenants killing another revenant was simply not done. Political spin would have to be applied consistently over time as Helms hid.

Now Fenerty was dead and wouldn't talk. It was time to blame his death on Helms; let the spin begin. He would stay close and listen using his new spell for hearing what the others were saying. His new magick had worked well on Helms, dulling his senses, leaving Gideon undetected. And nobody knew about it.

CHAPTER 60

1875

Gideon stayed away for three weeks and then made an appearance. He showed up at the cave that held the Book and checked in. The revenant named Webb stood guard and welcomed him in.

"You haven't been around, have you?" said Webb.

"I've been working very hard on a spell that will render the heart irrelevant, making us immortal. It takes a lot out of me, and I need long spells of recovery time." Webb nodded, then changed the subject.

"Have you checked your beads? You missed a lot. Helms is missing. Fenerty is dead. Newspapers said they shot at a child abductor, and we think it was Helms. Everyone is laying low. The townspeople are getting restless. Helms is awake, but we don't know where."

"Did Helms kill Fenerty?" Gideon planted the seed.

"Don't know. It seems possible, but I don't know why he would."

Gideon already knew that Helms was still out there and awake, hiding from him—most likely putting space between himself and Beverly Farms while he healed. How much time he would need, however, was a mystery. Fenerty had undoubtedly missed his shot, but the other two men had claimed to hit the target. The extent of the damage was unknown.

CHAPTER 61

1875

Almost two months later, Gideon pulled out his beads and checked again as he always did. Helms showed as sleeping—finally.

"Pleasant dreams," he smiled and breathed easy for the first time in quite some time. He'd been looking over his shoulder almost constantly. Now at least he knew Helms was most likely still hurt, and it took him two months to find a suitable place to rest. Gideon figured this bought him about a year to remake the revenant community in his image.

CHAPTER 62

1952

77 Years Later

Helms opened his eyes and moved his back ever so slightly, checking for damage. The last time he did this, it sounded like a bag of broken glass, but this time sounded much better. Hearing no grinding, he began to dig out. As he rose from the pit, he took a quick look around. The trees were much taller than the day he had gone to sleep. *How long?* He wondered. He dug in his pocket and took a reading.

What he saw troubled him. He counted again; thirteen walking—and four sleeping. *Shit.* Seventeen revenants. He shook the beads again: Seventy-seven years. He had been asleep seventy-seven years, and Gideon Walker had undoubtedly taken over by now, scrapping old rules and growing the population.

Helms wondered for a moment what number Gideon was shooting for and shook his head. More population meant less discretion. Sooner or later, they would clash with the human population, which greatly outnumbered their own. It would bring attention and problems.

He also wondered what else had happened while he was out; there was always something new after a long sleep. After seventy-seven years, everything would be new. Perhaps Bardelli had figured out the decay problem. If that was the case, and revenants could blend in with the human population, he might even support the expansion.

Helms looked again at the beads and wondered for a moment if one of the walking was still Mary. Was she alive? Had she found them? There was no way to know short of returning.

He had two choices: Remain on the lam, or crawl back and face the music. If he continued on his own, he would forever be visible as awake, and odds of a hunt would increase, especially if Gideon had revenants to spare. These facts spelled it out for him; there was only one real path, and it was back to Beverly Farms.

CHAPTER 63

1952

Gideon read his beads several times each day. He was a proud man now that his community was growing, and he was truly on his way to greatness. What bothered him most was that two of the revenants that showed in the readings did not belong to him, and he vowed each day to make sure that they would not one day prove to be his Achilles heel. Many of his recruits were out searching for them and would be until the mysteries were solved.

Two of the new revenants were recruited for their minds; one was a doctor and the other, a scientist. They were hard at work attempting to improve upon the spells left by Allemand. More specifically, and more than anything else, Gideon wanted them to find Helms. Secondarily, he also wanted to figure a way to know where everyone was at all times. As soon as they had it figured out, he would kill them discreetly, keeping their findings for himself. Two other recruits were nothing more than test subjects, rotating in and out of healing sleep.

Gideon did a double-take, surprised to see that one of the sleepers was missing; Helms had finally awakened. He felt a wave of anxiety. The man who used to tell him what to do—who had threatened to kill him on more than one occasion—was healed and on the move. Helms was smart and experienced, so Gideon had spent much of the last seventy-seven years catching up on various spells and techniques useful in fighting. He wouldn't be caught unprepared again.

The newest member of the clan was a giant named Saltz, even larger and more intimidating physically than Gideon himself, recruited to be his bodyguard. Saltz was an insurance policy. He had weapons hidden throughout the forest and became well-practiced in calling any one of them at a moment's notice. His magick was still weak but developing.

Two months later, Bergin came running into camp with news. It was Helms, who had surprised him in the nearby orchard and given him a message; he wanted to talk. Gideon was shocked, but this could be good news, he reasoned. It was at least better than a surprise blade in his chest at an inopportune moment. It was an opportunity to rid himself of the bane of his existence. Helms had insisted on the Salem Willows Park—at noon—on Friday.

CHAPTER 64

1952

Helms waited at Salem Willows Park, fully prepared to die. He didn't fear death, but he also didn't wish for it. His insurance policy had found an existence on her own, and that was disappointing, but Mary had, after all, always been a longshot. Thankfully, Gideon had never been aware of her or Helms's plan, and with the balance of power shifted in the cult leader's favor, it was time to kneel.

He prepared his excuse, which was easy to do because it was a partial truth—he'd been attacked and fled for his life. Depending upon how the conversation went, Helms would explain that he understood why Gideon would have wanted him dead, but it was time to wipe the slate clean. All he wanted was to live out his days without being hunted. He would pledge his loyalty, and if Gideon didn't accept, then he would most likely die on the spot.

Assuming he survived the meeting, he would be under scrutiny for decades, if not forever. He was not back in Beverly Farms to make waves—however, should the opportunity present itself down the road, all bets were off. Unless Gideon had devised a way to read minds, he should be safe.

A huge man approached as he stood near the water, far from pedestrians, so the ocean breeze could scatter the flies and mask the stench. The weather, too, was cool enough to help with both problems. Picnics were no longer in season, meaning fewer people. The big man stopped four feet away and stared at him.

"Where's Gideon?" asked Helms. Saltz said nothing. Helms wondered for a moment if this was a distraction or part of an ambush, or perhaps a test to see how he would react. He remained stationary and waited. Finally, fifty yards beyond the big man, he recognized the unmistakable gait of Gideon Walker. Saltz remained staring, intentionally blocking half of Helms' view. Ten seconds later, Gideon arrived, and Helms spoke first.

"Hello, Gideon. I think you know—I've been far away. I was shot twice in the back, and ambushed near the schoolhouse you sent me to, and I needed to heal. I wasn't sure who was after me. It could have been anyone. It could have been you for all I knew. When you're a leader, there are many reasons why you might be a target, but I'm not here to point a finger.

I realize things have changed in my absence, and I don't intend to challenge that. If you're the leader now, then so be it. What I don't want is to be hunted, and I also don't want you to think I'm doing the same." Gideon was privately surprised and pleased by Helms' sentiments. The pressure was off, and the challenge was all but over.

"You threatened my life," said Gideon. You blinded me and proclaimed your superiority after I had become a revenant. You don't respect me, Helms, and that is a problem."

"You're talking about things any father would teach his son. Of course, I threatened your life! But that was when you were human. I even took your life too, remember? It was because you wanted me to. Helms gestured at Saltz. You didn't just let this big one here walk right in without proper vetting and guidance, right? Tell me,"—Helms smiled—"Did you have fun watching the expression on his face on the day of his initiation?"

Saltz frowned. It wasn't often someone dared laugh at him. He glared at Helms, and Helms glared back, still smiling. Gideon didn't want to smirk but couldn't help it. It had been immensely entertaining, watching the big man fall. Immensely entertaining. What a wonderful tradition.

Gideon, fully satisfied with the peace treaty, felt a weight lift from his shoulders. Helms was no longer a dark shadow haunting his dreams. Perhaps he did have his respect. If Helms would publicly acknowledge Gideon's position as leader, it could work, and they would all be stronger for it.

CHAPTER 65

1964

Mildred dreamt under the dirt, reliving her entire life in bits and pieces. Mostly, her mind went back to her painful childhood and Gideon Walker's misguidance—she could remember it all now that she was dead and the spell was broken. Those were easy thoughts. They were someone else's fault—she was the victim, and dreaming of vengeance was satisfying.

Her marriage and motherhood experience was another matter. Those memories were even darker than her childhood. She did her best to stay clear of these thoughts, but not always successfully. Those dreams always ended in frustration. In moments of semi-consciousness, she felt anger, which meant that her energy was returning. She had no idea how long she'd been dreaming, but it was at least a break from her life above ground.

And then one early morning, a voice from her past called out nearby, too loud to be a dream. For the first time in ninety-nine years, she opened her eyes.

Everything was dark, like the aftermath of her suicide. Her body was immobile, held fast by the soil. The mound above her had fully settled as seasons had come and gone, turning the pile of brush and leaves to a rich layer of soil. The air pockets that had existed between the branches had been pressed out by decomposition and the weight of hundreds of feet of snow over time. The leaves that fell annually had rotted and sifted their way into the mix, creating a soft mound. She had unknowingly created the perfect revenant nest—ironic because she still didn't even know what a revenant was.

She listened again for the voice:

...(Daddy!)...

No. NO!

Fully awake, she began to work her left arm, the one that had finished the self-burial. Soon she began to break through the last layer of moss. The suicide burial of 1863 had taken her two days to dig out—she had mistakenly believed she would lie in that grave forever and had dug a much deeper hole with nearly a half-ton of soil to cover her. This time was different. In less than ten minutes, she was able to sit up and look around before freeing her legs. *And there he was.*

Elmer stood silently behind two young trees twenty yards ahead. Their eyes locked, but the boy didn't move. Chasing him had never worked, so she relaxed and remained a part of the earth for a few more moments. She raised her hand and reached out, beckoning. The boy inched toward her, and for a moment she thought he might approach. Then he stopped, looking off into the woods to Mildred's right. Mildred turned to see what he might be looking at.

Thomas?

She looked back at the boy, and he returned her gaze. Suddenly in what appeared to be a complete change of heart, he spun and ran off, disappearing between the dense green leaves. Her next emotion was anger. A lifetime of pain and disappointment flared back to life only minutes after she opened her eyes. Nothing had changed, *but something must!* Things could not continue this way. Fully rested now, she had energy and would do something about it.

CHAPTER 66

1964–1965

During her first three weeks of consciousness, Mildred fumed, deep in thought. Frustratingly, her mood was the same as it had been when she killed herself, but now she had to find a place for the negative energy. Because of her single-mindedness, it was nearly three weeks before she even noticed the family living in her house. A husband and wife, getting on in years. They had no children, or if there ever were children, they were long gone. The couple was boring but harmless, so she let them be.

For nearly a year and a half, she pursued Elmer with futility. Between Elmer sightings, she tried to release her anger in other ways and relive fonder memories of her short time in the house. Lonely, she even reenacted some of the more vivid scenes. Mildred became a one-woman show, to keep herself occupied. The peaceful drifting of the boat on the pond—even the day of the drowning gave her satisfaction, especially right after an unsuccessful chase.

Just after Thanksgiving of 1965, the mundane presence of the Smith family hit a bump in the road. Henry Smith stumbled upon their graves and began to excavate as Mildred arrived to lay flowers for Elmer's birthday. She had taken extra time and care to hide the stones and keep them to herself, yet he found them anyway. The little family plot was her fantasyland, the only reminder that they had once been a happy family, if only in her mind. It was her oasis, a symbol of reconciliation—her happy ending.

In a rage, she killed Henry on the spot. When her anger subsided, she realized his body would only call more attention. For the briefest of moments, she closed her eyes and painfully traveled back in time to the darkness of Gideon Walker's shed—for a secret that she needed to borrow. With her mind, she opened the *Book of Shadows* to re-read the twelfth spell, disguising the damage to Henry's body.

As soon as the spell was cast, the Book of Shadows slammed shut, and she was back in the comfort of her grove. The pain of being in the shed again for even a second cost her more than a minute of recovery time, and when it was over, she snapped to, realizing the old man's wife would come looking soon. The last thing she needed was a team of police discovering her holy ground.

Effortlessly she slung Henry's body over her shoulder and brought him back to the side lawn by the barn. She felt strong— much stronger than ever before. She could have carried five times the weight in her estimation. *There are some odd benefits*, she thought. As she set him down, she placed Henry's hands over his chest to make it look like a heart attack.

Henry's wife Annette surprisingly stayed in the house for three more years, living on the farm all by herself. Unfortunately, the sudden lack of a husband turned her into a bit of a busybody, and she got *nosy*. After Annette was gone, the house remained empty for three years, and in a way, it saddened her to see it fall into disrepair, but as long as her sacred plot remained anonymous, she didn't care.

CHAPTER 67

1965

Mildred walked alone through the forest and pondered her predicament. She'd been so wrong about ghosts and the supernatural. She'd never believed in any of it until she'd read Gideon's Book. She knew now that ghosts weren't made of vapor, nor could they disappear in the blink of an eye like all the stories said. The urban legends had it all wrong. Being a ghost was disgusting, clumsy, and far more physical than anyone imagined.

She'd never given a thought to any sort of afterlife, but now she *lived* one, and she also knew now that it was given to her by a rancid smelling man the night she escaped Beverly Farms.

The man cast two spells on her. One she wasn't sure of, and one that erased her memory. That unknown spell was the one most likely responsible for bringing her back. She remembered it all now that she was dead.

The mystery man helped her escape—but must have known what was happening in the shed all those years. Why did he wait so long? Who was he? Escape—and escape alone—would have been the doings of a good Samaritan. Allowing rape and keeping someone alive against their will was evil—and probably done for selfish reasons. An idea struck her—here was something to work on—a distraction from anger. Anything would be better than the frustration of chasing Elmer or trying to relive expired happiness.

CHAPTER 68

1971

In 1971 a newly divorced man named Tim Russell bought Mildred's house. She knew he was divorced—and many more things about him—by searching through his papers which he kept in the turret. He was a construction worker of some sort, and Mildred became interested in what he might do to restore her house.

In the end, however, the name Tim Russell would live forever in infamy. *Tim Russell*, and his girlfriend, *Holly Burns*. When it was all said and done, they would both be dead, but before that—they would suffer.

Tim Russell and Holly Burns had somehow, some*way*, conspired against her—partnering with the cowardly *Thomas Pike*—in the most devastating betrayal of her two lives—*no mean feat*.

Tim Russell and Holly Burns had helped Thomas. The more she thought about it, the more it all made sense. Thomas had recruited them, and they had worked together, moving the graves and hiding the bones. As anyone who has felt the sting of betrayal, it seemed she was the last to know.

Thomas Pike, the wannabe war hero—the man who had deserted his family under the false banner of patriotism—had returned for the first time in a century for one last dagger. Elmer was gone for good, and she could sense it. Any hopes at reconciliation were lost, and in the end, she was the villain—there would be no changing that. Her mind wandered for hours after the fact, trying to wrap her head around the events leading up to Thomas's premeditated masterpiece.

Thomas had scorned her not once but twice—The first was when he joined the Union Army. Raising a child—an unwanted child—all by herself—was too much to take. Thomas knew Mildred better than anyone, and even though he didn't know every dirty detail, he knew *enough*. He was equally to blame for what happened to Elmer, yet he ended up the hero after all.

She had relived the false family reunion in the grove hundreds of times, especially her thoughts at the time, step-by-step as they walked together side by side. Suddenly—they were gone. The confusion and denial that followed added to her humiliation—inexplicable but to those that have ever felt it—she'd been played the fool.

And the new owners that helped—*Do they think I disappeared too?* For several minutes she connected the dots, letting the anger flow. It all came together at once, and two powerful emotions collided within her—confidence—and *direction*.

So many possibilities and ideas; all she knew for sure was that her plan would be slow and painful. She would make it last because she had nothing better to do with her time. There was nobody left to chase—and no more graves to visit. The entire grove had been desecrated—stolen from her.

There would be *research*—and *travel*. She had to catch up with everybody who had taken advantage of her—catch up with the joke; the joke they all played on her. And it was time for a few jokes of her own.

Thomas had probably started on *his* plan more than a century ago. He had always been a patient man—*annoyingly* patient—it was so infuriating that it had *worked*. Another surge of fury bolted through her temples. She would have cried in frustration if she could have.

It was time to burn it all down, and everyone with it. When it was all over, they would all take a nice bite of her misery—and then choke it down.

CHAPTER 69

1971

Mildred stood alone in the grove that evening, still seething, in a trance. Her physical strength allowed the rage to burn on without fatiguing her. She hadn't moved in hours, but she had sorted many of her thoughts into separate plans. The first would be to double-check on their bones before Thomas took him away forever. Moving the bones had been the central part of his plan, and it had worked. Getting Elmer's bones back could still give her a chance to undo Thomas's work. If she did indeed find them, she would separate Thomas from Elmer herself and find somewhere hellish to bury the father.

Once again, she closed her eyes and in her mind returned to Gideon's dark shed where she opened the Book. Twenty-one pages in, she found what she was looking for and read aloud. An hour later—she could sense them—her family members. It took her another minute to calculate the direction, and when she had it right, she began to walk northeast.

Nine hours later, she arrived on the shore of Lake Kanasatka between two cottages. She wondered for a moment why Thomas and Elmer had ended up here, and then remembered that Thomas had help. *Was one of these places Holly's?* She would find out.

Looking out across the surface, she sensed the bones were

at the bottom of the lake and began to wade out. Forty minutes later, she surfaced on the other side, carrying the empty burlap bag recently dumped by Tim and Holly. Thomas and Elmer were indeed gone, their bones pulverized, then scattered.

In frustration, Mildred dropped the sack on the pebbly shore, and walked into the woods, headed back for Sanborn. *It all evens out in the end*, she told herself.

CHAPTER 70
1971

On her walk back from Lake Kanasatka, Mildred broke into the Meredith Public Library. When she couldn't find what she was looking for, she broke into the Laconia Public Library, which had a larger occult section. It took her an hour to find her answer.

She was not a ghost after all, and she should have known better. If she were a ghost, she would have been able to follow Thomas and Elmer. Thomas knew this—and she didn't, and that was the crux of his plan. Like a fool, she had mistakenly believed she was just like them, despite the flies and the physicality of the whole thing *and*—and just about everything, now that she realized it. How did he know this, and she did not? Had even Elmer known? The possibility made her sick. She looked down at the book again:

> *Rev-e-nant*
> /ˈrevəˌnäN,-nənt/
> *(noun)*
> *A reanimated corpse that has come back from the dead*
> *for the sole purpose of revenge. From the French verb*
> *revenir meaning "to come back."*

No wonder she could never catch Elmer. No wonder the flies followed her wherever she went.

It made perfect sense. The unknown spell that had been cast by the mystery man in Beverly Farms—the rancid mystery man—who was for sure a revenant himself. For the first time in more than a hundred years, she considered returning to the sleepy village. Yes, if Tim and Holly were going to pay, why not make them all pay? It had all begun with *Gideon Walker and his cult. Gideon Walker—and the missing children. Gideon Walker—and her beloved sister Sarah.*

The memories washed over her like a filthy river. Her sister, her mother. The food, the sermons. The three revenants that had pulled her into the woods and the returning revenant that had turned her into one of his own. Everything was there, bright and vivid. Mildred left the book on the library table and walked out of the front door. It was still dark out, but dawn was almost here.

Mildred sat down in the woods to think. Her eyes were open, but her mind was elsewhere—and everywhere. Her emotions held her hostage, but a plan was forming. It was still nearly impossible to think logically; there was too much emotion because everything was so fresh. The rug had been pulled out from under her feet, and chaos ruled her mind. The expression "Hell hath no fury like a woman scorned" was the closest phrase to the way she felt, but somehow it still didn't seem strong enough.

Would Gideon still be in Beverly Farms? He should be dead by now, but it was not hard to imagine that he might now be a revenant himself. Gideon Walker, the murderer. Gideon Walker, the cult leader. Gideon Walker, the predator. He would be extremely dangerous as a revenant.

She made up her mind. Gideon should die first because he started it all. The couple in the house could wait. Let them restore the farmhouse while she tended to other business. Their belief that she was gone forever would make it worse when they learned the truth. Their false sense of security would pay more dividends the longer she waited.

Mildred looked up at the last of the stars before the dawn broke and chose her direction. Sanborn was no longer the destination.

CHAPTER 71

1971

Tim noticed he was whistling while he was working, so when Holly called at lunchtime, he told her about it.

"I think she's gone. I was whistling while I was working, so I guess I'm relaxed," he said. Holly was a bit more on the cautious side.

"Even so, please be careful. Please tell me you check the field every five minutes!" Holly was referring to one of Mildred's favorite paths.

"Absolutely. Johnny's watching too, but I'm telling you, I feel something. I feel safer. She's not coming. Thomas could have killed me, but he didn't. We lived up to our end of the deal, and so did he. I'm not even the least bit nervous over here. I'm freakin' whistling while I'm working! I'm half expecting Snow White to come out of the woods with birds on her shoulders." Johnny laughed audibly, and Holly heard him.

"Don't encourage him, Johnny. He's not funny, remember that." Tim held the receiver so they could both hear her.

"I know he's not funny," Johnny yelled. "I'm working with Dopey here. And I'm gonna die of boredom, especially if we have ham sandwiches again."

"Grilling takes too long. And if I grill for Johnny, he's going to want a beer."

"What time do you think you guys will quit?" Holly asked.

"Eight o'clock sharp. A few more months of this and we're going to be in good shape. I'm paying Johnny overtime, and he isn't worth it, but that's the way it goes. God giveth, and God taketh away, what can you do? Honey, I will be at your place by 8:30 at the latest."

"Fair enough. I can wait for 8:30, but I'll be starving. I want payment for my sacrifice."

"And what is your currency, madam?" Tim asked.

Holly made him guess.

CHAPTER 72

1971

They woke in Holly's Laconia house the next morning. Tim hadn't renovated the bedrooms yet in his house, and in Holly's mind, there was no hurry. It would be quite a while, if ever, that she would feel comfortable sleeping there.

Things between she and Tim were going extremely well, and that was no exaggeration. A little *fast*—but great. They were both adults, and neither had any interest in playing games, frivolous arguments, or wasting each other's time. Holly couldn't recall if she had ever felt this level of connection with any man. Maybe twice, she corrected herself—and one was back in high school. It felt so good. The Mildred and Thomas episode had only brought them closer, proving to them that they had each other's back when things got ugly.

It was time to begin the daily routine. All-in-all it would be a happy day (they were all happy days now) interrupted by the need to try and make money.

"Honey, I'm gonna miss you today."

"Well, I'm going to miss you too, Lover-bun," he said. Holly couldn't keep a straight face and broke out laughing. *Lover-bun. Nobody says that.* Yes, the days were full of newly invented pet names for each other—and baby talk. Things only the two of them shared and would never want anyone else to hear.

"I win! You laughed first!" he proclaimed—Every day, the same cheesy bullshit, and...*she loved it.* It was so fun, so good... *The best part of life.*

"I'm going to miss you too. Why can't you quit at five o'clock like the rest of the working world?"

"Because I don't have an office job, sweetheart. This is the construction business. Slow projects mean *slow money.* I need to sell this beast! Just be thankful I don't work in the restaurant business—then I'd be working nights and weekends."

Money. Everything always came down to money, and she couldn't blame him. He bet everything he had on the house on Lancaster Hill Road, and she was his real estate agent. The intent was to refurbish the old house that had been empty for three years and sell it for profit. It was the beginning of his new post-divorce life.

Then the ghosts got in the way. Or the revenants. Or two ghosts and one revenant—it was all so confusing. She had never even heard the word "revenant" until two weeks ago; now she wished she could forget it. Mildred, Thomas, and Elmer had slowed things down and cost Tim money in the process—It would be a relief if Johnny could help Tim get back on track.

CHAPTER 73

1971

Tim arrived first to the house, and naturally, his eyes swept the field as he pulled in. A few weeks ago his eyes would *scour* the field, and he would check out the entire house room by room before starting work, but now he truly believed that Thomas Pike had lived up to his end of the bargain, and the house was ghost-free. Ghost-free and *revenant*-free.

Like Holly, Tim had never heard of a revenant. *I move out of one house with a banshee living in it, and I buy one with a revenant,* he joked to himself. The "banshee" was, of course, his ex-wife Sheila, the mother of his two young girls Olivia and Vivian. Sheila liked to make Tim's life difficult, so as far as Tim was concerned, she deserved his nicknames.

Who the hell knew there was such a thing as a revenant? *A bloodthirsty creature bent on revenge,* or something like that. He couldn't recall the exact words from the book Thomas had left him in the turret. A dead woman, stinking up the place, covered in flies, cooking weird shit in my kitchen. Thank you, Thomas, for taking her away. Tim stepped out of his truck and breathed in the morning air. Yes, they were gone now, and it was time for work. He opened the tool bin in the bed of the pickup and grabbed his tool belt.

The old hatchet sat on top, just another farm tool now that Mildred was gone—but Tim decided he didn't want to see the hatchet first thing every time he opened his tool bin, so he brought it back to the barn and put it in the drawer he originally found it.

"See you next century," he said out loud, then went in the house and up the stairs to what had become his favorite room, the turret. The vast majority of the house itself was a dusty mess. The bulk of the work done thus far was working on the inner walls, modernizing and re-insulating them. None of the rooms were even close to being finished. The turret was the only non-dusty room in the house, so Tim made it his office for the time being. The contents of the room included the desk that was here when he bought the place, a folding chair, and two boxes of files; one for his business and the other personal papers.

He came here to check one thing before Johnny arrived—his bank book. While the whole Mildred Wells episode had only taken two weeks, he had fallen behind money-wise on a plan that left little room for error. Buying, fixing, and selling this house was the key to his financial future, and he was beginning to sweat his money situation with more than a year to go before completion.

He opened the bank passbook—only $3,422.83 to his name. From this amount, he would have to buy construction materials and basic living expenses. There would be odd money trickling in from Johnny's jobs back home, but probably little more than enough to keep him on the payroll. He could freelance in the Lakes Region if need be, but that would take time away from the house. It was too close for comfort, but he had to make it somehow-he had no other choice.

He promised himself he would not skimp on his love life either. He and Holly were in their honeymoon phase, and worrying about money was the exact opposite of sexy. Their dinners out two or three times per week did add up, but at $12-15 a pop, it was an expense he would gladly incur. Their relationship itself was also an investment, something he and Sheila never realized during their marriage. It ended up costing a whole lot more money than the dinners ever would have, not to mention the emotional pain that racked the whole family to this day.

CHAPTER 74

1971

M ildred walked through wooded areas whenever possible; unwanted attention would only cause problems and interrupt her course. As she walked, she plotted, her thoughts jumping back and forth between where she went so wrong to the details of how she would make it right again. Her plans didn't end happily for anyone in the end.

She wondered what would be left when it was all over. Would she continue to walk the earth in torment, or could she rest? With no apparent answers, she cast the worry aside to focus her anger on those who had wronged her.

The woods were dense in some areas, at times marsh-like and thick. At one point, Mildred's dress caught on a snag, tearing the old rag completely off. Naked Mildred stood over the pile of fabric and pondered the predicament. A nude corpse would be immediately noticeable, even from a distance.

Mildred's swarm of flies capitalized on the new places to land as she picked up the dress. The clothing spell from long ago eluded her. Perhaps she would find a clothesline along the way. The walk from Sanborn to Beverly Farms was nearly ninety miles, and this was reason enough to detour. If she couldn't find a clothesline, she would have to break in somewhere.

She took her first steps over the soft ground and felt the wind on her legs. Three steps later, she felt the comfort of cloth brushing against them again. She stopped and looked down. There it was…a full-length farm dress. She dropped the ripped dress into the leaves and straightened up; she didn't have to remember the spell; it was still in effect. Mildred paused. What else did she used to know? What skills might be hidden beneath the surface? Also—some spells had been broken in death, and some had not—something to be careful of.

Mildred walked all night and into the next day. Most of the trip was a direct route through the woods, but on occasion, she would cross or run parallel to popular thoroughfares. She did her best to avoid farmsteads and neighborhoods.

CHAPTER 75

1971

Eric Enrico was twelve years old and grounded by his parents. He was not supposed to play outside after school or converse with friends, but Eric's mother didn't get home from work until after 6:30 pm, and what she didn't know wouldn't hurt her.

The first thing he did was phone his buddy Mark Gottlieb to tell him to meet at the stone wall in fifteen minutes. Eric and Mark were neighbors. Mark owned a BB gun, and the two of them had been caught shooting at street lights in front of their houses. Eric's parents had grounded him, and Mark's had laughed the whole thing off.

Mark met him at the arranged location with the BB gun. This time the two would head into the woods away from civilization and shoot stuff out there. Eric's brother Kevin had shot a red squirrel two years ago with a .30-30 rifle, and it blew a hole large enough to see inside the body cavity. He said he had watched the heartbeat for over a minute before it stopped. The two boys hoped to find a story like that of their own.

Spring had come early, and the forest was lush with new green vegetation. On a cold winter day, one could see nearly a quarter-mile through the woods, but now the visibility was less than ten feet in some areas, depending on how many low hanging branches there were. Some paths resembled leafy tunnels.

At 4 pm sharp, the two boys stepped into the woods and headed for the Birchwood Farm cornfield about a half-mile through. Eric brought his father's spare watch so he could keep a close eye on the time. Despite their best hunter impersonations, the boys made sounds equivalent to a drunken moose walking through the woods, and all the squirrels knew it.

Mark started things off by stepping on a rotting fallen tree and cracking it in half. Eric, a notoriously loud talker, unintentionally forewarned every living thing in a quarter-mile radius. With no squirrel sightings, boredom set in, and the boys began taking turns shooting at random objects.

Fifteen minutes later, it was Eric's turn with the BB gun. Tired of shooting at flaps of peeling birch bark, he vowed silently to make his next shot count. A fat gray squirrel chattered somewhere above but remained out of sight. Another rustled through the bushes, seemingly mocking them. Finally, another crunched its way through the leaves on the other side of some tall oaks, this time moving toward them.

This was a first for the boys. Most everything they had ever shot at had been running *away*. This one didn't seem to know that he was headed into a trap. Eric decided the best position to be in was directly in front of a treeless clearing. Hopefully, the squirrel would hit that open patch and run the length of it, giving Eric more than a fair chance at shooting him.

The crunching grew very loud, and Eric began to wonder if it was a squirrel at all—perhaps it was a dog or a coyote—Then the noise stopped altogether. Had they been detected?

Suddenly, a pale woman's face emerged from between two bushes—head high, six feet above the ground—the farthest thing from a squirrel. The face startled Eric, and the BB gun went off. He thought for a second that he had hit the owner of the Birchwood Farm and that he would lose his BB gun for good, but the face didn't flinch, even though he was sure he must have hit her.

A full second later, Mildred pulled back from between the

bushes and disappeared. Eric turned and looked at Mark, whose face proved he had seen the same thing.

Both boys believed they had seen a ghoul, and they weren't far off. It was only between the bushes for a second, but they compared notes and agreed that one eye seemed unnaturally low, like the capsule surrounding the eyeball had failed. Both agreed she was as white as a ghost.

A minute passed as the boys nervously chattered behind their wall of green leaves, wondering if they were in big trouble, or if it was indeed the face of a phantom. A living human would be howling mad right now—if they were conscious. *Had they killed her?*

Suddenly the crunching started again, closer than the last time. Eric pumped the BB gun as if it would protect them. Bravely, he raised it as Mildred parted the saplings and stepped into their hiding place.

It *was* a ghoul, thought Eric. Not only was the skin unnaturally white, but she was riddled with scars and imperfections as if the skin was peeling like a birch tree.

Along with the crunching footsteps came the buzzing of flies. They swarmed her, hundreds of them. *Had she rolled in something, like a dog?* Eric unwisely fired again, and the BB smacked into her right cheek. Three flies took wing as the BB sank into the soft flesh.

The woman did not flinch but lifted one hand to touch the spot the BB entered—there was no blood. She then left the wound alone and calmly let her arm fall back to her side. Her right hand suddenly flashed a long knife with a rusty blade.

In sheer panic mode, Mark and Eric scrambled wildly and unintentionally headed off in different directions. Eric, to the best of his knowledge, was headed toward home. He guessed that Mark had opted for the much closer safety of the Birchwood Farm.

Weaponless, Eric ran as fast as he could through bushes and trees, over stone walls, and through muddy marsh-like areas. He ran for five full minutes like a madman. When he reached a semi-open area on an embankment, he stopped, panting, listening.

The forest was quiet. Eric couldn't hear Mark—perhaps he had stopped too. The unsettling news was that he couldn't hear the woman anywhere either. With the embankment at his back, he sat down behind a maple to catch his breath while he listened. The embankment gave him the confidence to eliminate that direction from which the woman could approach.

There were no sounds in the forest, no birds, no squirrels, and no breeze. Eric wondered if Mark was alright. Had she caught him? *What happens now?* He couldn't simply sneak home to avoid punishment and leave Mark behind. The trouble he was in had just multiplied exponentially, and he knew it.

He couldn't stay in this spot forever—After four indecisive minutes, he realized he had to urinate, and he feared it would be the loudest thing in the forest—but he couldn't wait any longer.

Rustling as little as possible, he stood, half-covered by low hanging branches. Looking for a safer place to pee that allowed more reaction time, he hiked halfway up the embankment. Thankfully, there were several patches of moss that made no noise when stepped on. When he reached the halfway point, he turned to look back down and unbuttoned his jeans.

There was little or no view from this spot as there would be in a month like November. Even when he ducked to see around a leafy branch, there was another behind it to block his line of sight. Very quietly, he aimed for a small tuft of moss near his feet and relieved himself. He looked at this watch; it was 5:15 pm, and his mother would be home in a little over an hour. He had to gather Mark soon and get back home.

Eric found a baseball-sized stone on the embankment and headed back down. Not willing to retrace his steps, he stayed close to the embankment as he walked, looking back toward the general area from where they had come. He realized he wasn't even looking for Mark, but a gaunt, white face, peering out at him from between the leaves.

Searching in silence was a slow process. If there were any

chance of them both getting home in an hour, he would have to make some noise to cover more ground in less time. Twenty yards later, he heard a scream—Mark's voice, from the top of the embankment. The hill went as far as he could see to his left and his right, and there was no quick way to circle up and around quietly.

Cursing his lack of options, he bolted up the face of the embankment, picking up a second smaller stone on the way for backup. The final twenty feet were the toughest, and there was a lip at the top of the embankment like the edge of golf bunker where the soil had eroded. He could not see over the edge, so he stopped to listen. Mark had not called out a second time. He had no idea what to expect when he cleared the crest but had to imagine that whatever was going on up there, they'd heard him.

Suddenly, Mark cried out again, much closer but stifled this time. Eric, with no other choice, pumped his legs hard up and over the edge, arm cocked back and ready to throw. Mark was there twenty yards ahead, strapped to a gigantic oak by a length of barbed wire. It had him around the neck tightly. He was choking, and the barbs were cutting into his neck. He flailed at the wire with one hand, which was now also bleeding. His other arm was held close to his side. It appeared to be broken.

Eric rushed to his friend, dropped the stones at his feet, and circled the tree full-speed looking for the tail end of the wire. As he rounded the trunk, he bumped into something tall and bounced backward, stumbling. It was the woman with the white face holding either end of the wire, pulling hard, choking the life out of Mark.

As shocked as he was, there was no time for fear. Things had begun badly today, had escalated quickly, and had somehow passed the point of no return. One of the boys would probably die, if not both of them.

Recovering from the collision with Mildred, Eric scrambled back to the base of the trunk, where he grabbed the baseball-sized rock at Mark's feet. Mildred watched him, hands steady, wrapped in barbed wire as he fetched the stone. She knew what he would do and timed her counter perfectly.

Eric hurled the stone at her head as he dove for her midsection. With no concern for pain, Mildred ignored the airborne rock, never taking her eyes off of the boy in anticipation of his follow-up. She absorbed the impact of the stone just above her collarbone, and the rock dropped to her feet. As it fell, she nimbly dropped the wire as she sidestepped, calling the knife with precision, sinking it between two ribs. She let the blade go as his body passed her, allowing his momentum to take it with him, and landing on it hard.

It was a neat trick, being able to call the knife, the same one she hid in the woods near Gideon's farm so many years ago. It was the anger she felt when the BB struck her face. She didn't know how, but the knife was the first thing she remembered. It happened to be one of the only weapons in the world she knew the location. When it appeared, the blade was corroded and the handle semi-rotten—but it worked like a charm.

The boy she had strangled with the wire saw her roll the dead body over to remove the knife and fled immediately. Mildred let him go; the anger had left her, and these boys were not worth the attention she had already given them. It was a foolish occurrence because it would call attention, but it would not come close to stopping her and her grand plan. The brief flash of vengeance felt good; she could only imagine how good it would feel against her true enemies.

CHAPTER 76

1971

Mark Gottlieb ran all the way home, holding his broken arm against his body. His mother screamed when she saw him, with the blood, the holes in his neck, and the broken arm. Unfortunately, Mark's injuries were not the worst of the news.

Mark's mother called the police, and they recovered the dead boy, Eric Enrico. Mark told the authorities that a woman with flies all over her had broken his arm, strangled him with barbed wire, and stabbed his friend to death. She had also been shot in the face with a BB gun at least once and had not bled a drop.

The Hampstead Police put out an all-points bulletin for a woman with a white face wearing a full-length farm dress. The press picked it up just this way, although no mention was made that she hadn't bled, or that she was covered in flies. These details were omitted at the request of his parents as agreed to by the chief of police. *The boy must be in shock;* they all thought.

CHAPTER 77

1971

Robert Simmons went to the IGA grocery store in Laconia to stock up for the day's baseball game. Mike Nagy, his favorite player, was pitching for the Red Sox, and the game started at one o'clock. He grabbed some chips, some beer, some hot dogs, and some peanuts for an *as-close-to-being-there-as-possible* experience. It was too much food for one person, and the Chief had been on him about losing some weight, but he had little else to look forward to, so *fuck it.*

The Red Sox game was all he had going that day. There was no wife (anymore), no children, and Bob had slipped hard and fast into bachelorhood. The house was a mess, his diet was that of a fifteen-year-old, and he drank too much. He lived next door to his father, who was also single, geriatric and living his final years.

On his way to the checkout, he passed the newspaper stand. He wasn't much of a "Sunday paper" kind of guy, but the headline grabbed his attention: ONE BOY DEAD IN FOREST SLAYING. For a moment, he forgot about the Red Sox and the beer and the rest of the store around him. This story called to him for whatever reason, so he picked up the paper and read on.

One boy was dead, and one survived. The police were looking for *a pale woman in a long black farm dress.* He almost dropped his handbasket. Hampstead was about an hour's drive from here. That relieved him somewhat, as it seemed to be far enough away. But why had the headline caught his attention? Bob Simmons was a superstitious man and looked for meaning in most anything. Instinct told him it had something to do with his family history, but he could be paranoid at times.

Robert was raised hearing all about how two of his family members had been murdered by the neighbor up the road years back—a woman notorious for wearing long black farm dresses by the name of Mildred Wells. The first casualty was his great-grandaunt Elizabeth, a gossip who had gone so far as to create a scrapbook-diary dedicated to collecting everything she could about the mysterious Ms. Wells.

They eventually found Elizabeth's remains in the woods just across the street from the Wells (Sometimes referred to as Pike) house. Unfortunately, the police, including his Great Granduncle George, didn't have a lick of evidence that the Wells woman had indeed committed the murder. Many believed Elizabeth had finally gone barking up the wrong tree and was therefore, at least partially responsible for her own death.

Robert's grandaunt Emma picked up the torch—and the scrapbook—and was next to be murdered, or at least "suspected to be murdered." Emma's murder was never proven—she simply went missing, never to be found. Robert never knew either of them, of course, but the stories were engraved forever into his being—and the being of every other family member since.

Robert, now a Sanborn cop himself, placed the Sunday paper into his basket and paid, trying to get his mind back on the Sox, but the effort was futile. Mike Nagy gave up six runs in the first inning, and the game was over early. With nearly every food item he had purchased that morning uneaten, he shut off the television and reread the article.

CHAPTER 78

1971

By Monday morning, Robert Simmons was fully obsessed with the death of Eric Enrico. He didn't sleep well and even read the article a third time. The cop quoted in the article was the Chief of the Hampstead police named Anthony Luoma, and as soon as Bob got to work, he picked up the phone and gave him a call. He had no idea what he would say or where the conversation would lead, but what he hoped to hear was a good excuse to forget the whole thing.

"Hello Chief Luoma, my name is Sergeant Robert Simmons calling from the Sanborn Police Department. I saw the article in the Monitor yesterday, and, well, it strikes a tone with me, and I'm not sure why. I'm not sure I can help you, but I thought maybe by talking with you and hearing some of the details, I might come up with some thoughts. The whole situation seems familiar to me, and I'm not sure why" he lied. "Do you have a moment?"

"Yes, sure. Thank you. I know your Chief Galluzzo up there. Did he ask you to call?"

"Uh...no, he didn't. I wasn't aware you two were acquaintances. I'd say I could put you through to him to say hello, but he's got the second shift today. There's only three of us up here, as you know."

"I used to work in a small town like that. No, we don't need to speak. I've heard of you; Chief Galluzzo has mentioned your name. What do you have for me? Questions? Information? It's an ugly scene down here. Damned shame. People are shaken up—won't even let their kids out of their yards."

"I imagine. I guess I was wondering about the other boy, the one who survived. He must have given you the description of the woman; was that all he said? *'Pale woman/long black dress'*? Did he estimate her age, for instance?"

Chief Luoma shifted in his chair before answering.

"Look…yes…he did have more information that we intentionally kept out of the paper, but this is off the record; I don't want this getting out. It was crazy-talk. The boy was traumatized. The parents and I thought it would be best if we blamed it on shock. I'll tell you because you're a cop and I know your boss, but I'll say it again, keep it to yourself. I don't need Mr. and Mrs. Gottlieb up my ass."

"I hear you. Official police business."

"The kid said she was a ghost, or dead or something. He said she was covered in flies. She even smelled "rotten." These are farm boys don't forget, so they know the difference between *dead animal* and plain old body odor. They said her dress looked old fashioned, like, and I quote 'the painting of the farmer and his wife with the pitchfork,' unquote.

The Gottlieb kid had shot her accidentally with a BB gun and pissed her off. The woman started to chase them, and the kids got split up. The Enrico kid found them by a tree. She had the Gottlieb kid around the neck with some old barbed wire scrap. The Enrico kid took a run at her to free the Gottlieb kid, and the next thing he knew, the Enrico kid was on the ground with a knife sticking out of his chest. He says she was pulling the knife out to use on him when he ran for help."

Unfortunately for Robert Simmons, he hadn't heard anything that would allow his gut to let the episode go. Worse, the feeling in the pit of his stomach began to churn. As a fully grown adult—as well as a police officer—he was not supposed to believe in the supernatural. However, he was a Simmons, a name synonymous in Sanborn for gossip and conspiracy theories for over a century.

"A ghost story then. The boy says that the woman was a ghost—meaning there's no chance we could ever catch her? That, right there, is enough to make me wonder if he killed his friend. What's the kid like? Is he *all there*? Are the lights on upstairs if you know what I mean?"

"They are. Mark's a smart kid. I hear where you're coming from, and I thought the same thing at first. Then I realized that if I were trying to cover up my crime by blaming it on a ghost, I would be begging for a guilty verdict. No, my best guess is, like I said—it was the shock of the moment. The *fog of war*. People's minds play tricks on them in traumatic circumstances."

"So…do you think there's a woman out there in the woods?"

"Well, I do think a woman did it, but where she is right now is anybody's guess. We're only forty-eight hours into this. We're checking nearby farms, we have the length of barbed wire she used—but there's no evidence left on it, like her blood. There's no knife either."

"What about dogs?" Simmons asked about search and rescue canines. He had adopted an ex-police dog two years back; a German Shepherd named King.

"Yup. Had some down here from Manchester. There was a scent, and the dogs followed it about a mile to Big Island Pond, then lost it."

"Maybe she's smart and did that on purpose."

"Maybe. There are a bunch of cabins around there, however. We're in the process of asking around, seeing if anybody saw anything."

They didn't if she waited until dark—Simmons thought to himself—*That's what I would do.*

"Chief Luoma, do you mind if I take a look at the crime scene?"

"No, I don't. I'm going to be back out there this afternoon to shut it down. I think we've collected everything there is to collect. What time can you be here?"

"How does three o'clock sound?"

The two men finished the call and hung up. The dead-end he had been hoping for was now a two-lane highway. He didn't expect to show up at the crime scene and miraculously find a piece of evidence that Luoma and his men had missed, he just wanted to be there to see what his instincts told him, to feel the vibe where the atrocity played out. He wanted to see if his Simmons blood had an instinctual reaction when he walked over the same ground the killer had.

CHAPTER 79

1971

Simmons showed up at three o'clock at the Hampstead Police Department with his dog, King. Chief Luoma took them out into the woods, where they climbed the eroding incline and laid eyes on the tree that had recently been used to help choke Mark Gottlieb.

Sure enough, Simmons felt a chill, and this was a first. He had never considered himself psychic, clairvoyant, or "sensitive," and had never believed in ghosts. Nervously, he wondered if it was indeed his turn to write the next chapter of Simmons family history. Would he have to confront the family bogeywoman?

Most of the evidence was already packed up and taken away. There was still a minuscule bloodstain on the ground behind the tree, and some light scratches on the trunk from the barbed wire, but otherwise, it was just another forest—except it wasn't. The hair stood on the back of his neck, something Simmons hadn't felt in a long, long time. It felt real.

Someone had died here. Another boy nearly choked to death. To put an exclamation point on it, King was going nuts. He'd picked up her scent and headed south.

CHAPTER 80

1971

King followed her trail just as the official police dogs had, to a place in Hampstead called Big Island Pond. The scent ended right at the water in an overgrown area between two cottages. Simmons wondered if she had walked the shoreline for a while, or just swam across. Finding her exit point would be nearly impossible. Big Island Pond had roughly twelve kilometers of shoreline. It was not a simple oval shape, but more like a giant "C" with countless inlets and peninsulas. Not only would it take forever to walk the distance, but much of it was either on private land or clogged with vegetation.

He pulled out a map of New England, took a pen and drew a line from Sanborn to Hampstead, then switched to pencil and continued the line to the Atlantic Ocean. Salem, Massachusetts, was almost directly on course, and according to his great-grandaunt's scrapbook, Mildred Wells was supposedly from Salem.

There wasn't much more he could do at this point. He could ask to interview the Gottlieb boy, but the results would be predictable and painful for everyone. Besides that, Chief Luoma had already asked all the pertinent questions.

As an insurance policy, he called the *Salem Evening News* and ordered a subscription, for which he would drive down once a week to pick up. If Mildred had headed in that direction, she might leave some clues in the police log. In the meantime, he would head home and refresh his memory by reading Elizabeth's scrapbook again.

CHAPTER 81

1971

When Simmons got home, he walked to the over-cluttered bookshelf in the extra bedroom. He bought this house from his family years back but never redecorated. Many of the knick-knacks on the bookshelf were things that had been there for generations. His ex-wife had tried to replace some of them, but he had vetoed every one.

With his eyes, he ran a quick pass over the dusty old bookshelf but couldn't find it. It should stick out, he thought. It was thick with a quilted cover and had photos and dog-eared newspaper clippings sticking out every which way. He gave it another eye-pass, this time slower, bookbinding by bookbinding. Still not there. *Where the hell* was the Simmons Family Scrapbook?

CHAPTER 82

1971

As Mildred walked through the town of Wenham, she began to recognize the terrain and the foliage. She had never actually visited this town, but the trees looked familiar, and the houses began to look the same. Perhaps her senses were heightened now, but she could smell the ocean, something she never noticed during her first life. It must have been the stress, or the daily problems forced upon her by Gideon. Very soon, he would pay for every pleasure he had stolen from her, including small moments like this.

Gideon's memory-wipe spell had died with Mildred's human body, but even so, Mildred suppressed much of her past. But as her walk progressed, she allowed ancient memories back in. Everything *Mary* had suppressed, *Mildred* reviewed. Two hours later, she slowed her pace as she crossed into Beverly Farms. She was close now. It was time to hunt.

By evening she crept up on the old farm, now just one hill away. She wondered what it would look like, now one hundred and twenty years later. Would Gideon be gone? In the end, it didn't matter; her instincts told her to start here. First things first—she would figure the rest out later. All she needed was one good clue—a direction.

She wondered for a moment if he might even be expecting

her. The Book was only *so* thick the last time she saw it, and she remembered that new pages appeared almost regularly. There was a good chance that he knew things she did not, so she remained alert. She aimed to ambush, yet fully expected the same thing in return.

She recalled the tone that used to sound in her head every time Gideon was near. There was no tone as yet. Would there be one? Would he hear it too? Or had that spell died along with her body?

Mildred reached the bottom of the hill just after the sun disappeared, approaching at a rate of fewer than one hundred yards per hour. For every move she made, she waited five minutes in silence, anticipating—complications. Finally, ahead of her, halfway up the hill, she spotted a man standing watch. He stood against a tree that he might have blended right into if it weren't for her diligence. She had all the time in the world—fruitless years of chasing Elmer had prepared her for this.

After nearly an hour, the guard moved fifty yards to the other side of the hill. As he did, Mildred walked steadily toward the spot he had previously occupied. From there, she climbed the trunk and lost herself in the leaves. Thirty minutes later, she heard footsteps. Seeing in the dark was no problem, but the leaves that kept her hidden also obstructed her view. She listened carefully over the buzz of the flies for the footsteps to pause, then timed her jump perfectly. Halfway down, she called the knife, and it appeared in her hand as her boots connected with the guard's head.

He fell, stunned, dropping his weapon and a box-like device that crackled as it hit the ground. Before he could react, Mildred plunged the knife deep into his chest, twisting the blade for added damage. The fingers of her left hand found his eyes just in case as she pulled the knife out and re-sank it from a different angle. In less than a minute, Desjardins was not only blind, but his heart was in ribbons.

CHAPTER 83

1971

Gideon Walker sat in his renovated shed with a man named Lammi, a talented criminal, and the latest human apprentice. Lammi was addicted to heroin and in danger of squandering his opportunity at immortality. Gideon had called him in to remind him that death by overdose was a dealbreaker.

Gideon suddenly paused mid-sentence, sensing something. His hand instinctively went to the beads in his front pocket. Lammi was still high from his last fix and continued to drone on, apologizing incessantly, while Gideon ignored him and read. There were now only sixteen revenants awake and two sleeping. Someone was dead or missing. He had never seen anything like this.

"Lammi. Shut up and get out—*now*. And before you leave, remember this; I will kill you next time you use that drug—as simple as that. I no longer have patience." Lammi apologized three more times before letting himself out. Someone was gone, either one of his flock, or the mysterious "thirteenth revenant" as he had come to be known. The odds were not in Gideon's favor. He stood up and stepped outside, crossing the barnyard for the main house.

It made perfect sense to use the farmhouse as headquarters. There had been a never-ending stream of people coming through over the years, and the house was registered to a trust, and therefore, difficult to trace.

Helms sat at the kitchen table, checking his beads.

"I saw it," he said.

"What is it? What happened?" asked Gideon.

"I don't know. I was just about to radio the guards but then thought better of it—too dangerous. I hate these radios—too noisy. We'll give their positions away. I'll check on them myself.

But, Walker...the last time I saw a revenant die was the time you killed Sandberg. We need to figure this out by process of elimination, and quickly. Hopefully, it was the 'thirteenth revenant.' If one of our own was killed here on the farm, we've been compromised. Stay here and arm yourself." Gideon didn't argue. The knight should always protect the king.

Despite his hatred for the technology, Helms grabbed a walkie-talkie and hurried out; he would radio back only after everything checked out. Things had been good so far for him on the farm. Gideon had forgiven him, and he had—in the end—approved of Gideon as the leader. Gideon had made several moves that were good for the race, and moving back to the farmhouse was one of those things.

She's here, Helms thought. His plan had worked, although not the way he had imagined—the timing was off. She took too long, and things had changed since then. Now he had to choose his alliance again. He couldn't even imagine what Mary would be like—she would be the first female revenant that he'd ever heard. *Better the devil you know*, he thought. The phrase had never had such a literal meaning.

He rushed through the forest favoring speed over stealth. Reid was still at his post, and so was Reveley. He made them aware and moved on swiftly. Durant and Desjardins were the two remaining sentries. Without stopping—for fear of ambush—he ran on. Nine minutes later, he found Desjardins's body heaped beneath the maple tree. His heart and eyes were torn out and left beside the body. It would be a very chaotic night.

What to do with Mary? It would be best to kill her—avoid rocking Gideon's boat—but Helms had given away his position by running so noisily, and Mary might even be watching—deciding his fate.

A revenant's strength was supernatural, no longer dependent on gender or age, meaning Mary's strength was equal to his. Fighting skills were variable, however, and so was magickal aptitude. He had bested Gideon years back, but no longer held that advantage. Mary was a question mark, having been on her own for so long. There was no telling what she'd done with her time.

She was no doubt here for a reason, coming all this way from—who knows where—to seek them out. If she hadn't practiced the Book of Shadows, she would most likely lean closer to the primitive definition of a revenant—which meant revenge came first. Helms didn't have to be reminded that anger was a powerful and dangerous force with which to contend.

He shuddered, knowing he had to keep moving—but it was too late. As soon as he pushed off, a long wooden spear impaled him from behind, just beneath the ribcage—embedding itself in the ground as he fell, pinning him. He looked back in agony; Mary held the other end, lifting the spear, countering his every attempt to free himself, keeping him off balance.

"Mary, stop! We want the same thing! I set this up! You can have your revenge. I can help!"

Mildred stopped but angled the spear high, allowing Helms only one of his legs proper purchase on the ground.

"Where is he?" she asked.

"He's in the house, and he's armed. He knows you killed Desjardins…but…well, he doesn't know who died. All he knows is that someone is dead. He also knows there is a mystery revenant unaccounted for, but he doesn't know that it's you. I knew it was you because I made it happen."

"How does he know?" she asked.

It made sense, but Helms was surprised. Mary had been on her own all these years and was unpracticed. Her exposure to the Book of Shadows consisted of whatever she had learned as a child in Gideon's shed, maybe the first dozen or so pages. She had no doubt created her rune beads but hadn't learned how to use them.

"The beads. He read his beads. Walkers and sleepers—You don't know about this, do you." It was a statement more than a question.

Mildred relaxed her left hand and let it fall to her side. Her right hand still held the spear high, keeping Helms' skewered body off balance. *The beads.* She had forgotten about them because she didn't know what they were for. Memories came flooding back; she remembered making dice, or beads but had written off the process as a simple exercise.

Mildred shook her head, cursing her naivete, and flexed her hand. Her beads, still hidden beneath the corner of Gideon's house, appeared in her palm. The wood was warm with magick, and she could read them as well as she could read plain English. Helms needed to start talking and fast.

"I can help you kill him. I know what he did to you. He tried to have me killed once. I have wanted to kill him ever since, but I need help. We can do it tonight."

Mildred took her eyes off of her beads and looked at Helms. She let the spear fall, and he dropped, now able to get his footing and stand. Using both hands, he pulled the spear from his abdomen, staggering. He would need hibernation to heal the damage, but his bones were fine, as was his heart. He walked with a limp, however—weak and at her mercy. It would be difficult to pull off his original plan of staying with Gideon. Perhaps it was time to switch sides.

CHAPTER 84

1971

M ildred directed Helms to lead the way, slowly and cautiously. Several times she tapped him with the side of the spear to get his attention and direct him with hand signals. *Slow down.* The spear itself was Helms' little reminder that she was in charge.

Twenty minutes went by before Helms spotted Reveley. He turned to Mildred and indicated the sentry's position—a step closer to the point-of-no-return. The next hour or so would potentially change the fate of the race.

He turned back to face Reveley, who had no idea they were there and began to calculate a route around him. Another dead revenant would bring the whole clan, catching Helms in a compromised state. He would not be seen in a good light. He would be forever remembered for his failure.

He chose his detour and fell to a crawl, inching forward. Reveley was thirty yards to his left, intermittently blocked by the full May foliage. Five minutes later and a third of the way to safety, Helms looked back. Mary was gone. With no better ideas, he continued ahead.

Helms set visual waypoints. After he reached a low-hanging branch, the new waypoint became the fallen tree in the clearing. Time passed slowly, and it was difficult to be stealthy while injured, all the while wondering where Mary was. Suddenly a loud whisper broke the silence.

"Helms, what are you doing?" Reveley murmured.

"I…I'm hurt. Watch yourself. They pierced me through the back. I didn't see who it was. Stay quiet!" Reveley saw the blood, crouched, and raised his axe. Helms hoped that Mary had not heard the last exchange and taken it as a betrayal. "Help me up. I need to let Walker know."

"You're too slow. I can get to the house in five minutes." Without hesitation, he bolted. At the last second, Helms reached out and grabbed his ankle, tripping him. He'd passed the point of no return. The younger revenant looked back in surprise.

"Wait!"—Helms said loudly—"First I—"

Suddenly Mildred appeared over the two men holding Reveley's axe high over her head. Without hesitation, she brought it down quickly four times, smashing the ribcage, and inside it, the vulnerable heart. Casually she put her hand in her dress pocket and felt the beads, reading what Gideon would be reading. Reveley was almost dead, and she watched the final seconds as he passed. Helms last-second assist earned him a measure of trust.

"He'll be sending everyone now, but they don't know where to look. He might even come himself. I'd call it in to tell him you're the one who's dead, but there are still two more guards out here. Be ready."

Mildred lifted the axe high once again, and Helms thought for a moment that he might have outlived his usefulness. Instead, Mildred threw the weapon with force, sticking it high up into the trunk of the tree under which Reveley had stood. It lodged in the trunk with a heavy thud, embedded amongst the leaves and branches, invisible to passers-by. She walked over to the tree and examined her throw, then came back to Helms, who managed to pick himself up.

Mildred picked up her spear and gestured for Helms to take point again. He did as he was told, meanwhile trying to comprehend the magnitude of what was happening. Desjardins and Reveley were gone forever. Reveley was a Walker recruit, but Desjardins had been around for nearly as long as Helms. Helms' own life was also in doubt, and it seemed as if Mary had just begun. Everything had been easy for her so far, like a hot knife through butter.

Fifteen revenants were too many—that much he agreed. Twelve was the way it had always worked, and deep down, he felt a purge would do the clan well—but how far would she go? Would she stop with the death of Gideon—or just keep going? Helms began to wonder about with whom he'd partnered.

Minutes later, Helms spotted Reid and Durant hunting, weapons drawn. They saw him at nearly the same time. Mildred was nowhere to be seen.

"Helms! What happened? Walker needs you! He wants an update!" Helms looked down for his walkie-talkie and realized it was gone.

"I'm hurt. I think I hurt her too. She ran in your direction. Haven't you seen her? Tell Walker—I lost my radio."

"Her? A *woman?* Who is it?"

"Well, I didn't have time to ask her, but I know who it is. It's Mary. Little Mary, the one who escaped way back. You wouldn't remember." Reid appeared puzzled. "Be ready. She snuck up on me. I didn't hear her at all, and that should tell you something. I've got to get back to the house and tell Walker." Helms kept talking. "Desjardins and Reveley are dead. It's up to—"

Suddenly Mildred's spear sliced through the night and struck Reid in the chest, dropping him instantly—a direct hit. He was dead before hitting the ground. Mildred then appeared twenty yards to Helms' left. Durant, stunned, managed to raise his machete. Helms dropped to one knee, feigning further injury. Mildred began a slow approach, and Durant held steady.

When she had closed to within ten feet, Mildred paused, passively taunting, like a cat to a mouse. Durant, pathetically overconfident, took the bait and made his move, lunging, right arm back to swing, foolishly leading with his body. Before he could begin the swing of the machete, Mildred raised her arms, and in an economy of motion, began her double-armed motion before the ax appeared in her grasp.

The ax appeared in her hands a millisecond before she released it, sending it flipping end over end at Durant. When it hit, it connected just below his jawline, under his skull, cutting through muscle, and sending his charging body to the ground. She was on him before he could recover. With a flick of her wrist, the rusty knife from the woods appeared once again, and he was dead in seconds.

Mildred read her beads again as if she enjoyed the new tool. Four dead, eleven to go, but no telling how many were here on property. There were still two sleepers—apparently, killings like this didn't wake them. She could worry about them later.

CHAPTER 85

1971

Gideon slammed his runes down on the table. They were dropping like flies! Saltz, the bodyguard, stood beside him, weapon drawn.

"We're going out. Helms isn't helping. That's four dead. This is a coup. It's Helms—he's a part of this."

"Gideon, stay close. The worst thing to do is split up. The two of us together can take down ten. What's the plan?" added Saltz.

"We need to know what's happening out there. Who's dead? Who's left? I'm assuming that it's a coup, or that the mystery revenant is responsible. Maybe both." Gideon was near panic.

"We can't go into the woods. Too many hiding places. The guards are vulnerable out there. I say we sit here and wait. Worst case scenario, we lose only one more member before they make it here to the house. Everyone else is away, off on their own! There were seven of us on-property to start. Four at most are dead. That leaves you, me...and *one other*."

"We could also have the whole clan back on-property right now. We knew of seven, but that doesn't mean only seven were here. It could be Pratt and Sterritt. The *old guard*. *That* whole group—they could have convinced Webb, Bergin, and Lafleur too—I wouldn't put it past them. I bet they're back, and they want to go back to having just twelve again. Forget what I said about Helms, and don't repeat it."

Chaos reigned, and in the end, they followed Saltz's advice—they did nothing. After extinguishing the lights, each took a window on opposite sides of the house. Gideon kept his beads close on the windowsill and checked them every minute.

Things got quiet.

Even the woods were silent.

CHAPTER 86

1971

"It's Walker—and Saltz, his enforcer. They're going to expect you now," said Helms.

Mildred said nothing and turned in the direction of the house. Cautiously she came to the last knoll in the woods before the shed and the clearing that marked the beginning of the farm's property. *Gideon's shed. So close now...just over the tree line.*

Helms took note of Mildred's interest. She had suffered as a young girl in there, most likely the reason why she was back. The Book of Shadows was still in there along with many other unpleasant tidbits. "Go look if you need to, then come back to get me, and we'll finish him at the house."

Mildred crept up behind the shed to avoid detection from the house; there was no doubt they would be watching now. The old shed, in which she had suffered so, had been renovated, although the original structure remained. Gideon had outgrown it, needing more space for—the atrocities. The new door was now on the side facing the woods, which worked in her favor. She twisted the locked knob until it broke and let herself in.

Keeping the lights off, she stood in the original part of the building. Mildred looked down and recognized the original floorboards. Seven feet in, the boards changed—the new construction. Powerful memories came back, so strong she needed to remind herself to focus. Although beyond pain now, she felt sorry for herself—her younger self. She wanted to help, as no one ever had—and her anger flared. What was simmering—now bubbled.

The workbench along the wall was also original, and the Book sat atop it. She left it for now—it would be her reward for finishing the job. Gideon had a bed now across the room, and she wondered sadly how many others he had defiled. There was no food storage anymore because he no longer had to eat. Gideon's overcoat hung over a chair.

Between the bed and the workbench on the opposite wall were two doors. One was a defunct bathroom piled high with forgotten gardening tools, a lawnmower, and a cobweb-covered gasoline can. The second door was more of the same; boxes stacked high. Mildred opened one of them and pulled out a small skull.

It could be anyone, she thought. But it could also be *Sarah*. Mildred took the box out of the room and set it on the bed. In the window facing the house, she lined them up, assigning names to each: Sarah, Edward, Anna, Robert, George...*too many to remember*. There were more skulls than names and not enough windowsill. She wanted them all to watch what happened next. They all deserved to see him fall, and fall hard.

Looking at the children's skulls—she couldn't help but think of Elmer. She—had acted callously—it was true, albeit in another life. But—the illness, the mental weight—had been born in this room. But this was not the time for reminiscing. It was time for work. She grabbed the gasoline can, the blanket on Gideon's bed, and his jacket over the chair, then left.

CHAPTER 87

1971

Gideon smelled the smoke.

"We're on fire—*they're here*. But where? Can you see them? They're waiting—*be ready*."

Saltz did not like being surprised; he and Gideon were at a disadvantage, not sure who or what was coming for them. He left the upstairs bedroom at the back of the house and looked down the stairs. Flames engulfed the first floor making it impassable. He walked from the top of the stairs to the front bedroom to calm Gideon down and hopefully *shut him up. He was nervous and too damn loud.*

"Gideon, be quiet. Don't give us away. We have to be smart, or we'll be numbers five and six. The whole downstairs is ablaze, so we're going to have to either jump or climb down."

"We don't know where they are! Did you see anyone? I don't want to jump down into danger!" Gideon had a point.

"No, I didn't see anyone," Saltz replied.

"How long do we have? How long until the house collapses? We have to try and locate them first."

"I have no idea, but it's getting hotter and hotter in here. I'm guessing we have twenty minutes. The smoke is killing visibility. We should pick a random exit and make a break for it—but not the front window; it's too obvious."

Gideon didn't like having to run, but it was definitely the best plan. They each grabbed a weapon and decided the third bedroom would be the last place they'd be expected. It was a tiny room with a tiny window, and they were two very large men. "I'll jump first, and you jump immediately after. Don't worry about landing on me. We jump, we land, and we run—or fight if they're waiting."

After a short countdown, Saltz launched himself through the window and landed hard on the back lawn in front of the woods. Gideon was in the air before Saltz hit the ground and landed to his right. The two men raised their weapons, ready for ambush—but they were alone. Suddenly, Helms came bursting through the trees.

"Walker...it's Mary! She's back. She's *like* us—a revenant. She killed four of our men! She's hurt as well, but..." Helms coughed and dropped to one knee. He pulled his hand away from his abdomen and showed his blood-soaked shirt. "I...I will need healing time when she is dead. Surely she set this fire. Where is she? Have you seen her yet?"

"Mary?...*Little...*Mary? Alice's girl?"

"Yes, Gideon, it's Mary. Mary, *from your shed.*" Suddenly a loud bang echoed through the woods—the deafening report of a firearm. Saltz looked down and dropped to his knees, a bloodstain rapidly spreading across his shirt. Helms acted quickly and produced a knife, pouncing on Gideon's bodyguard and finishing him off. Gideon stood still aghast.

"It was *you*. I *knew it*. You never got over Boxford, am I right? Even after I took you back. You never had respect for me—did you." A bright light lit the back lawn.

Mildred stepped out of the house fully ablaze. Her eyes were beginning to *cook*, and a trail of smoke rose from the soaked blanket that partially wrapped her head and torso. The fire had not yet burned through Gideon's wet overcoat, but the charred flesh of her legs stung their nostrils. Dropping the smoldering garments and dropping the shotgun, Mildred doused the burning parts of her body with a pail of water she'd brought through the house from the barn.

Gideon was thrown for a loop. This was an unimaginable situation—the insanity—and the determination. The lengths she had gone for the element of surprise, the mad decisions she had made to get to this moment—The fire—Her burning body—Five revenants assassinated in a matter of hours, more casualties than any of them had seen—*in centuries.*

Hell hath no fury like a woman scorned, he murmured to himself. *Scorned, wronged, raped*; the words were for all intents and purposes, interchangeable. Now there were no more words. Anything he said now would sound like an excuse or an apology. There were no words to excuse what he had done—so he swallowed them. A woman with this much anger and determination wouldn't be interested in his side of the story anyway. Prepared for her next move, he hefted his ax.

Mildred's hot skin curled into a smile and cracked her lips. It was almost over—this phase anyway. To both Gideon's and Helms' surprise, she turned and headed around the house to the barnyard. The two men were left to wonder where she was going. They remained still for several seconds, staring at each other, then the corner of the house—wondering if she would come back.

Gideon leaped first, seizing the opportunity to rush Helms. The wounded former leader was no match for the current king and cried out. The ax landed hard, sending him to the grass, where Gideon punched a hole in his chest and held his heart until it stopped. To be sure, he borrowed Helms' knife and removed the organ so there would be no retaliation. Gideon stood and threw it into the raging fire that was the house and took one last look at Saltz, who lay a few feet away. *He didn't last long*, thought Gideon.

Mildred heard Helms die but continued walking. Helms had done nothing all those years to help young Mary in the shed and deserved to die. Mildred would not have let him live even if he *had* helped anyway. When this phase was complete, they would *all* be gone.

CHAPTER 88

1971

Helms lay dead in the grass at his feet, as the second floor of the house crumbled. His kingdom was falling apart, and the improbable cause was just around the corner. Brazenly, she had even fought and defeated his army on their home turf—but it wasn't over yet. Hefting his ax, he strode to the barnyard ready to dominate her the way he always had when she came to steal food from his shed.

Gideon rounded the corner cautiously but was hit with a projectile the moment he set eyes on the barn. The bottle smashed on his cheekbone, soaking him from the waist up. The burning wick lit the pungent fuel, and Gideon set the yard aglow. Naturally, Mary had made sure there was no pail of water handy. His already-dead flesh burned, peeled and blistered, rapidly deteriorating. A slow-burning timer on Gideon Walker's life had started.

Mary waited patiently just inside the barn, letting the fire do its damage. If he attempted to roll the flames out, she would be on him. He spun wildly, looking for water. The kitchen was gone. The shed was dry—The barn was his only option. She stepped out into the barnyard and showed herself. He halted nervously—time was of the essence! Gracefully, she swung her right arm casually

209

and conjured the ax, holding it barred across her waist between her two hands—relaxed, in a taunting sort of way—daring him to try.

Suddenly, his right eye popped in the intense heat, collapsing, and catching fire. Half-blind and out of options, he charged. Mildred freed her right hand as she called the hatchet from the barn in New Hampshire. With a flick of the wrist, she pitched the weapon, breaking his blocking arm, but still, he came, his remaining eye blurring under pressure.

Mildred whirled completely around for maximum velocity, swinging the ax with all the power she could muster. The ax head connected devastatingly just above his heart but crushed all bones in its path. The huge man flew backward, landing hard on the barnyard dirt. He hadn't time to realize the damage before she was on him wildly, closing the doors on his evil existence once and for all.

CHAPTER 89

1971

M ildred walked to the shed and stood outside the window, looking through the glass at the tiny skulls she had lined up to watch the Big Event. She raised her hand and showed them Gideon's heart. A victory for all.

She entered the shed and tossed the heart into an empty box, then piled the skulls on top. Four trips later, everything burned except the Book of Shadows, which she kept for herself. It was best to keep the humans in the dark—they would not be able to comprehend the truth of what had happened under their noses for so long, so she burned as much as she could, which might also serve her better in the long run. The sooner they'd examined the scene and left, the better. The remaining revenants would be here soon.

She checked her beads: Eight awake, two asleep. They would all notice the seven dead revenants eventually and would begin to stagger in. Until then, she would wait.

CHAPTER 90

1971

Sometime during the night, someone noticed the glow in the sky over Beverly Farms and called the fire department. Soon the closest neighbors were on-scene watching the house burn down. None of them had ever gotten this close to the remote farm, and most came to satisfy their curiosity. The BFD arrived shortly after and began battling the blaze.

Hours later, after the fire was out, the investigation began. Who lived here now? Were they dead? The rumor mill began to turn. To some, it seemed to be a murder-suicide, while others thought the owners had died of smoke inhalation before they burned.

The investigators found bone fragments amongst the ashes. Three people. Possibly as many as five. The rest of the evidence burned. The question of who these bones belonged to was another matter. The house was part of a trust, and the beneficiary was a man named Fenerty, who was shockingly already dead.

The authorities, along with the neighbors, were left scratching their heads, and it became big local news. How could this happen? The *Salem Evening News* wrote a piece entitled *House of Mystery Burns*, and from there, it snowballed. Within three days, it was broadcast on all three Boston news stations, and from there it was picked up by the *Associated Press* as a curiosity piece.

Mildred climbed a high tree on the top of the hill overlooking the farm and waited there for almost a week as police and press vehicles came and went. While she waited, she studied the book and listened carefully to the forest below.

On day four, the first of the wayward revenants returned. She heard him passing cautiously in the dark and finally saw him when he hid by the shed ten minutes later. He was no doubt shocked that the house was gone and appeared to be dumbfounded as to what to do next.

Mildred climbed down and met him as he snuck back into the woods. She walked confidently toward him as if he should know who she was, counting the seconds before he realized he did not know this revenant. It happened when they were ten feet apart, and when he realized, she tossed her beads at his face. He trained his eyes and attempted to dodge whatever it was she'd thrown.

LaFleur's distraction was Mildred's advantage. He raised his hands, and she was on him. After he was dead, she decayed him to hide the body.

CHAPTER 91

1971

Robert Simmons started his dinner on the stove just before six o'clock in preparation for the evening's Red Sox game. He'd already had a beer and a half and was feeling the buzz, and for a minute thought he should slow down. Disgustedly, he looked down into the pot of water. The hot dogs were always disappointing. Why did he always think they'd somehow remind him of Fenway Park?

Minutes later, the Channel Nine News out of Manchester began. Local news first, to be followed by the Evening News with Harry Reasoner and Howard K. Smith. Toward the end of the local portion, he saw the story about the house in Beverly Farms that burned to the ground, and none of the neighbors, nor the authorities had a clue as to who the dead people were.

The State Police were helping with the investigation, and the Chief gave a brief interview for the reporter on camera. Basically, he just shook his head, baffled by the circumstances. Simmons put down his beer and walked over to the television and turned it up, but the segment ended there.

The next morning he woke early to drive to Salem and pick up his newspapers. He dressed for work because he wasn't sure how long he would be gone, and his shift started at 3 pm. When he arrived at the newspaper, he picked up his seven-day stack and took a look at the edition from three days ago: *House of Mystery Burns*. *Dammit*, he thought. Three days had passed since then, and he wondered what he might have missed. The crime scene—or maybe just "the scene"—would be vastly different by now. It shouldn't be any of his business anyway. It *shouldn't be*—but it was.

He had never been to Beverly Farms before, so he bought a road map and drove across the Essex Bridge following the coastline to Beverly Farms, where he then turned inland toward the supposed location of the farm. He had to stop for directions twice despite the presence of the map, and in the end, it turned out the farm was not at the address it was supposed to be; the news had merely reported the location as the closest road with a name. The road itself wasn't even on the map anyway. *No wonder nobody knew them*, thought Simmons. Only the most local of locals even knew the place *existed*.

Simmons saw the mouth of a long driveway and took it. In a quarter-mile, he pulled into the barnyard and laid eyes on the pile of ashes that used to be Gideon Walker's headquarters. Everyone had left; the investigators had gathered all the evidence, and the press had written their articles. The story was at a stand-still, at least until there was new information.

He shut off the engine and stepped out of his cruiser. Grasshoppers chirped nearby, and the sun beat down on him directly. He walked over to the edge of the foundation and looked down. It was obvious that the ashes had been raked and sifted, looking for more bones. He didn't expect to find anything new.

He stepped into the small guesthouse and examined the four rooms containing two beds each. It resembled a seasonal summer camp. The furnishings were minimal—no rugs, curtains, or decoration of any kind. Did they even use this building? The shed was empty as well. Simmons surmised that the police had taken anything of evidence out for further inspection elsewhere. The barn was just that—a simple barn.

Despite the lack of physical evidence, Simmons felt a heaviness in the air. He'd always had a fascination for visiting places where something terrible happened. As a kid, he visited the Ford Theater in Washington, DC, on a high school field trip—the location of the assassination of Abraham Lincoln—and the museum even had the pistol that took Lincoln's life. To Simmons, there was something dark and fascinating about coming so close to something so infamous.

He felt the same feeling here. Something significant and evil had happened here, and he wondered if everyone who came here got the same vibe. It was the same feeling at the tree in the woods where the Enrico boy was killed, and the little memorial across the street from the house on Lancaster Hill Road where his great-grandaunt's—parts—were found. He looked at his watch.

He still had plenty of time before work. With his inspection over, he walked back to his Sanborn Police car and sat on the bumper to meditate. He peered into the woods as far as he could see, but it was almost like looking at a green wall. He looked up at the hill that rose behind the shed—examining the tops of the trees going up—and then froze.

Something big and dark was up in the tallest tree. It was much too big to be a squirrel's nest or a fisher cat. He sat up straight and squinted, but it was too far away to make it out. It might be a bear, he thought, but that was unlikely. *Something strapped to the trunk. A shadow. An optical illusion.*

He stood up and walked forward, never taking his eyes off it. Twenty feet, forty feet, fifty—he was almost to the shed—a few steps more, and he wouldn't be able to see the top of that tree anymore. One, two, three more steps, and he was too close to the forest. Now he had to decide if he wanted to continue through the woods and try to find that particular tree, or just quit and go to work.

He decided on the latter. Simmons turned and walked back to his cruiser. Before getting in, he found the tall tree up on the hill again. The shape was gone. He felt a chill and popped the snap on his holster. *Was he being watched?* He pulled the pistol and went and sat on the hood again, waiting and watching the tree line. He looked at his watch and started timing. Five minutes later, nothing had happened, and he decided to quit again.

A New Hampshire cop firing his weapon in another state might be grounds for termination, and he couldn't afford to lose his job—Massachusetts gun laws were tough, cop or not. He knew he would have this incident on his mind the whole drive back, and probably into the evening.

Now all he had to do was make himself believe that the shape in the tree was not Mildred Wells.

CHAPTER 92

1971

Mildred knew that the red-headed policeman saw her, but it didn't matter. She also knew he didn't get a very good look— but she had. She saw the hair, and the belly and the way he walked and the word "Sanborn" on the side of the vehicle. *Could it be?*

Oh, it can't be.

But she knew it was.

CHAPTER 93

1971

Tim was working in the breakfast area of the house when the phone rang in the living room. Seeing as it was Thursday night, and only two people knew his Sanborn phone number, he knew it would be bad news. He wished there was an affordable machine that could answer phone calls so he could listen at his leisure, process the information, and get back to Sheila after formulating his best response, but there was no such thing.

He answered the phone. Of course, it was his ex-wife Sheila, once his best friend and supporter, now a bitter soul that lived to make his life miserable. He was weak on the phone because he felt the need to tell the truth. Sheila didn't share that weakness and usually "won" every phone call.

"Hello?" he asked, knowing full well who it was.

"Hi, Tim? It's Sheila. I was calling about the pick-up tomorrow night. The girls have a birthday party after school, so they're going to be at Mindy Stevens' house, and she's on Route 110. The party's from 5 pm to 7 pm, so you can get them at 7."

Regular pick up was any time between 6–6:30 pm, as written in the Permanent Stipulations, but Sheila always pushed the limits without fail to piss him off. This time, however, the extra hour worked in his favor, so he let it go—for the most part.

"You know, one of these times, I'm not going to be able to go along with your special instructions. I'm not going to be able to go along with it, and you're going to have to keep them the extra night."

"That's fine with me, Tim. If you don't want to see your children, I'd be more than happy to take them." She was ready for all of his responses before she even made the phone call.

"Not what I said, and you know it. I'll be there Friday." He decided to quit before she asked for another favor in the name of the children. They hung up. The silver lining was that he hadn't been tricked into changing any plans with Holly. It had happened once a few weeks back, and Holly rightfully set him straight. He was left feeling humiliated that Sheila still held the puppet strings to some degree.

CHAPTER 94

1971

Tim picked the girls up at the Stevens house on Route 110 at 7 pm. The girls didn't come out of the house until 7:30, and when they did, they were still begging to stay longer. In the end, Sheila's change of plans had made him the bad guy. She was not supposed to schedule activities during his visitation time but continued to do so. The girls were in a bad mood for the first twenty miles, a hell of a way to kick off the weekend. Vivian broke the mood.

"Are you going to let us play outside this time, Dad?" This was the girls' third weekend ever up at the New Hampshire house. The first time was a haunted nightmare that he would never forget, and luckily the girls had no idea. The second time the ghosts were gone, but he wasn't completely sure of it, so he was nervous all weekend. He ended up yelling at the girls more often than not when they strayed from his designated areas, which were always moving. It had been a beautiful sunny weekend, and he made them stay inside most of it. The house was a real mess too, construction-wise, so that left them all but confined most of the time to the room at the end of the house. This third weekend would be different—he felt more confident.

"Yes, you can play outside this time. I know the house a

whole lot better now. I'm going to loosen up. Just be careful in the hayloft. And around the pond. And out in the grove. And…"

"Daaaaa-aaad!"

"I was kidding. I'm going to lighten up. Just be careful of any nails lying around." They pulled up the driveway between the two maples and parked around the side of the house in front of the barn. There were no lights on in the turret, no boats in the pond, and no woman walking through the field—*home sweet home.*

Like clockwork, Holly pulled up the driveway six minutes later. She didn't like to be the first one to arrive at the house, and he didn't blame her. Tim and Holly decided after the last visitation weekend to go public and tell the girls about their relationship. It was awfully quick, but it felt right. Tim and Holly had known each other for much longer than the six weeks they had been dating, and it wasn't like they were moving in together—yet anyway.

The only hesitation they had was that Sheila would find out, and the more Sheila knew, the more tools of destruction she had at her disposal. Tim was *happy* after all, and that would not sit well with Sheila. She would use the children to change pickups and drop-offs, book parties, and make life difficult in general. Holidays would be a nightmare when they came around, Tim had no doubt.

The other hesitation they had about telling the girls was the possibility that the relationship wouldn't last, and then daddy would have to introduce them to another girlfriend down the line—but Tim felt confident, and it didn't take much convincing to get Holly to agree.

"Hey, Holly's right behind us," said Tim.

"Yay!" said Vivian. Olivia wasn't quite as excited, but it wasn't anything personal.

"Hi, guys!" said Holly. "How's it going?" She carried two pizza boxes. Vivian ran up, grabbed her hand, and began to tell Holly about the birthday party. Olivia and Tim followed close behind. They all piled into the breakfast area, and Holly stepped aside, eyeballing Tim to give the house a quick but thorough pass-through. She didn't trust the house anymore and found it hard to relax.

Tim caught the signal and stepped ahead of the bunch as the girls innocently took their time. He stepped through the kitchen and rushed through the dining room and the office, clicking on lights as he went.

"Dad, where are you going?" asked Olivia.

"I'm just turning the lights on. I'll be right back."

Finally, he nervously jogged up the stairs, head on a swivel, even though he felt confident that Mildred was gone, and they were all safe. Thankfully he was right. "Okay. I couldn't remember if I made your bed up, so I had to check real quick. I did. You're all set." The girls looked at him as if he'd gone crazy.

Holly looked as if a weight had been lifted, and she pulled a bottle of wine out of her bag and winked at Tim. For the first time inside the house, she smiled and began to ease into the weekend. Olivia changed the subject:

"Dad, you're not going to change our nightgowns in the middle of the night again, are you? I didn't like them, and mom was mad you didn't return our other ones." Tim grimaced. That little episode happened a month ago now, and he thought the memory was dead and gone. *Apparently not.*

"No. No, I'm not going to do that again. I know you didn't like it, I thought I'd surprise you, but it didn't work out. Let's forget it, okay?" If they knew the truth—that a fly-covered dead woman had played with them as though they were dolls while they slept, they would never want to come back here.

"Daddy says he's not going to freak out this weekend when we go outside," Vivian added.

"Well, that's a step in the right direction," said Holly. She glanced at Tim with a look that said, *really?*

"Yeah, we're going to give it a shot. Naturally, you have to be careful on a farm, and I'm still going to worry a little bit, but I promise to be better." Olivia rolled her eyes.

"I don't like the geese by the pond. One hissed at us last time. And the little boy wouldn't even talk to us either," said Vivian. The mention of the boy spooked Holly, and her smile faded, prompting Tim to speak up.

"Uh, well, he moved away with his family. You don't have to worry about him anymore, but the geese are still there from time to time."

"Are you sleeping over, Holly?" asked Vivian. Holly blushed and turned her head to Tim.

"Wellll, yes, I was thinking about it. And then I can show you how to make my favorite breakfast—waffles. I brought my waffle iron. It's out in the car."

"Yay!" Both girls cheered the news.

CHAPTER 95

1971

Holly heard the girls wake early. They had the sunniest room in the house, and she wondered for a second if Tim had thought that one through. There were two other bedrooms at the back of the house right at the top of the stairs that were empty. Each girl could have her own room if they wanted, but it had been too late to move things around when it was time for bed the previous evening, and they were all tired. The rear bedrooms were plastered with construction dust anyway.

Holly heard Tim stir about a minute after the girls had not-so-quietly made their way downstairs. *The nervous father is up*, she thought. *He probably didn't sleep well, thinking he would not hear them get up.* But he did hear them, and—still believing Holly to be asleep—got dressed and quietly followed the girls.

He didn't go downstairs right away, Holly noticed. He's probably in their bedroom watching from the window. She dozed off. Five minutes later, she heard the stairs creaking and surmised that the girls had left his field of vision, most likely the barn or the grove. Thirty seconds more, and she heard the porch door open and close, Tim was outside.

She dozed again and began a dream about being left alone in the house on Lancaster Hill Road. The doors were locked, the

225

windows shut tight, and she couldn't break the windows. In her dream, she held the hatchet and swung it at one of the windows in the living room. At the moment of impact, she woke, and her hand hurt. She realized she was sleeping on it.

Stressed from the dream, Holly pulled her arm out from underneath her body and let it hang to the floor. The blood from the rest of her body began to refill it. There was no way she was getting back to sleep. Any dream of being alone in that house was enough to—*wait a second*. She *was* alone in the house. Suddenly in the window, a housefly began to buzz and bounce.

That was enough for Holly. She sat bolt upright and got dressed with urgency. With a severe case of bed-head, she made her way downstairs, opened the front door (the closest one) and walked outside barefoot onto the lawn. She used to hate spiders the most, but Holly's greatest household fear was now the common housefly. Mother of the maggot and harbinger of Mildred Wells—she now ran when she saw them.

She listened to the left and the right but heard nothing. Straight ahead were the pond and the meadow, two beautiful sights often ruined by the vision of the woman in the black farm dress. Now they were rid of her supposedly, but Holly's memories were vivid, and what should have been serene was instead tense and threatening.

In need of human contact and noisy family distraction, she walked along the driveway to the corner of the house and peered around. Thankfully Tim was standing in front of the barn barking reminders to the girls who had climbed their way up to the hayloft and were in the doorway high above the driveway.

"No, I'm not going to throw it back up to you. You're scaring me. Back away from the doorway, I don't want you to fall!" Vivian had somehow dropped her shoe. "Back up, back up, back up!"

"Dad, you're boring!" cried Olivia.

"Listen, I'm this close to calling the loft *off-limits*. All it takes is one mistake! There's plenty to do here that isn't fifteen feet in the air." With all the fun of throwing things down to the driveway taken away from them, the girls climbed down with disappointed scowls on their faces.

"I knew you'd be like this. I'm bored," exclaimed Olivia. Tim looked at his watch.

"7:52 am on Saturday, and you're bored. New world record," said Tim.

"Well, you won't let us do anything!" she complained. "You said you were gonna let us have fun!" Tim shook his head.

"I will. I will. You just have to be safe!"

"Is it safe in the front yard?" Olivia quizzed.

"Yes!" answered Tim.

"Is it safe in the field?"

"Yes!"

"Is it safe in the grove?" This time Tim hesitated—unintentionally.

"Uh—yes." It was difficult to allow. Henry Smith was killed out there. He and Holly themselves had been hatchet-threatened and bayonet-stabbed. "Here, I'll take you out there right now!"

"Dad, no! You have to trust us! We can't climb those trees anyway!" She had a point. The spruce trees were tall, thin with no weight-bearing branches. Tim looked to Holly for help.

"Go ahead, girls. But come back in twenty minutes, I'm going to make the waffle batter, and then you can cook them for us."

"Yay!" they said in unison again, repeating their seemingly favorite catchphrase. Both girls bolted for the trail at the bend in the driveway—the trail Tim had sleepwalked up—the trail that used to lead to two hidden graves—the trail right in front of which Annette Smith was killed. He made himself stop the constant stream of negative thoughts and turned to Holly.

"Good idea. If they're not back in twenty minutes, though, I'm going out there."

"I know," she replied.

"I thought I'd be better! I thought I could relax and handle letting them go!"

"Yeah, that's funny. You sound like I did last night when I offered to have everyone over to my house—*you know*—the one in Laconia where no one has ever been murdered?"

"You don't know that for sure, *do* you?" he teased. He referred to Holly's speech the day after he'd seen his first ghost. She shot him a glance that seemed to say *touché.*

"Well, Tim, I don't hear the confidence you've been spouting these last couple of weeks! *'Gone! I'm tellin' ya, she's gone—'* Even you're not sure you believe that! You drag me over here, and now you're not sure!" Holly had a point.

"Yeah, I hear you. I *am* confident, though, as confident as one could ever be. I work here alone every day, and it's different, I'm telling you. Maybe I'm just traumatized. The locations—the grove, the pond—are harsh reminders, even though they were just innocent bystanders—corrupted by *her*—like us."

"That's a poetic way of putting it," she mocked, still perturbed that they had all stayed here unnecessarily overnight.

But he might be right. There *was* evidence that things had changed. The previous week he pulled out all of Annette's journals and Holly's calendars and pieced together what he could of the month of May. Mildred, the creature of habit she was, was infamous for reliving her favorite moments on an annual basis, and it was all documented in Annette's journals. Tim managed to find one more predictable "anniversary"—as they had come to call them—and camped out in the guest bedroom to watch.

They called the anniversary *Thomas Pike's Funeral.* Unfortunately, Mildred's young family had only spent two significant Mays together in the house—they built the house in April of 1860, and Thomas died in early May of 1861. Tim plotted the day, double-checked the actual dates on the years Annette had witnessed it and calculated the corresponding 1971 date.

Holly proofed it to be sure; it was tricky business getting these right, and they had been painfully wrong before. She made up an excuse at work to be in Sanborn at the designated time because she couldn't allow Tim to witness it alone, and she wanted to see the proof with her own eyes.

Thankfully, Tim was right, and nothing happened. It was a significant sign that Mildred had indeed left the premises, yet it was only one day of proof and somewhat unsatisfying. Naturally, they wanted more evidence that Thomas had lived up to his end of the bargain—evidence that didn't exist—and they were forced to take things one day at a time.

"Honey, I've got more than a year of work to do on this house, and that's if I'm very lucky. I'd do it faster, but I can't afford to hire anyone to help me. We *have* to get used to this place!" Begrudgingly, she admitted he was right. On top of his reasoning, her house was not exactly child-friendly, and the thought of keeping the girls out of her stuff made his plan more attractive. She nodded and walked to her car, fetching the waffle iron.

"Okay. But come inside with me until it's time to get the girls."

CHAPTER 96

1971

Twenty-two minutes later, Tim left the kitchen, walking briskly for the path at the bend in the driveway. No sooner had he begun to cross the driveway, the girls appeared from the woods, walking casually. *Wow, not bad timing for two young girls without a watch*, he thought.

"Hi, dad, you can relax. We're back. Is it time to make the waffles?"

"I think so! Holly's in the kitchen, and she just mixed the—" he turned around to head back to the house, and Holly was out on the lawn. "Hey honey—uh, everything alright in there? Need some help?" He studied her eyes carefully.

"No, everything's fine. Just—wanted to see if the girls were coming." Tim realized that she *really* didn't like being in the house alone. That was unfortunate, but not imperative. Maybe they would only sleep here when the girls came up. At the very least, he would try to spare the girls Sheila's third-degree, where she grilled them on every detail of daddy's new girlfriend's house. Keeping Sheila in the dark was never a bad idea.

"How was the grove?" he asked when the waffles were ready, and they had all sat down around the barlike kitchen counter.

"Creepy!" said Vivian. Vivian seemed to like things such as

Halloween and *Casper the Friendly Ghost*. She also liked a new cartoon called *Scooby-Doo*.

"You like creepy stuff, don't you Viv?" he added. *Oh, if she only knew.*

"Yup!" she retorted.

"Somebody was digging out there or planting a garden or something. The forest is all dug up in the last row," added Olivia. Tim stopped chewing for a second.

"Oh, you made it all the way out there? You saw the whole grove?"

"Yeah, it's creepier out there!" said Vivian. Great, Tim thought.

"Girls, what do you think of your waffles?" asked Holly, who desperately wanted to change the subject.

"They're great!" said Vivian.

"You sound like Tony the Tiger," said Olivia. Both girls giggled. "These are even better than Frosted Flakes!"

"I like the way the dimples on the waffle catch the syrup and the butter," said Holly.

"Me too!" said Vivian.

"I don't know if I'm supposed to say something or not, but your dad and I have a surprise for all of us today." Holly looked at Tim, who exaggerated his excitement by bulging his eyeballs at them.

"What is it?" asked Olivia.

"Well, it's been a month since we've been there, so we thought you might like to go to—well, maybe I shouldn't say."

"What! Come ON! You have to tell us now! It's not fair!" complained Vivian.

"I'm only kidding you. We're going...to...*Funspot!*" Holly was referring to the Lakes Region arcade that also had go-karts and other fun stuff for kids. It was best to take the house on Lancaster Hill Road in small bites. Already they all needed a break, and it was only Saturday morning.

CHAPTER 97

1971

The little patchwork family enjoyed their day away. On the way home, they stopped for Chinese food, and all was well. Back at the house, nothing happened. Two geese landed in the pond and stayed for a few hours. The bats circled the inside of barn as they always did. No one walked the fields. No one left any messages in the turret, and the grove remained quiet. The property was as empty as it had ever been.

Holly's car pulled into the driveway and around the side of the house to park behind Tim's truck. They all filed out of the truck and into the house. The adults in the car had checked the turret, pond, and the field as they drove by—and everything checked out. Holly breathed a sigh of relief; she could get used to this. It was a very nice house when the previous owners left you alone.

They went to bed that evening without incident. Holly began to feel like she was getting to know Tim's kids for the first time. She listened carefully to their stories and found herself forgetting the recent problems.

Sunday morning came, and the kids woke early once again. Holly was surprised when Tim lifted his head to listen, and let them leave. He then rolled over and began to massage her.

"Don't you think they might be back? Did you hear them

leave? I'm not sure I—" Holly protested. He held a finger up to his lips.

"They left. The window of opportunity is open." Holly smiled. Tim really *was* confident that they were safe here. Without wasting any more time, they ran to the bathroom, brushed teeth, and jumped back in bed.

CHAPTER 98

1971

A month later, Diane Enrico, the mother of Eric (the boy murdered in the Hampstead woods), was angry with the authorities. Things were moving far too slowly in her opinion, and the trail was growing cold. Her son was dead, and there were no new leads. She checked with the police every single day, and they had begun to shun her—sure signs of the "cold shoulder"—which was unacceptable in her opinion.

After three angry, sleepless nights, she decided that she could do much better, and with that in mind, went to the local printer and had one thousand full-color flyers printed and mailed to every news agency she could find. She posted the rest of the flyers on every telephone pole in a ten-mile radius, and in short order, her story was picked up by the *Salem Evening News*.

Robert Simmons read the article and slept on it. He thought about the line he had drawn on the map that clearly intersected Sanborn, Hampstead, and Beverly Farms. He also thought about the Gottlieb boy's description of the woman and the shape he, himself, saw up in the tree.

When he woke the next morning, he affirmed his convictions and picked up the phone and anonymously dialed Diane Enrico. During the phone call, he recanted his version of the legend of

Mildred Wells and her Sanford history of killing. Purposefully, he held back any information having to do with the years his ancestors had lived or anything having to do with the paranormal.

Before he hung up, he was sure to mention that he believed Mildred Wells was responsible for the death of her son, and that he might have seen Mildred Wells recently at the farm that burned down in Beverly Farms.

Diane Enrico, already angry with the police, went right to the press with the information. From there, the information went in several different directions. First, the press once again swarmed the burned down house in Beverly Farms. On the second day, everyone spent their time gathering information on the new suspect, *Mildred Wells*. Finally, they threw out the Mildred Wells theory when they discovered she'd been dead since 1863. The press never gave Diane Enrico another minute of airtime, and the cold shoulder of the police grew even colder.

Simmons didn't care that he'd made a fool of Mrs. Enrico, or that the story made no practical sense to the general public. He didn't need everyone to believe it—not yet anyway. In the end, they would all see.

CHAPTER 99
1971

Neither Tim nor Holly were watching the Channel Nine broadcast featuring the update on the Enrico boy, but Robert Simmons sure did, and he was extremely pleased; things couldn't have gone any better. Before he put his shoes on, he celebrated by cracking one more beer before hitting the road, even though that only left an odd five in the six-pack.

Minutes later, he pulled up Tim's driveway and parked in front of the porch. The police cruiser would make an intimidating backdrop. He wore street clothes, but that was alright—he was only doing Mr. Russell a neighborly favor. As he parked, he grabbed the empty ring in the six-pack and dragged the five remaining lukewarm beers with him as he knocked on the door.

A saw buzzed inside, so he waited until it stopped and then knocked again. Tim Russell came to the door. He was working alone in the kitchen area.

"Hello...officer? Uh, can I help you?"

"Mr. Russell, my name is Robert Simmons. I'm your neighbor. I live about a mile down—" Tim smiled, recognizing the name.

"Yeah, I know who you are. It's nice to meet you finally. It looks like you came to party. Is this the Welcome Wagon? Haha,

I'm joking. Want to come in?" Robert Simmons froze for a second, appreciating the importance of the moment. No Simmons family member had ever set foot inside the Pike/Wells house, to his knowledge.

"Uh—sure, that'd be great—I—just—you're right, I stopped by to welcome you to the neighborhood, but I'm about, what—a month late? Sorry about that."

"Better late than never, Bob. Come on in. I just made my last cut of the evening, and I'm gonna start cleaning up. We can talk while I do that, is that okay with you?" Simmons nodded and stepped into the house nervously.

"Wow. You know, I've lived on this road my whole life, and I've never set foot on this property. This is a whole new perspective for me. I'm a little overwhelmed..." Tim looked at him sideways just for show but knew exactly who Simmons was, and much of his family history.

"Aw, it's just a house—hey listen—I'd offer you a seat, but I don't have much furniture." Simmons handed Tim one of the beers. Tim cracked it and took a long sip. "Thanks for the beer. Want to see the place?"

Simmons couldn't say no. Along the tour, he imagined Mildred Wells roaming the hallways, crazy, murdering bitch that she was, living free when she should be burning in hell. No one in his family knew anything about the inside of the house, so none of the rooms recalled any family tales. Simmons could tell, however, the difference between the original house and Russell's handiwork. The house was looking good—the work-in-progress was amazing. The two men made small talk along the way: neighborhood talk, the Sanborn Police, and the Red Sox. Finally, the tour ended, and they were back in the breakfast area.

"Do you know anything about the history of this house?" Simmons asked.

"Uh—a little, I guess. The last family here was the Smiths; it was empty for three years..." Simmons cut him off.

"No, before that. Like, way back. The people who built it and so forth."

"Well, I'm not sure. What do you want to know?" said Tim. A serious look washed over Simmons' face.

"My...family has a bit of history with the Pikes, or the Wellses, or whatever you want to call them. Some of the people in my family never got over it. Two of my ancestors were even killed, and many in my family think it all happened right here on your property. I don't mean to get all grisly on you, but—well, I feel like, in a way, I'm helping my family out. Thanks for letting me come over."

"Well, I can't say I know how I've helped you yet, but you're welcome." It was too early for Tim to spill all of the beans, especially because he knew the gossipy nature of Simmons' lineage.

"Yeah my great-grandmother Elizabeth, or great-aunt or something—I can't remember her actual relation to me, I'm terrible with that 'second-cousin-twice-removed' stuff—all I know is she was alive in the 1800s, and she was found just across the street from this place, murdered. My family always thought it was at the hand of the woman who built this house—Mildred Wells, a.k.a. Mildred Pike until she changed her name. My other uh, ancestor—her daughter, Emma, went missing and was never found either, but we Simmons' down the road always suspected the Wells bitch of that one too.

I admit my two ancestors had a bit of a reputation—they were nosy types, and everyone knew they didn't like Ms. Wells. A lot of people weren't surprised they got themselves into trouble. All this information is creepy as shit, I apologize—" Simmons slurred the last few words, and Tim wondered how many beers he'd had before stopping by.

"Hey, no problem. I'm sorry about your *ancestors*. That is some grim, grim stuff that happened here. That *is* a creepy story!" Tim hoped to wrap up the conversation and get rid of him. Then Simmons went darker.

"She killed her kid here too. In the pond. Did they tell you about that before you bought the place?" Tim decided it was time to speak up. Holly hadn't told him about the drowning because she didn't know, but they had both learned the hard way that it had indeed occurred.

"Yes, Officer Simmons, I know a lot of what went on here way back when. That's why nobody wanted to buy the place for three straight years. It sucks, and I try not to think of it. I'm hoping to help erase that past by making this place look completely different." Simmons didn't hear the edge in Tim's voice. For Tim, however, Simmons' visit was becoming uncomfortable.

"Please, Tim, don't call me 'officer.' We're neighbors. Call me Bob. Hey, did you read the news about the kid they found in the woods in Hampstead last week?" Tim hadn't but braced himself for another horror story. Since Officer Simmons was feeling so *loose*, Tim decided to speak freely.

"No, I didn't. All I do is work on this place all day long with a little radio in the corner playing *Top 40*. Bob—no offense, but *what's up?* You're depressing the hell out of me! I just met you, and we're talking about three murders! Are you the *Welcome Wagon*, or the *Meat Wagon*?" Tim tried to crack a joke, but Simmons looked at him with a blank expression on his face.

"I don't drive an ambulance—" he asked, quizzically. Tim didn't understand.

"What?"

"You called me the *Meat Wagon*. That's an ambulance." Simmons was feeling no pain. The last sentence came out like *Thatch an ambulanch*.

"Oh, right, sorry—I was going for *hearse*. Forget it. The point is, I work alone in this place until after it's dark. I don't want to think of drowned and dead people."

"Are you a superstitious man?" *Here we go*, thought Tim. *Great*.

"Not particularly, but if my back is to the door and I'm running a saw and can't hear for a few minutes, I might get anxious."

"Ah. Sorry about that. I could never do what you're doing. I *am* a superstitious man. I can't even watch a horror movie. Too realistic." *Fascinating*, thought Tim. "I believe in ghosts, do you?" Simmons continued—another personal question.

"No. I don't believe in ghosts, Bob."

"Yeah. Again, I apologize. You haven't seen the news. You were busy fixing up this haunted fucking house." Simmons was officially drunk.

"What news, Bob?"

"It was on Channel Nine about a half-hour ago. I came here to warn you if you believe in this sort of thing—but you don't, and I'll tell you anyway as a neighborly courtesy. First, there was a kid killed in Hampstead. Then there was a big house fire in Beverly Farms with bones found in the rubble"—Tim rolled his eyes—"If you draw a line on a map from here to Beverly Farms, Hampstead is pretty much right in the middle." Tim wasn't sure he wanted to hear the rest.

"Bones now. More dead people. Where are you going with this?"

"Mr. Russell—Timmy—you've been here since mid-April. Have you seen anything unusual?"

"Bob, is this official police business or something?"

"I'm talking about ghosts, and you think this is 'official police business'? *Fuck no,* Tim. I'm sticking my neck out here personally and professionally. The name 'Mildred Wells' was on the frickin' Channel Nine news tonight—and she's *dead!* I'm here to help you! Tell me, man! What do you know?"

"I don't know anything, Bob." Simmons studied his face for a reaction. Tim dropped his eyes instinctively, attempting to act his way out of the situation—but it didn't work.

"I *knew* it. What did you see, Tim?"

CHAPTER 100

1971

Tim put his beer down and stared at the floor, lost in thought. Without notice, he walked through the kitchen and climbed the turret stairs. Bob Simmons wondered for a drunk second if he might be fetching a gun to ask him to leave—so he rested his hand on his holster.

Tim returned fifteen seconds later with the *Simmons Family Scrapbook*. Bob's eyes widened, and he lost his breath for a second.

"How the fuck did you get that?"

CHAPTER 101

1971

Tim was in trouble on several different fronts. He wished Holly was here to help filter the conversation. Tim didn't really know Officer Bob Simmons at all, and yet somehow, they had become impossibly close over the last few minutes. Was this an unholy alliance? Would everything Tim said tonight become tomorrow's gossip? He had lost control of the conversation. The half-beer he had drunk went to his head—maybe he was tired? He shouldn't have produced the scrapbook, but now the cat was out of the bag.

"How the fuck did you get that?" asked Simmons.

"It was here when we moved in. I saw the name *Simmons* in it and put it aside. I didn't know it was important." Simmons took the book and looked it over as if he had discovered a baby on the railroad tracks.

"That's weird. Nobody from my family has ever been inside this house before. I'm not saying you took it; I'm just saying it's weird." Simmons put the scrapbook down on the counter and pulled his map of Northern New England out of his back pocket. "Check this out."

A thinly drawn pencil line ran through Sanborn, Hampstead, and Beverly Farms. It looked to have been drawn with a ruler, most likely on Bob Simmons' breakfast table. Tim noticed that the line ignored all roads and highways.

"You're saying Mildred Wells has something to do with a death in Hampstead, and a fire in Beverly?"

"Beverly *Farms*, to be more specific. I saw the Hampstead story in the newspaper, and it gave me a chill—I told you, I'm superstitious. Then I drew the line, thinking she was headed for Salem, Mass. Mildred Wells was supposedly from Salem, plus it's all about witches and shit, so it fits."

"You do know that the Salem Witch Trials were not really about witches, right? Innocent people were killed."

"Yeah, but tell that to all the crazies that want Halloween to be three-hundred-and-sixty-five days a year. It's way more than witches down there now. There's an underbelly of devil worshippers, the occult, Ouija Boards—the whole thing." Tim grew up in Ipswich, not that far away, so he thought he might know a few things about Salem that this hick from New Hampshire might not.

"Oh come on Bob, I don't agree with that." And then Simmons surprised him again.

"Yeah, well, look me in the eyes right now and tell me you don't think there's a chance *she's back*." Caught unaware—thinking he was simply condescending to a drunk man, Tim hesitated just enough to lose the stare down. "I'm telling you, Tim, it was on Channel Nine tonight. They're looking into it. They said her *name*—'Mildred Wells'!" I'm here to help. Obviously, I know who she is, and you do too, and I'm telling you she's dangerous!"

"You're saying that Channel Nine reported tonight that police are on the hunt for Sanborn's *Mildred Wells*—on suspicion of murder?"

"No, I didn't say that, Tim. They looked her up. They know she's dead."

Just then, the phone rang. Oh no. *Fifty-fifty chance it was Sheila.*

"Excuse me for a second, Bob." Tim strode out of the kitchen and into the living room to answer the phone. Thankfully, it was Holly.

"Oh, thank God. I thought you might be *you-know-who*. I'm almost done here. Bob Simmons, my neighbor from down the street, stopped by. He brought me a beer—uh—some beers. We're just getting to know each other." Tim knew Simmons could overhear his side of the conversation from the kitchen. Holly sounded upset.

"Lucky you. That's weird. I bet I know why he's there, though, and you're not going to like it."

"Uh, oh—I think I might already know what you mean."

"Channel Nine just mentioned the name 'Mildred Wells' in connection with a murder in Hampstead and a fire in Beverly, even though they know she's dead."

"Yeah—that's what Bob just told me"—Tim stretched the telephone cord to see through the dining room into the kitchen. Simmons nodded in agreement, hearing his name called. "Tell me something, Holly; Why are they broadcasting that name? Did they do their homework first?"

"It wasn't the police that was speaking—it was the mother of the boy in Hampstead. She seemed pretty pissed off at the police—said they weren't doing enough."

"What does this mother know about Mildred Wells?" Tim winced as he said it—he'd screwed up, and Simmons no doubt heard him mention the name.

"I have no idea. It's not like Mildred was a legend the likes of *Lizzy Borden*. Nothing was ever proven in Mildred's case— the police barely investigated anything. They couldn't even prove she drowned Elmer. Nobody today knows who Mildred Wells is except for—well, maybe the three of us—you, me, and Simmons! I've lived in Laconia my whole life and had never heard the name before all this."

"That's weird," was all Tim could think of to say. He was still dwelling on his slip-up, but the cat was out of the bag. "Hold on. Hey Bob—you saw the Channel Nine story, right? Do you personally know Diane Enrico, the woman who mentioned Mildred Wells? Is she from Sanborn, perhaps? How do you think she knows who Mildred Wells was?" Bob Simmons took the opportunity to approach the living room so that Holly could properly hear his response.

"The lady's from Hampstead, a half-hour away from Sanborn. I have no idea how she knows. I've never seen Diane Enrico before." Holly was surprised that Tim had invited Officer Simmons to the conversation. Were they talking freely about—*everything?* The sightings, the graves, and the bones?

"That's weird. I hope I don't get swarmed by the press now," said Tim. *What a shit-storm that would be*, he thought. It could be devastating to the market value. Tim's heart began to pound. He decided to get out and go back to Holly's house. "All right, honey, I'm almost done here. Cleaning up. I'll be over soon."

"Alright, see you," she said, and they hung up.

"Wow, this is a lot to process, Bob. What do you think the market for a haunted house will be in about a year? This could be really bad news for me."

"I wouldn't worry so much about the house as I would my safety," he rebutted. "And if you know what Mildred is capable of like I think you do, I'm betting you agree." *Very clever, Simmons*, Tim thought. *If I agree with him, he continues to pick my brain, and potentially, I become a laughing stock. If I deny Mildred as a threat, I'm lying to him, and he knows it.*

"Look, Bob, I appreciate you coming over tonight and getting to know you better. I'm a little late for dinner over in Laconia right now though, so why don't we continue this conversation some other time."

"Sure. Sounds good to me. Do you have a date or time in mind?"

"Well, you know where I'll be."

"Okay. I'm anxious to hear more of your encounters next time."

"Sure. Hey, are you okay to drive? I can run you back if you like."

"It's only a mile. I don't think I'll get pulled over." Simmons smiled.

Sanborn's Finest, Tim thought.

"Alright, take care, Bob, Thanks again." Simmons drove out, backing over part of the lawn before straightening the car to pass between the two maples. Tim closed the porch door and went back into the house.

Once inside, he grabbed his jigsaw and began putting it away. He heard something upstairs, then he froze, listening intently. He heard it again, a slight—*knock*.

With a touch of dread, he grabbed the machete on the top of the refrigerator, pulled it out of its sheath, and listened again. Two minutes passed.

Nothing.

Tim wondered: What would Mildred do if she *was* upstairs— *and he left for the night?* He didn't know the answer, but he knew that checking the upstairs was a battle he didn't want to fight right now, so he left through the side door, making sure the machete was out and ready on the counter for the following morning.

CHAPTER 102

1971

Holly was beside herself, but it wasn't so much about Bob Simmons as it was the possibility that Mildred had never left.

"What the hell was that Bob Simmons visit all about? Does he know everything now? I'm pretty sure exhuming bodies and moving the bones is illegal, or at least it should be. We have to be careful what we say around him. He might be a loon like his ancestors"—she wasn't finished. "And excuse me, but, *WHAT THE FUCK*, THOMAS PIKE?!? Where did *he* go? He was supposed to take Mildred *away!* Oh, what a horrible day. I hate everything. I hate Thomas Pike, I hate Robert Simmons, and I hate your house."

"Hey, you sold me that house," said Tim. Holly rolled her eyes—this was no time for jokes. He continued, "I'm pissed off too. He heard me ask you about Mildred. That proves we already knew who she is. It's not damning evidence, but it can't be good. I need to sell this place. Who the hell is this woman from Hampstead anyway?"

"I don't know, but I can't say enough about *Thomas Pike*. You *bastard, Thomas Pike,* wherever you are! If Mildred Wells somehow ends up being a better person than you are, I'm going to scream."

Tim, it goes without saying that I don't want to stay at your place until we're sure this is over. Maybe this lady from Hampstead is just crazy or was talking about a different Mildred Wells or something, but until we figure this out, I'm sleeping in Laconia."

Tim sighed. Holly still didn't know everything; the news was even worse than she thought. There was one thing that Holly didn't know yet that he'd been holding back.

"Honey, I have to tell you—there's one more thing Simmons showed me that backs the woman's story up." He produced a map from his glove compartment. He unfolded it, grabbed the dinner menu to use as a straightedge, and drew a line between Sanborn, Hampstead, and Beverly Farms. "Simmons says the farm that burned used to be a cult, and that Mildred might have been a part of it. It's right next to Salem."

"Oh, that's great. Look—she didn't even have to walk on the roads. She just took the shortest path between two points, straight through the woods—and right through a pond apparently! Tim— this isn't good. This isn't good at all. We screwed her over big time. And Thomas screwed us. I just can't get over it! She left, but she could be back—if what Bob Simmons says is true.

Tim didn't know what to say. They ate in silence and went back to Holly's house tired. Holly locked the door and had Tim drag the dining room table in front of it even though it would not have stopped an angry revenant. Despite their fatigue, they stayed up anxiously to watch the eleven o'clock news for a replay of Diane Enrico's piece. They couldn't believe their ears—everything that was said could be true. What a nightmare.

CHAPTER 103

1971

Tim woke early after a miserable night's sleep. Needless to say, there had been no lovemaking after the eleven o'clock news. Tim ran out to the gas station to get them both coffees. As he pulled out his wallet to pay, he glanced at the rack of newspapers.

The *Manchester Union Leader* was there, and Diane Enrico was the morning's headline. MOTHER SAYS DEAD WOMAN KILLED SON. It was a cruel headline, seeing as the woman had indeed lost her son and might not be in her right mind. Tim threw the paper on the counter next to the two coffees, paid, and rushed back to Holly's house.

They both hated that the name "Mildred Wells" was part of a front-page story in the state's biggest newspaper. This kind of attention could not be good. The writer touched on Mildred's history, but only that she had lived in Sanborn and that she had been a widow. It listed her death as 1863 but made no mention of her unproven allegations, namely the death of Elmer.

From there, the story went straight to Diane Enrico and as to why she might have floated such a preposterous accusation. It was an in-depth interview. Diane told the reporter that the name Mildred Wells had come from an anonymous phone call. The person on the other end explained that her son Eric's death and the fire in Beverly Farms were related, but they didn't say exactly how.

"That's got Bob Simmons' fingerprints all over it," said Holly. "Like I said last night, nobody outside of Sanborn knows who Mildred Wells is." Tim pondered that while they drank their coffees. Before long, it was time to wrap things up and head to work. Tim got in his truck and headed for the house. The only question in his mind was how long it would take before Simmons dropped by again.

CHAPTER 104

1971

Sure enough, the Sanborn Police cruiser came up the driveway shortly before 10 am. *This should be a productive day*, thought Tim. Simmons stepped out of the vehicle wearing the same thing he had been the previous evening.

"Good morning, neighbor," he said with a smirk.

"Hi Bob," Tim replied.

"Hey, I know you're just getting started with your day, but if you have a minute, I'd like to show you something. You busy?" Tim smiled through gritted teeth as if to say sarcastically, *sure I do. That's all I have is time. Stop on by!*

"Sure. What do you need?"

"Walk with me a minute. I want to show you something." Simmons walked past his parked cruiser and continued across Lancaster Hill Road. He didn't look both ways because he didn't have to. Lancaster Hill Road was made of dirt, and you could hear a car coming nearly half a mile away, which happened about four times per day. "Watch that right there. That's Poison Ivy." He gestured to a patch of plants, each with three shiny leaves.

"Thanks for the warning. Where are we headed?" But Tim knew.

"Well, I just wanted to show you something near and dear to the Simmons family, and that's the spot that they found my— relative, way back when. I come here about twice a year to lay flowers. This spot, more or less, is where they found Elizabeth Simmons."

A modest cross made out of metal pipes stuck out of the ground, anchored in a foundation of cement. A metal dinner platter was bolted to the cross, and the epitaph was hand-engraved, probably by Simmons himself.

Elizabeth Simmons
1835–1862
Vengeance is mine, sayeth the Lord

The Bible quote engraved on the tray seemed oddly inappropriate, yet very—*Simmons*. Tim turned back around to face the road, which was at most thirty yards away. The June foliage had filled things in pretty well, but if he looked hard enough, he could see white paint through the trees—a part of his house somewhere up near his master bedroom.

"Can you believe she got away with this? It's not technically her property, but give me a break! That was her bedroom window right there, I just know it. She probably got up every morning and flipped the bird at my great aunt. A damned disgrace."

"Wasn't your—wasn't her husband a member of the Sanborn Police at the time? How did he let this go?"

"You do know a lot, don't you, Russell?" Simmons smiled.

"Call me Tim."

"Right—*Tim*. Tim, tell me about your month of April. How was the move-in? Did you see anything?" It was an odd feeling being in the woods with no one else around talking to a man with a gun.

"Bob, look, I hate to disappoint you, but I haven't had any problems here. It's been smooth sailing the whole way. All I want to do is fix this place up and resell it. This 'Mildred Wells' business does not do me any favors. I want it to all go away."

"Well, that's the thing, Tim! According to my calculations, if she made it from Hampstead to Beverly Farms in a day or two, that means she was probably here very recently!"

"Bob, do you realize you're talking about a *ghost?* Something the *Union Leader* debunked this morning? Mildred Wells has been dead since 1863, and now they're making poor Mrs. Enrico look like she's crazy. Did you see the newspaper this morning?" Simmons had not. He'd gone home after his icebreaker with Tim and had a solo celebration. He spent the morning sleeping it off.

"No, I didn't see that." But he didn't care either. The anonymous phone call had gotten the ball rolling.

"Mrs. Enrico says she received an anonymous tip. Somebody called her and *gave* her Mildred Wells' name. The truth is, however, that nobody outside of Sanborn knows who the hell Mildred Wells *is.*"

"Hey, are you accusing me? I didn't call anybody. You'd better not be accusing me." Tim heard Simmons get testy and felt a drop of sweat run down his back. He didn't want to be alone in the woods with him anymore, so he started walking back. "Where are you going?" said Simmons.

"That sounded a little bit like a threat, Bob. I'm going back to work."

"Wait, Russell, uh—Tim. I didn't mean it that way. I'm just interested in some family justice. The woman beneath that cross you see right there is not even an entire body; they only found a few parts. The coyotes took most. My other relative Emma doesn't even have a final resting place—they never found her; she's probably scattered all over.

The Enrico kid *saw* her, you know. Mildred Wells. In the flesh. So did his friend, who survived. They said they saw a woman in an old-fashioned long black farm dress. They said the dress reminded them of that old painting with the farm couple holding the pitchfork. I forget the name of it."

"American Gothic" helped Tim. He didn't like these new details one bit.

"Right, I guess. Then, I did a little investigating myself. I took my dog to Hampstead, the place the kid was killed. There was still blood on the ground and everything. I should tell you, my dog used to be a cadaver dog. It was King's job to go looking for dead bodies—and he went nuts when he got a whiff of her. I followed the trail to a pond, and it ended there."

"So, you—"

"Wait, I'm not finished. Then I went to Beverly Farms—and *I saw something.*" Simmons paused, played up the drama, reading Tim's face. Russell *knew* what he was talking about, and Simmons was sure of it. *This guy even knew that his great-granduncle had been a cop back in the 1800s—All this and he had only lived here for—a little more than a month?*

"What did you see?" said Tim.

"Before I tell you, Russell, I just want to say that I know you're full of shit. I know you've seen her. The fact that you even know her *name* is more than enough to tell me I'm right. I know—it doesn't *prove* anything like, say, in a court of law, but I'm telling you right here, man-to-man, that you're lying to me."

"Bob, I don't want to get into a fight with my neighbor, the police officer, so I'm just going to excuse myself. Do me a favor and leave me alone." Tim was angry and frustrated. He was no longer thinking of Simmons' gun. If Simmons wanted to shoot him, then he'd have to shoot him in the back.

"I saw her, Tim. I saw her up in a tree. It was just her and me at the time. The firefighters were gone, the press had left—It was creepy as hell." Tim stopped and turned back around to listen.

"You know that feeling when the hair stands up on the back of your neck? It was *that*. I saw her up there in the tree, and she saw me too. We were like maybe a hundred yards apart. I pulled my pistol and walked up to the edge of the woods, but then I lost her—and, to be honest, I got spooked. Pistol or not, I got the hell out of there." Tim relaxed, no longer trying to act.

"Did she ever look at you like that, Tim? Do you know what I'm talking about?" Simmons stared at him carefully. "You felt the same thing, I bet."

"Bob, listen. I wish you luck. I didn't see Mildred Wells. And I don't believe in ghosts. I'm late for work."

"Can I take a look around your property? Maybe I can discover something, or keep watch for you. If I'm wrong, no harm, no foul. If I'm right…I could save your life." Tim stared at him for a few seconds, deep in thought. It was an honest offer if nothing else.

"I'm sorry, Bob. It's just not a good idea."

Simmons frowned and let him go.

CHAPTER 105

1971

Five more revenants trickled into Beverly Farms after seeing their population decimated. One by one they came, and one by one, Mildred killed them. After the five, there was only one more awake and two sleeping. She suspected the conscious one was hanging back for fear of getting ambushed—exactly what she would have done. The two sleepers would just have to wait.

Mildred stood in the tree overlooking the burned-out farm for the fourth consecutive day. She couldn't get her mind off of the Simmons cop, the one with the gall to drive all this way to satisfy his curiosity. She recalled catching Elizabeth Simmons on her property one snowless December and chasing her halfway down the driveway before dropping her with a kitchen knife.

Committing murder was more difficult back then because she was still mortal. All that action took a lot out of her, especially the long drag across the road and the body dump in the woods. Cleanup was easy because the woman's dress had absorbed most of the blood, but the real bonus was the length of time it took before they found her body.

It took them over five months! There were days when Mildred could see body parts in the woods across the street from her bedroom window. Even Elizabeth's father George, who was a police *captain*, didn't look at the unowned piece of land across the street. *What a stupid family*, she thought.

Emma, too, was quite a story. It happened just before Mildred's suicide. Mildred caught Emma in the grove, so the chasing was much easier. There were a lot of screams that went unheard, and when it was over, Mildred simply dug a hole in the middle of the woods and threw her in it.

Who would have thought that over a hundred years later, she might have to kill another nosy Simmons?

CHAPTER 106

1971

Tim sat at Holly's table and recapped his day in the woods with Bob Simmons. His spirits were low, and the outlook on his future had taken a nosedive. Now he wanted to buy more things to protect himself for his workdays, to which Holly thought to herself—*With what money? Why did I have to sell him* that *house?*

"Do I have a choice?" he asked. Holly couldn't argue much. She'd seen a Mildred attack first hand.

"If you're going to go out and buy stuff, you should have a plan. Don't go blow a bunch of money without a plan."

"It's going to get dark early in the fall, so I'm going to need floodlights. Half of my workday will be in the freaking dark. That takes time to set up. I can't wait for the last minute to install everything. Also, I'm thinking I'll need a rifle, some extra machetes, and either barbed wire or an electric fence. Maybe just around the main building where I'm working."

"If Bob Simmons sees all that, he's going to know who it's for."

"Yeah, well, Bob Simmons isn't invited. I should string wire across the entrance to the driveway. What do I care? He can get a warrant if he wants."

"Oh, we don't want that. If he gets a warrant, he's going to go looking around."

"So what? I rototilled the entire corner of the grove, we moved the bodies, and the gravestones are long gone. Even if he finds the gravesite, he still won't have any evidence of anything." Somehow, that comforted Holly. Somehow in her brand new strange life, hiding graves was good news. She smiled and asked him to turn off the light.

CHAPTER 107

1971

Sheila Palmer (no longer Sheila Russell) looked at her kitchen calendar. Her friend Sylvia had just called to let her know that she had an extra ticket for the Johnny Cash concert in Portland—but it fell on a Friday night, which happened to be Tim's visitation time, five days away. She bit her lip and planned her story.

Tim called every Monday evening just before dinner to speak with the girls. Sure enough, at 5:30 pm, the phone rang.

"Olivia, get the phone! It's probably your father!" she barked.

"Coming, Mom!"—Olivia picked up the receiver—"Hello?" Tim, on the other end of the line, was grateful Sheila had not answered.

"Hellloooo, Liv!" It's Dad. What's going on? Getting ready for dinner?"

"Hi, Daddy! Yeah."

"What are you having? Do you know?"

"Mom! What are we having for dinner!" Tim winced; involving Sheila was not his intention.

"No, that's okay Liv, you don't have to go find out—"

"Chicken and corn." The answer was fast and easy, and Tim was grateful. He quickly changed the subject so that Olivia didn't ask Sheila any more questions.

"So what are you up to? How was school? How's your boyfriend *Brian*?" Tim intentionally made up an imaginary boyfriend's name to tease her.

"Dad, I don't have a boyfriend! And there's only one Brian in my class, Brian Shaw, and he pulled my hair when we were in second grade!"

"I know. I was just teasing. I'm just checking in. I'm looking forward to Friday. I think we'll have some fun—we might even stay at Holly's house!" The girls had never been to Holly's house and had expressed interest in weeks past.

"Cool! How come? What's wrong with your house? You don't want us playing in the barn?"

"No, no, no. It's just all messy and stuff, and it's only going to get messier for a while. I've been doing a lot of sawing, and the sawdust is everywhere."

"Oh, okay. Hey Dad, do you want to talk to Vivian?" Olivia was getting bored on the phone.

"Uh, sure. Have a good week, Liv, I love you!"

"I love you too!" half of the sentence was blurted as the phone changed hands between the two girls.

"Hello?" it was Vivian now.

"Hi, Viv! How was school today?"

"Good. Um, Dad, Mommy wants to talk to you." *Dear God, no,* thought Tim.

"What, right now? You just picked up the—" Tim could hear Sheila's voice close to the phone now.

"Go take a bath, honey; dinner will be ready in a little bit. No—no. What? Because I said so, now start the water, I'll be right up. Be—because. Because I have to talk to your father for a minute. He can call you after dinner. Or tomorrow. And you're going to see him this weekend. Go.—GO!" *Dear God, what is it this time,* he wondered and braced himself for whatever curveball was coming. Visitation weekend somehow always managed to bring his blood pressure up.

261

"Hi, Tim. I just wanted to touch base with you about this Friday's pickup." Sheila always had a way of starting a conversation when she needed something with an annoying businesslike voice. It was falsely pleasant and extra irritating because it was so transparent.

'What is it? Another birthday party? I told you, please do not schedule birthday parties and the like during my visitation."

"It's not a birthday party, Tim. My parents will be watching the kids on Friday, and that means they'll be in Kennebunk."

"What the hell are you talking about? That is not in our Divorce Agreement. You do this shit every time, and I'm getting sick of it!" Kennebunk was a town in Maine that added twenty minutes or more—each way—to his commute.

"Listen, Tim. If you want to see your children this weekend, you'll have to pick them up in Kennebunk. I'm not asking my parents to meet you halfway in Rochester." Sheila had even figured the halfway point. Premeditated as always.

"Well, there's one more rule-switch for the list. We spent all that money on lawyers, and you don't even follow the agreement. This is bad faith."

"Tim, the children have a right to see their grandparents, and that's the only time that worked out for everyone. You're self-employed and make your own schedule. You can see the children any time you want, but for some reason, you choose to do so only every two weeks."

Her skill at twisting words and creating straw-man arguments was uncanny. It was written in their Divorce Agreement that Tim would see the girls every other weekend. The rest was simply Sheila-fiction designed to manipulate him and make him look bad. It was the shit she told all her friends.

"And where are you going to be?" he asked.

"I have some business to attend to," she retorted. Tim knew he would never get the full story, so he quit the pursuit. There was nothing he could do at the moment. She had to have guessed he was low on funds and could not afford to both renovate his house and take her back to court.

"Tell them I'll be in their driveway at 6 pm." He put the phone down hard but held back at the last minute, just short of slamming it.

CHAPTER 108

1971

It was a rough night's sleep for Tim. He managed, for the most part, to mask his problems in front of Holly and salvage the evening, but she noticed the dark cloud hanging over his head. He wasn't his usual self.

The problems had all come at once: Bob Simmons, Sheila's constant torment, and worst of all, the possibility that Thomas Pike had not taken Mildred with him. He prayed it wasn't true. It was, after all, unreliable news from an unreliable source. Tim had one neighbor, and that guy happened to come from a long line of gossips—busybodies obsessed with Mildred Wells. *Great.*

The three problems took turns on center stage in his brain as he attempted to fall asleep. Eventually, he compartmentalized them. The Sheila problem was said and done—until Friday—so he shut it down. Bob Simmons might not even be a problem anymore with the way the two men had left things—maybe he'd back off for a while.

The *Mildred Problem* was entirely different, however. It was a slow-burning threat hanging over his head that just might be financial death—or worse. Anxiously, he ran scenarios through his mind of her sneaking up on him as he worked alone. He would have to work smart, and it would cost money. Tim fell asleep just before 2 am.

When Holly's alarm went off, Tim awoke with a start and looked at his watch. He groaned. It was 7:45 am, more than an hour later than his usual wake up time.

"What happened to you last night?" Holly asked.

"I couldn't sleep. Busy brain—sorry. How'd you know?"

"Oh please. You're usually out cold before I even get settled. We didn't spoon as much. You seemed tense. Should I go on?"

"No, that'll do. It's just happening all at once. Sheila, Bob Simmons,—Mildred...*maybe*," he still wasn't able to fully admit to Holly that there was a possibility Mildred had never left. He wanted Holly to like his house because he needed to make it work. If she didn't want to visit him there, it would shorten their time together.

"Well, Sheila is just a bitch. Yeah, you have to drive a little extra this weekend and maybe have to buy a roadmap, but it is what it is for now. Bob Simmons is just a conspiracy-theorist with no right to even step on your property. He's a cop—tell him he needs a warrant. You don't need his friendship—but the Mildred thing is the one that gets me, as you know.

I wonder if we can follow up on some of the things Bob Simmons told you. In fact, that's what I'm going to do. It's bothering me, and I want to know if I'm wasting my time worrying. I'll make some phone calls or something." Tim felt a measure of relief with Holly's words. Sheila would not have been so helpful—she would have hounded Tim until he figured it all out.

"You just made my day; you know that? This may shock you, but Sheila wasn't this helpful." Holly dropped her jaw in mock surprise but did not smile. She was tired too, having fallen asleep not long before Tim.

"Let's just figure this all out so we can get back on track."

CHAPTER 109

1971

Tim kept the machete close by his workspace that morning and set up two nuisance barricades that would fall and warn him if anyone showed up while he was running the saw. The barricades consisted of the desk from the turret and the telephone table from the living room, both tilted onto two legs against two doors.

Every fifteen seconds or so, he checked the driveway through the window and looked around at the locked side door. He was a skilled carpenter, and his muscle memory with the power tools allowed him—unfortunately—to concentrate on his problems as he worked. Holly was right, however—he shouldn't just blow a bunch of money on fencing and protection without thinking it all through first—but he did need *something*.

At lunchtime, tired of feeling vulnerable, he jumped in his truck and drove twenty minutes to Concord. It would be an extended lunch break, but it would be worth it. Concord had a Sears department store. He found what he was looking for and informed the sales clerk. He forked over one hundred and seventy-five dollars and an hour later walked out with a double-barreled shotgun.

Back at the house, he leaned it in the corner and went back to work. For drill, he practiced grabbing the gun quickly and pointing it at the kitchen doorway, as if Mildred had approached from the porch. The gun was heavy and long, however, and took too much time to wield.

Four practice runs later, he decided to make some modifications. Taking his saw, he cut most of the buttstock off, making the grip more pistol-like. Still not satisfied with the necessity of having to use both hands, he took the next step.

Sawing the barrel off made the gun illegal. Tim would have to make sure Bob Simmons didn't see it if he happened to invite himself over again. He practiced a few more times and was satisfied with the improved performance.

Tim returned to Laconia that evening exhausted but with semi-good news; Mildred Wells hadn't shown up—maybe Bob's story was just gossip after all? Holly wasn't completely sold just yet. Bob Simmons hadn't shown up either, which was more good news. Tim was so full of good news and was feeling so much better about things that he decided to leave out the part about the sawed-off shotgun.

"How about *your* day?" he asked.

"I called the Chief of police in Hampstead," she said. Tim put down his beer.

"You did?" His face went serious.

"Yeah. I didn't learn much, though. I think I'm going to have to try and talk to the Gottlieb kid, the one who survived." Tim was temporarily at a loss for words. Holly remained humorless, understandably. She was tired, and the idea of picking a traumatized boy's brain was daunting if she even got that far.

"How do you plan on doing that?" he wondered.

"I'm just going to be honest, I guess. I'm going to say that I saw Mildred once too and I'd like to compare notes. I can't think of any other way of going about it."

"You are *tenacious*," he said quasi-mockingly in an attempt to lighten her mood. Once again, his attempt at humor fell flat.

"Yeah, I've been tossing it around all afternoon. I'm dreading the phone call. I was planning on doing it now as a matter of fact.

Before they go to work—and school—in the morning. I got their number from the operator this morning. Can you think of any questions you want to ask?" They wrote down a few that came to mind and picked up the phone.

CHAPTER 110

1971

"Hello—Mrs. Gottlieb? I'm sorry to bother you around dinner time. My name is Holly Burns, and I—well, my boyfriend—lives up in Sanborn. I've been following your story thanks to a police officer in our town by the name of Robert Simmons. This is a bit of a complex story, and I apologize, but—Officer Simmons said your son saw a woman who might be one of the previous owners of my boyfriend's house. I was wondering if we could compare notes?" Marcy Gottlieb started off skeptical.

"You say that a policeman from Sanborn told you this? I'm sorry, I'm just not following. I don't know any policeman from Sanborn."

"Well, you're right—you probably don't know him. Officer Simmons talked with your Chief Luoma because he also is familiar with the woman your son saw."

"Who knows a few things? Chief Luoma knows a few things about the woman?"

"No, I'm sorry if it's confusing. *Officer Simmons* knows about the woman; he compared notes with Chief Luoma."

"Does this have anything to do with that dead woman bullshit that somebody fed me on the telephone?"

"Absolutely not, ma'am. I'm talking about a woman I saw with my own eyes on my boyfriend's property."

"Well, how come I don't know about this? Chief Luoma never mentioned anything about any leads!" Holly realized she had just opened a can of worms. *Cat's out of the bag now. Luoma didn't share that because this IS about ghosts—but I can't tell her that.*

"I'm not sure—you can ask him though. I can direct you to Officer Simmons, too, if you like." Tim opened his eyes wide in disbelief. Now Simmons would be in his driveway again *tomorrow*. Not only that, but he'd want to know why they were willing to share Mildred Wells's information with Mrs. Gottlieb, but not *him*.

Holly continued. "So that makes three people you can question—no *four* if you include my boyfriend, Tim Russell. I just want to see this woman—put away." Holly was careful not to use any words having to do with the supernatural.

"Mark has not been well since his friend died. I hesitate to put him through this," Mrs. Gottlieb worried.

"I understand. I would be concerned too if I were in your shoes. Perhaps I should tell you what I know, and you can process the information as you like. My priority is to make sure we're talking about the same woman. My boyfriend bought his house about a month ago. Officer Simmons lives about a mile down the road and claims to have a history with the woman. He also says that he thinks the fire that happened in Beverly Farms is related to the uh—the Hampstead incident. Are you writing this down?"

Again Tim freaked out silently, and Holly turned away so he wouldn't distract her. Holly's complete-and-total-honesty-d own-to-the-finest-detail way of doing things was not the sort of approach he would use. There would be consequences for this—he wasn't sure what they would be, but he knew this was likely to bite him in the ass.

"Yes, I'm writing this down. Officer Bob Simmons, Sanborn.

Knows the woman, fire in Beverly Farms. Go on," said Mrs. Gottlieb.

"Okay, well, as I said, we've only been on-property for about a month, so this is all new to us too, but every day, we would see this woman walking through our field. It was weird. She wore a long black farm dress every day, and she'd trespass all over everything."

"Did she sell your boyfriend the house?"

"No, he bought the house from the bank. I guess she owned the place a while back, and I don't know all the circumstances yet." Tim started to relax as Holly's faux-innocence began to paint the picture. "Anyway, one day down by our pond, we see her, and she—I'm sorry about what I'm about to say, but she killed two Canada geese as we watched from the house. As if it was still her house and her property!"

"Well, what did you do? Did you call the police?" asked Mrs. Gottlieb.

"You know, I'm sorry to say that we didn't. Tim ran out there and told her to get off his property, or he would call the police, and she—seemed deranged or something I guess, and she took the geese with her and left! The whole thing was upsetting. My guess is that she's mentally ill or something. I wonder where she lives.

It breaks my heart that someone died because we didn't tell anyone. That's why I'm reaching out now. Maybe we can compare notes and get her apprehended before something else happens." There was silence on the other end of the phone.

"Mark, honey, can you come here for a minute? Just for a minute." Mrs. Gottlieb put her mouth near the phone again. "I have to warn you; I think he's still in shock. His description differs from yours in a few different ways, but I think you might be onto something. I mean, who wears an old farm dress and has recently been involved in two terrible incidents like this? Your police references won me over. You can be sure I will be talking with Chief Luoma tomorrow morning."

"Thank you, Mrs. Gottlieb."

"You're welcome. Now, here comes Mark. If you could perhaps tone down the gory parts of what you told me, I'd appreciate it."

'I certainly will Mrs. Gottlieb, thank you." Holly could hear the phone receiver handoff between the boy and his mother.

"Hello?" It was Mark.

"Hi, Mark. My name is Holly Burns. I think I've seen the same woman you did, but I want to be sure. I'm sorry, and I know this is painful for you, but can you tell me what she looked like?" Mark sounded groggy as if he had just woken up or might be taking something for his anguish.

"Yeah. She had a farm dress on like the lady in the painting with the farmer and the pitchfork."

"Was it just the dress that looked like the painting, or did her face look like the painting too?"

"No. Not the face. I didn't see her for very long—a couple of times from a distance, and then really close for just a couple of seconds. It was terrible. I made her mad. I shot her with a BB gun. She had a knife and started to chase us. She choked me with barbed wire around a tree."

"I heard that. How's your neck?"

"It's getting better. I'm going to have a scar, though."

"Oh, no. Well, in a way, you're lucky, though. Don't forget to look at the bright side. What else can you tell me about her face?"

"It was white—really white. And scary. Sometimes I wake up in the middle of the night because I dream about it. Mom got me some pills to help, though."

"Mark, is there anything else you can tell me about her?"

"Yeah, she killed my friend Eric. I didn't see it, but I heard it. I heard the air come out of his lungs." It sounded as if he might be starting to cry, and Holly realized her time was running out.

"Oh my gosh, that's horrible, how did you—" he cut her off.

"She smelled terrible like she was *dead*. And she was covered in *flies. Nobody believes me! Nobody believes me! Nobody—*" Mrs. Gottlieb took the phone away.

"I'm sorry we have to end there. I have to go. He's hysterical now. Thank you, but—it was too much for him. I have to go fix this now. Goodbye." The call disconnected before Holly could say anything with Mark still ranting in the background. Tim could hear him from across the room. Holly didn't look up; she couldn't take her eyes off of the receiver.

Mildred Wells had never left.

CHAPTER 111

1971

The next day, Tim kept the sawed-off shotgun on the counter underneath a kitchen towel just in case Simmons popped in unannounced. Sure enough, at 9:37 am, the cruiser pulled up the driveway. Tim went outside and met him on the lawn.

"I just got my ass chewed out by Chief Luoma of the Hampstead Police," said Simmons.

"Why's that?" asked Tim.

"Don't play dumb with me Russell, because your girlfriend called the Gottlieb woman and ended up talking to her son. Now he's all upset, and Mrs. Gottlieb is halfway up Chief Luoma's ass. He doesn't appreciate that, and neither do I."

"Mrs. Gottlieb was on Channel Nine of her own volition. My girlfriend called to ask about the woman who her son saw, that's all. It has nothing to do with you or Chief Luoma," Tim replied.

"Oh, yes, it does. You told her about Mildred Wells, but you left out the important parts—like she died a thousand years ago. You made it look like we held back information from her."

"You and your family scrapbook told me the name, 'Mildred Wells.' All I know is we had a woman trespassing on our property. She appeared to me to be alive, and I don't believe in ghosts. We were trying to find out if the boy's murderer was the same woman.

If it is, then she came from Sanborn. Now, I'm sorry if that upsets you, but it doesn't have much to do with you or Chief Luoma."

"Your girlfriend told Mrs. Gottlieb that Mildred Wells was the previous owner of this house as if she might still be alive today," retorted Simmons. Tim knew how to play the telephone game, and how a story changed the more people it passed through. Holly talked to Mrs. Gottlieb, Mrs. Gottlieb talked to Chief Luoma, and Chief Luoma talked to Simmons. There was plenty of room for misdirection.

"No, she didn't."

"Well, that's what Chief Luoma told me."

"Well, maybe Chief Luoma got it wrong—or Mrs. Gottlieb got it wrong."

"She told her I know Mildred Wells!"

"No, she didn't say anything like that."

"You're an asshole, Russell. I'm trying to help the two of us, maybe save your life in the meantime, and you stab me in the back."

"No, Bob, you want to destroy my investment by going to the news and reporting everything bad that has ever happened here. You also want to tell everyone there might be a murderous ghost on property." *And besides all that, I never want you to know I exhumed Elmer Pike's remains in the grove,* he thought to himself.

275

CHAPTER 112

1971

Bob Simmons spent the rest of the morning driving to Hampstead in full uniform in an attempt to console the livid Mrs. Gottlieb. Chief Galluzzo, embarrassed for the Sanborn Police Department, made him do it on his own time. When he got there, he denied everything, saying Holly Burns had lied. *Maybe Holly and her boyfriend were the ones that placed the anonymous call too, Mrs. Gottlieb. The police will look into it. No, he had no idea why everyone was trying to spin a supernatural element into her son's tragedy. Yes, he realized it only hurt the boy.*

As soon as he finished with Mrs. Gottlieb in Hampstead, he had to drive back to Sanborn and work his full shift. As he did, he fumed. He knew he was right about Mildred Wells; he just needed more information. Tim Russell was hiding something. Tim Russell was probably hiding a lot.

As soon as his shift ended at 11 pm, he headed home, passing the Russell house on the way—it was completely dark. For some reason, Russell wasn't sleeping there much anymore—now why was *that*? A mile later, Simmons pulled onto his private family road and parked in front of his house. King was there to greet him sleepily. Simmons went inside, changed his clothes to all black, then grabbed a flashlight and his Kodak Instamatic.

Fifteen hundred yards later, he could see the Russell house in the moonlight, and just in case Russell was indeed home, he cut up into the woods just before the property line where the woods ended, and the field started. The bugs were terrible, and he wished he'd brought repellant.

This was a first. Just as the other night was his first time inside the house, tonight was his first time exploring the land itself. It was not lost on him that at least one, if not both of his relatives had died most likely doing this same thing. His heart skipped a beat.

As soon as he'd crossed the corner of the field and was into Russell's part of the forest, he turned to see if he could see the house. When he could not, he clicked on his flashlight. A mosquito bit him good behind the ear, and he slapped it away in frustration, too late. It started to itch immediately.

He wasn't sure what he was looking for, but he imagined Elizabeth and Emma weren't sure either—somehow they just knew they had to be here. Had the women been looking for evidence of Elmer? He couldn't recall. He should have stopped home on his break and grabbed the scrapbook and done some studying before coming out, but *oh well*, too late now. He pulled his pistol and used it to move branches aside as he looked for any trace of a trail. Didn't anyone go walking out here? *There must be a trail.*

Suddenly, there were no more branches in his way. Across from him was a perfect row of overgrown spruce, their lowest branches several feet above his head. He shined his light to the left and realized he was looking down a perfect corridor—*an overgrown tree farm.* Simmons, already a superstitious man, felt the creep-meter climb. To be in this dark hallway in a quasi-natural setting was almost too much for him, and he nearly turned back. The flashlight wasn't powerful enough to reach either end—darkness yawned in both directions. Hefting his flashlight and his pistol, he began to count the rows as he cut through them.

He lost count somewhere in the thirties when something

flew over his head. He couldn't tell if it was a bat or an owl, all he heard was a whoosh as it passed his ear. Mosquitos feasted on him as his hands were too full for effective swatting. *I should have waited until October.* Finally, he began to see imperfections in the grove—trees growing between rows, different species, different heights. The grove finally came to an end, and only the darkness of the wild woods lay beyond.

He shined his light down the last row and noticed something out of place. There was a spot at the end of the corridor, not completely covered by brown spruce needles. He walked over it, and it sank a few inches under his weight, unlike the rest of the hard-packed forest floor. This patch of land was perfectly flat and rectangular, bordered by thick briars on three sides—someone had trimmed the thorns back in order to turn the soil with a machine. It looked something like a garden, but yet nothing grew. *What are you doing out here, Russell?*

He pulled out the Kodak and took a few flash pictures, then moved on. After, he jogged all of the other rows looking for similar *Russell projects.* Eight minutes later, he considered checking the barn but figured he might be pushing his luck. It was a longshot, but someone could be in the house sleeping. He looked at his watch; it was only 12:30 am. He still had time and plenty of it, to sleep in the next morning.

With that, he ran home and grabbed a lantern and a shovel. He dug until 3:30 am, then took some more pictures. He found bits of burned boards, some old feathers, and bits of fabric. He guessed that someone had been buried here, but now they were gone.

CHAPTER 113

1971

Tim bought a map of Southern Maine and made his way through unfamiliar towns like Alton, New Durham, and Lebanon. The whole ride, he cursed Sheila for her apathy and passive-aggressive taunts. When he pulled into her parent's driveway, he masked his anger. The Palmers had always been fair with him; he only wondered how the apple had fallen so far from the tree.

The handoff of the children went smoothly. In the back of his mind, he wished all the pickups could be so smooth—the extra driving would be worth it—maybe the kids should visit grandma and grandpa more often. It was so easy, he and the kids sang songs on the radio together all the way home. It was going to be a nice weekend—except for the Mildred tension in the back of his mind.

Holly understandably didn't want to sleep in Tim's house, and they'd had their first real disagreement as a couple the night before. Holly was, of course, adamant that the Gottlieb boy's story proved Mildred was still around. Tim countered that if Mildred wanted to get them, she could just as easily show up in Laconia at Holly's house, much the same way the scrapbook did one rainy night not too long ago.

"That wasn't Mildred, that was Thomas Pike."

"Well, if he can do it, she can do it too. And if she's able to make her way to Beverly Farms, she can certainly make it to Laconia."

Holly didn't take too kindly to being reminded that her *home sweet home* had been violated, and gave in—mostly because she wanted to believe it was safe there and didn't want to be proven wrong. Besides that, a visitation weekend was many things, including getting extra work done on the house in between family activities like going to Funspot and having meals together. Holly also had to admit that her house was too small for four of them, especially Tim, who couldn't seem to sit still. Holly silently compared him to a dog that had to be walked to the point of exhaustion. He could only fall asleep if he had worn himself out working; otherwise, he took on a different personality—lighter on humor and heavier on worry.

Tim knew he was bound to be "Nervous Daddy" this weekend once again, and—they would all get through it. The weekend began much the same way it always did except Tim stopped for the pizza this time. Holly once again showed up minutes after they'd arrived. Friday night was largely uneventful—they played some board games and went to bed. Tim made sure his many hidden weapons remained unseen yet ready for action.

The next morning Tim woke with the girls. Holly hadn't slept well, and both adults were mostly miserable. Holly brought the waffle iron again, promising herself it would be the last time for at least six months. She detested waffles and big breakfasts in general, yet—when you had children in the house, that's what you did.

Tim was outside supervising the girls when Holly, constantly watching her back, opened the wrong drawer looking for the electric mixer. She pulled out a long shape wrapped in a blue dishtowel and opened it. It was Tim's sawed-off shotgun. She wrapped it back up quickly and closed the drawer. Later, after breakfast in an off-minute, she pulled him aside.

"Tim, what is that in the blue towel in the drawer? Dear

God—you're going to hurt yourself or someone else. Do you know you made it illegal?"

Tim sighed. "Yes, I know it's illegal, but it makes me feel better when I'm working. Something like that would drop a bear. I need that kind of firepower if I'm going to take her down. I'll move it if you like, but I don't want to get rid of it."

"Well, yes, you should definitely move it. You don't want your daughters to blow their hand off looking for a spatula, right?"

CHAPTER 114

1971

Other than Holly's discovery, the day went smoothly. After another quick trip to the Concord Sears, Tim and Holly set up the porch, which meant the adults were doing something productive toward the house, and the kids were free to play in the yard.

It was a peaceful day—and everything was so different from the first two weeks living there that even Holly began to have her doubts about Mildred's return. Wouldn't she just come back right away and get her revenge? Would she abandon years of "anniversaries"? Everyone went to bed early that Saturday night, and things were relaxed enough for Tim and Holly to enjoy each other's company after the kids were in bed.

The following morning, however, ended up being a little too relaxed. Holly nudged Tim at 8:30 am, and Tim jumped out of bed in a bit of a panic. He ran across the hall to where the girls had already risen and then ran down the hallway while he put on his shirt, calling their names.

Five minutes later, Holly got up too, and Tim was still calling after them. His "daddy panic" might be justified. She bolted to the sound of his voice to help him reacquire the girls. As soon as Holly appeared on the lawn, Tim bolted for the grove. Another six minutes later, Tim returned with the girls at the trail in the bend in the driveway.

"What happened? Didn't you hear us calling?"

"No, we didn't," said Olivia. "I don't get it. Last time we went to the grove, you said it was okay. This time we're in trouble." Tim's face was pale, and he remained speechless for another few seconds as he caught his breath.

"They—they didn't hear me. It's true; we haven't been consistent. I guess we're just going to have to say 'no grove.' You can't hear us when we need you. There's nothing out there anyway. And another rule; wake me up before you leave the house."

"Why are you being this way? You never used to do this when you lived at mom's house." *At mom's house—nice.*

"Because this isn't mom's house. I'm going to tell you a story. A true story, and it's scary, but you need to hear it so we can all be on the same page. You see that pond over there? Well, a little boy drowned in it because his parents weren't watching him. I'm sorry, but that freaks me out, and I didn't want to tell you, but I feel I must. You guys don't have this much land or this many places to explore at your house in Amesbury. You have a little yard, and you're fine with that yard because that's all you have.

Let's pretend that my yard is this little front yard here—and the barn. I'll let you play in the barn, but I'm still going to be nervous about the loft. I might check on you from time to time as a father should. But no pond and no grove. That's your new yard. Agreed?" They had no real choice, so they agreed. Holly let the harshness of the "drowned boy" speech go.

CHAPTER 115

1971

Bob Simmons exited the Photosmith, got into his car, and opened the bundle of photos. He'd expended the whole roll snapping away in the darkness of the grove both before and after he'd dug it up. They weren't very good shots, but they were enough. These photographs, along with the Enrico boy and the Beverly Farms fire might be enough to get people talking. Maybe when that happened, Russell would be forced to open up.

He went home and added the photos to the presentation on which he'd been working. Much of the presentation's source material was newspaper clippings and happenings from The Simmons Family Scrapbook, but he tied it all together nicely with the most recent happenings.

He'd also spent some time with a locally-famous self-proclaimed witch in Salem, digging for answers as to the mysterious fire in Beverly Farms. The woman had never been a part of the farm but had heard things through the grapevine. Her answers were all rumors discarded by the police that dovetailed nicely with his project. Now all he needed was a little help from the media.

It took him a few weeks, but he finally got through to the person he wanted to—a young and popular radio DJ on a rock n' roll station in Boston that called himself *Orfeo*. Simmons was able to pick up his show in Sanborn on clear summer nights. Orfeo, whose real name was Scott Carson, spent his late-night-shift spinning cutting-edge rock 'n roll blended with four-to-five minute "true" ghost stories. The name *Orfeo* was borrowed from a supposed vampire in Romania for dramatic effect.

Simmons hand-delivered his work to the radio station's front desk to be sure it didn't get lost in the mail. The name "ORFEO" was written in large red magic marker and underlined twice, and he listened every night from 8 pm-midnight for two weeks before he heard the payoff. Orfeo came out of a Black Sabbath record with a "newsflash."

"Ladies and gentlemen, that was 'Sweet Leaf'—I'm guessing it has nothing to do at all with marijuana, but don't ask me. We've got more brand new rock 'n roll comin' at ya in a few minutes, but first—gather 'round—it's time for a *storrryyyy...*" Orfeo liked to drag the last word out nice and slow—the audience's cue to listen up for the next creepy tale.

"I just want to say—that a mysterious package was delivered to the station a couple of weeks ago, and it took us this long to get it on the air because we had to fact check it. We're not even sure who it was that dropped it off. I asked around, but Brinko—my intern and personal assistant—the man who accepted the envelope in his own grubby hands—just couldn't seem to remember—*cough* dumbass! *cough*—who left the package...But I digress." Brinko was intentionally left off mic and served as Orfeo's nightly *lamb to the slaughter.*

"Did you folks happen to read about the boy who was murdered in the woods up in New Hampshire two or three months ago? Brinko, did you? No? Oh, right, you don't read, forgive me. *Brinko, the intern, everybody!* Let's give him a hand!" Orfeo then stopped the show for five seconds to clap for the humiliated Brinko.

"Alright, well, for those of you who read as much as Brinko does, I'll recap. Two or three months ago up in Hampstead, New Hampshire, two boys went out into the woods to shoot some squirrels. You know, a typical Saturday night in *Cow Hampshire*—I mean New Hampshire. Haha—sorry about that New Hampshire—if you can even hear me. We're only a fifty-thousand-watt station, and we know most of you probably went to bed when the sun went down for lack of electricity. Pleasant dreams.

Anyway, these two boys saw a mysterious—hold on; I'll quote the document that appears to be on some official police paper with—very mysteriously—the jurisdiction—*the name of the police department that wrote it—cut off.* This makes me think a cop dropped off the packet, right Brinko? Did you think of that? Do you remember any cop-looking people? No? *Dammit, Brinko!* If you weren't free, I'd fire your ass.

Anyway, these two boys saw 'A white-faced woman who looked like she was dead, and had—*flies* all over her....' Think about that for a second folks. Brinko, have you seen a woman fitting that description? Other than every girl you've ever dated, I mean? Haha, sorry Brinko, I'll continue.

So this white-faced dead woman with flies all over her begins to choke one of the kids after he shoots her with his BB gun. Then the second kid comes over to help—and ends up knifed to death—and the shooter-kid escapes. I'm not going to give out the name of the kids, but this was apparently all reported in the *Derry News* newspaper. I have a clipping of it right here.

No wonder you didn't hear about it, Brinko, you're off the hook. You *canceled* your subscription to the *Derry News*, right? Just kidding. Man, does that sound like a New Hampshire newspaper or what? How do you spell 'Derry'? Is it *D-A-I-R-Y*? Wow, I am ruining this story, aren't I? Sorry, everybody, we're supposed to be getting scared here, and I'm cracking jokes—let's get back on track.

Where was I? Oh—A short while after the kid gets killed in the woods—and we're getting a little bit closer to Boston now, there was a housefire in Beverly...no sorry, more specifically; Beverly

Farms. According to my source, nobody really knows who lived at this farm, and I mean, like, the last town records are from the nineteenth *century.* A *full century* and nobody knows their freakin' neighbors. How does that happen in modern-day Massachusetts? This place, I guess, has a 'trust' as the owner or something; I'm no lawyer, so I'm not sure how that all works.

Well, the mystery person who dropped off the package did some digging, and it seems that the farm was some sort of *cult* that clearly didn't want anyone all up in their business. According to the modern-day-witches from Salem—yes, they do exist ladies and gentlemen—these modern-day-witches are saying *off the record,* of course, that the people on this farm—were basically slaves to an *army of the dead.* Beverly Farms is right outside of Salem, folks. Not too far from any of us. And this gets worse, so bear with me.

This unknown, unnamed source tells me that he or she went to Beverly Farms right after the fire—and everyone—the press, the police—were all gone—and he or she saw a—quote—white-faced lady in a dress—unquote—and they got the hell out of there because she started to come after them.

The key to the story of who this woman is, however, has roots in the *past.* My source tells me that they know who the fly-covered lady is, but the police can't—well, they're programmed to *not* believe this kind of thing, so nothing's going to get done. Watch yourselves out there people, especially if you live in the Beverly Farms area—" Orfeo lowered his voice and got serious. His horror-punchline was coming up.

"Here's the kicker that ties it all together. Here's the reveal on who this dark bitch is. Shut up Brinko; you're breaking the tension. I can say 'bitch' on the air. Sorry, everyone. The kicker is that this woman comes from a little town called Sanborn, New Hampshire. Hey, I pass this place on my way up to Loon Mountain when I go skiing, actually. Exit 20 off 93...sorry—Her name—write this down—is *Mildred Wells.*

Uh—it says here that back in the 1860s, Mildred Wells from

Sanborn drowned her son in a pond. Then she killed as many as four people, but nothing could ever be proven. The rumor is, she even buried two bodies in the woods somewhere on her property. Then she disappeared. Years later, an elderly widow was found dead in the very same house in 1968. She'd been in there for weeks before anyone discovered the body. Her husband was found dead there too a few years earlier.

Man, that's creepy as hell! This is happening right in our back yard! How come we're just hearing about this? Ladies and gentlemen, the source goes on to tell me exactly where this place is, but…I don't know if I can just put it out there on the air for legal reasons, uh, but—if you draw a line on the map from Sanborn to Hampstead to Beverly Farms, it's a perfectly straight line.

My question is, what happened between 1860-whatever and 1971? Who stirred this woman up? I mean, I don't know about you, Brinko, but when I don't want the lady to wake up, I've got mad moves to get out of there. I'm like the wind; you know what I mean? I'd even chew my arm off if I had to, right?

Ladies and gentlemen, if you want more information on, let's call this: '*The Legennnnd of Milllldred Welllls*'"—Orfeo dragged his words out and pressed the echo effect button as he said it—"don't come to me. It's in the *Derry News*. It's in the *Salem Evening News*, and it was apparently aired on *WMUR Channel Nine* up in Manchester. Ask them. Coming up after the break, more of the new Rock 'n Roll you want to hear. We've got The Doors, and 'L.A. Woman'!"

CHAPTER 116

1971

Bob Simmons was ecstatic about the radio broadcast. His patience finally paid off, and when he heard Orfeo's show opener, he eagerly pressed the record button on his shoebox-style tape recorder and held the built-in microphone close to the speaker. When the segment was over, he popped the cassette and called his friend-since-high-school Al Garlington, who had since become a private investigator.

Garlington, accustomed to catching philandering spouses, took the case at a ten percent discount to help his friend. He didn't believe in ghosts, but he knew Bob Simmons' family history. If his buddy wanted to fork out good money for this sort of thing, then so be it. It wasn't even that odd of a request, and the whole job required a day, maybe two of his time.

One thing he was asked to do was knock on Russell's door, ask questions about the radio broadcast and provide a copy of the cassette, and to not disclose who his client was. It was more of a ruse than anything, something he wouldn't do for someone he didn't know. His buddy Bob wanted to metaphorically shake the trees, and examine what fell out of them.

He was also asked to send copies of the radio show recording to the Beverly Police and the Hampstead Police. Maybe they would show some interest in the Sanborn connection, and Russell would feel obliged to let them in to look around, else arouse suspicion.

CHAPTER 117

1971

What Bob Simmons didn't know was that the national television program "Only If You Dare" was in Boston filming an episode about Albert DeSalvo, the notorious "Boston Strangler." "Only If You Dare" covered a different subject each week, everything from Bigfoot to Lizzy Borden to UFOs.

The producer of the show, Nate Hoginski, needed fresh ideas. The Bigfoot episode performed poorly in the ratings, and upcoming shows included equally well-worn subjects such as the Loch Ness Monster and the search for Jimmy Hoffa. Luckily, he was listening to the radio while driving back to his hotel after a rough day of trying to turn boring material into an exciting episode.

Immediately he scrapped the expensive Scotland trip. This New Hampshire ghost story was nearby, current, and best of all *cheap*. The nature of "OIYD" was to present open-ended topics, so there was no urgency to solve the mystery—only augment it. The better the mystery, the better the ratings. This show could become an "Only If You Dare" original.

CHAPTER 118

1971

There were three visitation weekends in July, and the girls obeyed Tim's "no pond, no grove" rules fully and completely for two of them. Midway through the third, Olivia got bored of the barn and the front yard.

"I'm bored, let's go to the grove."

"No, dad said we can't," answered Vivian.

"He always starts working on the house on Sunday afternoons. We aren't going to Funspot today, and we aren't going out to eat. I saw a chicken in the refrigerator. I think Holly's going to cook it. She'll be busy helping him too. This is so *boooooring*. Follow me to the barn."

Vivian stood, pretty bored herself.

"I don't want to go to the loft again. I get all itchy after."

"Just follow me, I have an idea," said Olivia. With that, Olivia led the way from the patch of lawn closest to the road past the entire front of the house. As they reached the bend in the driveway, she pulled a sharp right and bounded up the path. Vivian instinctively followed her but yelled out as her sister pulled away.

"We're not supposed to go there!" Olivia stopped in her tracks and turned to face her sister.

"Shhhhh! Come here; it's only for a second." Vivian slowly walked forward. Olivia took her hand, and it turned into forty-minutes of top-notch hide-and-seek.

CHAPTER 119

1971

A month passed—and Tim began to let his guard down. The sawed-off shotgun was still wrapped in the blue towel but hadn't left its designated kitchen drawer in over a week. There was not even a whisper of Mildred Wells in their lives. Was the whole Hampstead episode just coincidence? Was the Gottlieb boy simply mistaken, and the "flies" part of his story just a figment of his imagination?

Tim wanted to believe so, but Holly wasn't sold by any means—however, Tim's work on restoring the house progressed at an unprecedented pace—Which was about what he'd imagined he could do back when he bought the place—before all of the supernatural distractions. The kitchen and dining rooms were complete, and they looked great. Holly started to get excited; it was her first time seeing the fruit of Tim's professional talents (she already knew about his other talents), and she began to dream of the Open House—the beginning of the end.

Tim was now working on the turret, ripping out some of the old boards and installing a brand new hardwood floor while Holly was at work in Laconia at the real estate agency. Every once in a while, Tim caught himself glancing down the stairwell defensively, but all-in-all he wasn't concerned enough to go down to the kitchen to fetch the shotgun.

Suddenly he heard a knock from below. He turned down his radio and stood up to look out the window. A tie-wearing man he had never seen was at the porch door with a folder under his arm. *A salesman*, thought Tim. He put down his tools and marched downstairs to get rid of him.

"Good afternoon, are you Mr. Timothy Russell?"

"Yes, I am. What can I do for you?"

"Mr. Russell, my name is Albert Garlington, and I'm a private investigator. I represent an entity that is looking into the death of a young boy named Eric Enrico. I believe you're familiar with that case?" Tim's spirits sank.

"Yes, I did hear about that. Why are you asking me about this? That happened fifty miles from here." Tim had his suspicions but didn't want to mention any names just yet.

"Well sir, a radio show in Boston broadcast the story the other night, and they go into detail about the Hampstead death, the fire in Beverly Farms, and Sanborn. I've brought you a recording of it right here." Garlington pulled a cassette tape out of his folder.

"Alright, well, spare me a little time and tell me what it says," said Tim.

"In a nutshell, Mr. Russell, the radio show ties the Enrico murder to the fire in Beverly Farms and to a woman in Sanborn named Mildred Wells, and she used to live in this house, am I right?"

"I'm not sure," said Tim. The house was empty for three years before I bought it. How can I help you?"

"Well, sir, we're looking for this woman in connection with the murder. Would you mind if I took a look around your property."

"Look, Mr. Garlington—were you hired by a man named Simmons?"

"I'm not at liberty to say, sir, but I can tell you that many people are interested in finding Mildred Wells and bringing her in for questioning. The Hampstead Police and the Beverly Police as well." Tim knew damn well that Mildred Wells would not submit to questioning.

"I'm going to politely decline Mr. Garlington. If you can't tell me where you come from, I'm not comfortable as to what you'll do with the information I give you. Thanks for your offer but the answer is 'no.'"

"Mr. Russell, the police don't have to be involved in this. I have instructions to forward my information to the investigating authorities should you decline."

"So what you're telling me is you have information that you are not giving to the investigating authorities, Mr. Garlington? What is this, a shakedown? Are you blackmailing me? Do me a favor and get off my property. Right now. And tell Bob Simmons to go fuck himself until he gets a warrant."

Garlington could have produced the pictures of the excavation in the grove but was under instruction not to—that was *Plan B*, should they need it. Garlington tucked the folder under his arm and left. Tim spent the next hour building two sawhorses, which he placed at the end of the driveway, blocking the entrance.

CHAPTER 120

1971

For two weeks, Tim continued to make significant progress on the house, but there was still so much to do. He began to stress about the pressure applied by Simmons and desperately wanted to hold him off until the house was sold, but his most recent calculations had him finishing the house in a year at best. In the first week of August, Tim began work on the roof. He was surprised to hear a knock on the door below him just after 11 am. It was a policeman.

"May I help you?" said Tim. The two sawhorses had become part of his ritual. Bob Simmons knew or should know that he required a warrant if he wanted to search the property, but this man wore a different uniform from a different jurisdiction. The patch on his sleeve read *Hampstead*. The police car was parked on the road behind the sawhorses.

"Hello. I am Sargent Vendasi of the Hampstead Police Department. Are you Timothy Russell?"

"Yes, I am."

"Mr. Russell, we received a package from a—Mr. Albert Garlington—linking your property to a person of our interest."

"Okay. Is her name Mildred Wells?"

"Yes, sir. She is wanted for questioning in the—" Tim interrupted Sargent Vendasi.

"—the murder of Eric Enrico, I know. Sargent, forgive me, but I know who sent Mr. Garlington, and this man is basically harassing me. He's a cop too, right here in Sanborn. I'd call the police if I could, well, maybe I still should. There has to be a law against this. Or get a lawyer or a restraining order. Sargent, do you know that the woman you're looking for died in 1863? Did Mr. Garlington Tell you that?"

"I'm afraid I don't know anything about that, Mr. Russell, we're just looking for the woman who killed Eric Enrico. We're starting over, investigating every lead. Maybe it's a crazy person pretending to be the deceased Mildred Wells, or another woman named Mildred Wells, or another woman with a completely different name, but at this point, it doesn't matter, we just want to solve the case. There's a rumor a cult was involved in Beverly Farms, so we don't know who we're dealing with. The fact is, there are a few reasons why the evidence points to this property."

"Because the three towns line up on a map, right?" Tim asked with a touch of fatigue in his voice.

"Yes, and the Gottlieb boy's description of the woman. And the possibility there is a cult devoted to this woman and her roots. And because of your conversations about Mildred Wells with Officer Simmons." A lump formed in Tim's throat. He had never come right out and admitted to Simmons that he knew about, had seen, or had dealt with Mildred, but there had been—*inferences*—and Simmons had relayed the information as fact.

"So, you want to take a look around." Tim's mind raced. He knew nothing about *the law*. Would he look overly suspicious? Would they get a warrant anyway? These were questions for a lawyer. Lawyers cost money. He bit his lip and did what he thought was right. "I'm sorry, I think I want to talk this over with some people before you come in and start ripping the house up."

"Mr. Russell, what can you tell me about this?" Sargent Vendasi produced two pictures from his back pocket. It was a before and after set; one picture showed Tim's rototilled gravesite, and the other showed it dug up with a spade that was stuck into the dirt pile for added effect. Both pictures were taken with a flashbulb in the dark.

Tim froze, knowing full well exactly who had trespassed on his property and taken the pictures. The apple doesn't fall too far from the tree. He felt a rush of anger, and for a short minute, knew what Mildred Wells must have felt when Elizabeth (and perhaps Emma) Simmons did the exact same thing. What was the penalty for unauthorized exhumation? Most importantly, how much would it cost to defend himself?

"As I said, Sargent, I want to speak with some people before we proceed."

CHAPTER 121

1971

Nathan Hoginski, producer of "Only If You Dare," put his best employee on the show's first original story—working title: "The Legend of Mildred Wells." David Bonnette yearned to be a player in Hollywood, but at only twenty-four years old, he hadn't yet hit his stride. Eager to climb the ladder, he threw himself headfirst into any task given.

He was bored with the *Boston Strangler* episode and welcomed the chance to go out on his own and create a story from scratch. He knew full well that embellishment was encouraged in his line of work to prevent people from getting up and changing the channel.

It was amazingly easy to get the materials from the Boston radio station, all he had to do was slip a fifty-dollar bill to a disgruntled employee named Brinko, and in an hour he was handed photocopies of everything in the original folder. Fifteen minutes later, he was driving up Interstate 93 on his way to Sanborn.

Bonnette stopped for gas right off of the Sanborn exit and asked the attendant if he knew anything about the so-called local legend, "Mildred Wells,"—the woman who had drowned her child and committed a series of murders right here in town in the 1800s. The man looked at him as if he had two heads and replied with a single word: "Nope."

From there, Bonnette went to the Town Hall and searched for Thomas Pike and *not* Mildred Wells—seeing as Thomas was originally from Sanborn. Newspaper clippings in Brinko's folder narrowed the search considerably. What he was surprised to find in the Town Hall was Mildred's attempt at erasing family history. All the records for the house on Lancaster Hill Road from 1860-1863 were smudged and scrubbed out. *Creepy*, he thought. He snapped a few pictures and continued; step one was complete. He knew where Mildred had lived.

While he was still at the Town Hall, he also looked up Elizabeth and Emma Simmons, where he was happily surprised to learn they had lived just down the road from Mildred. He didn't know if the Simmons information would lead to anything, but it was good to get the logistics and the lay-of-the-land. From there, he could better concoct his embellishments and put things in the order he wanted for broadcast.

When he had found all the legal paperwork he needed and had properly photographed everything (to be used for slow panning shots of documents on the TV screen), he drove out to the house itself. On the way, he noticed a mailbox on the left side of the road that read "Simmons." *Well, I'll be damned*, he thought—*Could it be this easy?*—and made a mental note to check back.

About a minute or so more down the road, there it was—unimposing for the most part, a farmhouse like most any other on a nice piece of land. He drove right by without slowing in case the owner was outside. On his second drive-by, he noticed the pond which he'd missed the first time because it was on the other side of a stone wall—*murder spot. Nice and creepy*, he thought.

Not yet ready to knock on the door, he drove on for a half-mile, parked on the side of the road, and got out. Using nearly the same path Bob Simmons had when he took the original photographs, he snuck through the woods, snapping pictures of the field, the pond, and the distant house as he went. Like everyone else who had ever entered the grove, he was taken aback by its sudden appearance even though he'd known it was coming. Bonnette was relieved it was so close to the road and easy to find.

In the last row, he found the open grave left by Bob Simmons. There were small bits of charred wood in the dirt pile, but no headstones. It was very hard to tell that it was ever a grave at all, rather looking like someone dug a halfassed hole in the forest. The overall vibe of the scene was a bit disappointing—the night photos gave it more of an edge. Perhaps he would sneak back with a portable video camera along with some other well-placed props to spice things up later on tonight.

CHAPTER 122
1971

Bob Simmons slept in that morning. The previous night had been an exceptionally boring shift, and he had even fallen asleep parked in his cruiser for forty minutes. Luckily, not a single car had passed. The crackling radio woke him up, and just in time—his shift was nearly over. The thought of being caught by the Chief, asleep in his cruiser after the Hampstead embarrassment, was unimaginable.

He was surprised by a knock on his door at 10 am. King went crazy, barking with ferocity. For a moment, he thought maybe someone had seen him sleeping overnight, and he was in trouble.

"Hold on, I'm coming!" he gave a quick look in the mirror and patted his hair down. Looking around on the floor, he found yesterday's pre-shift sweatpants and put them on. His tank top undershirt would have to do, pepperoni stain and all. Finally, he put on his holster and locked King in the spare bedroom.

Simmons pulled the curtain aside and found himself staring at a man he had never seen before. *Good,* he thought. *Maybe just a flat tire or something—but wouldn't that suck for me.* He opened the door a crack. "Can I help you?" he asked in a purposefully disinterested tone. Bonnette looked Simmons over. *Holster. Belly. Sweatpants. Stains.* The word *trash* came to mind.

"Yes, excuse me—but are you Officer Simmons?" The man had no doubt seen the Plymouth Fury police cruiser parked, not ten feet away. Simmons looked him over, especially his hands, which were in plain sight. He didn't appear to have a weapon.

"That's right. Who are you?"

"My name is David Bonnette, and I am the production assistant for the TV show 'Only If You Dare.' Have you heard of it?" Bob Simmons couldn't believe his ears—it was his favorite show.

"Yeah, I love that show,"—he opened the door wide—"how can I help you?"

"Mr. Sim-, uh, Officer Simmons, I'm researching a potential upcoming show. The working title is 'The Legend of Mildred Wells.' Are you familiar with that name?" Again, Bob Simmons was floored.

"Did Al Garlington send you?" If he had, Simmons owed his buddy Al a couple of beers.

"No, I'm afraid I don't know the man." Simmons made a mental note to fire Garlington. This TV show development was so much more than he had imagined, and it was *free*.

"Ah, no problem. You want to come in?" Bonnette cringed, reminding himself to focus on his long-term career.

"That would be great, thank you," he said reluctantly as he stepped into the house. It was as filthy as he might have imagined. *No woman has seen the inside of this house in decades*, he thought. "As I was saying, Officer, I'm researching a show on Mildred Wells, and there are a couple of 'Simmons' already in the story. Do you know who Mildred Wells was or who Elizabeth and Emma Simmons are?

"You're damn right I do. Mildred Wells killed them. And a lot of other people too. Elizabeth and Emma are ancestors of mine. I know a lot about Mildred Wells. You came to the right place."

CHAPTER 123

1971

"**C**an I get you a beer? That's about all I have in this place," Simmons offered.

"Oh, no thank you, Officer, I've got a long day ahead of me, but it sounds like my first stop was the right one. What can you tell me about Mildred Wells?"

"How'd you hear about her?" Simmons asked, already three-quarter-sure of the answer.

"We heard it on a Boston radio station. A DJ named 'Orfeo' talked about it on-air. It captured our attention." Simmons mentally patted himself on the back.

"Great. This *Mildred Wells* thing was a great injustice to my family and several other families in the Sanborn area. She killed— allegedly—as many as six people, including her son."

"Six people? And who were they?"

"Well, there's her son, who rumor has it she stuffed like a taxidermist and kept him upstairs; also the Chief of Police—both Henry and Annette Smith just a few years back, um, Emma Simmons, Elizabeth Simmons—how many is that?" he asked.

"Six. You got 'em all. That's quite the body count. And the police couldn't prove it—even though—she killed the Chief?"

"Guess not," said Simmons. "He fell off a ladder, but they

were allegedly dating at the time." Bonnette liked what he heard so far.

"You're saying she stuffed her son and kept him in the house?" Even though it wasn't true, it was an attention grabber—on a show like *Only if You Dare*, this was *gold*.

"That's what I was told. My family has always been a little gossipy, though—if you know what I mean." Bob Simmons began to think ahead, worrying Bonnette would discover that he and he alone was the keeper of the *Mildred Wells flame* and that if only one man kept the "legend" alive—they would drop the story.

"Officer Simmons, if you were me, what would be the first place you would look?"

"I'd want to take a good look around that property—the whole thing. I'd treat it like a crime scene and look for bones. I'd get dogs in there, and I'd check basements and crawl spaces and attics and such. I'd look in the woods too. See if there are any unmarked graves—or the appearance of graves being moved."

"Do you think the current owner would let us look around?" Simmons frowned.

"No, I don't think he would. I talked to him recently, and he's all worried about fixing it up and reselling it without making waves. It's all about *profit* for him, while some of us are still searching for loved ones." Bonnette loved the drama, it would be great for the show—but he did not believe that Officer Simmons had ever shed a tear for two women he had never met—family or not.

"So, it's possible Russell is afraid of you finding something?"

"Yes, I think so. And I think the boy who died in Hampstead is related to this whole thing too—but Russell won't cooperate, and there's not much I can do about it right now."

"Officer Simmons, do you mind if I ask you a personal question?" *Uh-oh*, thought Bob.

"Go ahead."

"Did you send the packet to the radio station?" Bob Simmons hesitated, then gambled.

"Yes." He waited for Bonnette's reaction.

"That's fine. The fact that you're a cop lends this story credence. You'll look good on camera—we'll only use you for 'authoritative' shots. Do you have any more materials you could share with me? More like the stuff you gave the radio station?" Simmons breathed a sigh of relief. The story was *alive*. This kid didn't care where the information came from; he just wanted *juice*. Simmons stood up and left the room for a second, returning with the scrapbook.

"There's a lot of stuff in here. The whole 'Legend,' if you will. I bet you'll be able to spin this thing up pretty good. If you have any questions, here's my phone number. I work the third shift most nights. What's your plan?"

"I'm going to sneak into the grove tonight and film some *B-Roll*. I went in there today in the daylight, and it wasn't creepy enough. In the meantime, I'll read this scrapbook and start fleshing out a show. We might even have more than one with all this material. We'll have to see what we get for ratings on the first show, however." *'More than one show'*—thought Simmons, ecstatically.

"You're just going to sneak on his property, film it, and use the footage?"

"Only for reference, yes—but we'll use that footage to build a replica set back in Hollywood. That way, he can't sue us for trespassing, etcetera."

"Hey, don't let anyone know I took those pictures on his property either," said Simmons.

"Hell no, Bob. You're the only thing keeping this story going!"

CHAPTER 124

1971

Tim stared at the phone for several minutes before gathering the strength to pick it up. A year and a half of bad memories came flooding back when he finally heard the voice at the other end.

"Hey, Timmy, what's up? Are you keeping it in your pants? Or are you calling because you're ready to say goodbye to the latest Mrs. Russell? Just kidding, buddy—what can I do for you? How's New Hampshire?" It was Frank Turnbull, his divorce lawyer.

"Hey Frank, no—no lady problems as yet, anyway. I need— you're not going to believe this, but I need some help. You're not just a divorce lawyer, correct? And you're licensed in New Hampshire?"

"That's right. I do it all. Personal Injury, real estate, whatever you need. I am licensed in New Hampshire—you have to be when you practice so close to the state line. I'll see when I can fit you in, although I'm pretty busy. You happened to catch me at the perfect time—secretary's on lunch break." Tim had learned long ago to be dubious of Frank's small talk. He was a good lawyer, but he wasn't necessarily all that busy. And if he *was* busy, you would not get a call-back.

"Well, I'm not sure if you heard about the boy who was killed in the woods in Hampstead or not, but the Hampstead cops came knocking on my door yesterday, and they asked if they could take a look around." Dead silence on the other end, and then:

"Tim, maybe we should meet face-to-face. You never know nowadays, I—" Tim cut him off.

"I didn't kill the kid or anything like that. It's a very long story, and I don't have time to drive down and meet you. They want to search my property for signs that the killer was once here, but the problem is—I did a little digging in the woods recently, and I don't want them to know."

"What are you talking about?" Frank asked, for once not trying to crack a joke.

"I found two old graves in the woods on my property, and I *got rid of them*. I didn't want them here anymore. It turns out it might be some sort of evidence, for the Hampstead thing—I'm not sure. Then the cop knocked on my door, and he had pictures of the spot I rototilled in the woods. I think another cop snuck onto my property and took the pictures."

"Oh, wow. I wish you hadn't said that over the phone just now, but I think I can get the recording thrown out if there is one. Is your property sparkling clean now? No chance you left anything behind?" Tim thought hard for a moment. Elmer's bones were all within the confines of his coffin, and he had carefully transferred each and every one of them—painstakingly—into the burlap bag. Mildred, of course, took all of her bones with her, wherever she was.

"I'm sure. The bones are—elsewhere. I dumped the headstones in a lake in Massachusetts, and I rototilled the entire sight. The problem is if they see that, they'll think I'm covering something up." Frank Turnbull was quiet for almost a minute.

"Who took the pictures they showed you—*them?* Because they'd need a warrant for that. I can get that thrown out easily."

"No, not officially. The cop who showed me the pictures was from Hampstead, but I think a Sanborn cop—my neighbor—took the pics and sent them to Hampstead anonymously. I'm not sure, but that's what I think."

"And what are the pictures of, exactly? Just the spot you dug up? Or the entire surrounding area?"

"Just the spot I dug up. The pictures were taken at night. He snuck onto my property. He re-dug the grave again, too, to make it look sinister or whatever. There was no hole before he got there. I covered it and rototilled it. You can only see what the flashbulb lit, and it's all staged."

"Okay, that's good, buddy, ha-ha, you had me nervous there for a second like you were a graverobber or something—a necrophiliac. I'm relieved, man, I'm relieved! But I'm going to make your life easy. Go to a bookstore and buy yourself a book called 'Forest Gardening,' then throw the receipt away. My sister-in-law is a real hippie, and she does this sort of thing. Says it's better for the environment and all that crap. The forest is self-fertilizing, blah, blah, blah.

But even before you buy the book, take your 'tiller discretely back into the woods and rototill about five to ten times the land you already turned over. And rototill the gravesite again too to make it look like it was all done at the same time. Then go to a greenhouse and buy some spinach or collard greens or broccoli and replant them out there. Maybe some other fall vegetables too. I don't know much about what grows when—just ask the greenhouse. And there's your excuse right there. What exactly are you afraid of anyway? What crime do you think you've committed?"

"Well, mostly, I just want to avoid negative attention. I need to sell this place in about a year, and I don't want to upset the marketability. But I thought that it's probably illegal to exhume a body, or maybe they could hit me up for grave robbing or something—all problems that I don't need."

"Well, don't worry yourself too much, Timmy. I'll have to brush up on my exhumation laws, but it sounds to me that even if you were found guilty, you'd only pay a fine. Relax, this doesn't sound like a big deal to me." For all of Frank's obnoxious ways, a wave of relief washed over Tim. Maybe the police involvement wasn't the hazard that he had made it out to be.

CHAPTER 125

1971

As soon as they hung up, Tim jumped in his truck and drove to Franklin, where he'd rented the rototiller to turn over the gravesite. Jake's Small Engine Repair was a combination repair shop and rental center. Tim found the exact machine he had rented last time and made an offer to purchase. Jake accepted the offer, and Tim's next stop was Abbott's greenhouse, where he filled the bed of the pickup with vegetable seedlings. *More unexpected expenses,* he thought. *Hopefully, it will save on the grocery bill.*

CHAPTER 126

1971

David Bonnette entered the woods just after midnight along with the on-screen host of "Only If You Dare," Simone Infante. The two of them lugged the video camera, a spade, a single flashlight, a bouquet, and Simone's on-camera blazer. The props were reference pieces for the set designers back in Hollywood. Those guys didn't know their ass from their elbow about directing, and David had to spell it out for them. They built exactly what they saw in the reference video—no more, no less, every single time.

Simone was unhappy with this week's assignment, but she was paid well as the third host in the history of *OIYD*, so she kept her mouth shut. Branches brushed her cheek as David forged on ahead of her, holding their shared flashlight. They had done other night shoots before, but this was the first time they had to sneak onto a property or travel deep into the woods. Because of this, they left the official cameraman back in the hotel, and David promised a short twenty-minute shoot.

It was creepy, visiting a gravesite in the woods, and the fear factor doubled when the grove opened up. The long dark hallways were overly intense, so she caught up with David and grabbed the flashlight so she could shine the beam up and down each row as they passed through. They kept the talking to a minimum, and

David waved her in the direction of the back corner. Now that Simone held the only light, David slowed his pace and walked a half step behind.

It was quiet, the only sound being the soft crunch of the spruce needles beneath their feet. The bugs were bad too, and at one point, a large moth found the side of her face, buzzing like a helicopter until she dropped the bouquet and waved it away.

"What is it?" David whispered.

"A bug flew into my ear!" she replied breathlessly, picking up the bouquet. She missed David's eye-roll. He, too, felt the anxiety. This visit was much different than his daylight trip. He asked for the flashlight back, and she yielded. One by one, they cut through the rows. David knew he'd reached the last row when the flashlight began to pick up green leaves. They took a right and followed the corridor to the end—but something was different, and he wondered for a moment if he had the wrong spot.

"What the hell?"

"What?" asked Simone.

"This is different. It wasn't like this earlier today." Simone looked ahead. It looked like—a garden. There were even plant stakes in the ground labeled "lettuce," "spinach," "turnips," etc.

"It doesn't look like a grave to me," she added. David clenched his teeth at her overly-obvious remark, and the anger crawled his scalp—but he held his tongue for the most part.

"It's not a grave anymore, Simone—but thanks." He wondered for a quick second if it wasn't time to begin searching for the show's next host—Simone was beautiful, but she was a little stiff on camera, and the ratings hadn't jumped as they'd hoped they would. Just then, a mosquito bit his neck. He slapped it and examined the splotch of blood in his palm. *Gardens aren't scary,* he thought. He snapped a few pictures. He'd have to drag the set designers through it, to get it the way he wanted it, no ifs, ands, or buts. "Alright, let's get the hell out of here. The shoot is over."

CHAPTER 127

1971

Tim finished the cut and shut down the saw. Progress on the house had suffered due to the full day of impromptu gardening, and he hadn't had time to finish the roof. Mildred had become a distant memory—it was fully four months since they'd seen her, and his daily concerns centered more around another police visit. To be better forewarned, he kept the sawhorses at the end of the driveway. If someone wanted to visit, they would have to park on the street. It was too late in the day to be on the roof, so he found something to do inside.

He wondered what had happened to the Hampstead Police. Would they be back? Could they get a warrant, or were they denied by the judge? Bob Simmons had all but disappeared, but Tim felt in his bones that his silence was deafening. All-day long, he worked with the three-headed monster of Hampstead, Simmons, and Mildred hanging over his head. *That Gottlieb kid must have been wrong*, he told himself.

As soon as the ring of the saw blade dissipated, he heard a knocking. At first, he wasn't sure where it was coming from, so he descended to the kitchen and retrieved the shotgun, which was still wrapped in its blue dish towel. Moving quickly, he placed it next to the telephone in the living room, hidden from view but ready just in case. By now, he knew the knocking came from the front door at the bottom of the stairs. He peered out of the living room window and saw two people he didn't recognize.

The first was a distractingly beautiful twenty-something woman, clearly overdressed for rural New Hampshire. The other was a man, roughly the same age as the woman, but dressed in casual attire. The woman's hair, makeup, and manicure were perfect, yet overdone—she stood out like a plastic rose in a garden of weeds. Tim opened the door.

"May I help you?"

"Hi there,"—the woman did the talking—"are you the owner of the house?" Tim wondered if they were Jehovah's Witnesses, but he didn't see any pamphlets.

"Yes."

"Mr. Russell, my name is Simone Infante, and my colleague and I are from the TV show 'Only If You Dare.' Do you mind if I ask you a few questions?" Tim noticed immediately that she had used his name.

"You're from a TV show? Like the news? Are you from Channel Nine?" Simone smiled proudly, imagining she was about to blow Tim's mind.

"Ha—no, we're not out of Manchester, Mr. Russell. We're a *nationally syndicated program*, and we're here from Hollywood. We have over a million viewers each week. You've never heard of us?" David Bonnette cringed. It had been a colossal mistake to let Simone do the talking, but Nate Hoginski had suggested it.

"I don't understand,"—said Tim—"what are you doing here?" Bonnette cut off Simone just as she was about to answer.

"Mr. Russell, my name is David Bonnette, and I help produce the show. We are in the area looking for the potential makings of a new episode. We were in Boston producing a show on the Boston Strangler and heard about a woman from these parts with a particularly dark history. We did some research and tracked her back to your property—this used to be her house. Her name was Mildred Wells. Were you aware of that?"

Butterflies took flight in Tim's stomach as he imagined his investment and all of his hard work, broadcast nationwide. A million viewers—more than the entire population of New Hampshire. His property was on the brink of becoming unsellable.

"Uh, no, I don't believe in that sort of stuff. I'm just trying to get this place fix—"

"You don't believe in what sort of stuff, Mr. Russell?" asked Bonnette.

"I just don't pay attention to that stuff. Boston Strangler, ghosts, this woman, whoever she was. I'm not into these types of documentaries. How did you get my name, anyway?"

"As I said, we've been researching this episode, and part of that research was spending time in the town hall looking up records. So you're fixing this place up, huh?" Bonnette asked.

"Right. What can I do for you, folks? I hate to be rude, but I'm way behind."

"You know, Mr. Russell, I bet our show could help you sell this place. You'd be surprised by the money out there. You might even be able to sell it and make a tidy profit without even finishing it. Make a quick profit and move on to something else." Tim paused. Bonnette's idea sounded wonderful—if it were true.

"What do you want, Mr. Bonnette? Do you want to film the place and put it on your TV show? Set up cameras and record every shadow that moves? Brew up a good story? How can I be sure this will help me?" Simone Infante's head bobbed back-and-forth as if she were watching a tennis match.

"Yes, I'd love to film your property and the house. It would make a much better program. Rumor is, she drowned her son right there in that pond, so that would be a major set-piece. We'll talk about the death of the Chief of Police too, and of course the entire background of Thomas Pike."

David Bonnette purposefully left out the parts about tying

everything into the Hampstead murder and the Beverly Farms fire—and that Mildred Wells supposedly *"still roamed these parts."* The suggestion that a murderous ghost might still be haunting the property might not be to Tim Russell's liking.

As soon as Bonnette mentioned 'Chief of Police,' Tim knew he'd already talked with Bob Simmons and seen the scrapbook. Tim also knew that there was little to be found in the town hall and the library, meaning that Bob Simmons might as well be the executive producer of this hit-piece-to-be. He had never seen "Only If You Dare," but knew the type of show it was. Without a doubt, it was trashy, *tabloid television.*

"I'm going to pass, Mr. Bonnette. I'm not sure your show will help me. Thanks for asking first, though."

Irritated and on their way back to the car, David Bonnette spit into a large patch of poison ivy on the side of the road. He wasn't discouraged; this was the essence of his job. There was more than one way to skin a cat.

CHAPTER 128

1971

By late September, their visitation routine had taken shape. Every Friday night after Tim had driven down to Massachusetts to pick up the girls, they would get takeout and eat dinner together, catching up on the previous two weeks. On occasion, they'd drive to Laconia after dinner to watch a movie.

Saturday was usually the centerpiece of the weekend, and Tim and Holly did their best to come up with something fun. If it wasn't three or four hours at Funspot, it was the ice cream buffet at Kellerhaus. If the weather was good, they might drive over to Ellacoya State Park, a nice sandy beach on Lake Winnipesaukee.

Sunday morning was fun for a different reason—everyone went their separate ways somewhat and unwound in their own unique ways. The girls liked it because they got to explore. They didn't have much of a yard back in Amesbury, and Sheila didn't have the time to keep up with the amount they had any more. Dad's property was better—it was huge and had many different facets—the barn, the pond, the woods, the grove—even the house itself was big enough for an excellent game of hide-and-seek when the weather was bad. Dad had also calmed down considerably over the past couple of months and didn't seem as uptight as their first four or five visits.

Tim took advantage of this Sunday time to start his work week right after lunch. It was a nice way to get a jump on things—he'd put in a couple of hours setting up for Monday while the girls played on their own before driving them back. Holly would either lend a hand or sit at the kitchen table, planning out her week.

CHAPTER 129

1971

Durham, New Hampshire

Andrew Vaughn stuck his hands in his front pockets as he walked through the quad. He was excited about his thriving little business—selling drugs to his fellow students was profitable—and *so easy*. In his left pocket was what was left of the speed, and in his right pocket was a thick roll of cash. The pot was all gone—*sold out*—and he would use a good portion of this cash to reinvest.

Andrew came from a small town two hours north called Sugar Hill, and he enjoyed being away from it. Being this close to seacoast New Hampshire and only an hour from Boston was a genuine thrill in comparison—*hell*—just to have a local movie theater was a revelation. Sugar Hill sat nestled just outside White Mountain National Forest and Franconia Notch—beautiful country if you were a tourist but lacking if you were young and horny. Sugar Hill was a beautiful place—*if you were over sixty-five*, thought Andrew. Durham and its self-sustaining supply of women was exactly where he wanted to be.

Andrew's parents were Markus and Colleen Vaughn, and they owned a funeral home in Sugar Hill. They found the farm originally while vacationing—both were doctors from the Boston area yearning for a change of pace. It was a quaint New England farm with an adjoining apple orchard, and they renamed it the *Foggy Orchard Funeral Home.* They hoped one day for their two children (Andrew and his older sister Rebecca) to inherit what they'd created—but disappointedly, Andrew didn't seem to be interested.

Rebecca *was* interested in taking over the family business, however, and that left Andrew the odd man out. Rebecca graduated from UNH six years before and now worked full-time. Mom and Dad were very proud of her, as she had always been a model child. Their greatest worry was—what would become of Andrew?

Andrew was a very bright boy—perhaps the smartest in the family—but he had always been problematic. He got bored easily, was immature, and had a dark side. He was caught with marijuana early in his senior year of high school, and luckily Markus's good friend John Schutt happened to be the school superintendent and helped sweep the problem under the rug. Privately, the Vaughns worried that Andrew's ambitions would make Rebecca's life a living hell. She was such a good kid and so proud to be able to help them run the business—she did not deserve to have his reckless lifestyle sabotage hers.

Andrew saw the campus police turn onto College Road, so he took a quick right toward Hitchcock Hall. The campus police were everywhere and were most likely not after him or anyone in particular, but it was best to be safe. If he could make it inside, he could get lost inside and exit from any number of alternate doors. The car pulled over right behind him. Too close, he thought—and picked up the pace.

"Halt! You in the plaid shirt! Stop!" Andrew pretended he didn't hear. There were dozens of students in the quad—he could still play dumb—only forty more feet.

"*Andrew Vaughn*, halt." Panic flushed his face, *they'd used his name*—and he ran. The police didn't call out again—they didn't have to. Officer Paul Roberge was an ex track star from right here at UNH. In less than ten seconds, Andrew was down and cuffed. He recognized several students (and customers) as they watched him get taken away. *This was bad.*

CHAPTER 130

1971

Finally, after a four-month wait, she heard him. He walked with a noticeable limp and crunched through the forest, much noisier than the others had. It was Bardelli, the scientist, the man who spent much of his time hibernating to fix self-inflicted wounds.

His death was anticlimactic, and a measure of satisfaction was lost in killing her last peer as a result—like shooting fish in a barrel. To do it, she hid behind a tree, popped out at the last second, and brought down the hatchet, followed by the knife. She'd become quite skilled at murder. Bardelli had barely enough time to be surprised. He looked at her like an old man returning from the corner store—almost disinterested. In seconds, she was the last of her kind.

There was a satisfaction—a goal achieved—and it felt good. Mildred had destroyed Gideon Walker *and* his legacy. The farm was gone. The abductions were no more. She meditated for a moment over the memory of her mother and her sister, the closest thing to a spiritual moment in as long as she could remember.

There was only one more thing that had to be done before Phase Two could begin. She stomped down the hill, through the forest to the property. There was no reason to be quiet anymore;

her hunt was over. When she reached the shed, she pulled out the kitchen match in her dress pocket and struck it.

When the building was engulfed, she knelt, then sat back on her heels, savoring the closure. She watched it burn for twenty minutes until she heard the first siren, then she reached into her dress pocket and pulled out the beads for final confirmation. She was, indeed, the last revenant.

CHAPTER 131

1971

Mildred crossed into Northfield, New Hampshire, just after midnight—nearly home. The coyotes were out; she had seen three in the last two hours. Most of the predators left her alone once they got a good sniff, so she let them be. Forty minutes outside of Sanborn, she stumbled upon a den where she found a rabid male, near death.

The other coyotes had abandoned the area, waiting for him to die. The poor animal emerged from the hidden entrance suddenly and attempted to bite Mildred across the wrist. She dropped the Book of Shadows and put him down mercifully. After she returned the blade, she crouched down between the boulders and peered in.

It was a dead-end cave, shallow, with just enough shelter from the elements for a mother with pups. The rabid coyote had come here to die, and Mildred had helped him along. She took the opportunity to leave the Book of Shadows there and placed a large rock over it for protection. The rest of the band would no doubt return.

CHAPTER 132

1971

Six months had passed since she'd laid eyes on the house, and now, here she stood again in the corner of the field, doing just that. The slaying of Gideon Walker and the revenants had given her satisfaction, but only temporarily. Young Mary had been avenged—but Mildred as yet had not. Her anger still burned, and she was slightly surprised it had not weakened at all.

Tim Russell and Holly Burns were the reasons for her return—the reasons she'd been robbed of eternal peace. She had to promise herself to stay calm and recalculate the slowest, most painful way to carry it out. She, after all, waited over one hundred years, only to have the rug pulled out from under her—it was best not to rush things and make sure they turned out as intended. Perhaps waiting until his hard work on the house was finished would add an extra ounce of pain. She decided that before she made any final decisions, she would listen-in again—and before that, she would check out the neighborhood.

CHAPTER 133

1971

The Simmons compound was made up of three houses on a hundred-foot driveway. Decades back, the family had nailed a homemade sign to the tree at the end of the driveway that read, *Simmons Road*. The driveway had never been declared an official road by the town, nor did it show on a map. Mildred saw that the nearest house had a police car in front and decided to save it for last. She'd never been here despite living just down the road because she'd never had reason to—*they always seemed to come to her.*

"Simmons Road" was for all intents and purposes, a dump. The house on the left had an old toilet and a rusted out automobile in the back yard. Ugly, unkempt lawn ornaments cluttered all three yards, and a toppled birdbath had fallen from one overgrown lawn into the driveway.

The house on the left was also completely dark and looked as if it might collapse at any time—it had been Emma Simmons' house and hadn't had a resident for more than twenty years. Bob Simmons currently used it as an unheated storage shed.

The house at the far end of the driveway had a glowing blue light coming from the living room. Ralph Simmons, Bob's father, was an eighty-nine-year-old night owl that more often than not slept the entire night in his recliner. Mildred peered into the window unseen. She wondered for a moment if he was a Simmons from birth or had married one, then decided she didn't care.

Bob Simmons resided in the house with the cruiser parked outside, and he too watched television alone. There hadn't been a woman on Simmons Road since Jenny Simmons (now Jenny Incatasciato) had packed her things and left fourteen years ago. Mildred saw him through the window in his living room. Now she had confirmation that he was the man who had come to Beverly Farms and saw her in the tree—the man who left just as he was about to die.

Nosy like his ancestors, she thought. He must think he knows something about me, or he wouldn't have bothered to drive to Beverly Farms.

CHAPTER 134

1971

The windows were dark in her old house, and Russell's truck was gone. It was all hers for the *first time*—tonight there was no Tim, no Holly, no Thomas—and no Elmer. Oddly, she felt the sting of loneliness, despite the fact she had been alone for more than a century—but shook it off because there were things to do. She walked up the driveway and tried for a moment to imagine what it had looked like in 1860, just after completion. The memory wouldn't come—gone forever, with the rest of her happiness.

There was a newness to the outside—the roof—Russell had been busy during the summer months to prepare for winter. It looked good; she had to admit. She tried the doors gently, being careful not to break them. When she couldn't find an unlocked entry point, Mildred scaled the building where the porch and main building met and began to try the turret windows. The last was unlocked, and she let herself in.

The house felt empty. Mildred knew there was no chance Elmer would appear. Without him, despite their uneven history, the house—without him—was just a house. Russell had made much of it unrecognizable—but that didn't bother her. There was no room for sentiment. The answer to her happiness could not come from the past.

She found the sawed-off shotgun in the kitchen drawer but left it there, memorizing its location. After that, she climbed the stairs to the turret and began reading Tim's files.

CHAPTER 135

1971

Tim's work had progressed to the hardwood floor in the room closest to the road. It was all finish work now inside, but there was quite a bit of it to do. The good news was he'd winterized the outside and was ready for winter. Bad weather would be coming soon.

Tim shut the saw off and listened; there was an engine in the driveway—the unmistakable sound of a Volkswagen Beetle— Holly's car. Holly left work most days at 5 pm, and Tim worked until nearly eight. In recent weeks she'd begun showing up more, perhaps a sign that she too was on the way to forgetting about—*the things that used to make them worry.*

She helped Tim in her spare time more and more—anything to get the house on the market as soon as possible. Things were excellent between the two of them relationship-wise, but she knew he was increasingly nervous about his money situation and couldn't wait to put that mood-killer behind them. *Nobody likes a nervous Honey.* Tim opened the front door to greet her.

"Whoa—it's still warm out! What is this, an Indian summer?" said Tim. The sky was dark, but the temperature was a balmy seventy-four degrees—a near heatwave for October.

"Yes, it is. We're supposed to get colder next week, though. I heard it on the radio on the way over."

"How was your day?"

"An average workday. I'll take it. *Average* is good—it could always be worse, right? What about you? Almost done with the floor?" Holly entered the house and took a peek. "Oh, nice. You got a lot done today. That looks great. Now, where do you want me?" Tim paused and stared with a wolfish grin on his face. "No, that's later, Tim. At my house. Come on, put me to work, I'm getting hungry, and I don't want to think about it. And if I sit down, I won't want to get back up." Tim set her up with painting materials just across the hall in the living room. In between saw cuts, they conversed.

"Whatever happened with the Hampstead Police? Did they give up on looking around this place?" Holly asked. Tim sighed. He was juggling problems, and that particular ball was still in the air.

"I don't know, but if they come back with a warrant, I think I'm in good shape. Frank set me up with that garden idea, and I'm starting to get spinach out there. I hope you like spinach."

"And what about that TV show? Did you ever hear anything from them?" Another proverbial ball in the air.

"God, no. Bob Simmons put them up to it, I just know it. He's such a pain in my ass. I hope they realized it would be a boring story and gave up. I'm not letting them in, no matter what."

"I can't imagine knocking on someone's door asking to film their entire house. I wouldn't want the whole country looking into my living room! I don't blame you."

"I agree. Can you imagine what Sheila would do with that information? She'd make my life a living hell. She'd find something on camera and make a big deal out of it, just jealous my house was on TV. She's *that* kind of person. She would love to be filmed—loves that sort of attention."

"Not to mention she wouldn't let the girls come up here anymore without a fight. She'd say the girls were traumatized by spirits or something. I bet if they put Bob Simmons on camera, she'll track him down to compare notes on you. Those two would be fast friends. Even if she doesn't believe in ghosts." Tim hung his head. Holly was right.

"I don't know if she believes in ghosts or not, but she'll pretend she does if it makes my life more difficult."

"Speaking of the girls, has Sheila changed the pick-up time or location for this Friday?"

"Are you trying to depress me, Honey? It's only Wednesday. Give her time. You know she likes to throw her monkey wrenches later in the week. We'll find out last minute—remember?"

"Whoops, I don't want to depress you—you're right—it's only Wednesday. One day at a time."

"I can't afford to fight her right now. I'll have to, though, eventually. As soon as this place sells, I'll have to *invest* in my fucking freedom just because she doesn't want to get along. We need a new divorce agreement—she's not following the one we have. Maybe I can get her to drive half of the time, too, so she knows the sanctity of pick-up and drop-off times." *Uh oh*, Holly thought. She'd opened a can of worms.

"Honey, forget what I said. Hey, I have an idea. Let's shut down early tonight, and I'll take you out to dinner. We'll have some wine, some good food, we'll go to bed early, and you can get a fresh start tomorrow morning. What do you say?" She winked when he looked across the hall at her. She noticed he looked tired. Almost six months of ten-to-twelve-hour days, along with additional Sheila-stress was taking its toll.

"Come on, Tim, let's go. It will do you some good. You haven't taken a full day off since the last Saturday the girls were here. Twelve days. Call it a *sexual spa day*." Tim's eyes widened.

"Wow, you should be a salesperson for a living."

"Or maybe not. I sold you this house, didn't I?" He crossed the hall and hugged her.

"Let me lock everything, and we'll go." The house creaked on Tim's way back through the kitchen, but he didn't hear it.

He also missed the flies on the kitchen window that looked out over the back yard.

If he had used the bathroom in the kitchen, he would have heard them—hundreds of them buzzing up in the dark turret.

CHAPTER 136

1971

The only *good* news following Andrew's arrest was that the lawyer the Vaughns hired successfully kept him out of jail. The bad news was that Andrew was officially kicked out of UNH and back in Sugar Hill, unhappy and making their lives miserable. He was a black hole sucking the life out of the three of them, who had all been very happy before his return—having to take back the twenty-one-year-old manchild before his time was disruptive, to say the least.

Andrew seldom left his bedroom, claiming depression. He had no desire to take part in the day to day operations of the family business. The family had employed him most of the previous summers, and he had served a full legal apprenticeship at the funeral home before he had even graduated high school. It took him until just after his freshman year at UNH to realize he wasn't interested in pursuing the family business.

He hated comforting grieving families. He hated the wakes. He hated that his whole family had been on call twenty-four hours a day his entire life to do things like pick up dead bodies in the middle of the night. He hated dealing with sad people or worse,… angry people. But those were not the real dealbreakers.

What the rest of the family didn't know (because he never

dared tell them), was that he was afraid of Foggy Orchard. He was afraid every time a child died. And he was afraid of car accidents, and the *restorations* that followed. He'd witnessed several pacemaker removals and one artificial hip before cremations. He hated "setting the features," which meant massaging the dead person's face into a look of serenity. He hated sewing the mouth shut and inserting spiky "eye caps" under the eyelids to keep them from opening.

The building itself was ominous and intimidating. It was a large Victorian mansion, nearly eleven thousand square feet with a tall tower protruding out of the center of it. Andrew had always stayed away as much as possible. Rebecca thought it was quaint and often begged him to play hide and seek in the off hours, but he always declined.

He'd once been locked in the building unintentionally at age ten when he lingered in the bathroom too long. The family had locked up and walked back to the home across the parking lot. The office was locked, and he couldn't get to the telephone. He huddled by the door listening to the deafening silence. Every minute or so, a mysterious knock or click coming from somewhere up the stairs. There had been enough dead people in there to haunt it for a thousand years if they were so inclined. Andrew did his best not to think of these things as he waited a long twenty minutes before the rest of the family realized he wasn't in his bedroom.

The one incident that still gave him nightmares happened when he was fourteen. Andrew was about to assist with an embalmment when his father had to leave to take a phone call. It was the first time he had ever been left alone with a dead person. The deceased was an eighty-four-year-old man lying on the table stark naked.

For some reason, the lack of clothing made the corpse even more intimidating. Andrew tried to look away but would not allow himself to do so completely. Suddenly he heard a gurgling to his left and sensed motion in his peripheral vision. Panicking, he spun his head to witness the corpse rising slowly to a sitting position, a guttural churning coming from deep within.

Andrew screamed, fearing for his life. One of the man's eyes slowly opened, and the lifeless orb came to rest on him. He wondered if the eye could actually see. *Funeral homes are gateways—gray areas—*he thought, just as the corpse was about to stand. *Was his father already dead?*

Suddenly Markus ran back into the room—*and began to laugh.*

"Oh no, Mr. Fenton, no, no, no, lie back down. We'll take good care of you! But it's time to rest." Laughing, Andrew's father laid his full weight across the corpse and leveled the body out. A cacophony of escaping gas and gurgling bubbles filled the room. Andrew couldn't believe his eyes. His father turned to him with a huge grin on his face, laughing maniacally. *What was happening?*

"Welcome to Foggy Orchard, Andrew! Bad timing on that phone call. That was your first time, wasn't it? It's okay; it's rigor mortis. It happens once in a while. They'll sit up if you aren't careful. He scared you good, didn't he? Your sister's gonna love this story." Andrew didn't see the humor.

Little did he know that his life would change drastically in only eleven days.

CHAPTER 137

1971

Bob Simmons pulled into his driveway after another uneventful eleven-to-seven shift. He'd seen only sixteen moving cars over the eight boring hours. He'd gotten into the habit of counting them for lack of anything better to do. To make matters worse, every single one of them happened either before midnight or after 5 am. From midnight to 5, he might as well have been on the moon.

He pulled onto Simmons Road and parked beside his house, killing the engine, and grabbing his hat and clipboard. As he was about to open the door, he passed his eyes over his father's junkyard of a property—faded plastic flamingos, stolen milk crates, and his father's last recliner—*same old shit*. He'd have to be the one to clean it all up someday, but the inspiration had yet to strike him. Then, out behind the right-hand corner of the house, he saw her against the trees.

As still as a statue, she stared back—as if she'd been waiting. The pale white face, the long hair, the black farm dress—exactly what the Gottlieb boy had described. Mildred Wells in the flesh.

"What the fuck!" he said out loud to himself as he scrambled out of his cruiser to draw his pistol. In doing so, he moved approximately two feet to his left, and the corner of the house obscured her. Instinctively he ran to the front of the cruiser and knelt, pistol raised. She'd moved—and was gone. Simmons circled wide to the right, hoping for a favorable angle. Finally, he reached a vantage point where he could see his father's entire back yard, and still, she was nowhere to be seen.

Panting, he ran to the front door of his father's house and with his key, unlocked the door. His father lay in his recliner—asleep, but alive and untouched. He checked the windows in all directions with no luck.

Sweating heavily, he ran back out into the yard to check his own house. King, his dog, was gone. There was no sign of incident—the door was even still locked. For the next forty-five minutes, he lived on-edge, running between houses, looking behind him, and checking behind broken lawn ornaments. Finally, he came to accept that she knew exactly who he was—and exactly what she was doing.

CHAPTER 138

1971

"Yes, I need to talk to David Bonnette, and tell him it's urgent!"

Unfortunately for Bob Simmons, Bonnette didn't call him right back. He paced as he waited, his precious recovery time shot. He hadn't slept a wink in almost thirty hours, and his next shift was starting soon. He didn't want to begin to think about how hard the night was going to be to get through. Finally, near 9 pm, the phone rang, startling him badly.

"Bonnette, what the hell?! I called you eleven hours ago!"

"Relax, I'm busy out here. I'm working three shows at once, all in different phases. I'm scouting for one, shooting another and editing a third. What do you need?"

"I *saw* her! She was in my yard, waiting for me to get home! I saw Mildred Wells!" Bonnette didn't know how to process the information. He was up to his eyeballs in work, the Mildred Wells show somewhat on the back burner, and to top it all off, he didn't believe in ghosts.

"You what? You saw her?" He didn't know what to say, so he repeated what Simmons had told him, stalling for time.

"Yeah, didn't you hear me? She's stalking me! She was staring right at me, then she disappeared. My dog is gone. You've got to get

340

a cameraperson out here. I told you she was back!" Bonnette closed his eyes and pinched the bridge of his nose with his thumb and forefinger. Paying a cameraperson to fly out to New Hampshire for a week or two was not in the budget right now.

"Did you get a picture? I can't just send somebody, Bob. Everybody's busy. I need proof first." Bonnette thought for a moment. *The Legend of Mildred Wells* could use a shot in the arm, and anything this country bumpkin could snap a picture of, whether it was a shadow, or a shape or something else, might help move things up in the queue.

"Hell, no, I didn't get a picture! I've just got the little pocket camera with the flashbulb. I wasn't expecting her, I—"

"Hold on, Bob; I have an idea. Everything's closed out there now, right? Let me make some calls tomorrow, and I'll call you back. I'll wake up early and make some arrangements. I'll call you at about 10 am your time tomorrow morning."

Bob Simmons, extremely upset and overtired, brought a wind-up alarm clock with him in the cruiser. He set it every twenty minutes, and every time it went off, he reset it again. Even so, he didn't need it. Though he kept the cruiser's doors locked, he couldn't relax—imagining the horror of waking to a dark figure outside his driver's side window.

CHAPTER 139

1971

After he barricaded his front door and pulled all the curtains, Bob Simmons sat on the edge of his bed, shaking from fatigue, yet still, he could not relax. Would barricades be enough to warn him if Mildred Wells's ghost showed up again? He didn't know; so tired he couldn't think straight. He'd been awake so long he was beginning to hallucinate. Every shadow, every curtain, every single thing was starting to look like it might be the woman in the dress. Fearing for his long term health, he grabbed a three-year-old bottle of Nyquil from the medicine cabinet and chugged a third of it.

Exactly two hours later, the telephone rang. Simmons jumped groggily at the sound and answered on the second ring; it was Bonnette.

"I rented a video camera for you, but you have to go pick it up. It's in Manchester on—"

"Manchester? Why not Concord? Can you—"

"No, the Concord camera store didn't have what I wanted. You're lucky it wasn't Boston—but here's the deal. If you can get a shot of—whatever you think you saw—it will be *gold*. I don't care if it's long-distance bullshit like Bigfoot or the Loch Ness Monster, just get *something*. I really want to stretch this into two shows, and if you get a good *four-second* video of her—we're talking four-to-six. You get a video like that, and we can show it ten times during the show. We slow it down, zoom in on it, slow pan—the possibilities are endless. You know you get paid for being on the TV screen, right? It means big bucks for all of us."

It wasn't the help Simmons had hoped for. He wanted a cameraperson here, if for nothing else than to help him watch for Mildred.

"Right." He rubbed his eyes, head still spinning. "What time will it be ready?"

"It's ready right now. I'd get it now if I were you. Don't miss that shot! If you do end up filming her, I'll send someone to help."

"Right," Simmons said again. They hung up. The expired Nyquil still flowed through his veins as he got dressed and drove to Manchester.

CHAPTER 140

1971

Holly, thankfully, came to the rescue and set the tone for the second half of the week. Wednesday night was *refreshing*, to put it mildly, and she had rolled out the red carpet when they were finally alone together. She referred to sex as *spa-like*, and he was beginning to understand what that meant. The spa-night was capped off by a full eight hours of sleep, and he awoke the next day a new man.

Miraculously, pick-up went smoothly, and Tim and the girls were on their way back from Amesbury just after 6 pm. Tim breathed easy for the first time since Wednesday, and he felt a wave of happiness wash over him—all he needed now was a glass of wine, a nice dinner and maybe a board game or two with the kids—it was relaxing to sit at the same table and just *talk*.

The evening was as good as he'd hoped. The interaction between his girls and Holly was encouraging, and it seemed as though they all liked each other. They played a game of Monopoly in the living room, and Tim took note that everyone laughed more than once, and there was no boredom or complaining from the kids.

Mildred continued her education up in the turret as they enjoyed their evening down below her. Holly came to the kitchen once to get some more wine, but it was a cold day, and the flies were sparse. Mildred went undetected.

CHAPTER 141

1971

Tim and Holly took the kids out all day on Saturday. Mildred took the opportunity to go through the girls' overnight bag Sheila had packed for them. More ugly nightgowns with ugly designs on them. She abhorred the parents' taste in clothing, but more than that, she was disappointed they'd left for the day— she'd been looking forward to this weekend since finding out the girls were coming.

They returned just after 4 pm as Mildred watched from the hayloft. The Russells arrived with what appeared to be groceries, and the girls had balloons and oversized stuffed animals. Vivian was eating what appeared to be an apple on a stick. As Mildred stared down from the back of the loft, she still felt the same contempt for Tim and Holly. It would be so easy to swoop down, call the hatchet and even the score, were it not for the audience.

CHAPTER 142

1971

Olivia's eyes opened just before 7 am, and she nudged her sister. Sunday was what they had come to call "Exploration Day." Quietly, both girls rose and changed out of their nightgowns, tiptoeing through the house to the side door because it was furthest away from the bedrooms and made the least noise.

"Exploration Day" would have been called "grove day" if they hadn't noticed that the word *grove* visibly upset their father. Tim had relaxed his rules recently, and they didn't want to go back to *front-yard-only*. To ask them to stay away from a giant outdoor hiding place like the grove while he worked on the house was cruel and unusual punishment in their opinions.

They had it down to a science. It was a sort of unwritten agreement based heavily on denial—a sort of *don't ask, don't tell*. Tim and Holly woke up usually about an hour after they did, so they would rush back after a quick session of hide-n-seek to make it look as though they had been playing near the barn, or out behind the house. They'd have breakfast together, and then Tim and Holly would pull out the tools and paintbrushes.

When the girls snuck back out that afternoon, they knew the visitation weekend was down to its last few hours, and then it was back to Massachusetts that night and school in the morning. There was only time for a few more rounds of hide-n-seek, and then it would be two weeks of soccer practice and homework.

Olivia counted first and found Vivian almost immediately— Vivian's move was to try to hide behind a tree and then simultaneously step back into the row Olivia had just left, but it never worked. This particular time, Olivia saw Vivian's arm moving from behind the tree.

"Found you. Hey, where did you get that?" Vivian was eating an apple.

"By Dad's garden. They're on a plate; he left us a note. I guess he knows we come out here. Maybe he's not so nervous anymore."

"Show me," said Olivia. Vivian walked her to the last row, and they turned down it. Olivia could see one of their white-with-blue-stripe kitchen dinner plates on the ground just in front of the turnips. Underneath the three remaining apples was a handwritten note in block letters:

Found you.

"Oh well. Good, now we don't have to sneak. Your turn to count!" But Vivian wasn't ready to play.

"Who's that?" she said. Olivia spun around. Down at the end of the row closest to the barn, stood a woman.

"I don't know," said Olivia. The woman raised a hand stiffly as if to wave hello, then turned and left. The girls didn't even have a chance to wave back. She looked back at the plate of apples and picked one out. "Don't tell Dad."

CHAPTER 143
1971

Mildred left the scene prematurely—she enjoyed the girls' presence and didn't want to scare them.

In many ways, they reminded her of Mary and Sarah.

CHAPTER 144

1971

Bob Simmons crashed hard after his Friday night shift. He'd slept two of the last fifty (or was it sixty?) hours—he was so tired he couldn't even do the math. He slept all day Saturday, no longer able to care if it was life-threatening. When he woke at just after midnight on Sunday morning, he looked at his watch and cursed. His sleep situation was upside down.

12:37 am was a bad time to wake up for a person who believed he was being hunted by a ghost. Simmons didn't dare turn the lights on for fear of being visible from the outside. He kept the bulky video camera close by as he peered out the window into the blackness. He ate cold food out of a can and tried several times to go back to bed and sleep, even drinking what was left of the expired Nyquil. *Damn you, Mildred Wells.*

He wondered how it would play out between them. Did he stand a chance, or was it a hopeless proposition? With very few options, he unlocked his gun safe and pulled out a twelve-gauge shotgun. It would stop a bear in its tracks, but might be useless in this situation. He loaded it and stood it in the corner two feet from the bed. He was getting tired of hiding—of being scared—of everything.

A complete slave to his biology, he passed out just before dawn and slept for another nine hours. He woke at 4 pm. His next shift was in seven hours.

He searched Simmons Road once again, holding the awkward shoulder-mount video camera, looking for King, looking for signs of anything. He looked like a fool, according to his father, who shouted from his porch as he watched Bob attempting to wield the machine quasi-blind, eye-cup-to-eyeball. Simmons felt like a fool too—this was not his forte—Bonnette should have sent a professional, but then again, he hadn't seen her since the phone call anyway. Not a shred of proof for Bonnette and the TV show.

As he walked back to his house, he saw Russell's truck roll past his driveway toward the highway. Three heads bobbed in the cab as the truck bobbed its way down the bumpy dirt road. *Kids. He must be returning them after having them all weekend.* Simmons never had kids but was no stranger to divorce. Four seconds later, a green VW Beetle sped past close behind. *Must be the girlfriend,* he thought. And then Bob Simmons had his best idea of the weekend.

He walked and walked fast. In six minutes, he crossed the gully into the Russell meadow. The pond lay ahead, and then the house. He lugged the heavy camera on his shoulder, simultaneously hoping and hoping against the chance of seeing Mildred Wells. If she showed herself, he would hit and run— mission accomplished—escape and call Bonnette. If she didn't show, well, maybe Bonnette would get some good "b-roll," and Bob would get to live to fight another day.

Mildred watched from the grove. What was Simmons carrying? It was 1971, so it could be almost anything. She'd heard of cameras, but they were far from commonplace in the Civil War-era. Simmons had his eye planted against the mechanism, which had a long protruding tube off of the front. She rightly assumed he was looking through it.

Was he trying to photograph her? It had to be that, *didn't it?* Why else would he be here, after everyone else just left? Perhaps her appearance the other day had him feeling defensive—as designed.

She watched him film for another twenty minutes, pointing the contraption through the windows, touring the barn, and the grove. She could have killed him but decided that it was too early. She also didn't want him to have her picture just yet.

CHAPTER 145

1971

The phone rang at 9 am, an hour and fifteen minutes after Simmons had closed his eyes. He rose irritably, still recovering from the weekend, now five days ago.

"Hello?"

"Simmons—it's David Bonnette. Did you get her?" Simmons stared at his bare feet.

"No. No, I didn't get her. I saw her just the once. I even searched the property while they were gone. I didn't see anything."

"You searched the property? What do you mean? Did you get in there? The house?"

"No, not inside. I'd lose my job if I broke in. I'm risking it as it is. I'm a cop for God's sake."

"How'd you know they were gone?" said Bonnette.

"I saw them pass by my road, and I knew the house was empty. It was a Sunday night, and he was returning his kids, I think. He also leaves the house late in the evening every weeknight. I think he works on the house and then sleeps at his girlfriend's house."

"Do you ever go looking on those weeknights? Do you think you might be able to get in there and film the interior? It would be very helpful for my set designers."

"Fuck, no. I'm not doing that, David." Bonnette sensed Simmons' need to follow the written law and yielded.

"Alright, well, we're hurting here, and we could use some *news*—*any* news, Bob. I need you to get something on film, and get it as soon as possible, or this little project is going to suck, and it's going to be a one-shot."

CHAPTER 146

1971

Mildred was surprised to feel her anger subside the slightest bit. Her rage had taken her over completely in 1861 and had never let go. The happenings this past April had erupted and put her over the edge—however, the possibility of interacting with Olivia and Vivian was a welcome distraction. She spent her week constructing dolls made of corn and various bits and pieces from the barn.

Divorce had apparently become a common thing since her *time*. The documents were so cold and impersonal; they seemed to have been created with a boilerplate template. Even the names were left out—Russell and his ex-wife were referred to as "petitioner" and "respondent" in many sections.

Mildred also knew the girls would not be back this coming weekend. Normal visitation was every two-weeks.

CHAPTER 147

1971

Markus and Colleen Vaughn had just passed through Franconia Notch on Interstate 93 when they were killed by a drunk truck driver on Halloween night. In their will, they left everything in a trust, with their daughter Rebecca as the executor. They included a stipulation that Andrew would always have a job at Foggy Orchard as long as he wanted one.

Andrew, already dealing with many problems—was devastated, as well as angry. In his view, the family had boxed him out, leaving him with no options. It was a travesty the way they'd left things. The business was lucrative and *sellable*, and if sold would have set both children up handsomely—but they had given him no say in the matter. He tried talking it out with Rebecca, but she wouldn't hear it. She had plans to marry her boyfriend, and he too would be joining them on staff. Andrew was miserable on multiple levels and began to slip back into old habits.

CHAPTER 148

1971

Bob Simmons phone rang at 9 am waking him once again, painfully and prematurely.

"Who is it?" he mumbled, opening the curtain to peer out into the yard.

"Simmons—it's David Bonnette. I've got good news. We just got approved for a second episode—but I need your help." Simmons smiled. Two nationally televised episodes would mean more money, as well as a broader spotlight on all of the injustices against his family.

"That's good news, Dave. What do you need from me?" Bonnette braced before asking.

"Get in there and film—the house I mean. We need to build sets, and that takes time. I need the layout. Get the barn, too, if you can." Simmons pinched the bridge of his nose and frowned.

"I told you, I can't do that, Dave. I'm a cop. It's too risky. We haven't even talked about money. My job is all I have." It was Bonnette's turn to wince.

"I don't have that information yet. Bob, this is a team effort. The better the show, the more we have to work with. *It's your turn.* We're on the west coast, and you're right next door. Now, take the camera I rented you and get in there."

"Anything but that. I'm done talking about this, David. I'm tired, and I was up all night. I've been up all fucking week over this crap, and I don't even care anymore unless you're ready to talk about money. I'm going back to bed unless I can do anything else for you." Bonnette swore under his breath.

"No, that's it, Bob. That's all you can do for me." He slammed the phone down in frustration.

CHAPTER 149

1971

Bonnette's plane touched down at Logan Airport in Boston early that afternoon. *If you want a job done right, you've got to do it yourself,* he thought. He'd had plenty of time to stew on the Bob Simmons situation and tried to dream up ways to minimize the fat bastard's role in spinning this tale. Unfortunately, no matter how much he wanted to minimize his role, Bob Simmons would always be, at the very least, a strong supporting character.

He drove the hour and a half to Sanborn in his rent-a-car and parked it at the beginning of Lancaster Hill Road. From there, he walked through the woods parallel to the road lugging the movie camera, to avoid discovery by the likes of Tim Russell or Bob Simmons. He stopped by the lettuce garden in the grove and flipped it the bird. It wasn't scary at all, and it was definitely covering something up. He looked away to maintain focus on the story he wanted to tell.

Bonnette looked at his watch—it was 4:14 pm, and sunset was fifteen minutes away. Hopefully, Russell would quit work early, and he could get in and out quickly. Looking for a good place to while the time, he walked halfway down the path that led to the corner in the driveway and took a seat on the ground. From here, he could see Tim's truck and still be hidden. It had been a long day already, with the long flight and all. He laid back and closed his eyes.

CHAPTER 150

1971

An acorn fell from a tree and landed near his head. Bonnette sat up sharply. The sun was down, and it was dark. *How do New Englanders cope with such early sunsets?* Bonnette looked at his watch—it was 6:17 pm. *Wow.* He was flabbergasted. How could that have happened? He hadn't taken a nap since grade school, never mind in the freaking *wild*. Was it this easy to fall asleep in the woods for everyone? Or was it just he and Rip Van Winkle? Russell's truck was gone, and the house was dark. Mystified, he shook it off. It was time for work.

He grabbed the movie camera and crunched his way down the path, slowing his pace as the building loomed above him, and the time came to search for a viable entrance. He'd never believed in ghosts, but he, like everyone, had been a child once and remembered what it felt like to have his mind play tricks on him. The house seemed cold and uninviting—the windows might easily be eyes. Now—an adult—he squelched the thought and pushed on.

He found his entrance in the back yard—it was one of the unlocked windows into the carriage house, just off of the breakfast area. Bonnette crawled through and looked around. The room was unheated and unfurnished—clearly not part of the main house, and not much to film. From there, he tried the sliding glass door to the breakfast area and let himself in.

This was the main part of the house—the part that would be seen on television. Bonnette mounted the camera on his shoulder and turned it on. The eyecup was directly in his face and left him no choice but to look through it, and the body of the camera blocked all peripheral vision to the right. Slightly nervous, he pushed the record button, and the filming light illuminated the entire room, nearly blinding him initially.

Thank God there are no immediate neighbors, he thought; *otherwise, they'd be calling the police,* and he knew damn well that Simmons would do nothing to help him out. Bonnette was here for reference shots only, and he would finish as quickly as possible. The assholes in the set design department could slow the film speed or blow up individual frames if need be. This trip was over and above the call of duty as far as he was concerned. Ten more minutes, and he would be on his way back to Logan Airport.

He'd pass through each room once, spin around, and be gone. From there, they could plan a sequence. They'd have enough information to rebuild the entire home interior on a soundstage. He couldn't guess what the budget would be now that there were two shows on the calendar, so the goal was to film everything— they would figure the rest out later.

As he passed through the kitchen, Bonnette wondered when the last time was that Russell had taken out the trash. The can itself was not apparent—perhaps it was under the sink, or around the corner, but it smelled ripe. *You'd think he'd remember to throw it in the back of the pickup on the way out.*

He walked upstairs into the turret, temporarily pausing the camera so the lightbulb would go out, and the turret itself wouldn't resemble a lighthouse from the outside. *Not much up here but an old desk and a few boxes of papers.* Back at the bottom of the stairs, he paused outside the cellar door and tried the knob. The hairs stood on the back of his neck, and the goose-flesh crawled his arms as his heart hammered away. He was disappointed with himself that he was afraid. *It's just a house.*

He pulled open the cellar door, which squealed much louder than he anticipated. *Good thing you're alone, right? Now point the camera down the stairs and be done with it.* Bonnette didn't take more than one step down for fear the door would close and lock behind him. He panned the camera a bit too fast. *Good enough— looks tiny anyway. We won't be building that set, I guess.* He closed the cellar gratefully and crossed through into the dining room.

As he passed through the living room, the smell grew stronger. *Where the hell is that coming from?* Russell had left merely hours ago. *He couldn't have missed this.* Quickly, he stepped into the empty office at the back of the house, did a quick 360, and came back out. Deep down, he knew he had seen just about everything but the bedrooms in the *other* upstairs—but his body wouldn't let him go there.

Bonnette began to recall some of Simmons' background stories—the ones that had attracted him to the project. The horrible smell inconveniently dovetailed with all of them. *They're just bullshit stories*, he told himself—but here in the infamous house, alone, with all the lights out, it was hard to be the logical adult. *Five more minutes, and you're out of here.*

His head demanded it, but his legs wouldn't budge. He didn't even want to peek around the corner to look up the stairs—*but he did.* The smell was even stronger here. It was so surreal he would have thought this a prank, but nobody knew he would be here tonight. He began to rationalize.

Maybe Russell worked all day in the kitchen and didn't even come to this side of the house today. Maybe he left yesterday's lunch in a trash can up there and hadn't been back since. Or maybe a squirrel got in and died in the wall.

Suddenly he missed Los Angeles—He couldn't wait to lug the heavy camera into the studio and start replaying the footage. With that, he pushed all other thoughts out of his mind and started up.

With three steps left, he had a horrible feeling that he had left a safe zone—that he had crossed a point of no return, but even so, he had no real idea of how right he was. Mildred stood behind him as he climbed, in the front of the house, facing the top of the stairs. Her body blocked the hall window, and most of the light coming in. Bonnette reached the top stair and instinctively spun, sensing danger. He searched his surroundings as quickly as possible at the very dangerous intersection of the bathroom, stairs, the balcony, and two bedrooms. Death here could easily come from five different directions.

The light from the camera found Mildred immediately, and Bonnette screamed, startled as never before. The dark balcony was suddenly illuminated by the reflection off of her white face, and he shed the camera as if it were alive to prepare for flight. In doing so, he fell backward, landing hard on the hallway floor in front of the bathroom.

Like a cat, Mildred met him by the third bedroom's doorway and held his right shoulder to the floor as he attempted to escape her and wriggle his way back to the stairs.

Bonnette was now, of course, willing to accept the broken bones that would come with the fall. He knew now that the woman was, of course, the source of the smell, just as the Gottlieb boy had said. It permeated the upstairs. It hung in the air and his clothing, and it was a smell he would never forget—if given the chance. Flies buzzed, landing on him to try the taste of something alive for a change. She was everything Bob Simmons had told him—more even,—and it was far too late to appreciate the fat man's warnings.

With a flick of her wrist, the rusty blade appeared, and she wasted no time pressing it into his chest, hearing his breath shorten as if wading into a frigid sea. Bonnette sensed he was done and turned his head away, determined to let his last thought be something else—anything else. All he saw was the wallpaper pattern in the hallway as Mildred opened him up one last time.

CHAPTER 151

1971

Bob Simmons woke up tired after another poor quality sleep—
it was 3 pm. Sleep had been elusive ever since he'd seen her.
How many times had she passed through his yard since? He
had started leaving "booby traps" to see if she had gotten inside
while he was working—baby powder on the carpet, so check for
footprints (if she left any)—tape on closed doorjambs. So far, she
hadn't gotten in…if she had even tried. But was it even possible
to "catch" a ghost this way? He had no idea.

He spent his day inside on the couch watching television,
dozing off now and again. His breakfast was a box of macaroni
and cheese. He felt miserable, drinking two beers to help himself
nap. He couldn't remember the last time he'd felt rested. The sun
set two hours after he'd woken up—it was "vampire season" as
he liked to call it—he would see very little sunshine between now
and April.

Simmons dressed for work early and decided to spend some
time at the station before sitting in the cruiser all night. He stepped
out onto his rickety porch and descended the stairs, removing
the car keys from his pocket. He opened the door, dropped his
two-hundred and forty pounds into the driver's seat, and put the
key in the ignition—and then he screamed.

David Bonnette's face was pressed against the windshield, eyes dead, but open. Simmons leaped from the car and drew his gun, twelve hours too late. Bonnette was splayed across the hood face down. On the opposite side of the car was a movie camera nearly identical to the one in his living room. Bonnette must have come for some filming of his own, and it cost him his life. There was no blood nor any signs of physical wounds.

Simmons pulled Bonnette's wallet from his back pocket and went through it—inside, he found three of his business cards. He took one and put the wallet back, then grabbed the movie camera and put it inside the house. After that, he did the only thing he could do, which was to call it in.

CHAPTER 152

1971

Tim slowed his truck as he passed the Simmons house. Three police cruisers lined the road, and police tape had been unnecessarily strung across the driveway. *Are they expecting a crowd?* He slowed to a crawl, trying to get a good look at whatever the commotion was. He couldn't tell, so he pulled over and walked up.

"Crime scene. Sorry, you can't pass through here, sir." Tim metaphorically rolled his eyes.

"Hi, I'm Tim Russell. I'm the only other house on this road. Is Bob Simmons okay?"

"He is, sir. But I can't let you pass. It's a crime scene."

"I understand that officer. I don't want to pass. I just wanted to see if my neighbor was alright. What happened?"

"I'm not at liberty to tell you everything, but a body was found on the premises. The ambulance left a half-hour ago. It will be in the newspaper, I'm sure. I'm afraid we don't have any more information at this time."

Bob Simmons was nowhere to be seen. Tim got back in his truck and drove to the house. The first thing he did was call Holly.

CHAPTER 153

1971

Bob Simmons told the police the whole truth, minus the fact that he had taken Bonnette's movie camera and stowed it. When they left, he decided to visit his father. Eighty-nine-year-old John Simmons lay sleeping in his recliner as always. *Good*, Bob thought. *Less explaining to do.* Quietly, he snuck down the hallway and removed the fake electrical outlet that served as a hide-in-plain-sight safe. Not knowing exactly how much he would need, he took three hundred dollars and left.

He drove to Boston and paid to have the 16mm film developed, insistent on waiting. Three hours and two hundred and twenty-five dollars later, it was finished. He threw in an additional fifty bucks for the busy man to mount the reel and play it for him in a private side room. What he saw surprised him. *Son of a bitch—he snuck in there all by himself. That would have been me.* Simmons swallowed hard and continued watching.

He could tell Bonnette had been nervous. The camera was jerky and all over the place, hardly calm and measured. He could hear Bonnette breathing, but unfortunately, remaining silent during his final thoughts as he transitioned from life to death. The cellar part was self-explanatory, but the rest seemed relatively tame—until the staircase.

During the final steps up the stairs, Simmons heard something—a faint—*sniff* or two. Was Bonnette crying? Suddenly the camera whirled and fell, where it used the rest of the reel filming the wall sideways—recording a shadow or two and the grisly soundtrack of Bonnette's death.

Upon rewind, Simmons saw her for a split second, but it was way too fast. Quickly he hit the reverse button and played it again...and again. *Slower. I need it much, much slower.* Frustrated, he opened the door and went to fetch the clerk, even flashing his badge for the first time proclaiming police business.

The frazzled employee did as he was told, forgetting all of the questions he should have asked, and slowed the projector down. *Maybe this is what the show people need,* he thought. *If they can milk a questionable picture of some dinosaur-looking thing and call it the "Loch Ness Monster," maybe they can do something with this.*

He pulled Bonnette's business card out of his wallet and called the office number.

CHAPTER 154

1971

Nothing much was reported in the days following David Bonnette's death. All the public learned was that the dead man was someone from Los Angeles, and Bob Simmons was not a suspect. Tim didn't feel like asking Bob Simmons any additional questions for fear of encouraging him, so he let it go. Holly asked around in her Laconia circles but got nowhere.

CHAPTER 155

1971

On Sunday, November 7th, Mildred guessed correctly that the girls would be sneaking off to the grove for the first time in two weeks. She'd surprisingly been looking forward to their visit and had prepared some small gifts. It was still too early for a formal introduction, so she left the hand-made corn husk dolls in the same place she'd left the apples. She'd have left more apples this time, too, but the time for apples had passed, and the trees were bare. When the girls found the corn husk dolls, she waved to them once again from a distance and headed off into the woods.

CHAPTER 156

1971

The last two and a half weeks had been a nightmare for Andrew Vaughn. His parents were dead and gone, along with the love-hate relationship they'd shared. He missed them—but was angry with the way they had left things. He felt pressed into service with nowhere to complain, so indirectly, he took it out on his sister.

Two quality full-time employees short, their workload increased exponentially. Andrew had gone from full-time student to overtime funeral home administrator in a matter of months—trapped in the career he'd chosen to forego—trapped in the building he feared. He was pigeonholed, and it was almost too much to bear.

He left work in a huff early unannounced, with a pile of urgent paperwork still sitting on his desk. Rebecca noticed he was missing an hour later when she came up from the embalming room. She took one look at his desk and knew that he'd dropped everything. She searched the building, the house, and then made two desperation phone calls with no success. *Don't do this now, Andrew. I need you.*

Andrew spent the night in a bar three towns away. He didn't want the phone to ring anywhere near him. He drank alone for a few hours and then befriended a stranger who seemed willing to listen—an anonymous sounding board on which to vent his frustrations. The man's name was Jeremy Clary, and although he didn't share it with Andrew, he'd been recently released from the Concord State Prison for Men. Jeremy bought Andrew two shots to keep the stories flowing.

He seemed interested in everything having to do with Andrew's family and the funeral home business. *Foggy Orchard? Yeah, I know that place. What's it like to work on a dead body? What kind of hours do you have to put in for a career like that? Is there any money in it? Hey. Sorry about your parents, man. At least you have your sister. I'm sure you'll find some good help. The world is full of good people.* When Andrew occasionally lost his train of thought, Jeremy reminded him where he'd left off. Andrew even began to cry once, and Jeremy reached out and gave him a few friendly pats on the back.

They drank until closing and then parted ways. Andrew drove home drunk, so badly he wouldn't remember it the next day. Rebecca was still awake in her office, finishing the work Andrew had left her. She saw him pull in and park his car crooked. He'd been crying and was nearly incoherent, so despite her disappointment, she decided to save the lecture for later. She put him to bed, knowing he would be no help to her in the morning. Thankfully, she had already called a former employee, begging him to cover Andrew's shift first thing in the morning for triple the usual payday.

CHAPTER 157

1971

It was a surprisingly pleasant weekend. All parties seemed to have had a good time, despite the rapidly cooling mid-autumn temperatures. Nobody seemed bored—they played games, they played with dolls—and both girls were remarkably polite, despite their slightly altered awareness. They might have been rude otherwise. Worse, they might have treated her the way Elmer always had, and that would have been unbearable. Olivia and Vivian seemed just as happy as she to make new friends—and the afternoon surpassed her greatest expectations. It was confirmation that it had all been Elmer's fault, and not hers—since the very beginning.

The one caveat that fine Sunday afternoon was the father. He had no idea how close he had come, but it couldn't happen this way. The father had come yelling, and when he did, Mildred prepared herself discretely and then thought better of it. At the last minute, she sent the knife back to Beverly Farms. The girls let her go quietly, knowing somehow that if they mentioned her, it would be the end of their fun in the grove—forever.

CHAPTER 158

1971

The girls went home to their mother, and Mildred couldn't help but feel—lighter. Some of her anger had been—postponed for sure, yet she had certainly not abandoned her goal. They would still pay, it was just a matter of *how*, but she had not fully decided that part yet.

Mildred walked deep into the woods, well past the grove, and called the shovel from the barn. It took a minute to find the exact spot, but when she did, she began to dig. It was better to do it now and get it over with before the ground froze.

CHAPTER 159

1971

" **D** ad, come on! We're bored!"

"No, honey. It's twenty degrees out there, it's windy, and your mother didn't pack anything for you. I tell you all the time to check your suitcase before you leave. I can't go inside your house and check it for you. You don't have any hats, mittens or boots, and it snowed this week! You'd be frozen in fifteen minutes, and you'll be sick for tomorrow and miss school! No way."

CHAPTER 160

1971

Sunday, November 21st came, and Mildred waited, but the girls hadn't shown. It was a cold day. Thanksgiving was coming, and it had snowed seven inches this week. Mildred walked down one of the aisles, thinking about how odd it was that she was disappointed. She'd never missed Elmer; he was always there—more than she'd liked.

Deer tracks crossed her path in the snow. She turned her head and followed them. Then she turned around and noticed the tracks she had left—much deeper and more disruptive than the deer's. The girls had not come, and perhaps it was good they hadn't. The father would have noticed her footprints, and the friendship would have been over before it had a chance to develop. Winter was nearly here, and playtime outdoors would be reduced naturally. Mildred might have to find other ways to occupy her time.

CHAPTER 161

1971

Bob Simmons finished his shift and checked the premises thoroughly. His house had a brand new reinforced door, and he'd invested in a state-of-the-art electronic security system. If any door or window were opened, a telephone call would be placed directly to the police station. But would it make a difference? Couldn't she simply pass through the door anyway? The constant threat was grinding him down to a nub.

Finished but never fully satisfied with another property sweep, he climbed the stairs to the porch, pulled out his house key, and let himself in. He punched in the four-digit code that disarmed the security system and went to the fridge for an early morning beer. He didn't like that the security system couldn't be armed while he was home because of the motion detectors, but the beer would help him push that thought out of his mind.

He fell asleep eventually, even though he was exhausted— wrestling with the image of David Bonnette's face peering in at him through the windshield of his car.

CHAPTER 162

1971

He woke seven hours later after a restless sleep. He hadn't felt refreshed in weeks. After a quick check out through the windows, he went to the bathroom and peed. The garbage smelled bad. He hadn't taken it out in—He honestly couldn't remember. He removed it, put it in the trash can outside, and went back in. Then he went back to the kitchen for a bagel, which he split unevenly with a knife and popped in the toaster without washing his hands.

As soon as the bagel ejected, he grabbed it, burning his fingers. He cursed and then began to spread multiple tablespoons of cream cheese over the first half. When he was finished crafting his eleven-hundred calorie breakfast sandwich, he sat down at his tiny kitchen table and bit in, squirting cream cheese out in every direction. Two globs landed on his plate, and another hung on his chin. He stood up and crossed the room for a paper towel—and then he saw it.

Sitting neatly across the kitchen on the far counter was a long *bone*.

He wasn't quite sure what kind of bone it was, or whether or not it was human—but it was indeed a bone, and he was beyond-a-shadow-of-a-doubt *sure* he had not left it there.

His heart pounded, and his mind wandered as he struggled to come to grips. Could it be a dog's chew bone? Something his father found in the yard and—? *No, it wasn't a dog's chew toy. There weren't even any dogs for more than a mile, and it sure as hell hadn't belonged to King. A coyote's perhaps—but when was the last time his father had left his recliner to pick up the yard?* As much as he would have loved to justify any one of the possibilities, he knew this—*femur*, or whatever the hell it was sitting across from him—should not be there.

He spat out the bagel and threw the rest in the trash, not bothering to re-check his surroundings. Mildred Wells could be watching, but what did it matter? She was wearing him down— and there was not a damn thing he could do about it. He was beyond tired and on the verge of not caring anymore.

Against his better judgment, he skipped reporting the bone. Chief Galluzzo had chastised him over the Bonnette incident, and he didn't need any more headaches. The Chief might be working on getting him fired—once the written warnings started, they usually didn't stop until you were *gone*. Luckily, he wasn't working with Bonnette that night. Bonnette had acted alone, and Simmons was allowed to keep his job.

CHAPTER 163

1971

Tim was pleasantly surprised that the holiday visitation season had gone so smoothly. Sheila hadn't thrown any monkey wrenches yet, but it was still far too soon to count his chickens. She was scheduled to have the girls for Thanksgiving break, so of course, *that* went well. Tim and Holly took advantage of their time alone and enjoyed a cozy and romantic long weekend together.

Christmas *Eve* was also Sheila's, but Christmas *Day* was Tim's. Thankfully, both of those occasions went off without a hitch as well. The biggest holidays of the year were history, and they were almost into January.

But, *it ain't over 'til it's over* as Tim's dad used to like to say, and it wasn't long after that before Sheila ruined all that good-faith. The issue this time was the terminology surrounding the phrase "New Year's."

Tim hopped into his truck on the morning of December 31st to go pick up the kids. He'd intended on picking them up at 9 am, but Holly required some extra loving attention that morning, and he was running late. In a defensive move, he took the Londonderry, New Hampshire exit to find a payphone—he didn't want Sheila to be able to claim he hadn't communicated. As the only parent doing the driving (Sheila refused to drive ever since Tim's move to New Hampshire), unexpected delays were bound to happen.

"Sheila—it's Tim. I'm going to be about ten minutes late. Sorry, but I'm coming. Don't go anywhere."

"Uh—Tim, it's not your year. I have plans with the girls."

"What do you mean, it's not my year? It says it right in the agreement that I get the kids for New Year's on every odd year—this is 1971, and that's an odd-numbered year." Tim felt the heat rising through his temples. *Here we go.* This was so premeditated on her part. They had even spoken of New Year's a month or so back—but it wasn't in writing, so it might as well never have happened.

"Tim—New Year's *Day* will be in 1972, and that's an *even* year. We've made plans. We're leaving for them as we speak."

She'd found and exploited a technicality, even though it wouldn't fly in court. The divorce agreement officially stipulated that Tim would have the kids on "New Year's" every odd year, and Sheila would have the kids on "New Year's" every even year. Anybody who *wanted to cooperate* understood that "New Year's" was the counter-balance of Thanksgiving in the divorce agreement. If you had the kids for Thanksgiving, you didn't get them for "New Year's," much the same as if you had the kids on Christmas Day, you didn't get them on Christmas Eve.

Sheila didn't want to understand, or cooperate for that matter, because she had always dictated the terms of everything they had ever done since the first day she met Tim, and she wasn't about to give that power up. *If he wants to argue over a stupid holiday like New Year's, he can take me back to court—but he won't because it costs money—just like he never took me back to court for fifty-percent of the driving duties.*

In bad faith and going against the spirit of their court-approved agreement, she had simply changed things to be selfish and difficult. The same phrase must have worked in thousands of other couples' agreements—people who could cooperate and get along.

Lawyers always work off of templates, don't they? *Only Sheila*. And what about his New Year's Eve?

"Dammit Sheila, what about tonight? At the very least, *tonight* is my night—" He heard the line go dead and saw red. He slammed the receiver into the faceplate of the telephone three times, cracking it. She said she was leaving *right now*. Whether it was true made no difference. If he showed up and she was home, she would call the police. *Maybe that would be a good thing, in the long run, he thought. Let's let it play out. I'll win.*

It started to rain, and Tim looked around before yanking the handset hard, breaking the telephone. Blood dripped down his palm, and he dropped the broken handset underneath the phone shelter. She could press his buttons like no one else.

He paced back and forth for four minutes, trying to squash his anger and re-formulate his plan. He couldn't call Holly, at least not from this phone. In the end, he decided not to show up in Amesbury. He was in no position to take her back to court right now. Tim didn't like to say it unless he meant it. Shaking with anger, he got back in his truck and drove back to Sanborn. *Maybe I'll just fucking work all day.*

CHAPTER 164

1971

M ildred was about to exit the woods when she heard Tim's truck. *Almost*, she thought. She liked keeping him in the dark about her very existence, for now—until she figured out her plan of action. She was in no hurry. He was a young man, and she could wait forever—but she couldn't wait to see the surprise on his face when that day finally came.

She watched his truck as it pulled into the driveway, wondering if he had the girls. According to his divorce agreement, he should. She was a bit disappointed to see that they were not there and wondered why. Even though her friendship with the girls had been put on hold by the weather, she looked forward to the spring, and the brief nighttime visits as they slept—all winter long.

Tim got out of his truck, walking with purpose, and she could tell he was angry. He ran to the side door, opened it hastily, and ran inside. Something had happened. Mildred snuck through the woods around to the back of the barn and climbed to the roof. Carefully and quietly, she made her way to the turret and let herself in. Flies were no matter this time of year as long as she didn't stay inside for any length of time.

She heard him on the telephone, clearly heated. Sheila had "hijacked" his visitation time—some new slang, perhaps, but she understood the meaning. *He must be talking with Holly*, she thought.

"It's frustrating—it's just fucking frustrating. What if Sheila does this some Christmas day? I'd have to take her to court immediately. I'd *have* to spend the money. This incident is going to embolden her. She's going to know she can get away with anything she wants as long as she thinks I'm strapped! She'll call my bluff until the cows come home—*but she shouldn't*. What a waste of money!"

"You're right, Tim. You're completely right. I have some money—I could—lend you some if need be. In fact, if she does it again, that's what we'll do. That's all you can do for now. Pick your battles—this just isn't the right time.

Now—let's redo our plans for tonight. Why don't you work on the house for a few hours, and I'll get my shopping done. Instead of dinner for four, we'll have a special romantic dinner for two, followed by some TV, and—*special privileges*. What do you feel like? Sirloins? Baked potatoes with sour cream? A nice bottle of red? See? We can improvise. It's a blessing in disguise."

She was right; at least there was a silver lining to every one of Sheila's infuriating last-minute switches. He didn't want to be angry anymore. It took a physical toll, so he breathed deeply and counted to ten. His hands shook, especially the one he had injured today on the payphone. Dried blood ran crusted down the side of it, and some had soaked into his sleeve. *I need to clean up*, he thought.

"Yes. Yes, yes, yes—YES! You're right. I'm pissed, but I need to let it go. Nothing I can do right now but try to enjoy the moment—some *other* way. Some other *happy* way. Thank you, Honey. You're the best. If I were alone right now, I mean like, not dating you, I'd be punching holes in my brand new walls. I love you."

It wasn't the first time he'd said it. In fact, he said it all the time. The first time was in August, on their four-month anniversary.

Holly waited another month before saying it back. They had a good thing going, other than this Sheila crap and of course the money situation. She realized that because both of them wanted the relationship, the trying times—made them even closer. It might not make every couple closer, but it seemed to work for them.

The *Sheila bullshit* problem was a good example. Holly got to witness firsthand what he was going through in real-time, and his reactions to each episode. More often than not, she agreed with his reactions and backed him up—it was emotional support, but at the same time, so much more. It was another brain working on a shared problem—*teamwork*. She realized she had never had a better teammate.

CHAPTER 165

1972

Rebecca Vaughn was up to her eyeballs in business yet had to find time to babysit her brother Andrew. Andrew was twenty-two years old but acted as if he were only fifteen. The loss of their parents was devastating on many levels, and she alone struggled to hold things together.

Andrew's low point was the day he left work unexpectedly to go to a bar three months back, but he had recovered somewhat since then and had shown up for all of his shifts. She knew his heart wasn't in his work, however, and kept searching for a reliable full-time replacement. Perhaps she could afford to buy him out one day, and it would be best for both of them. What he chose to do with his life was up to him—nobody could magically make him happy—only he could do that—and she wished him the best.

Her ears perked up two months back when he began to mention a new friend that he'd met. Suddenly she'd heard the name "Jeremy" at least once a day for two weeks or more.

"Who's this Jeremy you keep talking about?" she asked.

"A guy I see at the bar. Good guy. His parents died too not too long ago, and listening to him has been therapeutic in a way."

"What's his last name? Is he from around here? Did either of us go to high school with him?"

"I'm not sure exactly where he's from. I think he said Concord, so no, I don't think either one of us went to high school with him."

Rebecca frowned as she turned away. Andrew had a propensity for trouble, and she worried about him now the same way their parents had when they were alive. He had a poor track record of choosing friends, and the entire family had been pleasantly relieved when he was accepted at the University of New Hampshire. Rebecca herself had privately bet that he would be left with no other options than to attend the much closer but far less prestigious Plymouth State College—either that or join the military. The ultimate safety net would, of course, be to skip everything after high school and go right to work at Foggy Orchard, but nobody— especially Andrew—wanted that, at least right away.

The very next day, she walked upstairs from the embalming room to see Andrew with a skinny man, thirty-ish with a thin mustache. He wore a baseball hat, a hooded sweatshirt, blue jeans, and well-worn Timberland boots.

"Rebecca, I'd like you to meet Jeremy. He's the friend I told you about—good guy. Jeremy, this is my sister Rebecca—she pretty much runs the place, now that, uh—well, you know the whole story."

"Yeah, I know the story. Hello Rebecca, nice to meet you. I've heard a whole lot about you. You sound like a great sister. Andrew speaks well of you." Jeremy reached out and shook Rebecca's hand.

"Nice to meet you too Jeremy, I—I've heard Andrew speak of you too actually. He says you've been a help to him in a difficult time. Thank you." She didn't know exactly why she'd thanked him, but she had, perhaps because she'd been taken by surprise. In truth, she'd gotten an immediate vibe that she didn't like him. He seemed weasel-ish, untrustworthy. Smooth-talker. She didn't trust him—not one bit. He was shifty, didn't dress well, and didn't have the good sense to take his hat off inside the funeral home.

"He says he can start tomorrow, so I was just about to give him the tour. Having him on board is going to lighten the load. We'll be stronger with three solid full-timers plus the rest of the staff. Jeremy used to manage a restaurant." Rebecca's jaw hit the floor. She couldn't believe her ears.

"Uh—you've hired him, without introducing us first?"

"I, uh—yeah, but I told you all about him, and I just introduced you. And you've been saying we've been shorthanded for months now. I can vouch for him. He's used to dealing with customers and a large number of employees. Plus, he's a handyman." It was incredibly awkward discussing this right in front of Jeremy, but Andrew didn't seem to mind, perhaps because of his inexperience. Not so surprisingly, Jeremy didn't mind either. He smiled a nice big smile as if he even appreciated the awkwardness. Rebecca felt he had pushed his way into their lives. He even took over the sales pitch.

"Ms. Vaughn, I used to manage the Howard Johnson's in Darien, Connecticut. That location was number four in the whole company and pulled in nearly fifteen thousand dollars a week. We had a staff of nearly fifty employees, and I was in charge of training. We also had the lowest turnover in the company. I won't let you down. I'll be the first person to work and the last person to leave. I'm an extremely hard worker." Rebecca couldn't hear everything Jeremy was saying because she was angry for even having been put in this situation.

"Do you have a resume, Jeremy? Usually, we make some phone calls before hiring a new person. Andrew hasn't been here long enough to have seen a new hire." Surprisingly Jeremy reached around to his back pocket and pulled out an off-white envelope with a perfectly typed resume inside. The paper was quality— cotton, or linen perhaps, and had a nice weight to it. There was a six-month gap between his last job and today's date.

"Are you currently employed, Jeremy?" Rebecca was still angry that this had turned into a job interview—right in the middle of the foyer.

"No, ma'am. I'm unemployed. My wife wanted to move us up

to Northumberland to take care of her mother. I didn't have much choice, as there aren't any Howard Johnson's up here. I couldn't transfer my employment. Family first, I guess, right? I've been looking for employment since."

"Alright, well, if you'll excuse us, Jeremy, I'd like to do my due diligence with your resume here, and I'll be in touch with you tomorrow." She glanced at Andrew, who had caught the mood and was now clearly embarrassed if not angry. Jeremy thanked her and left.

Neither said a word to each other as Rebecca carried the resume into her office and sat down to call the Howard Johnson's in Darien.

CHAPTER 166

1972

Jeremy Clary had earned a lukewarm recommendation from the manager of the Darien HoJo's. The man, whose name was John Lallo, seemed distant and distracted—tired, perhaps. He said that Clary had worked there for one year and two months but had to give a sudden two-week notice for family reasons—nothing more.

Rebecca picked up the phone again and called Lum's Restaurant in South Portland, Maine. Clary had put his dates of employment as April 1963-June 1970—seven years. *Not bad,* she thought. Apparently, they'd found value in his work if they had employed him for so long. Unfortunately, three shrill beeps sounded from the headset, and she pulled the phone away from her head. The phone was disconnected. *Out of business,* she recognized.

There was one other restaurant on the resume called Valle's Steakhouse, also in South Portland, but they were under new management, and the phone call turned into more of a chore than anything. Rebecca dropped the inquiry. She left Jeremy's resume on her desk and went to find Andrew.

"You've got to discuss things like this with me. You can't just go and hire someone without talking first—I would do the same for you." Andrew sat at his desk, brooding. "You're barely twenty-two years old, Andrew. I've been doing this for five years.

I got to see mom and dad running the place, at least. I'm only twenty-eight myself—but we need to be smart, or we'll go out of business, and I don't know about you, but I don't have any better ideas than to make this place work." Andrew nodded, still slightly humiliated that she had pulled rank in front of Jeremy—but deep down he knew she was right.

"I called his employers, and…he checked out. Call him and tell him he can start tomorrow, but we've got to get him started on his certifications right away." Andrew smiled and picked up the phone.

CHAPTER 167

1972

In mid-April during a funeral service, Rebecca checked in with Andrew and Jeremy to make sure everything was ready graveside. Jeremy had been very hands-on during his first month-and-a-half, and she was happy with his performance—yet still did not trust him. She kept it to herself and didn't share her concerns with Andrew, and continued to keep a close eye on Jeremy.

The priest began his graveside sermon, and the employees of the Foggy Orchard Funeral Home took their places, watching the attendees, ready to assist in any way. Jeremy had adopted the proper stance: Feet shoulder-width apart with arms clasped at his beltline. Rebecca stood ten feet behind him, observing everything.

Something caught her eye under the cuff of Jeremy's jacket. He wore a watch—something she was quite certain she had never seen him wear before. In the post-funeral staff meeting, she went over everyone's performance (including the part-timers) and thanked them all for an error-free ceremony. During the meeting, she made it a point to compliment staff appearance.

"As always, make sure jackets are pressed and shirts are starched. Keep jewelry to a minimum: no dangly earrings or hoop earrings. I know you've all heard this before, but it bears repeating. A watch or a ring is fine, but not *seven* rings. Jeremy here has the look we're looking for down pat. Jeremy, I'm not trying to embarrass you, but—everyone, take a look. His jacket is pressed, his shirt is starched, and he has only a modest watch. I should also note, please remember to not look at your watch during a service. It comes off as rude. Nice watch Jeremy, by the way. I don't think I've seen you wear that before, have I? Very handsome."

"It was my grandfather's. I don't know why I put it on today—I guess I just kinda threw it on." He smiled proudly. Rebecca worried; if it was indeed his grandfather's, then God bless them both—but if he had stolen it somehow from the body they had buried that morning like she thought he might have, then he was a very dangerous man with a heart of ice.

CHAPTER 168

1972

As May 1972 rolled around, Mildred looked forward to the girls' return. She'd spent the winter checking in on them but missed their lively eyes and excited voices. The three of them had been on to something last fall, something that made her feel right—like the mother she always knew she could be. She needed more interaction to prove that she'd had no choice when it came to that fateful day on the pond. A person can only take so much, and she'd been pushed to the limit. *A lapse in judgment can happen to anyone*; she rationalized.

"Can we please, please, please, please play in the grove, daddy? We can plant seeds in your garden for you. You've lived here for more than a year, and we've never hurt ourselves or anything!" Olivia attempted to negotiate with Tim, who was having a good morning. The house was coming along nicely, and he'd begun to dream of the end of the project—and Holly's open house.

He did quality work and was proud of every nail and cut. When the general public finally got their first look, people would talk. He was confident. Thankfully, Bob Simmons had disappeared. So had that damned TV show. The Hampstead Police had never come back, and most importantly, Thomas Pike seemed to have done his job after all. Mildred Wells was not in his life after all. For these reasons, he reconsidered Olivia's plea.

"Go ahead. Go play."

CHAPTER 169

1972

Four more peaceful months passed, and Tim was excited—one year and five months of construction were over, and he was mere weeks away from finishing the work and putting the house on the market. The culmination of his new life's plan was nearly here. On Friday, September 8th, he quit work early, drove to the IGA supermarket and bought some salmon fillets for the grill. While he was at it, he also bought a special bottle of wine.

After dinner, he and Holly retired to the couch for some television and more above-average wine. Tim didn't care much for television but always used the occasion to get close to Holly and play with her hair—something he referred to privately as *pre-foreplay*—and his success rate was off the charts.

Holly read the new TV Guide. New TV shows always debuted in the fall, and this was only the second Friday of the month. Eight o'clock was coming right up, the beginning of the season's prime time lineups. She read the descriptions of each show to Tim out loud.

"*The Brady Bunch*," said Holly. It was the show's third year, and Tim hated it.

"*Nope. Next!*" he said in exaggerated disgust.

"*The Sonny and Cher Comedy Hour.* This is a new show."

"I don't know, honey…*comedy?* They sing songs, don't they? I kinda doubt they can be funny for a whole hour." Holly continued her search.

"*Only If You Dare.* We watched this show last year a couple of times. Documentary type—This week's show is about—" Holly froze and put her wine glass down.

"What?" Tim looked up at her. Holly's face was as white as a ghost.

"You're not going to like this. *A ghostly woman haunts a sleepy New Hampshire town.*" Tim spilled his wine and swore aloud. Holly visibly witnessed his blood pressure rise.

"Can I see that?" he read it again. It was just one sentence, so there was nothing more to glean from the description. Without saying a word, Tim walked over to the television and turned the dial, remaining on his feet.

> "*Welcome, ladies and gentlemen. Tonight on Only If You Dare—a sleepy small town in New Hampshire is haunted by the ghost of a woman who allegedly drowned her child back in Civil War times. Mildred Wells— born—1836—died—1863—the mother from Hell— but even death didn't stop her from terrorizing the town of Sanborn for more than a century after that.*
>
> *Welcome folks, and thanks for watching Only If You Dare. I'm your host, Simone Infante.*"

Their hearts sank as the TV screen panned past the front of Tim's house. The camera appeared to have been right smack in the middle of the field in front of the house, but with the zoom lens, it was hard to tell—they might have been just over the property line. Tim was beside himself.

The show recapped Mildred's life, according to Elizabeth Simmons' scrapbook. They attempted to back it up with a cheesy looking Hollywood set attempting to recreate the two graves in the grove. Then the show burned a segment attempting to tie-in the Hampstead murder and the Beverly Farms fire. Tim's refusal of their interview on the front steps was included with his name not mentioned, and his face blurred-out with special effects.

Only If You Dare was sure to include an entire segment to David Bonnette's death and a long segment interviewing Bob Simmons, who explained his entire family history. Finally, the show closed with Bonnette's footage of the real-life Mildred inside the house. They showed the final scene no less than twelve times, slowing the blurry, low quality shot and squeezing it for all it was worth.

"Did you see that?! That last shot was real, wasn't it! The other scene with the graves looked fake as hell, but that was my house! *Fuck!* Holly—that—that was Mildred, wasn't it?" Tim was upset, but Holly was right there with him. She got nervous immediately but wondered if it could possibly be true. They had no means of rewinding or replaying the show—all they could rely on were their memories of what they had just seen.

CHAPTER 170

1972

On Saturday, September 9th, the Foggy Orchard Funeral Home facilitated the ceremony of Gerald Nye. Jeremy was a bit late to the hearse, and Rebecca went looking for him, finally finding him in her office of all places, hanging up the phone.

"Sorry. I left the front burner on the stove lit. I had to let my wife know," he pleaded.

"Let's go. The procession is waiting," Rebecca barked. She hated to be behind schedule. Thankfully, the rest of the funeral went off without a hitch.

CHAPTER 171

1972

The very next day, Rebecca made a follow-up call to the Nye widow as a professional courtesy. Much to her horror, Mrs. Nye was upset, but not for the reason she had imagined.

"We were robbed! We were robbed while we were at the cemetery! Nothing was broken or trashed, but they must have known we would be away those few hours. I lost my jewelry. We had a little bit of cash. They even took tools from the garage! How can people be so cruel?"

CHAPTER 172

1972

B ob Simmons woke at 3 pm after his normal shift. He had a little extra pep-in-his-step since the *Only If You Dare* show aired despite the initial ribbing he had taken from his coworkers. They were right, he was not a natural on camera, but they were also jealous, and the unexpected result was that Chief Galluzzo began to treat him with more respect—the heat was off professionally for the time being. The extra three grand for the video of Mildred felt good too—he went out and bought himself a bottle of eighteen-year-old scotch first thing.

Although he'd just woken up, he couldn't resist—and poured himself a glass of the expensive stuff right after breakfast. He hadn't tasted *any* scotch in more than ten years, and it was so good he poured another as he took a seat on the couch and flipped on the television. An hour later, he dozed off.

He woke just after 8 pm, and it was pitch-black again outside— just part of life working the *Vampire Shift*. An episode of *The Mod Squad* was playing on the television, so he shut it off. He had a headache now and regretted his empty OIYD celebration. The scotch-fest hadn't been worth it—now he'd have a miserable night in the cruiser. Upset and slightly nauseous, Simmons went to the kitchen to fix something to eat. Maybe some food in his stomach would smooth things out.

As he left the light of the living room, he couldn't help but notice a glow coming from the kitchen. Had he left a burner on? He saw the flame as he entered the room and flicked the wall switch—it wasn't the stove; it was a candle. Not quite—it was a candle and something else. *What the hell is that?*—Squinting his eyes, he looked closer—it was a *skull*—the eyes and crevasses, packed with dirt—dirt that had once been part of its grave.

Simmons charged back into the living room and ripped his pistol from its holster. Then he turned back to the kitchen, weapon still ready for something already gone. Pointing the gun unnecessarily, he saw something written on the forehead of the skull. It looked to have been fingerpainted—and there were four letters in total.

E–M–M–A.

CHAPTER 173

1972

The girls came for visitation in mid-September and never saw the house on Lancaster Hill Road. They all stayed at Holly's house in Laconia, and the excuse was that they had just polyurethaned the floor, and it wasn't safe to breathe. Tim was nearly finished—less than a month away from completing the refurbishment, but the unwanted attention from *Only If You Dare* made him nervous.

Mildred took note that the house was empty. She knew the schedule as well as anyone and had been fully expecting the girls. The weather was good, and there should be no reason they wouldn't be here—unless her secondary considerations had worked much sooner than anticipated. Maybe Simmons had shared the camera, and word had already gotten out. Maybe too, Emma's skull was public knowledge. If that was the case, then so be it. It was time for a focus on the original plan anyway.

A lifetime of suffering had yet to be fully avenged, but it certainly would be soon. Besides that, it had been a boring winter. Whatever traction might have built with Tim's girls was now ancient history. She was back to ground zero, losing what little patience she had.

CHAPTER 174

1972

"One more, buddy, come on. I'm buying." Jeremy Clary waved to the bartender and paid for another shot. It had been a long day at the funeral home, and the boys needed to burn off some steam. In twelve hours, they'd be at it again, however, so this had to be the last drink.

"Last one. We have to work tomorrow, so this has to be it," said Andrew.

"Yes. Last one, but we deserve it, man! Those people wouldn't leave the cemetery today! We should have gotten overtime! Hey buddy, pass the Beer Nuts, would you?" Andrew looked to his right. About three feet out of reach was an unattended bowl of Beer Nuts. He got up, took a few steps, and retrieved it. As he did so, Jeremy sprinkled a pinch of *mind-eraser* into his tequila. It was a combination of Quaaludes and something else he couldn't remember, yet always worked in a pinch. His brother swore by it.

"Here you go, Jeremy. Hey, what are you, a bottomless pit? Didn't you just have a double cheeseburger? I can't even look at those things. I'm feeling nauseous." Jeremy took a handful to make it look good and raised his shot glass.

"Cheers, buddy. To life and death." They drank up and left soon after.

CHAPTER 175

1972

Where the hell is Andrew? Rebecca wondered. Jeremy was on time—early even—but at least there was someone there to help greet. Mourners would be showing up soon.

"Jeremy, hold the fort while I check on Andrew. I'll be right back." She ran across the parking lot to the house and found him in his bed—catatonic. She checked his breathing, and it was fine, but she couldn't shake him. "What time did you get home last night?!" He didn't answer. *Pathetic,* she thought. He was useless—again.

"Dammit, Andrew—I need you!" She shook him one more time with no success. Things could not continue this way—there were three more funerals this week. In frustration, she left him to suffer his hangover and ran back to the funeral home.

As she reentered the building and climbed the stairs to the main floor, Jeremy was nowhere to be seen. Elderly mourners often arrived early, and it was policy to have an employee as a greeter. Working quickly, she checked the bathroom and the sitting room with no luck. Finally, she tried the office and noticed that the petty cash drawer was open on top of the desk—and it had been emptied. Sadly, she wasn't surprised—she'd seen this coming since Day One. Jeremy was a street rat, and she knew one when she saw one. *Had he set this day up?*

Thinking fast, she looked out the office window. Jeremy's Ford Pinto was backed up to the loading bay. *Still here.* She ran downstairs to intercept and found him loading supplies—embalming fluid and anything that wasn't nailed down—into the back of his car. She'd already known that criminals had somehow found a way to use the fluid to get high, and here was living proof. She ran downstairs and surprised him—he didn't think she'd be back so soon.

"What the hell do you think you're doing, Jeremy!" Jeremy knew he'd passed the point of no return at Foggy Orchard, as he had at several other occupations in his dark and illustrious past—and it was time to run again. He was nearly untraceable at this point—no address or phone number, the way he needed it to be. He'd sell the embalming fluid and the rest of the stuff on the street, then move on. The funeral business wasn't as lucrative as he thought it would be—there wasn't as much jewelry. Not much worth stealing.

He waited, timing his move, pretending he was busy loading something—until the last second. Just before Rebecca got close enough to put hands on him, he sprung, lowering his shoulder, lifting at the last second, up and under her ribcage. The well-timed hit cleaned her clock, taking her off her feet. Rebecca fell hard and hit her head on the curb. The lights went out.

Jeremy slammed the hatchback and sped away. There were no witnesses, but with Andrew's help, the police arrested him a week later in the city of Dover, attempting to sell the embalming fluid on the street.

Rebecca, still in a coma, had emergency brain surgery. She died nine days later.

CHAPTER 176

1972

There was no proof the skull was Emma's, but Bob Simmons had no doubt. He was beside himself, ranting to anyone who would listen. *Only If You Dare*'s Nathan Hoginski flew in himself, drooling at the unforeseen *escalations*. The police confiscated the skull but were only able to determine that it was that of a female.

Simmons felt less safe in his own home than he ever had, and sleep only came when his body collapsed. He moved into his father's house for a night, but a mouse ran over his face as he slept, so he went back to his own house, defeated and afraid. His anger for Tim Russell grew.

Russell knew something, he was sure of it—he was hiding something from the good citizens of Sanborn in the name of his wallet. Now that "The Legend of Mildred Wells" had aired, he had to smile a bit. The asking price of Russell's house would drop like a stone, and he would get what he deserved—bankruptcy. Now that the OIYD crew was back in town to film another episode, he took comfort in the power of karma.

Simmons asked again about a chance of getting a warrant, and his lawyer friend once again laughed at him.

"You still want a warrant? A warrant for what? *Your* property is where you found the dead guy and the bones, not his! Those things have nothing to do with Russell's house—and that video the dead guy supposedly took doesn't prove shit. The best thing you can do is wait for the Open House and pretend you're interested in buying to take your look around, but you already saw the whole inside, right? He gave you the grand tour himself, didn't he? Hey, let me know what he did with the place. It looks great from the road!"

CHAPTER 177

1972

Andrew couldn't bear to take the responsibility of burying his own sister and wisely hired another funeral home fifteen miles away. Aside from the upcoming funeral itself, he was wracked with guilt, never suspecting that Jeremy had drugged him, and the whole incident was only indirectly his fault. He went into a mild depression and closed Foggy Orchard for three days while the Vaughn extended family made their way to New Hampshire for Rebecca's service.

Nobody came out and said it, but he felt he was looked at as pathetic and a disappointment. He heard the buzzing words behind his back. Only his Aunt Jenny spent any quality time with him, asking him how he was and how he was dealing. Andrew hoped she would relay the information to the rest of the family over time. He felt foolish, and he missed his sister, and he missed his parents. He had done a lot of growing up—but it was too little, too late.

The day after the funeral, everyone had left except for Andrew's uncle on his mother's side—Uncle Roy. To say that Roy fell into the disappointed camp was an understatement—Rebecca had always been his favorite niece, and to make matters worse, Andrew had once—as a child—been caught going through Roy's wallet.

Since then—even without the added guilt of Rebecca's death—it had always been a shaky relationship, even though Andrew had only been nine years old at the time.

It was uncomfortable being with Uncle Roy, but Andrew decided that it was better than being alone. Even negative attention was better than being alone in the orchard right now. Andrew made himself some breakfast and put enough out on the counter for two. Uncle Roy was in the bathroom upstairs. Andrew stirred the eggs and jumped out of his skin when Uncle Roy entered the kitchen finally and spoke.

"So what happened that night, Andrew? I thought I could avoid this conversation, but it's eating at me. I guess I need to hear it." Uncle Roy had obviously been stewing. He looked tired and haggard. The dark circles under his eyes made him look even angrier than he usually did. *Here it comes*, thought Andrew. He'd felt so much pain these past few days he felt like an empty eggshell. He would cry soon, of that he had no doubt. The tears began sooner than expected.

"I wish I could say I knew, but—I don't. We were drinking tequila—something I don't usually—We had a couple of shots, and—and a couple of beers, and, like that—I blacked out." He held the tears as best he could because he didn't want Uncle Roy to think he was playing for sympathy.

Uncle Roy impatiently threw a coffee mug violently at the wall—pieces exploding and landing across the kitchen. Andrew dropped the spatula in shock as Roy's face went red as a beet. The man couldn't hold his emotions anymore.

"God…*dammit*, Andrew."—and he went silent and put his face down onto his forearm, shedding tears of his own. "I hate saying that word. I hate saying 'Goddammit' Andrew, but I hope God will forgive me. *You make me that mad, Andrew.* You're a smart guy, right? Maybe the smartest in the family? I mean, you got kicked out of college, but you got *in* first, didn't you? Your parents gave you everything—every opportunity—and all you ever did was walk around as though everybody owed you a living. Do you know how much that pisses me off?" Andrew nodded, daring not to speak. Uncle Roy continued.

"I consider myself a Christian, so I'm not going to say everything I'd like to today, but I hope you feel *one-tenth* the sorrow that I feel right now. This thing—hurt us all, Andrew—it hurt the whole family." He stopped just short of blaming Andrew directly.

"What the hell were you doing hanging out with this guy anyway? Did you think you were cool, or different? Couldn't you tell—being the smart one—that he was bad news? We all know what Rebecca thought of him—why didn't you realize? Maybe you didn't give a fuck? Were you having *fun* cutting across the family grain? Go ahead, *tell me*. Tell me what's going on in your head right now."

Andrew knew this was a lose-lose situation; there was nothing he could say or do to make things right—he'd only add fuel to Uncle Roy's fire. But he was on the spot, so he tried.

"I'm not sure, Uncle Roy. I know I didn't want to be a funeral director—and I didn't want to live so far in the country anymore. I thought I was cooler than that, you're right. Jeremy was an audience, I guess. A distraction from having to think about that. There aren't that many people who live up here—it's not easy to find friends—and everyone's a buddy when they've got a beer in their hand. I—I fucked up. I know I did, and I have no excuses, and I'll regret it for as long as I live."

Uncle Roy seemed to steep on Andrew's careful words with no immediate retort.

"And what are you going to do now?"

"I don't know. I suppose I'll sell Foggy Orchard and live somewhere closer to Boston—maybe Wakefield or Reading, and commute from there. I like the city." Uncle Roy was silent again, hanging his head momentarily, elbows on the kitchen counter. Andrew couldn't see his face but sensed the words were coming.

Uncle Roy finally picked his head up with a smug look on his face as if he had a secret—and then he let it out.

"Andrew, I'm afraid you're not moving to Massachusetts, at least not with the family money. Arrangements were made years ago to protect your sister from you fucking her life up. Your parents always intended for the two of you to inherit this business—the one they worked so hard to create with their bare hands—and they planned on you being an absolute pill about it.

They even had a plan in case Rebecca died, and you fucked it all up, which, let's face it—nobody thought the two would be related. How sad is that? It turned out worse than they could even plan. And Andrew—that's the reason we're having this conversation right now. I came for the funeral, but I also came as the bearer of bad news. Your mother took me aside years ago and set me up for this talk. She knew you were going to be a problem. Andrew, I'm here to tell you that the funeral home is set up in an irrevocable trust. Do you know what that is?"

Uh-oh. Andrew shook his head.

I'm the trustee, Andrew, and you're the beneficiary. That means I make the call as to what happens. Your mother and I..." he trailed off, getting emotional for a moment. "Your mother and I were very close—very close. She told me that if you survived your sister, that I was to make the call.

She told me to give you the funeral home and nothing more—but no selling. You can work here for as long as you like. You can have all the profits of the business. You can even abandon it and let the business die if you want, but she wanted me to be clear that if you did let it die, you would be doing so against her wishes. If you go that route, the property will be sold, and the proceeds will be given to charity." Andrew's jaw hit the floor, and despite all the guilt and sorrow flowing through his system, he felt a layer of anger underneath it all. Uncle Roy continued:

"They did this to make you an honest man, Andrew. They were good, hardworking people, and so was your sister—and there are no shortcuts when running a business like this. You earn every penny, and it builds character. It makes you a better person by teaching you the right way to *live*. Your mother had faith that you would someday be that kind of man—someone of whom she could be proud. Today is obviously not that day, but you have the rest of your life to go find it."

CHAPTER 178

1972

Friday, September 29th came, and Mildred listened in on Tim's phone call with skepticism. It was another visitation weekend, and the girls should be coming over, but they had been kept at Holly's house last time as a result of all the Simmons-related hubbub that had churned its way into their everyday lives. Mildred's expectations were low concerning the weekend, and her impatience was back in full force.

The pleasant distraction that the girls had afforded her had been taken away, and the bitterness began to bubble once again under the surface. In the meantime, she'd had over a year to ponder her original plan of vengeance and refine it for maximum effect. It was a powerful plan, the perfect payback for what they had done to her, and they weren't going to like it one bit.

Listening carefully from the turret, she heard the phrase "bring the girls right to your house," and "lose a half-day of painting Sunday because we'll be in Laconia"—confirming her suspicions. Mildred balled her fist. She *could* walk to Laconia and simply *disrupt* it all if she wanted to, but she'd already seen Holly's house (thanks to Holly's unlocked car and handy paperwork), and it was far too small for Mildred's purposes. There was no privacy, and showing up in a congested neighborhood to wreak havoc was boring and far inferior to her original plan. Tim was still on the phone, and Mildred would have to leave soon. Flies were beginning to swarm.

"...I...right. I don't know how I'm going to sell it. One day at a time, I guess. I'm still hoping it's not true, or...Yeah. I know it's morally questionable but that TV show brought out the crazies. I get at least one call a day asking if I want to sell. What? I don't care! They can have it! I can't save their lives if they knowingly buy a...okay. Okay. I have to leave soon to get the girls. I'll see you at around seven. Love you too."

Mildred heard Tim put down the phone, grab his keys, and leave. She didn't bother to duck down as his truck passed the turret—she almost wanted him to see her—but he didn't look up.

CHAPTER 179

1972

The following Wednesday, Tim took a final look around. He had finally finished refurbishing the house, and it was spectacular. Despite the accomplishment, the specter of Mildred Wells hung over his head, and he worried about the final steps—the Open House, the offers—and the final sale. He would have to be completely honest with prospective buyers about the haunting, and it would no doubt be a dealbreaker for many—but all he needed was *one*.

CHAPTER 180

1972

Holly considered hosting open houses her strong suit, and this particular open house would be especially satisfying.

It had been a very long year. Selling Tim's house would mean they could begin to forget about the horrors they had faced. The stress of the dead geese and the drowning would all be sold off with the house—not that they had to disclose every last detail. It had been eight months since the last incident that *they* knew of for sure.

You could justify anything if you wanted to, especially when sixty-thousand dollars was on the line. She and Tim hadn't seen Mildred Wells since Thomas had supposedly taken her; it was all second-hand information from dubious sources. Tim and Holly hung their hat on the fact that nothing (other than their own experiences in April of 1971) had been proven. Holly wanted to believe that the ghost of Thomas Pike had taken his wife Mildred and their son Elmer to go wherever the dead go to rest peacefully.

Everyone on God's Green Earth knew that Bob Simmons was a conspiracy theorist on his best day. There was no real evidence of what the Hampstead boy claimed to have seen. No one could clearly make out what was in David Bonnette's film. His death could be written off as an exaggeration of a simple heart attack. It wasn't proven that the footage was real, or where it was filmed, and the studio withheld any comment as they waited to see if Tim would sue.

Even with all this justification, both Holly and Tim remembered their phone conversation back in April 1971—the conversation that led to their first date and several more after—about the morality of selling Tim's house—or any house—with such a history. Together they agreed to warn *qualified* potential buyers first. It wouldn't be a blanket statement read aloud to an open-house crowd or the general public, but rather a discreet *one-on-one* discussion for people placing serious bids. Regardless of whether or not they believed in ghosts, all bidders would get "the talk" before signing on the dotted line so that they could sell Tim's house with a clear conscience. After the warning, the bidders could make up their own minds.

Because of this, the money worry remained. Tim would be on edge until the minute the money was in the bank. The moment of truth was coming, and the sale was imperative. He had bravely returned every day after the Mildred trauma to finish the refurbishment in a year and a half. His work was fast, efficient, and beautiful. The housing market was favorable, and pending the all-important final *talk* with the prospective buyer(s), it seemed like things might just work out.

A good crowd arrived that Saturday; close to twenty people in fact, but Holly was skeptical as to how many were qualified buyers when she saw a policeman in full uniform. His nametag read SIMMONS, and she drew the connection immediately. *A policeman like his grandfather, and nosy like the Simmons ladies. The apple doesn't fall too far from the tree. I know who you are, Bob Simmons.* Was it his grandfather who was the cop? Or great-grandfather? She couldn't recall. Maybe it was even great-great-grandfather. It didn't matter—Simmons was finally able to gawk at the entire "Wells property" and its infamous past without it being trespassing. Holly shrugged it off. Today was a good day; let him gawk—but she would keep a close eye on him nonetheless.

She had already shown the house privately twice, with both couples submitting bids, despite hearing her version of *the talk*. Tim was not there—house owners were typically not on-site during showings—but he would deliver the "final talk" when the time came. Holly was slightly encouraged because she'd given a fair amount of background information, and they seemed unfazed by it. She'd prepared (but did not hand out) a special page that read like a warning:

> *You may have seen this house featured on the TV show Only If You Dare, in an episode titled "The Legend of Mildred Wells." In it, a cameraman is allegedly killed in the upstairs of the house by "the ghost of Mildred Wells." It is unclear if the footage shown was filmed inside the house, or in a Hollywood studio. No permission has ever been granted by the owner for the studio to set foot on this property, and the studio refuses to comment for fear of legal retaliation.*

> *There is also a claim of a boy drowned in the pond by his mother (Mildred Wells) back in 1862. This did happen. Like the owner of the property, I, Holly Burns, have seen the woman known as Mildred Wells here on the property and urge you to consider this danger when making your final decision—whether or not you believe in ghosts.*

Holly had originally included the sentence, "I believe she has the potential for violence," but decided her statement was strong enough without it. She also left out details having to do with the bayonet and the geese. The bayonet was something she thought long and hard about—Tim had actually been stabbed with it. It was *real* and *dangerous*—but Thomas Pike was most certainly gone forever, so she no longer considered it a threat.

The kitchen splattered with goose blood seemed a thing of the past too. It seemed that Mildred—if she *was* still around—had abandoned her "anniversaries." She and Tim had even watched from afar a year after witnessing the incident close up, and nothing happened.

After reading her warning over and discussing it with Tim, they both agreed that there was enough information included to allow the prospective buyers to make an informed decision, as well as allow the two of them to live guilt-free lives.

She read it to each of the potentials with a straight-face. Both times it was met with nervous laughter and a bad joke by the man in the room attempting to break the tension. Holly hadn't joked back and wouldn't joke going forward either. If the warning ended up sounding like a spooky gimmick to help sell the house, then it would go against what they wrote it for—and wouldn't do her conscience any favors.

There would be two more private showings after the open house before they would select the winner. Things were looking up—fingers crossed—but she couldn't wait for today to be over so she could get the hell off the property.

She avoided showing areas like the pond and the grove, announcing to potential buyers that they were free to check things out on their own if they chose to do so; she hung back and pointed people in the right direction. The kitchen and the turret were also painful for her, but Tim had done such a wonderful job on the interior that it was almost easy to pretend that what had happened in there occurred someplace else.

She waited on the front lawn for her latest guests to return from the outskirts. Bob Simmons had disappeared somewhere inside the house. *Already seen the grove, Bob?* she wanted to ask but kept quiet. One couple ambled through the field, past the pond area and straight through the spot that Mildred had slaughtered the geese. When they passed the stone wall and arrived at Holly's lemonade tent, she turned to them, composed herself, and prepared to answer questions.

"It's beautiful. Do you agree? Romantic, even?" Holly spoke of the grove the way she *used to* feel; her current opinion would not be as positive.

"Yes…it is, and very peaceful. I can see myself taking walks up there to de-stress after work," the woman commented. She was not as yet a qualified bidder and had not received *the talk*. Holly wondered if the woman would indeed be able to take those stress-free walks one day.

"Yes, perfect, and with the sunset? Wow…"

Tim's "forest garden" was now growing in the spot the graves used to be. No one needed to know there had ever been headstones out there. Not many people had *ever* known, come to think of it. Looking back, Holly reflected on how hard it had been to get to this very moment. The whole Mildred/Thomas ordeal had happened in approximately *two weeks*, but it had felt like much longer. Now it was all but over. The house was finished and *finally* up for sale; the bids were rolling in. Maybe now they could move on to bigger and better things.

"Excuse me…Holly, was it? I have a question if you don't mind." It was one of the potentials who had not yet encountered *the talk*. Holly turned. "Mrs. Wallace. Yes, how can I help you?"

"How close are the nearest neighbors? I don't recall seeing another house on this road, except right at the beginning," she asked.

"Those *are* the closest neighbors—a Mr. *Simmons*, I believe. You can ask that police officer right over there if you like, I believe that's him!" Bob Simmons had come back outside, apparently finished with his self-guided tour. "There are three houses down that driveway, but he might know more than I do. It is very private out here, no congestion of any kind—just plenty of New Hampshire peace, quiet, and fresh air."

"And you said the whole meadow comes with the property, correct? To the trees?" Mrs. Wallace continued her questions.

"That's right. You get the meadow, the pond, the house,

the barn, and a big chunk of woods, which includes the grove. Twenty-three acres in all. You can even tap your maples right here in the front yard if you want to make homemade syrup."

"No close neighbors, you say? Well...who do you suppose that lady is out near the corner of the field? She's been standing and staring at the house on and off since I arrived. That was forty-five minutes ago. First, she was over there...and then she moved over there. It's kind of creepy—I mean, as you said, it's not her land!"

CHAPTER 181

1972

"It's her! It's Mildred Wells!"

Bob Simmons shouted it out as Holly turned to look, a chill running through her blood at the mere mention of the name. As Mrs. Wallace said, there, in the shadow of the corner of the field, stood Mildred Wells, her dress blowing in the breeze. She was staring in their direction; her face the brightest thing in the dark shadow. It was too far to read her features, and from this distance, she resembled a skull. Wisps of hair blew across her face, hiding any trace of emotion.

Holly had an immediate flashback to the first two weeks they'd been on the property—when Mildred sightings were as common as blue jays. There she was. Had she been here the whole time? Before Holly could react, Bob Simmons was waddling down the lawn on the way to the pond. *Where was he going?*

Everyone at the Open House had now stopped what they were doing to watch the portly policeman run into the pond area.

"What's happening?" said someone who hadn't heard the whole conversation.

"Not sure. Where's he going? After that woman out there?"

Holly's heart sank as she realized their worst fears had come true. The Open House was a disaster, and there were enough witnesses to spread the word—if they all survived. Her heart pounded, as there was nothing she could say to diffuse the situation. Bob Simmons ran alongside the edge of the pond on the way out to the meadow. All eyes were on him and the woman who seemed to be his destination. When he reached the back end of the pond, huffing and puffing, he pulled his pistol, and the crowd gasped.

Several people began to make a move to find their cars. Mildred stood firm in the corner, still a hundred yards from the lumbering Bob Simmons. Four seconds later, she turned and stepped into the woods. Bob Simmons could be heard, yelling, "Halt." Frustrated, Holly did her best to hide her emotions, one of which was contempt. He was a pathetic man and had no idea what he was doing. On top of that, his ignorance was now interfering with her life.

"Ms. Burns—What just happened?"—a man she hadn't met yet asked—"What's going on?" Holly sighed, and in the heat of the moment, improvised.

"Has anyone here seen the TV show *Only If You Dare?*" Two people raised their hands. Twelve people had decided to stick it out and watch. Bob Simmons had stepped into the woods and was out of view. Holly only hoped the next sounds would not be his screams.

"For those of you who don't know, *Only If You Dare* is a national TV program that recently did a show based on one of the previous owners of this house—a woman named Mildred Wells. She lived here around Civil War times. According to the show, she was a troubled woman who—unfortunately, did some bad things while living here. It wasn't much of anything anyone remembered until the TV show aired. Officer Simmons is the star of that episode." Holly unconsciously looked down at the pond as she spoke.

"So—uh—you're saying that woman out there in the field— was Mildred Wells, and she's from Civil War times? The man had a skeptical look on his face. Holly searched for words, but someone beat her to it.

"That TV show is garbage! It's tabloid trash! It's almost Halloween for God's sake! It's just a prank. Somebody watched the show, and they're having fun with us. Something we'll have to get used to if any of us buy the place, I guess. I think I'd have to install an electric fence." Holly was still at a loss for words and held back, just as Bob Simmons emerged from the woods. She breathed a small sigh of relief, even though a part of her hoped he would have disappeared.

"If you'll excuse me for a second, ladies and gentlemen, I'd like to speak with Officer Simmons. I don't feel safe with a loaded gun being waved around during my open house. I'll be just a minute. Feel free to look around and help yourself to the refreshments inside if you'd like to wait for me. I'll be right back." Holly trudged down the lawn to intercept Simmons before he could return and give everybody the absolute worst version of the legend of Mildred Wells.

She met him just past the pond. His pistol was holstered, and he was out of breath. Holly was angry.

"Was that necessary, Bob? *Pulling a pistol* at my open house? *Running with it* across the field? Was that what they train you to do? Because I'm guessing it's not." Simmons talked tough even though he knew she was perfectly capable of getting him fired. He was on thin ice as it was, and his goodwill was all used up. The Chief would side with her in a second.

"You and your boyfriend should be ashamed of yourselves. She's a killer, and I think you know it. You're hiding information, and I'm going to figure it out."

"We're *hiding* something, Bob? You were at the open house. You toured the whole property by yourself without supervision. Did you find anything? You're a policeman, aren't you? Did you find *anything?*"

"You were digging in the grove. Moving graves. And you know it."

"It's a fucking garden, Bob. A fucking *garden*. The open house is *over*, I want you to walk straight from here to the road and leave the property, or I'm going to call your boss myself, *right now*. If you're lucky, we won't seek a restraining order." Simmons bit his lip angrily but didn't say a word. He did as he was told and cut across the field directly to the road, got into his cruiser and sped home, spraying gravel as he went.

Holly walked back to the house, checking over her shoulder twice before arriving on the front lawn. Only one couple was left of the original twenty or so people, and they looked like they were leaving too.

"I'm sorry about that; I just didn't want a gun being waved around anymore. That was some unwelcome excitement. Did you folks have any questions about anything?"

"Uh, yes, Ms. Burns. We saw the TV show, and to be honest, it's the main reason we're here today. We're real ghost story freaks, and that was just—well, it was *amazing*, and it made our weekend! I have to ask: Do you think that was *really* Mildred Wells, or do you get that sort of thing all the time now? I'm freaking out right now!" Holly looked at the young couple and cut her losses—they were only here for the free haunted house tour anyway.

"It happens all the time."

CHAPTER 182

1972

"Tell me you're joking," said Tim. Holly said nothing and remained straight-faced. "You *personally* saw everything you just told me?" Holly nodded. "It was her?" Holly buried her face in her hands and began to cry.

CHAPTER 183

1972

Bob Simmons was scared, angry, and frustrated. He feared Holly would report him to the Chief for pulling his weapon—if not today, then sometime soon. Unfortunately, she was in the right, and he imagined his days as a Sanborn police officer were all but over. Today's sighting, along with the fatigue and stress of Mildred's taunts had culminated in one very bad decision. Still, he knew what he had to do. With nothing to lose, it was time to double down.

At four minutes past midnight, he parked his cruiser north of the house and left it running with the parking lights on. From the trunk, he grabbed the movie camera, his hunting rifle, and his ax and fast-walked the half-mile to Russell's property, approaching from the rear, making his way through the brush around the side of the barn. Russell was not here—he was with Holly in Laconia, where he spent his nights, and the house was dark.

His heart pounded as he considered perching in the hayloft, but realized he would not be able to see the front of the house from there. Attempting to enter the house was out of the question. He'd seen how quickly she had taken down Bonnette and wanted no part of a close-quarters confrontation in the dark. He wanted to capture her unaware, not only for the TV show but to perhaps save his job. To be safe, he unscrewed the filming light—hopefully, the moonlight would be enough. It would have to be—there were no other options.

Unsatisfied with the hayloft, he walked down to the pond and camped under one of the huge bare willow trees. From here, he could see the house and the field. If she was in the house, he could film her when she came out, and if she came from the woods, he had plenty of reaction distance. The hanging willow branches even provided a bit of camouflage.

CHAPTER 184

1972

Mildred stood in the dark turret and watched him search for a place to be. Back and forth from the barn to the lawn to the pond, overloaded with useless tools and equipment—ten minutes of indecision, unaware he was already being hunted.

She waited until he settled under one of the willows before slipping out.

CHAPTER 185

1972

It took her ten minutes to quietly sidestep the cattails and enter the water, but only one to cross the bottom of the pond. She thought about Elmer as she passed the spot she drowned him, then began to ascend. A moment later, she broke the surface and found him again beneath the tree. His back was to her as she knew it would be. His head was seemingly on a swivel, pivoting from right to left—woods to house, house to woods.

Simmons didn't hear her. He felt a pressure in the middle of his back, followed by a raspy exhale—his own. He coughed, and with that came the pain. He looked up and around helplessly as she grabbed his left shoulder with her left hand and pushed the blade in again with her right. He tried to reach for the ax stiffly but coughed again, immobilized. His failure washed over him, and he realized the game was over—but he might still be able to even the score.

In one last act of desperation, he lurched for the ax. Mildred stepped to her right and caught him mid-reach, pinning his head to the ground. Helpless, he saw stars and intense heat behind his eyes as Mildred applied the eighth spell. Simmons died in seconds. A minute later, he was a messy pile of decay.

With no reason to disguise the body, she left him under the willow. She didn't want Tim Russell moving just yet.

Turning, she looked for the moon and began to walk.

CHAPTER 186

1972

By Tuesday, October 10th, Bob Simmons was reported missing, and Nathan Hoginski—producer of *Only If You Dare*—took note. He contacted his sources at the Associated Press and suggested they look into Simmons' disappearance and compare notes with *Only If You Dare*'s findings. It was just a "suggestion," but it was also genius marketing, and it was free. It didn't matter if *OIYD* was right or wrong—just the suggestion that a policeman's disappearance might be related to Mildred Wells would blow the immediate ratings through the roof.

CHAPTER 187

1972

Tim had finished his work on the house, and with nothing else to occupy his time, he drove daily to Massachusetts to help Johnny. Holly called him with the bad news. He couldn't believe his ears.

"Simmons is missing?!" Holly could hear his anguish. "Holly—that's it. I'm gonna go broke. The house won't sell. The *'Legend of Mildred Wells'*—has become—a *'thing.'*"

"Not yet, Tim. I'm still getting phone calls for showings—we just have to separate the qualified prospects from the gawkers."

"How's that going to happen?" he asked.

"Well, for one, I'll find out if they're pre-approved for a mortgage. That will save us a lot of time." Tim changed the subject, his mind wandering. Holly's attempt to make him feel better didn't fix the Mildred problem.

"Holly—a hick like Bob Simmons hasn't left the town of Sanborn more than ten times in his entire *life*...and Elizabeth Simmons was found across the street. If you were Mildred, what would you do with his body?" Holly frowned.

"Well, they didn't find him on *his* property. Tim, I was thinking; you're in Massachusetts now, and the police might be trying to reach you. What are the odds he's on your property? And what about the whole search warrant thing? I'm not down with the legalities, but you might want to check in with the police."

She was right, and Tim got nervous even though he had nothing to hide anymore. He would gladly open the door for them now—but if Simmons was missing, and the police thought Tim had skipped town, they might get off on the wrong foot. He thought of calling Frank Turnbull for a second but held off.

"You're right. I have to go. I'll call you when I get there." Tim got in his truck and left for New Hampshire. He prayed Simmons' body was anywhere else.

CHAPTER 188

1972

It had been three weeks since Uncle Roy's talk, but Andrew Vaughn hadn't learned his lesson yet. He was ashamed, and he was low, and after a day at his desk arranging an upcoming Saturday service, he pulled out the bottle from the bottom drawer and began to drink.

Half of each workday was spent dreaming of ways to get out of his family's morbid way to make a living, but at twenty-two, he was as green as could be—a child dealing with adult matters. He hadn't figured out how to break free yet, but until he did, he would at least run the funeral home correctly.

Come Saturday, he'd fret, hoping all the part-time employees would show up and not leave him hanging. The most important of those was Claude, a fifty-nine-year-old semi-retired Marine that he designated the unofficial face of Foggy Orchard. Many of the patrons mistook Claude as the new owner, and that was exactly what Andrew wanted—he was still too babyfaced to earn the trust of potential patrons even if they hadn't heard of his recent checkered past.

Even if all the employees did show up, his nerves would still ebb and flow for the duration of the service. He would leave the majority of the *corpse care* to Claude, but even so, he would have to double-check on the body, as much as he loathed it. Hopefully, in the end, all would go smoothly, and nothing would tarnish the public perception of Foggy Orchard Funeral Home. The pressure was intense and seemed to come from all sides.

Business aside, the macabre old building itself was enough to drive him to drink, and there was too much work to be done to simply pick up and go at 5 pm to leave with Claude. Even if he could leave, the house next door was almost as eerie and uninviting, full of rooms he loathed to visit. The office in Foggy Orchard was at least small enough so that he could put his chair back against the wall and only have to worry about the doorway to the hall—and beyond.

Andrew finished three strong drinks before he dared to leave, and as he stood, the room spun. It wasn't just about alcohol. He was exhausted emotionally and physically as well—tired of *thinking*. And when he got right down to it, he was afraid. The last thing he wanted to do was go back to the empty farmhouse, but after Jeremy, he was too gunshy to go out on the town. Deep down, he knew rest was the best medicine. Socialization wasn't right—he was only running from his reality, and was in no shape to become someone's boyfriend or buddy—he hadn't even found himself yet.

The house seemed especially empty since Uncle Roy had left. Even though they didn't particularly like each other, Andrew didn't want to see him go. Andrew had grown up here, but back then, he'd always had the family for background noise—for *life*. They were gone now, of course—*dead* and gone, and the house was equally so. On top of that, it seemed four times its normal size. He fixed himself a lackluster bowl of noodles in the home kitchen along with three more drinks, then collapsed on his bed upstairs, drunk.

He was usually afraid to go to sleep—or better put, *go to bed* because sometimes sleep didn't come. Many lonely hours were spent staring at the ceiling. This time he passed out fully clothed, but awakened five minutes later, feeling sick. He'd overdone it with the whiskey again, and he could not afford to be sick anymore. Andrew rose and went to the bathroom, forcing himself to vomit. Then he downed two glasses of water and took his clothes off and showered. Perhaps now he had salvaged part of his morning.

After the shower, he managed to fall asleep again, but it was a restless and unsatisfying sleep. At 4:30 am, he woke, his mouth bone dry. A dull ache nestled behind his eyes as he kept them shut and attempted to ignore the pain. Soon his bladder joined the interruptions, and it took him twenty minutes of procrastinating before he surrendered and got up.

Andrew swung his feet out onto the floor. The house was painfully silent, and all his true-life problems came flooding back. The room was cold, so he put on a t-shirt as he passed the bureau. He left the bedroom and took a right into the bathroom, just missing the figure in the dress as she came up the stairs. He relieved himself by the dull glow of the night light.

When he finished, he washed his hands and gulped water, hoping the extra hydration would further salvage his morning. Whiskey was *always* a bad idea—it was too strong, and he could never handle it, always paying dearly. Everything was a blur as his contact lenses had dried to his eyes. He opened the drawer by the sink and applied eyedrops. *More damage control*, he thought.

Andrew left the bathroom, took a left down the hallway, and walked back into the bedroom. A dim gray twilight had begun to illuminate the dark curtains meaning that sunrise would be here before he knew it. He opened the bureau again as he passed and took out another t-shirt to throw over his eyes, again missing the dark figure by the closet as he crawled back into bed and prayed for sleep.

Eyes covered, he couldn't help but listen to the room, and the house beyond it. The furnace shut down after finishing a cycle, bringing new meaning to the word silence. Still, he didn't hear her approach.

The woman opened the book she held over the bed and loudly clapped it shut. Andrew, already wide awake under the t-shirt, threw it off and sat up straight, heart pounding. Three feet away was a dark figure he couldn't quite make out. He screamed in surprise.

"Who is it!? What do you want?!" he looked to his nightstand for any sort of weapon with no luck. The figure said nothing, but stepped out of the shadows, dimly illuminated by the dull light that made it through the dark curtains. He looked twice, recognizing her posture—her hair—but the face remained in the shadows. She paused to let him *realize*.

The ghost of Colleen Vaughn stared at her son with disgust. She could still smell the alcohol. He wallowed in self-pity—despite the pain he had caused them all, especially Rebecca.

Colleen was dead, but not finished raising her son.

"Mom?" Andrew thought he might be hallucinating. The budding hangover was enough to remind him he wasn't dreaming, but—he remembered how he felt the morning Rebecca was killed. This experience was equally hellish—a second self-inflicted nightmare. Perhaps he'd let *himself* down this time.

She took a step closer to let him see how angry she was. He could make out her furrowed brow and the edge of a frown. She glared unblinkingly, and he knew exactly why. Andrew had thanked God his mother wasn't alive for his sister's murder—but his mother back from the dead was unimaginable.

She loomed over him, threatening, staring, stepping closer. He backed up into the headboard. Now she held the book out to him. He froze, wide-eyed in disbelief. *Was this happening?*

The ghost of Colleen Vaughn dropped the book next to his leg and waited, curtains beginning to illuminate behind her. If he couldn't manage this simple task, she was more than ready to guide him through it. Finally, he reached out and retrieved the book.

The first five pages were blank.

On the sixth was written one word—"John."

On the opposing page was the word "Sherman."

Andrew flipped the page again. "George" was the next word. Then "Brown."

He turned the page again—"William,"…and then "Lincoln."

He paused to look up, as much as he didn't want to.

"Mom…you're angry. I know I've let you down. I know you blame me for Rebecca's death—and I'm…" he stumbled on his words, choking up—"But tell me, *please*—what *is* this?"

CHAPTER 189

1972

Tim sped down Lancaster Hill Road with a lump in his throat—
something bad was happening—he could feel it in his bones.
Simmons Road was taped off as expected, but much closer to his
house, a Belknap County Sheriff's cruiser partially blocked the
road just before the pond. Unable to pass, Tim parked and got out.
There were several more vehicles up ahead, including three in his
driveway—and there was a team of official-looking people under
one of the willow trees. His worst nightmare was upon him. Chief
Galluzzo of the Sanborn Police saw Tim arrive and intercepted
him as he hopped the low stone wall.

"Mr. Russell? I'm afraid I can't let you over there. It seems we
might have a crime scene on your property. Can you tell me where
you were for the past twenty-four hours?"

"It's Bob Simmons over there—*isn't it*. What's he doing on
my property?"

"That's what we're trying to determine, Mr. Russell. We'd
appreciate your cooperation in the matter—in fact, we require it."
Galluzzo handed Tim the search warrant.

"Yeah, you don't need a warrant anymore. You guys can look
around all you want—I just didn't want Bob Simmons stirring
up shit about some ghost on my property—but it looks like he

440

managed to sabotage me anyway—him and that damned TV show. I've been working on this place for a year-and-a-half, and—now this." Tim gestured toward the mob under the willow. "I take it he's dead?"

"I can't officially comment yet, Mr. Russell, but I can tell you we're probably going to be here all day. I'm going to need to ask you some questions. Do you want to do it in your house? It's roomier than the station." Tim agreed, and the two men weaved between the vehicles to the side door. Along the way, Tim craned his neck to try and get a glimpse at Simmons' body under the willow, but all he could see were two men crouched while three others looked on. The two men went inside and stood around the breakfast bar. Tim continued to look out the bay window.

"Where were you for the past twenty-four hours, Mr. Russell?"

"Please, call me Tim. Twenty-four hours ago, I was working on a job in Newburyport with my co-worker Johnny Upson. The owner of the house was also there. Then I drove back to Laconia from about 6 pm-7:30 pm. From that time until 7 am, I was with my girlfriend, Holly Burns. Then I drove back to Newburyport and came back quickly as soon as Holly told me Bob Simmons was reported missing. I haven't been alone at all except for the drive-time."

"Alright, well, I'll have to corroborate all this, but it sounds pretty tight. Tim, I'm well aware of Bob Simmons and his family history. I saw the TV show too—I know the whole deal. I also took a walk out into the grove and took a look at your garden. Not planting anything this year?" Tim paused for a second, wondering if he should simply tell the truth—then thought better of it.

"No, I'm selling the place, so I skipped it this year," he replied. Chief Galluzzo took some notes.

"Any reason why you wouldn't use that great big meadow to plant a garden?" Tim left the room and came back a minute later with the "Forest Gardening" book Frank Turnbull had told him to purchase.

"It's apparently a great place to grow lettuce and such. Who knew?" Galluzzo took more notes. Tim looked out the kitchen window again. The officials were coming up the lawn to their vehicles with only a five-gallon bucket—no body bag. What looked to be a long bone protruded over the rim. Tim reacted.

"What the hell is that? Is that supposed to be his body?" Tim bolted out of the front porch door. Chief Galluzzo shouted after him too late. "Excuse me—excuse me! Is that—Bob Simmons?" The man in the hazmat-suit holding the bucket froze. They hadn't expected anyone to be in the house, let alone come running out of it. Tim got close enough to see. The femur sat on top of a skull, some hair, and a host of shorter bones.

"Russell, step back. Let them work." It was as if Simmons had been dead by the pond for a month. He looked back at Chief Galluzzo, who seemed regretful he'd conducted his questioning here.

"What the hell *is this* Chief?"

"I was about to ask you the same thing, and then you took off like a jackrabbit. Now, you know. Come back inside, or we finish this down at the station." Tim lowered his eyes and walked back in, taking a seat for the first time.

"I believe what you're telling me, Tim, and I'm sure your alibi will check out. I was about to tell you about Ol' Bob's condition and get your take on it. What do you suppose might have done that to him? My first thought was lye, but even lye doesn't work that fast, plus he'd be all covered in white powder. On top of that, the boys said they didn't detect any foreign agents in their preliminary observations. Bob Simmons was here just the other day for your open house, wasn't he?" Tim nodded.

"He was. I wasn't here, of course, but everyone who was here will confirm it. Holly said he pulled his gun and went running across the field after someone dressed up as Mildred Wells." Galluzzo's jaw dropped, and Tim realized he shouldn't have offered that bit of information.

"Now, why the hell would you not report that to me?!" His eyes bored into Tim's. "Why did he pull his weapon?"

"We...we just want to sell this damned place. We don't want to be in the news." Galluzzo shook his head in disgust.

"And that asshole pulled his gun over a prank. I should have found a reason to fire him years ago. Show me where it happened." They walked outside to the lawn, and Tim apologized to the young hazmat suit as they passed.

"The woman came out of the woods in that back left corner of the field, and then—hey—what the hell is *that?*" Tim saw a reflection coming from under a tree, just over the property line way out across the meadow. It was two people, holding something. Tim couldn't quite make it out but pointed, and Chief Galluzzo saw it too.

CHAPTER 190

1972

Nathan Hoginski had already been to Boston and rented the most powerful movie camera available when the police scanner squawked. Officer Bob Simmons, the hero of "The Legend of Mildred Wells—Part 1," was missing, and he had to turn up sooner or later. *Chance favors the prepared mind*, thought Hoginski. *Better to be proactive than reactive.*

The police spoke cryptically, but the address was unmistakable—Lancaster Hill Road. They arrived on the scene just after Tim, and parked up and off the road under cover of the woods themselves, hidden from view. The camera was mounted on a heavy-duty tripod, and they began filming. They got hundreds of feet of mind-blowing footage, including a bone, sticking out of a bucket, and a skull being turned over in the gloved hands of an official.

"Oh shit!" Larry Sandberg, the cameraman, swore and ducked down. They were the first two words he had spoken since entering the woods.

"What is it?" Hoginski looked out across the field and saw the two men standing in the driveway, one of whom was a policeman.

"Okay, that's it—let's go. We can't lose this footage." In ten seconds, they broke down the tripod and were on their way out.

Hoginski watched the cops try to get around all of the extra vehicles in the yard and estimated they might be alright as long as the cops didn't get a look at his license plate.

This *Mildred Wells* story was rapidly developing—and he had enough new material to make three more shows. The next step was to get it out of here, and then get it edited and narrated as soon as possible. After their surprisingly easy getaway, he found a payphone and called Hollywood.

The plan was to bump tonight's episode of *OIYD* ("Stonehenge") for a rerun of "The Legend of Mildred Wells," except that they would rename it "Part 1" for tonight's broadcast and have a dramatic voiceover at the beginning and end promising important new developments forthcoming—then bust ass all week making the new shows. The way things were going, they could get a whole season out of it. The ratings would be through the roof.

CHAPTER 191

1972

The kitchen garbage needed to be taken out, and Sheila Palmer knew her procrastination must end. There was only one thing she missed Tim for, and it was *this*. It had been two days since her last trip to the backyard cans, and tomorrow was garbage pickup—the number one reason she hated Thursdays. Scrunching her nose, she flicked on the kitchen light, put on two reusable yellow dish gloves, and pulled the bag out of the can.

Suddenly the phone rang in the living room, and she gratefully put the bag down, exhaling heavily to answer it. Any distraction was welcome at a time like this.

"Hello?" The person on the other end was her best friend and co-conspirator Judy Larson.

"Sheila, it's me. Turn your television to channel seven *quickly!*" It was five minutes past eight o'clock, and Olivia and Vivian had just gone to bed. The TV wasn't even on yet, so she pressed the button and waited for the old Zenith to warm up. Judy was bursting at the seams and took the opportunity to fill Sheila in.

"It's Tim's house! In New Hampshire! It's on TV!" Sheila immediately thought it might be some sort of home showcase program and felt a twinge of envy. She and Judy had driven by his new house one weekend he had the girls, just to snoop and see how well his life was going. They'd taken Judy's car to make it less conspicuous, and in the end, she was glad they did. The dirt road was not built for rapid drive-bys, and the potholes were numerous.

Sheila's initial reaction was, of course, envy, but she hid it from Judy to maintain her illusion of strength. Sheila could tell Judy also adored the house by her lack of commentary—she didn't dare piss Sheila off. The two of them could carve up just about anything with words, but neither could deny Tim's talent with construction. Sheila felt so bad she almost wished she hadn't come. The new house would most certainly be gorgeous when it was finished.

Finally, the television picture came into focus, and Sheila turned the dial to channel seven. The first thing she saw was the house, and then Tim, his face blurred out, refusing to be interviewed. Over the next half hour, she learned everything about the house: The drowning, the haunting, the Beverly Farms fire, and most importantly, the recent deaths of the Enrico kid and the TV show cameraman.

The end scene was especially creepy—the found footage of the Bonnette death. Something about that scene struck Sheila, and after five angry minutes of venting to Judy, she hung up the phone and dialed Tim's new number.

CHAPTER 192

1972

Tim had canceled his phone service in Sanborn and installed a separate "business" line in Holly's house—for his use only. One reason for the separate line was that he sometimes made costly long-distance work calls, but the real underlying reason was he didn't want to immerse Holly completely into the *Sheila Universe*. The rule was, if Tim's phone rang, only Tim would answer it.

It was eight-thirty-six, and the phone rang. Tim had no idea they had just rerun "The Legend of Mildred Wells" on national television and that Sheila had seen it this time around. Another phone call, another blindside about to happen.

"Tim? Do you have something you want to tell me because I think this might be your last chance to see your children for a while." *Oh, the agony.*

"What are you talking about, Sheila? Refresh my memory. What fire can I extinguish for you tonight?"

"I saw that TV show. Two people have been murdered up there this year, and it's all related to your haunted house! I'm their *mother*, Tim, and I can't let you put my daughters in danger! You need to run these things by me because obviously, you have no boundaries and don't know any better!" Tim's heart froze. She was a bitch on her best day—at least since their marriage ended—but there were several degrees of difficulty beyond that, and he could tell this time she was out for blood. Even if the court eventually sided with him, everything between now and then would be hell on Earth.

"We aren't staying there anymore. We sleep in Laconia! Relax, it's a tabloid ghost story! A bad TV show! It's fake! They make shit up!"

"Two people are dead, Tim. And you let your daughters sleep there. You didn't think to consult me. We can't trust you anymore, obviously." Tim noted that she'd switched to "we" mode. "We" could mean many things—Sheila and the girls, Sheila and Judy Larson, or Sheila *and the whole world*—versus Tim.

"Excuse me—*YOU* can't trust *ME*? Weren't you the one who was bouncing from bed to bed while we were married? Give me a break Sheila. I'll be there on Friday—you have a good night."

"I don't think so, Tim. We won't be here. We're going up North. You do know I could get a restraining order if I wanted to, don't you? And I don't even need a reason. And when I do, they come and take your guns, no questions asked. Don't fuck with me, Tim, because I'll do it." Tim, now fully wound up, saw red. He was done with her threats and ready to spend the cash in court if need be. *Let's burn it all down then*, he thought.

"I'll be there on Friday, Sheila, and you'd better be there too unless you want to pay my legal fees. You're wrong, and that's the way the court will see it!" Sheila slammed the phone down, and Tim did everything he could to avoid doing the same. The shit had hit the fan *hard*, and life as he knew it took a giant step backward. He swallowed hard as his pulse continued to race. How long would it be before he saw his girls again?

CHAPTER 193

1972

Sheila's hand hurt from slamming the phone down, and she removed the yellow dish gloves to rub it. Even though she was supposed to be the one messing with his life, he always seemed to say one or two things perfectly and end up pissing her off. How had she ever married him? He knew where her buttons were and how to press them. Tim Russell was the only person she had ever known who had never bent to her will—even her parents let her get away with murder.

Now she would have to go out of her way to find something to do outside the house on Friday evening so that when Tim showed up—*if he showed up*—they would not be there. She reached for her wine on the table by the couch and killed the entire glass. As the adrenalin began to subside, her sense of smell returned. *Tim Russell and the kitchen garbage—back-to-back.* She grabbed the yellow dish glove and put it back on, heart still pounding, mind still wandering, replaying in her mind every word they had said to each other.

Sheila stepped into the dark kitchen and stopped dead— *Weren't the lights left on in here? Too angry to remember.* She reached over and flicked the switch.

Flies swarmed, taking flight with the sudden illumination.

Her eyes were overexposed as she attempted to gauge what was going on. It was surreal, like the confusion of a dream. *Is it the wine? Am I hallucinating?*

The flies were so numerous that several flew into her, bouncing off and circling back. She braced to run when she realized the dark figure in the corner, just inside the unlit pantry. She attempted to draw a breath and stumbled, backing into a chair, falling awkwardly underneath the breakfast table.

With the tabletop now blocking the overhead light, Sheila could better see the intruder, but only momentarily. It all happened so fast there was no time to react, or even to scream. The flies came from *her*—and the stench was far more than garbage. Her face was pale, her skin was mottled, and before Sheila could attempt to try and sit up, it was too late. A rusty knife disappeared into her chest, went through her heart, and sank into the kitchen floor.

Mildred waited several seconds, holding the knife in Sheila's chest until it was over. When Sheila was gone, she stood and walked through the living room, looking up into the stairwell. She half-expected them to be at the top of the stairs, but luckily they still slept. Now, she would hide the body so that when they passed they wouldn't see. And then they would have to leave.

1972

The first five pages of Annette Smith's flipbook were blank.
On the sixth was written one word—"John."
On the opposing page was the word "Sherman."
Andrew flipped the page again. "George" was the next word.
Then "Brown."
He turned the page again—"William,"...and then "Lincoln."
He paused to look up at his mother, as afraid as he was.

"I know you're angry. I know I've let you down. I know you blame me for Rebecca's death—and I'm..." He stumbled on his words—"*Please*—what *is* this book about?"

She said nothing but reached out and took it back. Andrew recoiled as he felt the cold radiating off of her hand. She tore the pages he'd already read, then turned deeper and ripped out several more without taking her eyes off him. When she finished, she handed it back.

Andrew opened it again and began flipping to find her message. Suddenly, something caught his eye in the hallway to his left—a tall figure in the doorway.

Father?

—*No.*

Andrew was surrounded now—caught between two ghosts,

one on each side of the bed. They loomed over him as his eyes darted right to left, and his heart pounded.

His mother pointed to the book, reminding him to continue. He read the name but didn't recognize it. His mother raised her arm and pointed to the man on the other side of the bed. Andrew turned his head to acknowledge the guest.

The dead man was tall, bearded, and dressed in old fashioned farming clothes. Andrew noticed that his eyes were blue.

His mother spun suddenly and walked away, body language suggesting deep disappointment. She was through, leaving him alone with the stranger. She walked directly into the closet passing between the hanging clothes—gone, at least for now. *What have you signed me up for, Mom?* Andrew wondered.

The tall man stared, and Andrew was at a loss for what to do. He took another look at the name in the book and closed it. Out of ideas, he offered it to the visitor.

Colleen Vaughn's guest ignored the gesture. The flipbook was and would be again, a useful communication tool between the living and the dead. It helped get Elmer to safety—but it was time to help the others that had once helped him. Russell and his girlfriend stood no chance against Mildred, and things were about to get much worse, now that they had her full attention. Thomas was about to return to Sanborn alone when suddenly, Andrew Vaughn's services became available. Unfortunately, Andrew didn't seem to know this.

Andrew put the book down, unsure of what came next. The ghost had rejected the book and continued to stare. Was he here to kill him? Finally, the ghost moved, slowly opening the drawer on his father's night table. Andrew knew there was a pistol there and began to slide to the opposite edge of the bed. The ghost stood tall again as if catching him in the act, then pointed something from the drawer at his face. Andrew braced for gunfire, but it never came.

Thomas Pike held out a pen, and Andrew stared at it for several seconds before reaching out to take it.

As ever, for Josi, Karil, Ed, Addison and Olivia

Also, special thanks to my "early feedback" team:
Darlene Saltz, Sherry Pratt, Erin Bergin, Laura Sterritt, Dawn
Goodman, Ron Desjardins, Steve Hoginski, Tony Vendasi,
Sally Reyer, Darci Davis, Marion David, and Bill Gottlieb
...and Philippa Middleton for my fantastic website.

Michael Clark was raised in New Hampshire and lived in the house *The Patience of a Dead Man* trilogy is based on. He is enjoying this new writing gig, has several ideas for future works, and plans to continue until you finally give in and "like" his Facebook page *@MichaelClarkBooks*.

He now lives in Massachusetts with his
wife Josi and his dog Bubba.

Mildred Wells will return in:
The Patience of a Dead Man—Book Three.

In the meantime, read some free short stories at:
https://www.michaelclarkbooks.com/
and follow:
https://www.facebook.com/michaelclarkbooks/
Twitter: @MIKEclarkbooks
Instagram: @michaelclarkbooks
Reddit: u/michaelclarkbooks

Made in the USA
Columbia, SC
03 January 2020